Alexander Fullerton, born in Suffolk and brought up in France, spent the years 1938–41 at the RN College, Dartmouth, and the rest of the war at sea – mostly under it. His first novel – *Surface!*, based on his experiences as gunnery and torpedo officer of HM Submarine *Seadog* in the Far East, 1944–5 – was published in 1953. It became an immediate bestseller, with five reprints in six weeks, and he likes to recall that, working for a Swedish shipping company at the time, he wrote it in office hours, on the backs of old cargo manifests. He has lived solely on his writing since 1967, and is one of the most borrowed authors from British libraries.

WAVE CRY

Alexander Fullerton

To Charlie and Dawn,
with affection as well as sincere thanks for their help –
not least, the tracking down of our man to Co. Galway

WARNER BOOKS

A *Warner* Book

First published in Great Britain in 1999
by Little, Brown and Company
This edition published in 2000 by Warner Books

A CIP catalogue record for this book
is available from the British Library.

ISBN 0 7515 2977 X

Typeset in Palatino by
Palimpsest Book Production Limited,
Polmont, Stirlingshire
Printed and bound in Great Britain by
Mackays of Chatham plc, Chatham, Kent

Warner Books
A Division of
Little, Brown and Company (UK)
Brettenham House
Lancaster Place
London WC2E 7EN

1

In Frank's arms on the narrow bunk in black thrumming darkness she'd woken to Tom's crying out and Frank's response to it, Frank's sudden movement, disengagement from her. She had no idea he was reacting to something he and Tom had heard, because *she* hadn't; she'd have slept on if it hadn't woken her husband and her son. Tom was in the other bunk, secure under a tight blanket and with a bolster on the outside; Eileen's assumption was simply that he'd called out in his sleep and Frank was going to him. Frank off the bunk now, murmuring in his deep, Irish voice, 'He's back asleep, I'd say.'

'So *you* come back, and quick!'

Non-committal grunt in the darkness. Giant shadow moving around. Dressing? A big man in a confined space, pulling on trousers and a sweater: there was in fact a scraping of light at the foot end there, a leak of it through slats low in the cabin door. There was less vibration than there had been: you might even have thought they'd stopped the engines. She reached out, found an arm and held on to it: 'What are you after doing, Frank?'

'Take a look-see, see what that was.'

'See what *what* was?'

'If I knew, I wouldn't need to look.' He'd moved out of her reach and she heard him open the door of this narrow third-class cabin – in the huge ship's forepart, six decks down, closer to the engines and the keel than to God's fresh air – and saw the widening vertical slab of light, his shape filling it for a moment and then the snap of the door shutting. Dark again, but with none of the rattling there'd been before – ship's rattles, the ship and all the fittings inside her trembling under the engines' power – none of that now at all. Could be the engines *have* stopped? she wondered. What had Frank gone to see about? He would, of course – having worked on trawlers, and involved as he was with engines and suchlike, naturally enough he was mad to know everything about the ship and how it worked, and to have herself and Tom understand it too; he'd even tried to explain to Tom – aged two and a half, for heaven's sake – how the ship was driven by two different kinds of engine, all that stuff. Thinking of Tom again, reaching long-armed past the washbasin that fitted without a half-inch to spare between the heads of the two bunks, her hand feeling its way over the bunk-board and the bolster to the small body's warmth and stillness: to her surprise Tom's hand came groping to find hers. 'Did ye not hear it, Ma?'

She was out in the space between the bunks then, crouching over him, smoothing back his hair . . . 'I did not. What did you think it was?' Then before he could tell her: 'How about you come over and keep us warm while your daddy's gone?'

Warm bundle in her arms. Eileen, who was tall enough, stooping almost doubled to gather him up and lift him over, Tom informing her meanwhile, 'Must've been we hit on something.'

'Hit?'

'Might've been a whale?'

She hugged him. 'Old whale'd come off the worst, I'd say. If we hit anything at all, mind you!'

'Something, all right.'

Not three years old yet, already talking the legs off donkeys – and often with more than a little of his father's quiet certainty in the tone of his squeaky voice; one squeaky-piping and the other a deep bass, yet boy and man so alike that she knew how this one surely *would* be, given another dozen years say. A dozen *glorious* years, please God – and a few more dozen after that! She was assuring him, 'Not as there'd be cause to worry, no matter *what*.' She had him cuddled warm against her. 'Back to sleep now, Tommy boy. Dream of the fine life we're heading for, the three of us together. *Sweet* dreams now, my darling!'

She'd only thought to reassure him because he was such a tiny soul and might be worrying, having heard whatever it had been and his father then gone wandering in the night. For her own part, no possibility of any danger occurred to her at all, no matter *what* was going on out there. It wasn't even a rough sea they were on: more like a vast pond than the feared Atlantic ocean, and this great vessel safe as houses on it. Colder on deck than it had been earlier or yesterday, but that was only because they were passing close to the ice that lay to the north of their route – so a steward had explained. Her worst imaginings at this stage, in fact, was that if the ship were to lie stopped for long, her arrival in New York might be delayed, with Frank's uncle Matt maybe hanging around waiting for them and going mad: he had a fearful temper, so Frank had told her, wasn't a patient man at all. But then again, he might not be coming to meet them, either: Frank's mother, Matt's sister, had suggested that he might, but it was quite likely they'd have to find their own way there. 'There' being Philadelphia, where Matt McGrath had his motor repair business.

But they'd have the engines running again soon, for sure. She was listening for it, for the thrumming to start up again, as well as waiting for Frank's return. Giant of a ship, giant engines. *Surely*. Though who Frank might find to ask, down here in the ship's bowels in the middle of the night – that might be what was taking so much time, she guessed, finding someone who'd know. There'd be others like him nosing around with the same questions, no doubt, maybe dozens of them, but the engineers would only be getting on with it. Frank might have gone down to the engines, she supposed: that was where the heart of it would be. Well – not engines, boilers. Engines were farther back – farther aft, one should say. End to end, the ship was about the length of Patrick Street, for God's sake. Imagining that – from Saint Patrick's bridge to Old Queen's Castle, *that* distance! Boiler *rooms*, though, was what they had lower down in this part of the ship – men stripped to the waist, running with black sweat from the harsh labour and stifling, blinding heat, shovelling coal by the ton after ton into the furnaces that raised the steam to power the engines.

And ourselves here idle, in the lap of luxury, she thought. Nothing like the bad old days when emigrants had been battened down in sailing-ships' dark holds and left to fend for themselves through weeks-long storms, sickness and starvation. Eileen had heard of it from her mother, whose father Josiah had been a sailor himself and seen it all, seen the dead landed with the living often enough and had himself drowned at sea when his daughter had been eleven years of age.

Nothing like *that* now. Third class it might be, this was still luxury. Tom sleeping peacefully, his breath fanning his mother's neck. Come hurry back, Frank my darling. They'll tell us in the morning what it was that stopped the engines for an hour or two. Voices out there – women's, then a banging – on a cabin door? – and a male shout of 'Are ye in there, Deirdre?' She shut her ears to it: once the engines started up again they'd all settle down, and meanwhile Deirdre'd do well to stay put *and* keep her door bolted. Eileen Maguire yellow-eyed in the darkness – cat's eyes, Frank called them – consciously happy, *excited*, on the way at last to their own new world. Remembering the excitement of embarkation and departure from Queenstown on Thursday, three days ago, having come off the train from Cork and boarded the tender – tall-funnelled steamboat, she'd thought at first it was a tug – that carried them from the harbour-front to this great vessel lying at anchor four miles out, close off Roche's Point. Frank pointing out the ship's main features and warning herself and Tom, 'The cabin they're giving us will be a long way down in her. You'll see. Five, six decks down. That's third class, what's called "steerage" – although where they're putting us is nearer the bow than the stern, as it so happens. Could have been either, there's third-class cabins both ends. "Bow" means the front, Tom – remember? "Steerage" used to mean right aft, where the rudder is – for steering, see – because in the old windjammers it was the crew lived right for'ard, in what they called the forecastle. Still do, mostly . . . But all right, so – in the middle of her there's second class, and up top is first, the grandest cabins and staterooms and God knows what else, where them as can pay a small fortune for it has everything a man could ask for. So listen now, Eileen, it's a promise I'm after making you – and you, Tom, you're witness to it. When we come back to Ireland—'

'*Will* we?'

Tom had asked this. Eileen only shaking her dark head, gazing over ruffled grey water at the huge liner lying there at anchor. Frank telling his son – telling her too, although he knew how she felt about it – 'For a visit, like. Maybe. Why not? After I've made our pile . . . But all right, let's say *if* we come back: what I'm telling you is we'll come in the first class, so we will!'

Coming back wasn't in *her* mind. The way she saw it, America was to be their home henceforth and for ever more, and that should give them enough to be thinking and talking about right now. Whereas in Frank's mind it was the politics, of course, the part she didn't like – and hoped to God he'd put out of mind once he was there and had his hands full. Maybe he would, too. But there and then, on the tender taking them out from shore, the last thing she'd wanted was another argument about it – in Tom's hearing, at that – and she'd changed the subject, asked him why the ship was anchored so far out from shore. She'd visualised embarking right there at Queenstown, filing up a gangway from the quayside, the way she'd seen pictures of it at places like Southampton. Frank had explained – to Tom as well as to her – that there wasn't a sufficient depth of water so close into the port, or for that matter room to manoeuvre a ship of such size. Out towards Roche's Point was where all the big liners anchored: this one's White Star Line sister-ship the *Olympic*, for instance, had lain there often enough: and the Cunarders *Mauretania* and *Lusitania* – even though they were only about thirty thousand tons apiece, and this *Titanic* half as big again. Frank was pointing out headlands and islands then: Haulbowline Island, which like Queenstown itself was a Royal Navy base, then Spike Island with the military fort on it, another fort on a bulge of land to port soon after, and on the starboard hand the entrance to Crosshaven, inside Ram's Head. Others who didn't know the place were listening too; with them on the tender were a hundred and twenty other steerage passengers, and a few second-class as well as three Americans travelling first: those were in some cabin, getting not nearly so fine a view of the grand harbour, or probably hearing much of the music, bagpipes that were being played by a fellow by name of Eugene Daly. Daly was from County Westmeath, and they'd come to know him and his wife Marcella quite well in the last few days, but on the tender he'd been only a tall, red-headed stranger livening the half-hour passage with his piping – 'Erin's Lament' he'd played, and then 'A Nation Once Again'.

One of Frank's favourites, that. Politics again. It so happened that the Irish Home Rule Bill was to have been presented to the English parliament by Prime Minister Asquith this Friday – day before yesterday, when the *Titanic* was one day out of Queenstown, and although there'd been no mention of it in any news bulletin – according to a steward whom Frank had asked to enquire of the Marconi operators – he'd said it wouldn't amount to anything more than a monumental swindle. Seemingly his friends in Cork had fed him all this stuff. He'd had Eugene Daly play a lot of old Republican ballads that night, and again this Sunday evening – back aft in the third-class smoking-room, which opened on to the after well-deck, giving easy access to the poop. It had been too cold for Daly to play up there as he had on Friday, on account of the proximity of the ice, of course.

Frank had been gone an awful long time, she thought. And there was a huge noise out there now. *Up* there – a blasting, roaring sound. She put a hand lightly over Tom's ear, for fear the noise might wake him again. Working it out for herself though – that it must be a letting-off of steam. Anywhere near it, it must be truly thunderous. With the engines stopped, and fires still lit in the stoke-holds, she supposed—

Frank burst in, and light flooded the cabin. Frank, dishevelled, darkly unshaven, grim-looking, telling her, 'Best turn out, love, get dressed, the both of you. They're saying it's not serious but – we hit ice, over there starboard side, been *that* side you'd 'a heard it all right! Fact is, she's holed, so—'

'*Holed*, is it?'

'Starboard side from the bow well aft. Come here to me, Tommy. Warm clothes now, Eileen – and quick, eh?'

'All right. Although I don't see how—'

Tom's squawk: 'Are we after sinking, Pa?'

'Here, put your arms in – reach up now. That's the way!'

'Merciful God . . .' Eileen had tried to help with Tom, but Frank pushed her away, urged her, 'Dress *yourself* . . . Now, Tom – sit, stick your legs out – there now . . .'

'*Will* we sink, so?'

'No, Tommy, we will not.' There was pandemonium outside, cabin doors slamming, women yelling and a man's repeated shout, 'All of you *out*!' Eileen seized Frank's arm, pointing – guardedly, not for Tom to see – at water spreading in under the cabin door. Frank nodded. 'I know. I was down below here – to the orlop deck. Mail-room's filling fast, they've moved up to the sorting-room – G deck that is. But you see we're bow-down with the water that's already in her for'ard—'

'All out!' The door flung open. A steward – name of Humbert, little fellow, bald as a plate and pink-faced: he'd recognized Frank and nodded to him. 'All to go aft – along the E-deck corridor – all right?'

'Will the ship sink then?' Tom had asked it.

The steward gazed at him, wordless. Eileen demanded, '*Will* it?'

'No, missus. But at this end where the water's coming in, see – well, *see*.' The water – all of them staring down at it. It was already right across the cabin floor. 'Hurry along aft then – all right?'

'Did you get all the women out of their berths?'

Because third-class single women and girls were all at this end, single men in the after section. The steward told Frank yes, all on their way or will be. He ducked out, calling to someone else out there. The water was an inch deep near the door, two or three inches at the basin end, owing to the deck's slope, the ship's increasing bow-down angle. Eileen was ready – in a skirt and a shirt with a jersey and her coat over that; she was rolling a shawl to stuff it into a pocket of the coat. Headscarf – round her neck . . . Frank picked up Tom, ready to go, but she had him wait while she pulled the child's bobbled woollen hat down over his mop of ginger hair. Ginger like his father's. The noise of escaping steam would have been frightening if you'd let it be: she had a picture in her mind of the mail-room flooded, and maybe by now the sorting-room above it, which was only one deck down from this one. So after *that*—

Checking the thought. A smile at Tom. This ship was known to be unsinkable: Steward Humbert had surely been telling them nothing but the truth, it was a matter only of getting to the other end of it where it would be dry. Frank obviously with similar thoughts in mind, telling them as he ushered them out, 'Fact of it is, I'm sure enough she'd *not* sink. This forepart can fill with water but there's bulkheads and a heck of a lot of ship abaft them as'll hold the rest up. And there'll be pumps at work. As long as they can keep power on the engines—'

'But if they're letting out all the steam—'

'Step careful now.' To get to the iron staircase they were having to move closer to the bow – down-slope. Overhead lights brilliant on white-painted walls and ceiling and the swirl of water underfoot. Frank in the lead with Tom in his arms was already up to his ankles in it. Tom silent, big-eyed: staring back at her over his father's shoulder: she gave him a smile, reminded him, 'It'll be dry at the other end, your man said.' In any case the staircase was only two cabin doors along now, it wasn't going to get much deeper: although it was just as well they'd moved when they had, she thought: these cabins here would have it halfway up to the bunks by now. Frank telling her – telling *them* – 'Letting off steam, you said. That's only venting excess pressure. Sure, there's six great boiler-rooms down there, you know?'

Tom asked him, 'What if *they* get full with water?'

'Well, they will, the forward ones. Others won't, for the reason I said. Here, now – up we go. Eileen, come on past me now, go on in front?'

Knee-deep, edging round them and on to the stairs. The first two or three iron steps were under water. The stairway was made of iron at this level: higher it became much grander, where it led on up through second- into first-class accommodation. Not that you could just walk up from steerage into second or first – you'd come up against locked iron gates at certain levels. In any case E deck was their destination, just one level higher than this, F deck.

'Will you listen a minute now.' Frank with some new thought in his head: she was above him, three or four steps up, pausing to look down at him as he came up another step out of water and made to pass the boy to her. 'That's the way – you go to your mummy now, just for a minute – keep an eye on her for me, will you so? Eileen, go on up, wait for me at the top there, I'm going for our money and that, papers and such – y'know?'

'No – *no*, Frank—'

'Damn fool I was not to think before. Go on now, there's time, stay here fussing we've lost the lot *and* God knows what else.' He'd transferred Tom to her, had been saying all that as he went back down – glancing back up now, a wave goodbye and a smile. He was knee-deep in it at *least*, down there. Eileen calling, for Tom's sake trying not to sound as frantic as she felt, 'We don't *need* the money, Frank! *Please*, don't – Frank—'

'*Hell* we don't need money!' His voice and a laugh like a bark echoing back: steam gushing again above them: something else he'd called too, but she hadn't made it out.

Tom with his mouth open, panting, close to tears. Most kids would be howling their heads off, she thought. Hugging him tight, telling him, 'We'll go up just a little way, I doubt he'll be long. He's a big strong man, your father . . .'

Up a few more steps. Even then, not far above the water. Tom with his face in the angle of her neck and shoulder, hidden from her. She didn't want to climb too high, for fear he'd think they were deserting his father – or it might even feel to *her* they were. Bellow of escaping steam cut off again, voices from higher decks loud but also remote, incomprehensible for the most part, echoey; close to her ear Tom's shrill 'Why doesn't he *come*?' She was patting him all the time, his back and shoulders, murmuring to him: 'Well, he *will*, my darling, any minute now he *will* . . .'

Please God, he will. Does he know what he's *doing* to us?

A noise like a groan. From the forward end – which had to be all flooded. Long drawn-out, a giant's groan – or creak, say. The lights flickered, then steadied again – maybe even brighter that they had been. The groaning – creaking – sounded frighteningly close. Steel straining against rupture? She'd gone up another step. Water came in a wave then – below, piling along the corridor of E deck, bursting around the staircase and smashing against the bulkhead there that blocked it off. But coming from the drier end of the ship – how? Maybe forced up from below and further aft – the hatchway from the flooded mail-room, for instance, flooding up *there* maybe – where Frank must be, near enough? The water-level down there, she reckoned, had to be at least a foot higher than it had been when he'd left them: you could measure it on the staircase, the steps it covered. She was doing so as well as watching desperately for Frank when something like – well, an explosion, an almighty *thump*, from the flooded section, the forepart. She'd not only heard it but felt it, a solid jarring through the iron under her feet and where she had her hip against the railing for support.

Like running into the iceberg might have sounded?

Tom had begun to cry.

'Tommy me darling, angel-boy, he'll be with us *very* soon, you'll see . . .'

He could surely have got that stuff and been back by *now*. Imagination suggested a buckled door or somesuch, trapping him – or that flood half a minute ago, whatever had caused *that*. But he was a big, strong fellow, and resourceful – as well as bloody obstinate, strong-headed, risking his life – hers and Tommy's for that matter – for a bit of saved money and some old papers—

'You all right, there?' Below her, staring up, wild-looking. A wave of one hand: 'So go on higher. Go on – I'm with you and I have it all!'

Turning, climbing . . . 'See, Tommy – did I not tell you?' Tommy was craning his head around her upper arm that side to see down to his father. He'd stopped his crying. Eileen climbing slowly, step by step, not having a hand to spare so using the rail by pressing her hip against it. Being tall, long in the leg, she could do that. Hearing Frank's boots now on the iron treads as he closed up behind: telling her, 'Cabin's half full, but I got it. *And* your watch!'

Expecting congratulations, for having put her and Tom through that agonizing wait?

Well. How he *was*, that was all. And special enough at that – her man, and this one's Da – for better or for worse, but darned near all of it was for better. The reason it had *mattered*, for God's sake! Like the thought she'd had a minute ago that he'd been chancing not just his own life but hers and the boy's too – in other words that it was the three of them or nothing?

Tell him, when there's a chance, tell him from now on stay *together*.

E deck. The wide working passage that ran its whole length along the ship's centreline was known to the crew as 'Park Lane', or 'Scotland Road'. Eileen was off the stairs, and in the bare, bright tunnel of it: seeing a whole crowd of people gathering – well, milling around – having she supposed only just been cleared out of the cabins on this deck. Familiar faces, most of them – and Steward Humbert there, urging them to go on aft. Some of them were taking baggage with them – suitcases and bundles. Humbert spotting her and Frank now and beckoning fiercely as if they should have been up here long ago. She smiled, wagged her head at him, while transferring Tom to his father.

'Safe now, Tom. Home and dry. Not *far* off dry. You're a grand, brave lad.'

'He is, of course. What else'd you expect?' Frank had him in his arms, and was thrusting a package towards her in his right hand. It was the canvas roll in which he kept his razor and shaving-brush and a few other bits and pieces; he'd filled it with money and papers, and fastened it in a tight roll with string. Telling her, 'You have the pockets for it, and I have not.' He was soaking wet up to his waist, she realized. So much for 'dry' . . . 'And here – your watch!'

It was half-hunter sized, made of gun-metal. Her late father had bequeathed it to her; she felt shame now at having left it down there in the cabin. Then after pushing the canvas roll into the pocket that didn't have the shawl in it she looked to check the time and was ashamed again at not having wound it last night.

'What time is it, Frank?'

'Quarter after midnight. Getting near an hour since we hit the 'berg.'

'And she won't float more than another hour.' It was another steward – white jacket, from first class evidently. A middling-sized man, with brown hair slicked back and a narrow moustache. Stewards, even first-class ones, had cabins somewhere in this region: and he was going forward, towards the staircase. He'd have a key, of course, he'd go right on up into those palatial upper areas, opening a gate or two and re-locking them behind him. He jerked a thumb the way the steerage crowd was supposed to be going, told them, 'Get along, if I were you.'

'You say an hour?'

'It's the captain's opinion, so I heard.'

He was an Englishman, and for a steward, she thought, unusually well-spoken. Her own Irish ear being attuned by the early influence of her father having had strong English connections.

'And the ship *will* sink?'

'I'd like to be able to say no, she won't, but—'

'Will we be let up on the boat-deck now then?'

Frank staring down at him, delaying him with a hand on his arm – a wet hand, from which the man freed himself, glancing at the jacket-sleeve with disfavour. At Eileen then: and back to Frank and Tom. 'Your own stewards will direct you. Couldn't say where, exactly. But – ' pointing aft, the way all those others were crowding along now – 'best not to hang around, eh?'

'Wait – please . . .' Eileen: he'd been turning away but paused, cocking an eyebrow at her. She asked him, 'Would you ever let us up there yourself – through the gate? No one to know of it, you'd go on ahead and we'd take care of ourselves from there on?'

'Great heavens, but you'd have me *shot*!'

Frank said, 'There's worse deaths.'

Eye to eye: the steward staring at him for a long moment: then glancing at Eileen and back to him again. 'You'll be all right. If you hurry along now. Don't want to be left behind, do you?'

He turned, went on for'ard, down-slope. Frank jerked his

head, 'Come on. Like he said . . . Eileen, you had a cheek, to ask him that!'

'If we don't get to the boat-deck, how'll we get into boats?'

Heading aft, close together, hurrying now. 'He didn't say we would not be let up there. Only not by *that* route. They'll get us up there but by way of our own parts of the ship – that's the answer to your question. Up the stairs back aft to our smoking-room, I'd say, out on to the after well-deck—'

'But that's nowhere near any boat at all!'

'*From* there, I'm saying, up to the boat-deck by whatever route's opened to us. That Humbert's not leading us back aft for no purpose – huh?' Striding on, Eileen having almost to run to keep up with him. He told her, 'Another thing is there's ways through the ship's side at lower levels than just the boat-deck and A deck, there's like big doors they call "entry ports". They can stop lowering a boat at this or that one, and if a bunch of us is waiting there and there's room left in the boat – there y'are. One thing I'd tell you though – so you'd be ready for it – it could be as they'd split us up – me from the pair of you. How it goes, at sea, always has, it's women and children they put in lifeboats first.'

'I wouldn't get in a boat without you, Frank.'

'Oh yes, you would – having the lad with you – of *course* you would, for Tommy's sake!'

'So what'd you do then?'

'Well, after all the women an' kids is safe away—' Shifting Tom in his arms, smiling at him: 'Look, don't either of you worry now, it'll pan out all right.'

Ahead of them the crowd was slowing, bunching up. From the slant of the deck she realized the ship had to be leaning sideways, as well as the slope that had been making them walk uphill. A *list*, was what you called it: this one. a list to *port*. She saw Steward Humbert coming back towards them with his arms full of what looked like bedding but turned out to be life-jackets.

'You'd best put these on. On the boy too, if you can manage.'

'Show us how?'

'Pleased to. See – over your head like this – arms through then – so. Now the tapes – pass 'em round behind, and secure 'em good an' tight in front. All there is to it – see?'

'Thank you . . .'

'With the young lad you can pass the tapes round him two or three times, maybe.' Looking at Eileen: 'But you'd do better to wear yours under your coat, missus. Up to you, of course, but you'd find it easier. I'm having a job persuading some of 'em to wear the things at all – would you believe it? And as for those as doesn't speak English – well, God help us!'

'What happens now, then?'

'Oh – up to the boats.' A gesture, pointing upward. 'Women and their children first, of course.' Shake of the head as he turned away. 'Won't be long now.' He moved away, still with a few jackets to get rid of. Frank said as he set Tom down, to put the life-jacket on him – it would be like a strait-jacket, immobilize him completely, Eileen realized – 'Up the stairway there, see, when our turn comes.'

Tom said, 'I don't *want* it!'

'Come on, Tommy lad. Keep you warm, and—'

'No! No, *please*—'

'Frank, it's not necessary. He'd be lost in that. You or I'll be his lifebelt – if there was any need – which God forbid—'

'All right. All right, Tom.' Straightening, leaving Tom down there knee-high but with the small hand clasped in his; Eileen moved round to the far side of him and took the other one. Stooping to explain, 'Only a matter of how best to set about it – no matter what, we're going to be all right, Tom.' Frank was giving the unwanted life-jacket to a young man who didn't have one and was thanking him for it in a foreign tongue. They were in the thick of the crowd here, hemmed in between the steel walls like cattle patient in a yard. As well as Irish there were Finns, Norwegians, Dutch, French, Italians – and English, and French who'd embarked at Cherbourg, where the ship had lain at anchor for a couple of hours before coming on to Queenstown. Frank had lowered himself again to squat and murmur reassurances to Tom; two small girls, maybe eight and ten, holding a stout mother's hands, were watching the little boy and the man curiously – admiringly, Eileen thought. Asking herself who ever *had* such a son – two and three-quarter years old and so steady, such a *man*-child? She was distracted then by movement up ahead, something happening near the foot of the stairway, which was where this steerage crowd had halted – or *been* halted. On her toes, looking over the people's heads – and Frank rising too – but simultaneously there was a crash like a clap of thunder, now reverberations like shudders running through the ship. Voices had begun to hush before this, for whatever was happening up front, and now you had dead silence, folk gazing around and at each other. Frank up on his feet with a hand still down to Tom, Tom with his other hand clinging to his mother's skirt. A steward called from the front, 'Will you listen now? Don't worry, that wasn't anything to concern us.' Frank's derisive grunt close to her ear: but she could see the steward, a man by name of Hart, he'd climbed a few steps on the staircase to address them. 'Listen – captain's orders – women and children to the boat-deck. But you wouldn't find your way, through parts of the ship you were never in before, so I'll lead you up in groups – say twenty at a time. Twenty females from the front here now – and I'll be back for more. Let's have you now – you, miss – and you two—'

'Wait our turn.' Frank said it stolidly. Eileen murmured, 'What would that noise have been?'

'A bulkhead going. One boiler-room to the next one aft, I'd say.'

A whisper: 'So we *will* sink?'

Frowning: and a shake of the head. 'Maybe not for hours. High and dry this end – the whole afterpart to hold her up.'

'But if it goes on like that, smashing through—'

'Who says it will?'

'The slope's steeper, isn't it?'

Shuffling forward, up-slope. Girls and women, some with children, thronging up the stairway, the rest shifting along nearer to it. A young man – Dutchman, or maybe a Swede but anyway he had some English, they'd chatted with him on deck and in the smoking-room a few times – put a hand on Frank's shoulder, asked him, 'Women, children, very good, but we?'

'Take our turn,' Frank told him, 'It's the way of it, always was.'

'We stay here?'

'Sure. Get them away first, see?'

'Why you not take up your wife and small one?'

'Well – as your man was tellin' us—'

'How long, wait here?'

She'd seen the barely contained panic in his eyes, and turned away – crouching, to converse with Tom. On their way along the corridor she'd set her watch, and caught herself glancing at it again now; but why bother, when time itself might finish – explode – at any second? That last booming crash could have been a prelude to the sea smashing *all the way* through. Seeing it in her mind: an overwhelming flood, break-through and invasion of solid ocean – the weight and power of it, nothing man-made standing a chance against it . . .

Stop it, now. *Stop* it. The Dutchman had left them, making his way through the crowd towards the staircase. Not seeming to hurry, excusing himself as he shouldered through the tighter groups, but within seconds – she'd risen to her feet again – he was on the stairs and climbing, not glancing back or down. Gone. She met Frank's blue stare, hesitated momentarily before whispering to him, 'Couldn't *we*?'

'They'll have the gates locked. Steward'll unlock 'em, lock 'em again behind him. We'd get so far, no further.' Frank was whispering too. 'You can see what for, they're controlling the rush, else they'd be swamped up there. Be easy now, love – steward'll be back any minute.'

'We won't make the next group if it's only twenty again – and *you* won't make it at *all*, at all. Not with them saying who goes, who stays. Well. *I* shan't go, not without you. And look, that's our third-class stairway, we've a *right*! Frank, if we just *go* – same as that Dutchman—'

'Dane, he is.'

'Dane, then.'

'There's no point. On his own, maybe he'll find a way up from the well-deck to the promenade deck above – up the outside, that is. Not that it'll do him much good, when they aren't letting men into the boats in any case. And with Tom we can't climb ladders – uh?'

Looking into his eyes: conscious of the clutch of Tommy's arms down at her knees. Shaking her head: 'It's not the wild man I married, is it. *He'd*'ve fought a way up, wouldn't he?'

'No, he would not.' Back down to a whisper now. 'Because that way would be to start the rest of 'em at it too, a panic maybe. He may've been wild, that fellow, but he wasn't a damn fool and what's more he was a seaman, he'd've cared more for saving his wife and child than acting the bloody idiot!'

Pronouncing it 'eejit'. Which on occasion he *had* been,

even if he didn't know it. She acknowledged, 'You could be right. He was always a thoughtful man – as well as wild.'

'Sounds like a contradiction, did I ever hear one.'

'*Not* at all! What I loved him for – and still do!'

When he smiled that way, she saw the man she'd fallen for, all right. Frank seeing her the same way maybe – touching her lips with his. From above, the sound carrying down the stairway, a renewed thunder of escaping steam so loud she could imagine it whitening the night sky. She said, 'You'd think they'd've let it all out by this time. But I suppose the lights – and the pumps—'

'There's engineers still at work down there, all right.'

'Would *you* have?'

'I hope I would. In any case, God bless 'em. Listen – we might advance ourselves a bit. Quietly like – see if we can't get you in the next crowd to go up. Might *just* do it, see—'

'Get *me* in it?'

'The pair of you I mean, of course. Don't be silly now, you heard him – women an' children *only*. At *this* stage, mark you. It's Tom you should think of – and I'll be along by and by, God's sake—'

'Second party ready now please!'

Steward Hart. The other one, Humbert, had gone up with him and not returned. There was a start of general movement: Frank stooping to pick Tom up and put him on his shoulder, Eileen on tiptoes to give her son a kiss. 'All right, pet?' She heard Hart's voice again, a more urgent note in it: 'You ladies, *please*!'

Extraordinarily, some were refusing to go up. Arguments were in progress in various languages, women either refusing to leave their husbands or just not understanding *why* they were required to leave them. Many not speaking English: *and* scared half out of their wits. Hart was losing patience: 'Come on then, some of you others!

Twenty I want – I'll be back again but twenty I want *now*. Look, boats are being lowered already, some's down in the water!'

'Hear that?' Frank was pushing forward with Eileen at his side and Tom on his shoulder: up there he was clear of the life-jacket which otherwise made it awkward, carrying him. Quite a few women were standing aside, although all the single girls were clustered at the stairs' foot, more than ready to go up. Women with children had all gone in the first party, it seemed – except this stout one with the two small girls. Hart saw Frank coming, and pointed at him: 'Women and children only, mister!'

'I'll carry the lad up, see my wife away and come back down with you. That all right?'

'I'm sorry – contrary to my orders. It's the crowd up there, you see. The lady can carry your son, can't she? You'll all be brought up in the end, only it's women first. The way it is, that's all! Now – you ladies—'

Eileen told Frank, 'I'm not going.'

'God's *sake*, girl—'

'Excuse me.' A woman who'd been refusing to move had changed her mind, was pushing through. Then several others. Maybe Hart's assurance that the men would follow in due course had done the trick. He'd got enough of them together now. Frank trying again, pushing Tom at her: 'Eileen – take him, will you?'

'Take you any time, Tom my pet.' From Frank's arms into hers. 'But we won't go up there without your daddy, will we?'

'Mr and Mrs Maguire – excuse me . . .'

A short, broad-shouldered Welshman, name of Davies: he and Frank had been finalists in the dominoes tournament, evening before last. Reaching to ruffle Tom's hair: 'Fine lad, you have.' Dropping his voice then, and a jerk of his head towards the stairway. 'On their way up now and Hart's at the front, see – and no eyes in the back of his head – uh?'

'You're saying—'

'Go on up, I'm saying. Tag on the end. When you're there you're *there* – right?'

'By God—'

Eileen nodding: 'Yes. Yes . . .'

'I'll stand rearguard.' The Welshman was broad enough, solid enough, to do just that. 'Don't want a whole crowd pilin' after you.' His hand out: they both shook it. Frank muttered, 'See you, Taffy – I hope.' He was taking Tom back from Eileen, telling her, 'You go first.' To the foot of the stairs, then climbing, with Frank and Tom close behind her and Davies taking up his own position with his fists on his hips and his eyes on the people below there – who'd fallen silent, watching the Maguires climb on up and out of their sight. Frank telling Eileen, 'Faster, love. To be at the gates before they shut 'em.'

'All right.' Glancing back at him: and at Tom, but only at the back of his head, since he was facing backwards, over his father's shoulder. Eileen envisaging Frank being sent down from the locked gate, maybe: and his offer to Steward Hart that he'd voluntarily return with him. If Hart believed that, she thought – on the next flight now, from D deck up to C, and with the tail-end of the bunch ahead, that woman with her girls, in sight but not looking back – he'd believe the moon was made of cheese. Time by her old watch, ten minutes past one. Why they should have had to wait down there on E deck she couldn't understand; a whole deck higher now, they were still in third-class territory, right up to the staircase lobby and the smoking-room inside the poop. Hart could as well have mustered them up here – you'd have thought.

Maybe they'd *had* a crowd up here, and sent them up

first? Married women and families from this end of E and F decks, maybe?

Up into the lobby now. Wicker chairs stacked along the far side – starboard side, and the heavy steel door leading forward to the well-deck shut now behind those others. Eugene Daly had played his pipes in here: it struck her that she hadn't seen him or Marcella – or quite a few others either – down on E deck. Frank had passed her, going ahead to cope with that heavy door, swinging it open to freezing-cold night and the down-slope of the well-deck glistening with sea-dew or – God, *frost*, it could've been. Light streamed out from the door the other side of it, was cut off as the last of the women ahead of them pulled it shut; there was light flooding from above in any case, from windows in the rear end of A and B decks, while closer here a crane slanted skeletally against the sky – and rigging, and the mizzen mast and beyond that the rearmost funnel high and massive against stars. One funnel was a dummy, Frank had told her: she'd asked why in the name of God they'd want any such thing, and he'd told her, 'Because without it she'd look peculiar.' They'd reached the door the women had gone in by: from here on would *not* be in third class. Frank muttering, 'Might be locked – if there was a feller there to do it.' There wasn't though, and he had it open, his shoulder to it for Eileen to get in ahead of them, and it was she who saw Humbert shutting a steel gate across, just a short way along this passage. The big woman was shepherding her daughters around a corner of the passageway further along, Steward Humbert had a hand on the cage-like barrier pushing it across but with his back this way, bawling after them, 'Good luck to you too, lassies!' Eileen had snatched Tom from Frank as he pounded forward: the gate had clashed shut, Humbert unhurriedly turning back and locking it. Eileen clutching Tom, and mortified: seeing then that Frank had an arm through one diamond-shaped aperture – had Humbert by the throat, Humbert clawing at that wrist and mewling, gasping. Frank growled, 'Unlock it – or you won't need drowning!' Eileen was up with them by then, and saw surrender – terror – in the man's bulging eyes, told Frank, 'He'll do it – *let* him!' The key was attached to the steward's wrist on a chain; Frank had loosened his grip but still held him while he fumbled at the lock. She didn't hear it click over, partly because at that moment and for about half a minute there was a new trembling, juddering – as if the ship was shuddering in its own stark fear. But the gate was *open* – Frank sending it crashing back, Humbert standing back purple-faced, massaging his throat. 'You'll pay for this! By God, you'll—'

"T'was not by choice, Mr Humbert – and I'll not be getting in any boat, only making damn sure *they* do. Let's say you didn't let us by, we came some other way?'

Open-mouthed, gasping, speechless – as the tremor ceased. Humbert still quivering: Frank twice his size and ten years younger – and on this side of the gate now, with Eileen and Tom; Eileen thinking ahead, aware there might be other gates. Humbert found his voice: 'Go on then.'

'Thanks. Good luck.'

'Wouldn't've wanted to stop you, only—'

'Frank, come *on*?'

No one to follow now. Those others would be well ahead, guided by Steward Hart. But they had the down-slope towards the bow for guidance: you could hardly go wrong, on that. The list as well, of course. Hurrying through a lobby, then past a library, its doors wide open – spines of books in glass-fronted cabinets and a table with chairs around it. Second-class restaurant, then, on their left. Then another of the sliding gateways but this one mercifully standing open: they were passing into first class, through what she guessed (from notices on doors) were the surgeon's quarters and the hospital; then after turning a couple of corners – right into a transverse passageway and then left on the down-slope again – past a saloon for the use of first-class passengers' maids and valets: the inscription on that doorway was 'Servants' Hall'. Then cabin doors widely spaced, and the grand stairway was in sight ahead. No bare decks here, carpets all the way, and Eileen heard music – a band playing ragtime, above them somewhere where an enormous glass dome crowned the stair-head. Wide, deeply carpeted stairs, glossy mahogany banisters, oil paintings in gilt frames: Tom once again on his father's shoulder with his eyes shut, ignoring all such wonders; not fully asleep, she thought, but drowsy. Reaching B deck, now: the ragtime music louder as they climbed, and glimpses through open doorways of luxuriously decorated and furnished public rooms – all deserted, empty, until in one open double doorway a middle-aged man in evening clothes, smoking a cigar, removed it from his lips and bowed slightly to Eileen: 'Good evening, madam.' A nod to Frank: appraising eyes back on Eileen then. 'Charming. Absolutely.' He pointed with the cigar at Tom. 'Fine little chap you have there. You'll take very good care of him, I'm sure.'

'We will so.' Eileen smiled at him. He was an American, she thought; and behind him in the room lit by wall-sconces she had a brief sight of three other men sprawled around a gleamingly polished table – cigar smoke floating, glasses that glowed amber, playing-cards, and a voice calling, 'Should we expect you back, Charles, or are you too well occupied ogling pretty girls?'

Frank had muttered, 'They've had a good few, I'd say!' Eileen reflecting that to have found her charming in her present state the Yank must have had a lot more than just a few. It was plain enough *they* wouldn't be getting into any boats. Imagining it: water filling that big room, the table and chairs floating away, playing-cards dancing on the swirl of foam.

What could she do to get *Frank* into a boat, when he seemed half resigned to being prevented?

Boat-deck, finally. Something in common with a fairground: hurdy-gurdy ragtime from the band, which she couldn't see because of the crowd but had to be somewhere close, and people all over – more men than women, she noted – milling around or just standing in groups or on their own, moving between groups, dressed every way you could imagine – nightclothes and dressing-gowns, overcoats, caps and hats, women in evening dress with shawls or rugs over them, even in one case a bath-towel. Most were wearing life-jackets. Near them a stewardess was pleading with a stooped old man to accept the one she was offering him and which for some reason he didn't want. It was *extremely* cold. Tom was covered, all right, but not all that well: she hadn't foreseen this degree of cold. All she had was the shawl in her pocket; she got it out, to wrap it round him. Frank nodding towards empty davits: 'Your man was right, some's gone down already.' Having to shout: and shifting Tom so she could get the shawl around him. There was a lot of noise – men's and women's voices competing with the band, and the shouting of orders and so forth mostly around the boats. Now a great *whoosh* and a streak of flame, a rocket that exploded brilliant white overhead, momentarily whitening upturned faces. A man near them told another, 'Distress rocket. Been sending 'em up this past hour. To bring other vessels to our assistance, I understand.' Eileen and Frank were opposite a boat that was being loaded, crew-members straddling the ship's rail to help women over: two embarking now, handed up by their husbands who then stepped back, raising their hats – as if just seeing the the ladies into a carriage, for heaven's sake. But to Eileen's astonishment she saw they'd already

let two men into that one; and now a married couple –
elderly, both needing help: while a youngster, couldn't
have been more than about sixteen, was stopped by the
officer, sent back into the crowd.

There seemed not to be any firm policy. They *said* women
and children, then let men go. Or let some go and stopped
others.

'Frank – see, not only women!'

'Hold on.' He was watching a tall man in a suit and
carpet-slippers waving his arms about and bawling, 'Lower
away! Lower away!' That same officer yelled at him then,
'It's all right, sir – it's me here gives the orders!' Turning
to a bosun or some such then, demanding, 'He aiming to
drown those people?' Frank muttered, 'Damn right!' The
tall man was moving away, shoulders hunched, shuffling
in his slippers. Eileen hugging Frank's free arm: 'They've
put men in that one as well as women!'

'I know, I seen 'em. Mind you, you'd need a few seamen
to steer, handle the oars and that.'

'But those weren't—'

'Maybe old, or sick. God knows. Listen, we'll try the
other side. This side with the list the way it is a boat as
much as halfway down will be scraping the ship's plates.'
He nuzzled Tom's sleepy face: 'We'll be all right, Tom boy.
You'll look to your ma, huh?' To Eileen then: 'Come on.'
He'd spotted a way across from this side to the other,
under the loom of the huge third funnel; carrying Tom
and hauling Eileen, pushing through or around clusters
of people; passing now the windows of a gymnasium,
with folk inside – clearly first-class passengers – sitting
on exercise machines with seats like bicycle seats. And at
the corner here, an old couple – couldn't have been less than
in their seventies – on steamer chairs with one rug covering
the pair of them, by the look of it holding hands beneath it.
The woman smiled at her, and she hesitated, would have

stopped to talk but Frank was pulling her along. Growling, 'Mind yourselves now, please . . .'

Addressing a clutter of men filling that thwartships passage. One, standing aside, advised him, 'Best get the lady and the kid away, so. Ye don't mind me saying?'

Irish – and he'd have recognized Frank's intonation, that 'Mind yourselves', as Irish. He was a stoker, or trimmer: a big man, huge belly. Frank assured him, 'What I'm after doing this very moment, believe me. Thanks anyway.'

'Good luck to ye, then!'

'And to you, my friend.'

Through the gap, out on this port side. Telling her, 'This side, see, the way the list is, a boat'd swing clear on its way down. Lowering 'em isn't child's play, from this height – specially if the weight's not spread even—'

'He said get us away, and you—'

'Why would I dispute it with him?'

'You are coming with us, Frank—'

'Sure, I am. Other men going, why wouldn't I?'

The situation on this side seemed tense, with groups of men looking as if intending to rush the boats. A lot of them must·have been waiters or kitchen hands. Seamen were standing ready at the boats' falls, an officer with two stripes on his sleeves was perched up on a bollard or somesuch, supervising the whole deck, and there were more junior officers at individual boats. Repeating time after time, shouting over surrounding noise, 'Men to stand clear, women and children only now: and hurry! McLellan, you'll take charge of this one!'

A sailor acknowledged, climbing in, 'Aye aye.'

'Start the falls!'

She saw the boat next to this one starting down half-empty. Each could hold forty, he'd told her, or even fifty, but there weren't more than a dozen in it, including a seaman and three stokers – to handle the steering and so forth, he'd said. At this nearer boat meanwhile they'd stopped lowering, were holding it where it was while a stewardess embarked with two little girls who had to be lifted down into it. The surrounding crowd – *threatening* crowd you might say, and all males – edging forward as if in preparation for a last-minute leap. The officer was on the rail, a leg each side of it, one hand resting on the davit gear and the other with a pistol in it – waving it in the men's sight and repeating, 'Women and children *only*!' You could see how it could happen – a sudden rush in such force and numbers that it would tip the boat over, spilling those women down the ship's side. Eileen turned her back on it: Tom was awake now on Frank's shoulder, and despite the shawl still looked and felt icy cold. When they got in a boat, she'd loosen her coat and have him inside it. She heard the sharp *cracks* of pistol shots, whipped round just as the officer fired a third time – downward between the boat and the ship's side, not endangering anyone, but a clear warning to that rabble. There was a bellow of 'Lower away!' and the boat lurched, was on its way down again. She yelled at Frank, 'Isn't the other side best, after all?'

Despite the hazard of the list, Frank agreed: 'But no shilly-shally, if they'll let me go with you, well and good, if they won't you and Tom must go and I 'll see you later. Once all the women's away, see—'

'Then there'll be no boats left.' She insisted, pulling at him, 'You'll come *with* us, Frank!'

Back to the starboard side: Frank swearing again that if they let him, he would, of course. God's sake, did she take him for an eejit? He was only warning her – again – in case it turned out different. Like over there, buggers with guns even!

'Excuse me . . .'

A blond stewardess put her hand on Eileen's arm: and saw Tom perched up there on Frank. Back to Eileen, looking anxiously into her face. 'Time to get going – eh? That boat there – there's room for you and your boy—'

'For my husband too?'

'Oh. Well—'

'Get *them* away, you're right.' He'd shrugged. 'If they'll let me too – we seen men taken, mind—'

'I think when a boat's going down near-empty.' Shaking her head: and a hand up to Tom's cheek. 'Your little boy's cold!' Tom opened his eyes, stared at her, looked for reassurance at his mother and shut his eyes again. Eileen admitting to the stewardess, 'I should've brought up a blanket. Didn't expect *this* cold.'

'I'll try to find one.' Looking at Frank: 'Take them to the boat now? I'll find *something*, and throw it over. Put them in now – won't you?' She'd gone. Frank had his spare arm around Eileen, coaxing her towards the boat, which looked crowded already although they were still waving women forward. Must *be* full, just about, she thought: seamen who'd come from what were now empty davits were stooping to the falls, freeing the ropes for lowering. Frank told her, 'If they won't take me in this, I'll find another and be with you later, somehow. Be content with that, Eilie, please, believe it, if I can come, I will. And there'll be rescue ships along soon enough – that rocket then—'

The last of the rockets, she supposed, since there'd been no more and they'd been at it for an hour, someone had said. Who was to know there'd be any other ship near enough to see them? She followed in Frank's wake as he shouldered through towards the boat – until an officer of sorts – junior purser, she recognized him, he'd taken their tickets and allocated cabins when they'd boarded at Queenstown – barred their way. 'Only women and children, sir!'

'I've one of each here.' He added – up closer, more quietly – 'Don't give *her* that stuff. I'll be passing the boy over, *then* coming. It's a fact he wouldn't want a stranger handling him.' Eileen was beside him then: 'What's this?' He told her, 'You in first, then I'll hand Tom over.'

'And follow?'

'I was telling him, Tom wouldn't want a stranger slinging him around.'

'You'll *follow*, Frank?'

'When they're set to lower – maybe.' Eyes on each other's faces, and in the crowd as jammed tight as they could have been. There'd been a lot of new arrivals on this deck, a whole pile of them suddenly. He kissed her, repeated, '*Maybe*. If there's places left. Like we saw along there?'

'Frank, I'd *die* if—'

'Ready, are we?' The purser gestured to a steward, who took her arm: there was a sailor on her other side. Frank standing with Tom, watching them less help her up than *fling* her up: Eileen twisting to look back at him imploringly, while a woman already in the boat – thickset woman in a fur coat, a felt hat jammed on her head – helped too, hauling her over and in, and Eileen through trying to look back again stumbled – her foot missing a thwart maybe – went sprawling into the whole mêlée of them. There was a degree of rush in it you could have called panic now: and through the women's yelling an officer's bark of 'Stand by!' and then 'Start the falls!' Meaning, Frank knew, to inch the falls out a little, see the ropes ran clear through the blocks, as a preliminary to the order 'Lower away'. The boat jerking a little as they did it. Eileen still somewhere in that free-for-all behind the woman in the felt hat, who was holding her arms out for Tom, shrieking at Frank to pass him over. She was no beauty – mouth like a spade-gash in a turnip, and solid enough to be obstructing any sight he might have had of Eileen – and the steward who'd helped was on the rail again to assist in Tom's transfer. But Tom didn't get that far. Frank had eased him down off his shoulder, assuring him it was his ma he was handing him over to – Tom in a bit of a state of course, having seen not his mother but that huge creature reaching for him – and as Frank let him down to the deck in order to get a better sort of hold on him he twisted free and bolted like a rabbit into the crowd. Eileen up beside the heavy woman with her mouth open in a shriek, then struggling to climb out, but she'd have needed help, not the restraint several others were exerting on her – and Frank gone, charging into the rabble bellowing their son's name; *gone*, both of them, from her view of it virtually driven off – and over the pandemonium including her own shrieks suddenly a renewal of that high-pitched howling from the tall one in the suit, his arms whirling again like a windmill's sails – to Eileen unbelievable, a death sentence from a total stranger – 'Lower away! Lower aw-a-a-y!'

2

Numb, exhausted, after prolonged hysteria that had left her soaked in her own sweat and with her own screams and the other women's extraordinarily varied reactions – aggression as well as kindness – a jumbled, barely comprehensible background to the nightmare. At one stage she'd been trying to get out, and they'd had to restrain her physically. She couldn't understand why her pleas had been ignored, why they hadn't stopped lowering despite at least one of these crewmen bawling up at them to do so. She'd had – Jesus God, *still* had – a nightmare vision of Tom scuttling through the foundering ship's interior, the maze of passageways and stairs and vast empty rooms – little boy in terror, Frank having been handicapped to start with in getting through the crowd, Tom fleeing like some small terrified animal through the forest of trousered and skirted legs, and Frank then having no track to follow, only blind alternatives at every corner or cabin door. Frank racked by the same horror and guilt that was racking *her* – Tom thinking his mummy had deserted him, his daddy then trying to hand him over to this strange female with her loud voice and savage grin. In the nightmare was also the wave she'd seen flooding through F deck and bursting around the ladder's foot, but ten times the size and force, the kind of inrush of ocean there *would* be now: not on E deck, which would have been full, not D either, but C maybe – Tom racing and maybe tumbling down the wide sweep of stairs, and not a soul to stop him. In any case strangers scared him. That tiny figure, and the thunderous rush of sea . . . She had her head in her hands, shivering, the sweat like a film of ice on her now, aware of the big woman tentatively putting a thick fur arm around her – carefully, because the last time she'd done it Eileen had fought free – as Tom would have. The woman was telling her in her rather deep, American-accented voice, 'They'll have him in a boat by now, I'm sure. As like as not the both of them – they'll understand he *needs* his daddy. Honey, it stands to reason . . .'

Other boats were widely scattered – dark, distant shapes on the shine of the starlit ocean. *Frozen* ocean. There was none visible in the close vicinity of the ship, although she knew that at least one had been lowered since this one had.

Whitish flickerings here and there would be the splashing of oars. Eileen, with her breathing under control now, told the big woman, 'Tom's advanced for his age in a lot of ways and brave too, but when he's scared he's *really* scared. And only Frank looking for him, you see. Well, that stewardess maybe, the pretty one. All the others only out to save themselves or getting boats launched. Like they wouldn't stop lowering this one no matter what!'

'Guess they could not have, honey. They were having to go from one boat to the next – if they'd stopped for you there'd be the next one delayed as well, left dangling there full of people and with the danger of being rushed, d'you see. There was that danger, I swear there was, even if you didn't see it. Then again, how long would they have to wait? They'd say no, get this one down, when the little boy's father comes back with him we'll put 'em in the very *next* one . . . Huh?'

'I think Mrs Dalby's right.'

'Mrs Dalby?'

'*My* name, honey!'

The big woman. This one on Eileen's other side was younger and a lot slimmer, and English. She had a scarf tied over her head and what looked like a man's jacket on her. Eileen had put her scarf on too – or someone else had, Mrs Dalby maybe. She wasn't answering them now, only thinking that Tom *would* hide. Not from his father, but from the fear of being handed over to strange people. So little, he could hide *anywhere*. In a cupboard, for instance. How many cupboards in a ship that size? How many empty cabins with cupboards in them?

The ship was still ablaze with light, and the band was still playing. Figures like ants all over her decks. Decks slanting more steeply now, the ship's bow buried deeply in the sea and her stern lifting right out of it. At some point she'd seen a lifeboat at A deck level – lowered that far and held there, the way they had *not* held this one – with passengers being helped into it through one of that promenade deck's big windows. It must have gone on down since then. She couldn't see *any* boats up there – not on this side. But maybe *that* one had had Frank and Tom in it. Poor little half-frozen creature. She hoped the stewardess had found a blanket for him. It was a *good* thought that she'd have helped, would have come back with a blanket and heard what had happened, then helped find Tom – helped look after him too, maybe persuaded them to let Frank go with him in the next boat there was. They couldn't have refused – seeing Tom would have fought like a wild thing against being put in without his father.

It seemed to make sense. It was the way it *would* have happened.

The stewardess might have got in the boat with them, too?

Eileen felt she was emerging from an interval of semi-consciousness and even lunacy. Welcoming the logic that made such a sequence of events really quite probable. The nightmare element was still there, but she felt she was coming to terms with a less harsh, less terrifying reality. Feeling also a touch of shame at having lost her head as she had, needed so much tolerance from the others.

'Listen – I'm sorry, the way I acted.'

'Honey, you have *nothing* to apologize for. My God, what you were going through back there!'

'Dreadful.' The English girl. Woman, maybe. Mrs Dalby had called her Susan. By starlight and the radiance of the doomed ship's lights reflected as they were in the barely moving mirror of the sea Eileen couldn't see all that well, even in close-up, but she thought Susan had a long neck, small face and little pointy nose. The headscarf covered quite a lot of her face. Repeating, 'Dreadful. But it *will* all come right, I'm sure.'

'No boats left up there now, are there.'

'There would be, miss.' Voice of the steward who was rowing – after a fashion – although he'd admitted never having touched an oar in his life until now. There were three crewmen with them in the boat, this steward from second class and two stokers or greasers, one of whom was at the helm, although as far as she could tell they weren't going in any particular direction – or making much progress either. Initially they'd wanted to get well clear of the ship, but they'd had a subsequent discussion between themselves as to whether to remain at a distance from which it might be possible to return to pick up people from the water when she sank; the other school of thought was to get much further away so as not to get caught in the suction when she went down. One of the arguments in favour of rowing on had been that with the sea as cold as it was – below freezing, literally iced water – no swimmer was likely to survive for more than a few minutes anyway.

The steward was telling her, 'When the timber boats is all sent away, miss, there's collapsibles too. Canvas boats, that is. I seen one go down – on number one's davits, that was – but there's three more. Boats is numbered, one to sixteen, collapsibles has letters – A, B, C and D. I don't see none *now*, but port side maybe . . .'

Somewhere nearer the stern a child was sobbing, the mother crooning to it. Around them, women were offering items of clothing to mothers whose children needed greater protection against the cold; one piping up now to ask whether anyone had anything they could spare – *please* . . . Mrs Dalby was on her feet suddenly, making the boat rock: 'Put 'em close together, why don't you, cover 'em with this coat?'

Her outsize, ankle-length fur coat: she was taking it off. Eileen protested, 'You'll freeze!'

'With the blubber I have on me, honey?'

Laughing like a banshee: passing the bundled coat back to that mother or those mothers, to a chorus of thanks. Mrs Dalby sitting again, Eileen and the English girl huddling closer for mutual warmth. Eileen reflecting that nothing on earth would have induced her to divest herself of *her* coat. Well – nothing except Tom, if *he'*d been here and—

'Oh, my Lord . . .'

'What is it?'

All staring at the stricken ship – her bow buried deep now, forward well-deck under water up to the level of – counting from the top, boat-deck then the promenade deck, then B, then – God, it was as high as C deck, at the front there. And the slant definitely steeper than it had been only minutes ago.

Something else, too. The band had stopped playing.

'I'd thought she was going.' Mrs Dalby wide-eyed, staring. 'Some sudden shift, I thought. But maybe I was—'

The band had struck up again. Here in the boat there was a sigh, general murmur of relief. This wasn't ragtime, though: more like a hymn. Eileen recognized it: 'They're playing "Autumn".'

'*That*'s what it is. I knew I *knew* it . . .'

Those decks would be too steep to climb now, Eileen thought. But all over them, figures like maggots were trying to. Along the sides – they'd be dragging themselves up along the rails. To get higher, away from the water, towards the stern. She *was* going: at least, her angle in the water was steepening so fast that you could assume the process had begun. *Begun* a long time ago, all right: with the impact that had woken Tom and Frank – when *she'd* had no notion at all of any danger. Ignorance being bliss: there *had* been bliss, or something very like it – hope, expectations, happiness – up to about the moment Frank had burst back in, telling her, 'They're saying it's not serious but . . . fact is, she's holed . . .'

It was indisputable that they'd be in another of the boats. Nowhere else they *could* be. There could be no one below decks by this time, in any case. No one who'd live. Those men in the smoking-room for instance: she could imagine the swift influx of sea . . .

She'd been impressed by them. Had liked that *one*, for sure.

The steward said – addressing her again, while just paddling more than rowing – 'Them canvas boats, if they got 'em on deck from where they're stowed – which is on the roof of the officers' quarters, abaft the bridge like – see, if they didn't get to lower 'em from davits, might just *float* off. So *there* you'd have another hundred or more saved.'

Nodding – without comprehension. Nothing in her mind except the *fact* that Frank and Tom were in one of the boats that were down already. They *had* to be: it was logical, in no way wishful thinking, you could accept it absolutely. While the mystery – scary as well as hateful – was that berserk creature's insistence on the lowering of the boat – the man in the suit and as she and Frank had seen earlier, carpet-slippers, therefore obviously a passenger, but—

'What did you say?'

Mrs Dalby pointing. 'She *is* going!'

A spook, Eileen was thinking. A spectre. In her lasting, visual memory, that was about the nearest she could get to it. That and the fact he'd drown. Imagining him in the sea still howling 'Lower aw-a-a-y!' The band had stopped, she realized. Stopped *again* – or finally. A roaring noise, in the place of those brave men's music. The girl on her left had been humming the hymn tune with them and was still doing it, on her own. Stopped, now. The women exclaiming, weeping, some looking away or covering their eyes. Snatches of prayer were audible as the great ship's bow dug deeper and her stern lifted. Poop deck still black with people clinging to the rails and other fittings. The rush of sound rising, floating out across the sea to the wide dispersal of lifeboats – covering by now maybe a square mile of it. Going – going . . . The ship's bridge dipping under. Frank will be watching this too, she told herself. With Tom in his arms, well wrapped up. He wouldn't be letting Tom see it – she hoped he wouldn't. Shivering, thinking suddenly of that old couple on their deckchairs under a rug; she didn't think they'd have allowed themselves to be forced into any boat. That roaring – caused she supposed by the sea rushing through and air rushing out – and heavy weights sliding, falling maybe clear through the ship: she envisaged pianos and other heavy furniture hurtling down, smashing through.

People, too – their screams part of that noise?

Mrs Dalby grated, holding tight to Eileen's hand, 'Don't wanna see it but I can't – can't look away . . .'

The stern was still rising, but there were still people clinging – on the poop especially – clinging to whatever . . . Well, notably the railings along the ship's sides and around her stern. But some falling: like ants being shaken off. Whole clusters of them falling. Amazingly, the lights still blazed. Mrs Dalby let go with that hand and put her arm round her again: 'Isn't it the most terrible thing you ever saw?' Remembering then and assuring her, 'Mind you, your husband and your little boy will be watching it just like we are, I'm convinced.'

'So am I.'

'Good girl. Good girl. Oh, sainted aunt—'

The foremost funnel was toppling, breaking off. The ship near-vertical in the water: *was* vertical. Nearly fifty thousand tons of her: and that funnel swaying over and crashing down on this starboard side – huge impact, the sea leaping in a sheet of white. And the lights – they'd flickered, then steadied, were bright again for a few seconds, now went out. Darkness alleviated only by the stars as the huge liner began her dive. The roaring had ceased. But there'd be live people still on her stern – had been just seconds ago, at any rate. Women all round were gasping, crying, praying. And the huge propellers high out of the sea slowly turning and catching starlight, a measured flash-flash-flash . . . She was very clearly going now – the downward slide had started almost imperceptibly, but gathering momentum: slipping away faster – faster still . . .

Gone.

Small upheaval in the dark sea, Eileen saw, a flicker of white that subsided quickly. Boats and litter floating, boats dark smudges widely separated on the surface shine. There wasn't a single one within – she guessed – a few hundred yards. Here in this boat some of the women were sounding almost like *she* must have. They'd include some whose husbands had brought them to the boat, kissed them goodbye and then stood back.

But some of those too might have got away in later boats – as Frank had, as she knew he must have. She put her hand on that of the girl on her left: 'Do you have a husband, or—'

'No. I'm so lucky – and believe me, so conscious—'

The steward called to the man at the helm, 'That's us off the payroll, eh?' There was a silence: only the girl's explanation to Eileen, 'My fiancé is in America already, you see.'

'I'm so glad . . .'

The steward was telling Mrs Dalby, who must have queried the statement he'd just made, 'Fact, missus. To the minute, they'll figure it out. Standard practice – no ship, no pay. Signed off, we are.' Mrs Dalby's comment was, 'I call that *mean*!'

A wave like a foot-high ripple came like a shadow curving across the sea and passed under, rocking them. It was Eileen then, following the shadow with her eye as it rolled on, who saw the ice.

'That's floating *ice*! Isn't it? Look – all around us!'

Pointing: out to starboard, and all down that side. Amazingly, this was the first any of them had seen of it. Because all their attention had been on the ship, of course – and they'd have been to some extent dazzled by her lights. They were all excited now, gazing round at the low patches and humps, starlight giving it the look of an uneven landscape – patches of sea as flat land, ice-shapes the humps and ridges on it. She was looking around again now to see what other boats might be in sight – and could see only one – if indeed that *was* a boat.

Thinking that if it was, Frank and Tom might be in it. Boats launched earlier would surely be those most widely dispersed. Therefore the ones nearest—

'Listen!'

Mrs Dalby cupping her ears . . . 'Oh, my word!'

The cries of the lost and drowning. A wailing, chilling cry, on a note that barely fluctuated. She'd thought at first of seabirds, the weirdness and sadness of gulls' cries, but those were *human* cries. Cumulative, no individual voices: she thought, *Hundreds* . . . Seeing again those tumbling black ants – and the men who'd stood back or been turned away – or not allowed up on deck in time.

As *they* would have been, if Frank hadn't acted as he had.

'Can we get back there, save at least a few?'

That had been an Englishwoman, calling back from somewhere in the bow, and the man at the helm's response was, 'That what you all want?'

The response sounded like general assent. With additions such as 'And quick, at that!' and an American voice 'God's sake, can't just sit here *listening*—'

'Hang on. If you'd allow me.' The steward, half up to his feet but still grasping his oar . . . 'Ladies – excuse me, I gotter say this. We got a fair load already – now if you get fellers 'auling theirselves aboard like, tippin' the boat like billy-o as they well an' truly *might* do—'

'We're twenty-eight in this boat – I've counted – and you three make it thirty-one. It's supposed to hold fifty, isn't it?'

'So they may say, missus. But see how close up you are with only thirty! See, we *could* find a whole mob around us—'

'Then we should take 'em!' Mrs Dalby could make herself heard all right, when she wanted to. 'There was some talk about this before, wasn't there, but you didn't speak out then, as I recall?'

'But I been thinkin', since. For your own safety, see – what me and my mates is here for like – well, that's it, I said it.'

He'd sat down.

'Let's take a vote, then.' The helmsman invited, 'Hands up them as says go back!'

Eileen's, Mrs Dalby's and the English girl's hands went up; a lot of others too. The helmsman again: 'That's clear enough. Get pullin', you lads! You ladies up for'ard, will you keep a lookout ahead – for men swimmin', or – hobjects we might strike, so forth?'

Eileen was looking again for other boats – low, relatively dark shapes amongst the ice-field. But she couldn't see any. Maybe they'd look just like boat-shaped ice. It *was* very dark, starlight didn't help all that much; if there'd been a moon things would have been different, but there wasn't. Might they not have hit the iceberg in the first place, she wondered, if there'd been a moon? She'd have liked to cover her ears against that dreadful wailing, but to do so might have been cowardly. Oars thumping in the cut-out rowlocks, blades splashing awkwardly and the boat hardly moving; it would need to be going well before the rudder could take effect and turn them towards that continuing, ghastly sound. The cries of men freezing to death: men and women too, probably, but most of the women she guessed would be in boats – except those who'd refused to go, hung back. That crowd on E deck, for instance. She didn't think there'd have been time for Steward Hart to bring up another group. Although there *had* been what had looked like a sudden flood of new arrivals – third-class at that – at the time she'd been following Frank and Tom over to the starboard side, eventually to this boat. It was one reason she'd taken it almost for granted that he *would* embark with her, at least *try* to – having seen that lot crowding out on to the deck and keenly aware there weren't all that many boats still to go.

Steward Humbert might have let them all up, finally?

Frank *would* have made it, though, because of Tom. And

with the blond stewardess's help. She'd have seen to it, all right. All she'd have had to do was yell at the officer in charge that Tom couldn't be embarked without his father.

This boat was moving now, beginning to turn – slowly – towards the cries.

'Listen.' She grasped Mrs Dalby's thick arm. 'There must be more than two oars, so why don't *we*—' Breaking off: 'You – steward—'

'Name's Starbridge, Miss, Henry Starbridge.'

'Well, Starbridge – ' Mrs Dalby, leaning forward – 'what this lady is proposing is some of us could help with the rowing. Some of us could do at least as well as you're doing, I guess. Darn sure *I* could! And four or six oars instead of two, for Pete's sake! Hey, you back there – I wanna *row*! All right? Me and this lady here, and there must be others—'

'Ma'am, if you don't mind—'

'I *do* mind! We'd get to those poor wretches a whole lot faster!'

'Ma'am – beg pardon, but I'm in charge and I say it's best keep on as we are. We're not trained seamen, I 'll admit it, but we're doin' good enough, I say. Any road, gettin' you all shifted around we'd *lose* time. D'you follow my reasoning, ma'am?'

Mrs Dalby asked the steward, 'What do *you* say?'

'Same as him. Well – ' another stroke – 'see, we got her movin' now.'

'So be it.' Shrugging, turning to Eileen. 'At least we're moving *some* . . .'

Less of that sound, now? Fewer voices in it?

Oars clomping, Steward Starbridge grunting at each stroke, breathing like a horse. Frank would be rowing in *his* boat, she guessed. That, or in charge of it, at the helm, and the stewardess with Tom in her arms, wrapped in his blanket. Come to think of it, if Frank had only told

them he was a seaman, wouldn't they have welcomed him
into this or any other boat? Seeing as they'd come down to
putting passengers in the hands of men who clearly were
not seamen?

She told Mrs Dalby and the other one, 'My husband was
working in a fishing trawler when I first knew him. I mean,
he *is* a seaman.'

'Well, for the love of God, why—'

'I know. I know. He should be here with us. If I'd only
thought to tell them . . . But *I* didn't. Never thought they
mightn't have enough seamen of their own, I suppose.'

'Well, you wouldn't.'

'Something in the sea out there – to the right a bit!'

One of the women up front had shouted this. Another
then: 'There's a *lot* – I don't know – a whole *lot*—'

'How far off?' From the helmsman, that. The women were
discussing it between themselves; one thought fifty yards,
the other at least a hundred. Eileen was standing, trying
to see whatever they'd seen – with a vision in her head of
Frank in the water holding on to wreckage – and Tom on
his shoulders, or maybe on whatever –

'C'mon, you lads – *pull*!'

The steward muttering between gasps, doing his best, but
apart from his own inadequacy as an oarsman it was far too
heavy a boat to be managed by just two oars. Mrs Dalby
commenting to Eileen, 'Simply on account we're women,
didn't want us showing 'em up, eh?'

'All the same, we must be *very* close—'

A shriek from one of the women in the bow: 'It's a whole
string of boats!'

'A *what*?'

'You're right! Three – four – no, *five*!'

And men's voices audible now: from these other boats,
audible above the cries of the dying. A male shout carrying
clear across the water: '*There* – see? To port there!' Sounding

close, but Eileen still couldn't see them; she was standing again, with a hand on Mrs Dalby's shoulder. This boat's helmsman called, 'Easy, there, 'vast pullin'!' The steward stopped rowing immediately, but there was the clunking sound of one further stroke from the other side before he stopped too, The steward agreeing jerkily, 'With them others ahead of us, no *sense*—'

'To the left! All by itself – heaven knows, *some* object—'

'Give way starboard, then. *Pull!*'

Eileen sat down again, hugging herself against the murderous cold. She heard the English girl's teeth actually chattering. No protective blubber on either of them: Mrs Dalby, coatless, would be needing every ounce of hers. The helmsman was calling to the women in the bow, wanting to be told when he had the boat pointing the right way. Both his oarsmen were at it now: this boat diverging from the direction of those others – which she, Eileen, still hadn't seen. Had in fact almost dreaded seeing – or communicating with, finding that Frank and Tom were *not* in any of them.

'How many boats altogether?'

She was asking the steward, but a woman behind her said, 'Sixteen. As well as the canvas ones I heard him mention. So twenty. And if each holds fifty people – ' fractional pause – 'heavens – a *thousand*?'

Susan exclaimed – stammering from the cold – 'But I doubt a single one has fifty in it!'

Eileen agreed: 'From what *I* saw—'

'Any case, there were about fifteen hundred passengers on board. I heard the captain himself say that. So, supposing the average number to a boat is twenty-five – which would be more like it—'

'More to the left!' Women up front giving the orders . . . Eileen thinking less of numbers of passengers than of boats: twenty of them, and that was a string of five that they'd seen: so chances of Frank and Tom being in that lot would be four to one against. How many to one *on* that they'd be in one of the other fourteen – no, not counting *this* one, thirteen?

'Right ahead now!'

'Don't wanna ram into 'em . . .'

Into *them*?

'Steer a fraction to the right, then!'

Dizzy. Stooping forward, head down by her knees, waiting for the sick dizziness to pass. Beyond it, the thought of Frank, and the haunting vision of the individual with the circling arms . . .

'How far now?'

Mrs Dalby called, 'If you weren't all standing, the poor man might see for himself!'

About twenty yards, had been the immediate answer. Then: 'Or ten. Yes, say ten. Oh, God—'

'What is it?'

'Some sort of raft – and I think two – persons . . .'

'Couple more strokes, lads, then get up front there!'

'Aye aye—'

'Ladies, leave it to us now?'

The steward stopped rowing, slid the loom of his oar across the boat and squirmed off his seat, clambered forward over thwarts, between the women on them – forward and to the other side, where the stoker was already. 'Let us at it, ladies?' The stoker then – a Scotsman, by the sound of him. 'Timber grating. Two fellers on it, but – reckon they're done for.'

'Got life-jackets on, though—'

'Get 'em inboard, Jock, make sure?'

'Nah. Both gonners.' The steward's voice: and women's shock. There was a thumping in the boat that Eileen felt through its timbers: the stoker telling the steward, 'Lay hold there, lad. That arm . . . Right – together, now . . .'

The boat was heeling to port; they'd be dragging the bodies on board, she guessed: half standing again, to see – but Mrs Dalby pulled her down. 'You know yours are going to be all right, honey, don't you. No matter what other terrible things—'

'I know Frank and Tom will be in a boat, so.'

'*Exactly*. You're *splendid*, I'll tell you that!'

'Oh no, I'm—'

'Man's dead, for sure. Big heavy geezer. Other's a young lad—'

'*How* young?'

The English girl, on her feet, reacting fast probably for Eileen's sake: 'young lad' could mean a young man, could also mean a child. Eileen with the breath tight in her throat and her heart pounding: but not trying to rise again, while the girl repeated insistently, '*How* young?' After a further pause the answer came from one of the women: 'Sixteen, seventeen, no more.' Then to herself more quietly, 'Oh, God in heaven . . .'

The English girl kissed her – icy kiss on an icy cheek. 'It's going to be *all right* for you, my dear. Just keep telling yourself so. It will be, I'm *certain*—'

'I know. I mean – I am too. And thank you—'

The helmsman had called, 'Best leave 'em, then. All right, Jock?'

Meaning – put them back?

Eileen, sitting normally again, felt the boat lurch and heard the sound not so much of a splash as of a slither in the water, water movement. And the men grunting. Women up forward – back here too now – were reciting the Lord's Prayer. Eileen joined in, as did Mrs Dalby and the English girl as well.

They were turning the boat: there was ice all round them, close enough to be easily visible, and the helmsman was trying for a way out of it. 'Back-water, port side! Starboard there, *pull!*' Getting out of the close encirclement but also giving up as far as rescuing swimmers was concerned. With that string of other boats in there anyway, closer to where the cries for help were coming from.

Or *had* been coming from. The sound was muted now, and seemed to come and go, no longer continuous as it had been.

'Pull together, lads!'

Ice scraped along the side: the other rower, the Scot, stopped pulling and used his oar to fend the boat off. *Bitterly* cold. How anyone in the sea could have lived this long – or have the strength to moan, or call . . . Maybe they weren't *in* the water, but on floating wreckage? The steward had talked about canvas boats just floating off as the sea swept over, and the same would apply to anything else that was buoyant. Those stacks of steamer chairs for instance – and what they'd said was a 'grating' those others had been on.

But even with that – something to hold you up – it seemed to Eileen incredible that flesh and blood, however resistant or resolute – when even here, in the boat and dry, the cold actually *hurt* . . .

Her rosary was inside her clothes and she couldn't nerve herself to open them to get at it. So do without it. She started on the first paternoster – her lips moving, head bowed, hands pressed together to start with below her chin but then rebelling, thrusting back into coat pockets – the left one grasping Frank's money-roll. Her prayers were for Frank and Tom, pictures of them both flickering through her brain – through that paternoster and into the first *ave* when Mrs Dalby suddenly lunged forward, responding to the steward's sharp 'Ah, *Christ!*'

The blade of his oar had hit something solid. He was reaching over the side with one arm, head and shoulders right over – Mrs Dalby too, and the boat rocking as others leaned over, peering . . .

A call from the stern: 'Ice, was it?'

'Nah. Soft, like.' Then after a moment: 'Yeah. What I thought. See – *there*.'

Using the oar then, probing at it, tilting it up. Eileen with her eyes shut, struggling to continue with the prayer but hearing 'Crikey. Little kid . . .' Mrs Dalby shifted around on the thwart, making sure Eileen *didn't* see it. Not that she would have anyway. Another American voice querying. 'How would a child have gotten this far out, Lord's sake?'

'On a man's back, likely.' The steward – Starbridge. He wasn't attempting to fish it out. Calling to the helmsman, 'Face down an' awash – wasn't nothing to see, not till me oar 'it it!'

'Kid about six or seven, honey.' Mrs Dalby. 'Guess she *would*'ve been on her father's back. He'd've been swimming to find a boat, I'd guess.'

'*She*, you said.'

'Sure!' Mrs Dalby swivelled her bulk around, asking a woman behind her who'd also been leaning out over the side, 'Little girl – right? *Right*, dear?

Assent, after hesitation. 'Well – I guess . . .'

Eileen was visualizing Tom on Frank's back, skinny little arms tight round Frank's neck. Frank was a powerful swimmer, all right. It *could* have been, although it had *not* been. Couldn't have been because – well, *couldn't*, that was all. Obviously Mrs Dalby had thought it might have been, or that she – Eileen – would jump to that conclusion. Eileen told her – as much as anything to reassure *her* – 'Frank and Tom are in one of the other boats. It's just a fact they *must* be. My heart breaks for the little one you saw, but on my account don't concern yourself, Mrs Dalby.'

'Call me Elizabeth?'

'Why, thank you. And I'm – well, you know.'

'I'd like you to know I admire you greatly, Eileen.'

'You're very kind.'

'It's not kindness, honey, it's a straight reaction to your situation and the way you're handling it.'

Slow and steady clumping of oars in rowlocks. Hardly any conversation now, elsewhere in the boat. At least such exchanges as there were were dying out, people retreating inside themselves. The sea was quiet too, littered palely with the ice. No sound at all from out there now, she realized.

One woman was reported to be in a coma from the cold. Those around her – back in the stern there – were tending to her: sheltering her with their own bodies, rubbing her hands and feet, talking to her continuously in the hope of bringing her out of it. Others were moaning and whimpering some of the time, and a few of the children were becoming fractious. Elizabeth Dalby said quietly, 'It's not going to go well with some of us if we don't get picked up soon. And how we could be, in the dark, heaven knows. Mind you, they were sending out wireless messages all that time – Captain Smith himself told me that.' She shook her head. 'Poor man. Poor dear man. After the fine career he's had. This would have been his last trip before retirement, did you know that?'

'Yes. I heard.' Susan – the English girl. 'I only spoke with him once, but he seemed *very* nice, I thought.'

'Sure was. A fine seaman, and a gentleman.'

'You say *was*, but –'

'Went up on his bridge, and he'd've stayed there. Kind of man he was – you know?'

Eileen broke the ensuing silence. 'Frank said there'd be rescue ships along all right. One of the last things he said to me.'

'And he'd know, I guess, being a sailor. Or having been

one. You said he was sailoring before you were married, but not after?'

'Yes. A fishing trawler, he was on. He worked on deck but looked after the engine too. He has a natural facility with engines. His boat worked out of Dungarvan – that's to the east of Cork, halfway to Waterford.'

'And how did you and he come to meet, honey? Did you know each other long before you married?'

'No, not long. But you don't want to hear all that, now . . .'

'I'd like to.' Susan Harper, this one's name was. The fiancé she was on her way to America to marry was a Scotsman who'd gone on ahead and had now established himself successfully in an insurance business in Seattle. She was twenty-four, Eileen's own age.

'Well – how we met was – oh, I was working in Cork city—'

'Working at what?'

'In a store. The biggest in Cork. I started there selling hats and dresses, but I was studying shorthand and type-writing – nights, when I finished in the store – and I ended up doing only that – secretarial work.'

Like another world – distant and vague in memory even before this had now wiped it out altogether. Still, if they wanted to know about it . . . Elizabeth patted her shoulder encouragingly: 'That was smart of you, Eileen.'

'It was not my first choice. I'd thought a lot about nursing – well naturally, my father being a doctor as he was, and other girls we knew had gone for it. But then my father said to me why a nurse, Eileen, why not be a doctor?'

'Good for him!'

'Well, I was doing better than most at school then. And I read a lot, as he did, and he talked with me a lot. He was a fine man, Elizabeth. A *marvellous* man. But he had a weakness in his heart – of which I'd never known – and he collapsed and died in the hospital at Bantry when I was thirteen. It broke *my* heart, I tell you: it was a terrible loss to me. Then my mother married another man, and – well, I left home. I was seventeen then, and in Cork I shared a room with a girl called Betsy O'Flaherty, who was a sort of cousin to Frank. Well, he was at sea in his trawler – March of nineteen oh-eight it was, when there were terrible storms, ships sunk and all sorts of damage all along the coast, and they put into Unionhall – west of Cork, that is. They did well to get into shelter before the worst of it, so. And the weather looked to him to be set as it was, he took a chance on it not improving that week or anyway a few days, and got himself into Cork where he'd never been but had an old friend he hadn't seen in years—'

'*And* Betsy, huh?'

'Oh, yes. He came to visit her, and—'

'And there *you* were!'

Their interest had to be feigned, Eileen realized. Wanting to distract their minds from the cold, or hers from Frank and Tom, or both . . .

'You and Betsy still on speaking terms?'

'Oh, of *course*. There was nothing like that at all, at all. I mean not between him and Betsy. But he was – sort of wild. Still is, but – more so then than now. He'd take awful chances – like leaving the trawler that time, just taking a chance the weather'd stay bad – well, that's not such a good example, but – wild things, and yet – well, he'd work it out, then, he'd never just walk away from it. Like if he'd done something crazy when he'd had a few pints more than he should have, if there'd been harm done he'd put matters *right* – you know?'

'And you married, and he left the sea?'

'I was scared of him being out there in all weathers – winters and all, the storms we'd get. And being apart so much: that was mostly what persuaded *him*. Well, I said, he's good with engines, all that, and he took a job with the Cork bus company. We have tramways in Cork, still do, but the motor-buses had started up – there'd been horse-buses of course, before that – anyway, Frank got talking to a man in a bar – pub called the Western Star, where it so happened Betsy's uncle worked—'

'That's how he heard about the job, eh?'

'Same as when he came from his family home – near Nenagh, Tipperary that is. He was in a pub in Waterford that time, when a fellow who'd put in there in a trawler from Dungarvan—'

Susan Harper put in – signalling the limit of her interest – 'Getting light, isn't it? Sorry – interrupting—'

'It *is*, you're right.'

Lighter overhead and on the sea too: the ice plainly visible, and some of it substantial. Not ice*bergs* exactly, but from this low level seemingly quite big. Would a rescue ship come steaming into this lot for us? she wondered. Her inclination – habit – was to put any such question to Frank, and she'd almost done so – on the point of *turning* to him – despite being achingly aware –

And scared as well as half-frozen. Scared of the coming daylight, too.

'What does your husband's father do, Eileen?'

Glancing at Susan, who'd put the question: wondering how she'd give a damn, Except you didn't want to just sit and think about cold, hungry, exhausted, frightened. Above *all*, frightened . . . She shrugged. 'Farmer. But I never met him.'

'Never *met* your—'

'He didn't come to the wedding. Frank didn't want him to either. His mother and some others did but his father didn't. Because the last they'd seen of each other they'd had a fist-fight and Frank gave him a thrashing. That was when he left home.'

'But – Eileen, that's *awful*!'

Mrs Dalby asked her quietly. 'What did they fight about?'

'His father wanted him to stay and help work the farm, and Frank had no such intention. He'd no wish to end up – well, like his father – and if he hadn't made the break then he'd have been trapped, he felt, he'd *never* get away. It was his father started the fight – he was going to beat him, teach him a lesson so he thought!'

Frank had told her, 'Change my mind for me that way, was his idea. There's contempt in that – you know? He'd drink taken, of course. And since I thrashed *him* – see, that put the lid on it, we were finished good and proper.'

'D'you love him, though?'

A gesture . . . 'A dog can love the man that beats him. I wouldn't think a man can. That he could *allow* himself – a man that had the contempt for him to think he could – look, make a slave of him, you might say – by going for him with his fists. Well, my mother understands that, I'll tell you.'

'She knows *you*, is what that comes to. Better than I do – yet.'

'Yet.' A nod. '*Yet*'s the right word there, all right . . .'

Three years ago, that conversation. Eileen explained to Mrs Dalby, 'Frank's mother wanted him to leave the farm. She could see how it might be if he didn't. She wanted the future for him that he wanted for himself. Besides, there's two younger sons growing up, as well as three daughters, his father wasn't to be left bereft . . . She writes quite often, does his mother. She's a dear. It's through her we have this chance in America – her brother, Frank's uncle Matt, has a business that's doing well, and he's asked Frank to join him in it. So . . .'

Thinking then – without pleasure – of her own mother, who'd strongly disapproved of her marriage to Frank: hadn't *liked* Frank anyway, but had thought her daughter should have married a man of better social standing and with money, prospects, all that. Which *she*'d done all right – married a complete *bastard* with money by the bagful . . . Shifting on the thwart, and rubbing her legs: standing then, exercising her arms, moving herself around. Shivering cold, aching all over. She'd have touched her toes, done physical jerks, but there wasn't room: besides, the steward had been staring at her like a hungry dog. She sat down again, careful not to look at him. There were streaks of silver in the sky, and the sea in its open patches between outcrops of ice looked like polished marble. Susan asked her, smiling, 'Better for all that?'

'Blood might be circulating a bit better, I hope.' In this greyish light, Susan looked haggard. Eileen thought, How I look too, probably. Or maybe worse. The thought of Tom and Frank – the torment of anxiety and the need to control it – because surrender to abject fear might seem to validate it – although dear God, if one only *could* – could let go, let the tears flow in rivers . . .

She asked Susan – to put her off, whatever next question *she*'d been about to ask – 'Have you left a big family behind in England?'

'I wouldn't say big.' A smile. '*You* wouldn't, I'm sure. In Ireland don't you have enormous families?'

'Some do. And I've a lot of cousins, that's the truth. But what I was meaning – you're not sad to be leaving yours?'

'A little, I suppose. But then, it doesn't have to be for ever. They might come and see us, some time. Or we might make visits home. Depending how things go, of course. What sort of business is it – your husband's uncle's, you said?'

'He has a motor repair works, in Philadelphia.'

Mrs Dalby, who'd seemed to be slumbering, showed interest: 'What's the uncle's name?'

'Matt McGrath. McGrath Motor Works, the business is.'

'Well, *we* have friends in Philly. Matt McGrath. I'll tell 'em that's where to go!'

'We could have moved over three years ago, as it happens. Frank's mother wrote her brother that Frank was settled down, wasn't the harum-scarum he had been – or that Matt McGrath had thought he was – and working hard, well thought of by the bus company, all that – and Matt wrote and said all right, come on over. But I was carrying Tom and I wanted him born in Ireland, so Frank wrote back asking how would it be if we went in say a year's time. Well, the answer came saying no, if you haven't the sense to grab a chance when it's offered you – etcetera . . . He's not an *easy* man, Frank says. So we stayed as we were, Frank at his job and me back to mine after Tom. But as it turned out, Frank's mother was still at it, and lo and behold didn't we get a letter from Philadelphia saying all right, if you're coming at all, come *now* – Uncle Matt giving Frank six months to prove his worth or he'd be out. Well – no question, he *will* prove his worth!'

'We'll send him customers, you bet your life.' Elizabeth Dalby patted Eileen's arm. 'We'll tell 'em to request the personal attention of Frank Maguire – so his uncle will have no doubt who's bringing in the business, eh?'

'How far's Seattle from Philadelphia?'

'Huh!' A laugh. 'About as far as you could get, dear!'

'Pity.' Susan shrugging. All of them gazing out across the sea, the ice-field slowly heaving. You could see that motion now as well as feel it, the slow swell with the shine of dawn on it and the stars fading into pink and silver spreading from the east. There was a breeze coming up too, Eileen had noticed – which wasn't making it any warmer; all you'd need now would be to have a rough sea whipped up, she thought. She was looking for other boats, and not seeing any. Mrs Dalby murmuring, 'Drive a motor from Seattle to Philly, you'd just about need a new one when you got there!'

'What was *that*?'

Susan – pointing. Eileen had seen it too, and so had others – a yellowish streak in the southern sky. A woman called 'Shooting star!' but there was another exactly the same: and general stirring, excitement. The steward – who'd hardly been paddling even, of late – was craning round to peer in that direction. He croaked, as yet another fizz of yellow showed against the southern darkness, 'Signal rocket. Ship, some kind!' There was cheering then, although Eileen stayed quiet, wondering how much *he* knew about it. Mrs Dalby however, was on her feet, bawling to the helmsman, 'Now I *shall* take an oar! And these two ladies here would like to, please. One other oarswoman we'll need. All right – *you*, dear . . .'

3

They'd been rowing for about two or two and a half hours, rowing into the Atlantic dawn, and with the sun up now the rescue ship was clear to see, a steamer with one tall funnel, lying stopped with a number of the *Titanic*'s lifeboats already alongside, their white outlines clearly visible against the black paint on the ship's hull. Even from a distance of several miles and with the blinding effect of the newly risen sun – sun's brilliance due east, rescue-ship southeast. But how all those boats had beaten this one to it was a mystery. Must have been well to the southeastward before the rocket-firing had started, perhaps: or seen earlier rockets which had not been spotted from this boat? The rowing had been back-breaking work anyway, the women changing around several times and the helmsman taking his turn and turn about with the other two as well. Eileen and Susan had each done two half-hour shifts, but had stopped now with blistered hands; while Mrs Dalby had rowed almost continuously and was back at it now. Mrs Dalby, Susan had whispered, could have gone a few rounds with Jack Johnson and not necessarily have come off worst.

The wind had got up, and it cut like knives. It was squally, arriving in gusts that fairly lashed across what was now a choppy as well as ice-littered sea. The ice wasn't only small stuff either; several 'bergs stood as high as two or three hundred feet, glittering ice-mountains in the early sun – and good enough reason for the rescue-ship's captain to have stopped in the ice-field's periphery and let the boats come to him.

The ship's decks were dark with people. The foredeck anyway – which one could see more easily than for instance the promenade deck, the foredeck being open to the sky, not shaded by any deck above it. But there'd be people all along those rails . . .

Frank among them?

If this was the last of the *Titanic*'s boats, she could imagine him watching its approach just as anxiously as she was waiting for a sight of him and Tom. He'd be assuring Tom in that deep, soft voice of his, '*Sure*, your ma'll be in this one!'

She checked the time by her father's watch. Coming up for eight a.m. The ship had foundered at two twenty, someone had said; so she'd been in this boat about six hours. The longest six hours of her life, undoubtedly.

Blinking, wiping her eyes with her fingertips. Salt crystals gritty in them.

'Should have a telescope, Eileen!'

'Yes.' Looking round at Susan. Who meant well: but of all the silly, inconsequential remarks . . . Wondering if she could even begin to understand the *reality* of the agony – from which there was by no means any certainty of relief, and which would very soon be getting to its peak: which Susan said then – again, in a casual, even flippant sort of way – 'Won't be long now, anyway.'

Might not seem long to her. Eileen heard herself agreeing: 'No. Not long.' But half an hour at least, she guessed. Thirty more minutes of *not knowing*. Or even longer – forty-five, maybe.

What if they are *not* there?

She thought, *I don't know. I don't know if I could live . . .* Eyes shut for a long moment, clenching her mind against accepting that such an outcome was even possible: but none the less still needing to prepare oneself – or try to. Meeting Susan's enquiring look again, she changed the subject to *her* situation: 'Will your fiancé have heard about the *Titanic* being sunk, I wonder?'

'I've been wondering.' Blue eyes, fair complexion, freckles on her nose and forehead. 'I suppose – if they were sending out wireless messages—'

'Would he have been coming to New York to meet you?'

'Oh, yes. But—'

'Wireless would be the answer, wouldn't it. Just a message that you're all right, put his mind at rest. At least when we know where that ship's going to take us – might depend which way it was going, I suppose . . .'

If the ship's own passengers had embarked in New York, say, bound for – well, London or Liverpool – wouldn't they have priority over another ship's survivors?

'What does Frank look like?'

'Oh – he's tall, big shoulders on him – hair's sort of ginger—'

'Would he be wearing a hat?'

'A cap, more like.'

Mrs Dalby, rowing doggedly, met Eileen's eyes and puffed her cheeks out. 'Phew!' Eileen smiled, used sign-language, pointing at herself and offering to take over. The offer was immediately rejected – shake of the head, a quick, savage smile and a glance over her shoulder to see how far . . .

Half an hour crawled by. She thought she might have dozed, even, slumped on the thwart leaning against Susan. Maybe her head had rested on Susan's shoulder. Coming to then, pulling herself upright: 'Sorry. Was I—'

'It's all right. Just a sec, though—'

The steward was talking to her – to Susan – pointing at flags on two of the ship's four masts, telling her, 'Red duster, o' course, and I reckon that'd be Cunard's house-flag.' Adding – while Eileen strained again to recognize a figure, a face, thinking that if you could pick out the details of a flag, then *surely* . . . – 'I sailed Cunard, couple o' times. Wouldn't surprise me if this ain't the *Carpathia*.'

Frank most likely would not have Tom with him up on deck, Eileen was thinking. They'd have found a bunk for Tom. Maybe the blond stewardess keeping an eye on him. Alternatively Frank himself would be: in which case he won't be up there on deck and I don't need to panic if I don't see him there.

Effectively, giving herself licence to go on hoping. They aren't there, but may be *there*. Anything *but* the end of the road, the ultimate surrender.

To what? To ending up screaming mad?

A crane was lifting one of the boats on to the ship's forward deck. Dangling meanwhile like a big white toy. There was a number of them in the water near the bow, where that one was being lifted from. There *had* been one or more amidships, half an hour ago; she guessed there'd be a disembarkation point in the middle somewhere, and then the empty boats would be shifted along there out of the way of new arrivals. The rescue-ship's own boats were easy to see on davits more or less abreast the funnel, on the top deck – boat-deck, one up from the promenade deck. To which the gangway did not reach – she could make it out now, a light-coloured diagonal against the black paintwork, from the waterline to about halfway up the ship's side. Where no doubt there'd be what Frank had called an 'entry-port'. But you *wouldn't* see any faces of people on the promenade deck, since it was darkened through being roofed by the deck above it and the rising sun being on the other side. A man would have to be leaning right over, looking down, and you'd need to be directly below him, looking up: which you would not be, because by the time you were that close you'd be busy disembarking.

He'll know I'm in this boat, though – if it is the last one – and he'll come down to the entry-port to meet me. *Please God?* Let him come down to meet me and take me to the cabin where Tom will be asleep?

Day-dreaming, or praying: but no reason it shouldn't turn out like that, even though it *would* mark the beginning of heaven on earth. Not to be counted on, exactly – but not unlikely either: and this whole episode being bearable only if one could believe in that *sort* of outcome.

The crowd on the forward deck was just a mob, from which hands and hats were waving at the boat as it approached. Oddly, you could see the waving but not the people who were doing it. But the ship was moving, she realized: then heard the helmsman telling the women near him, 'They're giving us a lee', and explaining what it meant, that the captain was turning his ship to provide shelter against the squalls, making it easier for the boat to get in alongside. Eileen still searching: gazing up at the blur of faces along the rail. Hands waving, mouths open in shouts of greeting or just hope . . . And the helmsman shouting orders now – the ladies to stop rowing, only the two crewmen to carry on – and stand by to come alongside, there! She could see several men standing in the entry-port, the aperture at the gangway's head, and right above it a derrick projecting from the ship's side with a rope sling dangling.

She could see the ship's name painted in white capitals on the plating at the bow, and the steward had been right – *Carpathia*.

'Guess I worked my passage home now – didn't I?'

Mrs Dalby: dabbing at her palms with a lace-trimmed handkerchief patched red. Gushing with concern for Eileen though, showering her with instructions: this was not to be the end of their friendship, Eileen was not to go hiding herself and her family in steerage class; they were certainly to dine as her guests in first class, and if the accommodation they were offered wasn't adequate – 'You hear me now, Eileen?'

Looking up at the entry-port. Frank *might* have been able to get down there to meet her. But there were only ship's staff in view, that she could see. An officer had come out on the gangway's top platform now: and a seaman with a coil of rope, two others coming down.

She nodded to Mrs Dalby. 'Thank you very much, Elizabeth. But—'

'No "buts"!'

No Frank – yet. Telling herself of *course* they wouldn't want passengers there, getting in their way. Any case, if no other husbands had managed to get down there . . . The boat was drifting in at an awkward angle, and these three men didn't know what to do about it. But lines were being tossed down now; the helmsman had caught one, and the stern was being hauled in. Now another fell across the bow; two sailors had come down the gangway, on to the wooden grating at its lower end, and the sling from the derrick was being lowered. They were going to use it for the woman who'd been unconscious, someone said. Meanwhile children were being disembarked first, with their mothers: Eileen looking round at a sailor who'd leapt over with the sling – swift and agile, giving her no chance to button-hole him with 'Anyone called Maguire up there – big man with a baby boy?' but hearing one of those women tell him, 'I'm afraid she's dead. Wouldn't have done for the children to have known.'

'Your turn, Eileen.'

From Susan, that. Mrs Dalby was already out and stump-ing up the gangway. They'd given her back her fur coat: she had it bundled under her arm. A sailor put his hand out: 'Ready, miss?' She was out then, climbing the timber steps, and he was helping Susan over. She – Eileen – craning her head back trying to see vertically upward to the faces at the rail; in fact seeing nothing except the black steel plating and the rounded heads of rivets: then she'd stumbled, and from there on took care to look where she was going – crossing the gangway's head into the entry-port: iron deck, white paint and a steward directing them all to a staircase while repeating over and over, 'You are requested to muster in the first-class saloon, ladies, for your names to be registered and berths allocated. There's hot soup ready too. Ladies, you are requested to muster . . .'

Faces loomed close: none of them was Frank's. Not *yet*, Frank's face. She left the queue to ask a seaman who on the promenade deck was pointing them towards the saloon, 'Was ours the last boat, do you know?'

'No, ma'am – one to come. *That* way, please . . .'

So even if they were not on board – well, that was a possibility one *could* accept now, with another boatload coming. Not that their non-appearance was any proof of their not being on board: this was after all a first-class area: after giving her name she'd no doubt be packed off to third, and Frank wouldn't have been hanging around in first. He'd have his hands full with Tom anyway: might not even know another boat had arrived. He and Tom both out to the wide, even.

If they were, it would be a long time before they heard the last of it.

'That's my girl.' Mrs Dalby – furred and hatted. 'Caught you smiling. *Much* better, honey. Here, you go ahead—'

'No, *why*—'

'I'll grab us some of that soup. You have questions to ask 'em, don't you? Go *on* now!'

Into the queue to register. Aroma of chicken soup. Not only Mrs Dalby had gone to the buffet table first. She was right though – except it was *the* question, singular, as important as any she'd ever asked and with elements of dread in putting it. There were two others ahead of her in any case. At the table a purser and a senior-looking steward had lists of names and line-drawings of the ship's decks with cabin numbers marked on them, and a foreign woman – a Finn, she guessed – was giving them a hard time, not understanding anything she was asked or told. But finally she'd been induced to write her name down; they gave her a slip of paper with the number of her berth on it, and a stewardess who'd been discreetly summoned was taking her to the buffet.

One more, then it was Eileen's turn. Susan, she saw, was at the buffet with Mrs Dalby.

The purser looked at Eileen; he'd glanced briefly at her wedding ring. 'Welcome aboard the *Carpathia*, madam. May I have your name, please?'

'Maguire.' The thinness of her voice embarrassed her. 'My husband's Frank Maguire and our son Tom's two and three-quarters. He'd have been asking after me? I think they must be on board – unless—'

'Just a moment, Mrs Maguire, and I'll tell you. May I ask in which class were you travelling?'

'Oh, third . . .'

As he'd have known at a glance, she suspected. Shabby old overcoat bought second-hand from a dealer in Cork City, for instance. Although, God knew, there were enough strangely attired women around. Bath towels, blankets: but smart hats as well, lace-topped dresses: all some of them *didn't* have on were tiaras.

'Maguire, Frank, son Tom two and three-quarters . . .'

'Not *here*.' The steward murmured it quietly, having run his eye down a column and a half of names of those who *had* made it. The purser had glanced through some others too. A shake of the head: 'Mrs Maguire – I'm sorry, but at least to the best of our knowledge this far—'

'Still one boat to come. I know.'

Mrs Dalby was beside her – soupless. Must have left it over the other side. 'Is that a fact, young man, another boat to come?'

'Yes, there is. But may I ask, madam—'

'Mrs William K. Dalby – I'm a first-class passenger. I have no husband for you to look for, he's safe in New York. Incidentally I'll want to wireless him, by and by. But Mrs Maguire is a very special friend of mine and I'm concerned to help her in any way I can. Is it possible her husband and child might have come on board without you knowing?'

'It's unlikely, madam. But there is this other boat – it's in sight from the bridge, but apparently very heavily loaded, therefore making particularly slow progress. Mrs Maguire, I'm allocating you a berth in cabin 218. It's a four-berth cabin and the other three berths are already allocated. You'll find it two decks down and right forward; any steward or stewardess down there will show you to it. If your husband and child *are* in this last boat we'll have to make different arrangements – may I say we will do so with the very greatest of pleasure?'

'Well, as *I* was saying—' Mrs Dalby wagged a forefinger – 'If there's difficulty with that and it's easier first class, I'd gladly give you my note for whatever difference in the fare there might be.'

'First class is more difficult than third, as it happens. Despite some of our own passengers having given up berths – doubled-up, and so on. But we'll bear that in mind. Mrs Maguire, there's hot soup at the buffet over there, and of course a more substantial meal when you're ready for it in the third-class dining room. If you'd like me to show you here, on the deck plan—'

There was plenty of room at the rail on the promenade deck, now interest in the boat's arrival had faded. She wasn't in any hurry to locate her cabin, or get breakfast. The soup had done her good: and she'd needed it. Couldn't see any boat though. The sun was well up, and its blaze reflected on the ice-field and the huge drifting 'bergs was dazzling. Refraction came into it too, all the colours of the rainbow refracted through ice and mirrored back from the glittering surface. How you'd see *anything* . . . Glancing round, she saw a steward passing – the rather dignified-looking one who'd been working in there with the purser. He saw her too.

'Mrs – Maguire, isn't it . . . You didn't get to see your cabin yet?'

'I wanted a sight of the boat that's coming. But the light's so blinding . . .'

Other people further along the rail were looking for it too, she realized. The steward suggested, 'Perhaps if you stood back a little.' He was tall, with greying hair. Pointing . . . 'There. There's a 'berg shaped like – well, like a castle. Jagged top rather like battlements?'

'Yes – *yes* . . .'

'Two fingers to the left of that. No, your face is in the sun again – come back a little. That'll be better. Two fingers to the left of the castle. See that flickering there? That's the swirl of water and ice from the boat's oars. Unfortunately it's white and so are all the life-jackets. But if you can make out just the shape – and that movement—'

'I see it!'

'They're rowing strongly enough, you'd think. But one of our officers using binoculars from the bridge mentioned that they were very low in the water – the weight of so many people, d'you see. Some of the passengers who were in – oh, boat number four, I believe – said that a boat which had been close to them had changed course to take a number of men off some floating object. One of that boat's crew said he thought it might have been a collapsible boat floating upside down. But you see, if the boat that went to take them off – *this* one you're looking at – had been loaded to capacity already—'

'They were lowering most of them half-empty!'

'Well—'

'Do you know which boat that is?'

'Yes.' Putting his mind to it. 'It was mentioned – by those others. Boat number twelve, I think. Yes – I'm sure. Mrs Maguire, would you like me to show you to your cabin, and the dining saloon in third class? I'd imagine you'll have at least an hour to wait, for—'

'Thank you, but' – pausing, getting her breath – 'I'll find my way.'

'Very well. May I say how fervently I hope—'

'You're very kind.'

'No, Mrs Maguire. In circumstances such as these—'

'Say a prayer for me? For *them*?'

Gazing at her: she'd surprised him. Not a request often put to stewards, perhaps. Nodding then: 'I will. I will. And meanwhile, anything you may need—'

She'd thanked him, and turned to look for the boat again: tears in her eyes. Kindness did that: when you were on a knife-edge as she was: and boat number twelve being her last chance. Frank's and Tom's lives and her own too – all of it in boat twelve, that insect crawling across the fiery, multi-coloured seascape.

'Excuse me?'

She'd seen them when she'd arrived here, leaning over the rail a few yards away: a sharp-faced man in a suit and a light-coloured cap, and a pretty young woman in a somewhat over-decorative dress and a hat with a bunch of feathers in it. The man had lifted his cap: he had brown eyes and a small dark moustache, carefully trimmed. Cigar smell. The steward was on his way, leaving her to them.

'George J. Parry, ma'am, and this is my wife *Mrs* Parry. We couldn't help but overhear: you're kind of anxious, for that last boat—'

'My husband and our little boy may be in it.' Glancing at Mrs Parry, and the blond curls escaping from under the hat and across her forehead. Baby face, little pouty mouth. 'It was kind of you to enquire, but—'

'Only wondered if we could help any. That is, if you'd like company, for instance. To be alone when you're really up against it—'

'Must be *awful*!'

'Well—'

'We're so *lucky*. To be here together. See, our boat was about to be lowered with room for a lot more people than were in it, and Muriel – Mrs Parry, that is – kicked up such a fuss at me not coming too – well, the officer said what the heck, jump in!'

'I'm glad for you.'

'May I ask what class are you travelling in, Mrs—'

'Maguire. I'm Eileen Maguire.'

'From Ireland, would that be?'

'Yes. County Cork. But I'm travelling third. Shouldn't be on this deck at all, I know.'

'Well, I don't know anything about that. Fact is, we're living it up some – first class. Scraped it together somehow. Well – it's a honeymoon trip we've been on!'

'Ah. Are you from – New York?'

'We sure are. But how come – your husband *and* your little boy—'

'They wouldn't let Frank get in. They were turning away

all the husbands. He had Tom in his arms though, he was going to pass him over to me, but I'd tripped and fallen into the boat and another woman reached out for Tom and – it scared him. He wriggled out of the hold Frank had on him and – they began lowering, wouldn't stop. Frank had gone chasing after him—'

'I'd've gone *crazy*!'

She nodded to the girl. 'I *did*. Believe me . . .'

'But now—'

'They *have* to be in that boat. Who'd leave a two-and-three-quarter-year-old child to drown? And he would *not* have got in a boat full of strangers, they'd have *had* to have taken Frank!'

Nodding: 'I guess . . .'

'Oh, Mrs Maguire, I do so *hope*—'

Behind them a door in the white-painted superstructure was pushed open, and two men came out on deck, heading aft. One was an officer in uniform – with red colouring between the gold stripes on his sleeves – and the other a bigger man in a dark suit – and under it what looked more like a pyjama jacket than a shirt. The uniformed man was telling him, 'Best thing for you, sir, would be a bowl of hot soup – which as it happens is being served now in the saloon. Or a glass of brandy, as good if not even better!'

'No. No thank you. But look here – ' a hand on the doctor's shoulder – 'you mentioned allowing me the use of your cabin. Privacy is what I crave, doctor – if it wouldn't inconvenience you too greatly . . .'

It was *him*.

Incredible. She gasped, reaching for support. Glancing at the Parrys, seeing their eyes were also on that pair: on the tall man especially, a creature therefore *not* of her overstrained imagination. Passing her now without even looking at her: *still* with only slippers on his feet. Hatless, with wavy greying hair, moustache still dark with waxed, upturned ends. The first close-up view she'd had of him, but it was definitely the same man; her memory was superimposing on his tall, shuffling figure, the image of the waving arms and his high-pitched, insistent 'Lower away! Lower aw-a-a-y!'

She had one arm around a stanchion: was staring after him wide-eyed and still only half believing that it was no hallucination. Parry had glanced at his wife, lifting his eyebrows and muttering, 'The big white chief!'

'You *know* that person?'

'Sure. That's to say, we know who he is, all right. Joseph Bruce Ismay. Boss of the White Star Line – owners of the *Titanic* – right? They call him "Managing Director" – it's not a term *we* use, so—'

Mrs Parry simpered, 'So my hubby christened him big white chief. Get it?'

'They let *him* into a boat . . .'

'Guess they'd have to. Heck, he *owns* 'em!'

Laughing, both of them. Eileen staring at them for a long moment, for a moment barely understanding her own reaction. Dizziness again, and ready to faint, or scream, or –

Well, Christ . . .

He and the doctor had vanished, anyway. She was trembling, and short of breath. Parry noticing it suddenly, asking her was she was all right.

'Yes. Thank you . . .' Shaking her head, telling herself that boat number twelve was all that mattered: *only* that. She'd turned away from the Parrys, was facing the ice-field again, that dazzling panorama now churned by the gusting, knife-like wind. Edging back to shade her eyes. She could see the boat more easily now. Hardly surprising – several hundred yards closer, surely. Very *much* like some wounded insect or animal though, the oars its flailing, spindly legs inching it along.

Frank pulling one of those oars?

She turned back. She'd need to be up here, and clean, and sane, to meet them. Wife and mother, not avenging fiend . . . Telling the Parrys, both of whom were watching her rather strangely, 'I'm going below now, find my cabin – if you'd excuse me . . .'

'Why *sure*, Mrs – er—'

'You certain you're all right, dear?'

Cabin and a bathroom, she hoped. Clean up a bit, get her breathing back to normal and not looking and feeling like something out of an asylum.

She was back on the promenade deck not far from the entry-port after only about forty minutes. She'd found the cabin – with three Dutch women in it, who'd obviously been expecting to have it to themselves. There were two lower bunks and two upper ones, and no washbasin of course; that had been a strictly *Titanic* luxury. A cabin like this would do perfectly well for the three of them though, when those two arrived. Or a two-berth: floor-space even. Leaving the cabin, she didn't leave anything behind in it – least of all her overcoat with the money and papers in its pocket – but a stewardess whom she met in the corridor fetched her a towel embroidered CUNARD STEAMSHIP CO. in red capitals, and a piece of soap, and showed her to a washplace where there were lavatories and washbasins and two baths in cubicles, one of which luckily was vacant. The stewardess lent her a comb as well, telling her, 'Let me have it back later.' People *were* being kind . . . Eileen stripped while running a shallow bath – shallow to save time, and it was salt water – as it had been in the *Titanic*, in third class, anyway – and ordinary soap, which didn't lather too well. But it was still heavenly – relaxing and steadying as well as warming. Having got herself more or less into shape, when *they* arrived she'd be able to concentrate on Tom's needs while Frank attended to his own.

She dressed herself then, in steamy heat – wishing she had some of the clothes that were now at the bottom of the ocean – and combed her hair. It was a black tangle, sticky with salt. Should have washed it. Yellow eyes watching her in the mirror, telling her *Stupid*, not to have. Her eyes were what she called light brown, but Frank had always insisted they were yellow. Cat's eyes, he'd called them, and pretended that they scared him. When soon after they'd got together he'd asked her why her mother's re-marriage had necessitated her leaving home, and she'd told him it had been because of the new man's attitude to herself – suggestive remarks whenever they'd been alone, and the way he'd stared at her – Frank had at first looked angry, and then shrugged: 'Well, I wouldn't blame him, not *al*together. Might *kill* him for it, but—'

'Ah, go *on*!'

'When he was doing his staring, did you give him the evil eye the way you were doing then just telling it?'

Maybe they did glow yellowish, at that. In some lights, certain moods. Love-making too – so *he*'d said. He'd asked her more than once, 'Can you see in the dark, same as the four-legged kind?'

She took the towel back to leave it in the cabin – the Dutch were all snoring – and went up one deck to the dining saloon. The quickest things to get were porridge, bread and tea: it would be enough to keep her going. Probably eat again with them later. They'd be famished. There were other Irish whom she recognized in the saloon but kept away from, to avoid having to explain everything all over again. Nobody was doing much talking anyway. Maybe from having too much to think about: or in shock, in varying degrees, from what they'd been through.

People they'd lost, or seen drown, had to leave to drown.

How could that man have got himself into a boat? she wondered. The head of all this, responsible for all of it –

and when other men had handed their wives and children into boats, and they themselves stood back or been turned away? Being around the boats as he had been he'd have seen that happening, all right – enforced it even, him with the orders he was giving!

Frank had been turned away. She'd realized, since, near enough what he and that purser must have been saying to each other. Hence the calamity with Tom. And your man there dancing around, yelling fit to bust . . .

As for people keeping to themselves, it was the same outside, on the ship's decks. They were all courteous enough, acknowledging each other when they met or passed, but not speaking, or seeking company as the Parrys had. She went out on to the forward deck, to start with; there were people all over it, sitting or reclining, in steamer or basket chairs or on the deck itself, many wrapped in blankets. The sun was brilliant, sky cloudless, but the wind was bitter: having passed over all that ice, of course. Some passengers were dozing, and a few were engaged in desultory conversation, but most seemed purposefully to be avoiding contact. As she herself had in the dining saloon, of course. Many, she realized, would be in a similar predicament to her own. Poor things, poor darlings: she crossed herself, unobtrusively. Mary, mother of God, comfort them. And *please*, let Frank and Tom be in that boat? I'll never ask another favour, God, I swear it! Making her way to the ship's side, hands up to her eyes against the glare and the gusting wind. She saw the boat at once: no more than five or six hundred yards away, she guessed, deep in the water, packed with people, four oars each side labouring to keep it moving. Rowing wouldn't be too easy, in that pack of people: and from this distance there wasn't a hope of spotting let alone identifying any individual. But a lot of them would be men – the steward had said as much. Men rescued from some other capsized boat, he'd intimated. She was looking round, wondering whether to stay here or go back up on that higher deck – which was first-class territory, of course, might have been shut off by this time. On this deck meanwhile – further forward, up where it narrowed – several lifeboats were already on the deck and in the process of being lashed down, while another was being hoisted on the crane. Anyway – promenade deck, she decided. Try, anyway. If she was challenged she'd say she was looking for Mrs Dalby, who'd invited her. Whom in any case she'd like to see, to whom felt enormously obliged, even to some extent dependent upon.

Running aft along each side of the ship from here was a side deck with cabin portholes all along it – first-class state-rooms, she supposed. Then, a ladderway leading upward – with its gateway standing open and latched back. She climbed it: two stewards with their arms full of folded linen standing aside at the top to let her pass; she murmured thanks, and one of them said, 'A pleasure, miss.' Miss – not madam. Astonishing, the difference a few gallons of hot water and a comb could make.

Although she still felt weak, and shaky. Would do until she had her arms around *them*, she guessed.

She paused – seeing it was a lot more crowded along there, closer above the entry-port. Whereas here, quite a length of ship's side-rail was as yet untenanted. She stopped leaning on it, gazing out across ice and glittering, jumpy sea to the boat struggling this way through it, the boat with Frank and Tom either in it or not in it, and facing the question *What if they are not*?

It was out of her hands, her control. Foot of the rainbow if they *were* in that boat, but if they were not – then, no starting point, no destination and no answers. Only in her ears again the cries of the drowning – amongst whom *they'd* have been.

Live the rest of your life with *that* in your head?

If you have to, she told herself – if you have to, *yes*. If it's going to come to that, you'll gear yourself to it, that's all. Eventually, you will.

Leaning back, hands latched on to the rail and arms out straight, she could see another space between people ten yards or so further along – further aft, closer to the entry-port. So move quick, before it fills up . . . With the boat's approach, people were crowding out again.

Others – other women – facing *their* last chances.

'Eileen!'

Mrs Dalby, coming from a group of bizarrely dressed people further along. She'd been titivating *herself* up, all right. Looked as if she might have just come from a hair-dresser's. 'Why, you *do* look better, Eileen! Truly, you look *swell*!'

They were together at the rail, in the space Eileen had just spotted. The captain was turning the ship again, she realized – feeling the engines' vibration as the propellers churned, angling the ship so as to provide shelter for the boat on this side. Mrs Dalby linking her arm into Eileen's and assuring her, 'They'll be in this one, don't you doubt it for an instant. Why, they reckon there are in excess of seventy persons in it! The Chief Officer made that estimate, using binoculars from the bridge up there. At *least* seventy, he said. More than twice as many as we were – imagine that? Honey – excuse me, the way I prattle on – I do, I know it – but I'm *certain* as far as you are concerned the happy ending's coming up in just *minutes*!'

'Please God it may.'

'Well, you know – the way you had it worked out they *had* to have gotten away in *a* boat—'

'I'm saying prayers that I was right.'

The vibration was continuing, though less noticeably, but the quarter-turn had put boat number twelve almost right astern of the *Carpathia* now. Eileen was having to lean further and further out to keep her eyes on it, past the heads of others doing the same. Mrs Dalby, for whom leaning far over was impossible – since she was quite short as well as stout – was asserting that they'd see it all right when it came in closer: she held out her hands with fingers crossed on both of them, added, 'See *them*, I should've said.' Hands together as if in prayer then, shutting her eyes for a moment. Then: 'It *is* going to be all right, honey. My heart *and* my brain tell me so, they really do!'

'But you see, there are dozens of other women in my position. Here and now, along the rail here. We can't *all* be so lucky, can we.'

'A whole bagful can, and you'll be one of 'em. Although you're right, there's a dozen at least *I* know – one who was at the same table with me even, she and her husband – see, *he* might be in this boat now, along with your Frank!'

Just as Frank *might* be . . . 'Might' was the key word. Mrs Dalby was as good-hearted as anyone could be, but what her heart told her didn't add up to a row of beans. Leaning well out again, watching the boat approaching – clearly in need of shelter, the ship's lee, waves actually lopping over the gunwale on this weather side. They'd have to be baling, she supposed. Not easy, being so tight-packed.

'See any that *might* be them, can you?'

'No.' She pulled back, to rest for a minute. 'But – close now. Getting some of the oars in. I still can't make out . . .'

Back over the rail, trying again. The only individual standing out clearly was a man upright in the stern, weirdly dressed – some sort of hood over his head. A woman's evening cape, over a ship's officer's uniform? That was what it looked like: but her eyes weren't focusing properly, the whole boatload of now suddenly upturned faces was only a greyish blur – *and* people here leaning out even further, obstructing her own limited view. Then a line fell across the boat's bow – she saw *that* – and a man was reaching to grab it – not a seaman, but tall – long-armed anyway – in a black or navy-blue working jacket. It *could* have been Frank – just for a split second it could have been, then clearly was not – not Frank's light ginger head, but shiny-black, Italian-looking. She heard Mrs Dalby shout something to her – shouting was necessary, there was a lot of it going on, people yelling down to those in the boat or just calling names, wanting them to look up, reveal themselves; but no one hearing much of it. Mrs Dalby was suggesting, fairly hooting at her, 'Try farther along?' Eileen shaking her head – in tears – leaning dangerously far out to see something of the start of disembarkation: seemingly all women coming first, men remaining for the most part seated – to keep the boat steady, or whatever that strangely clad person was telling them. Although with the crowd in it becoming less dense she was beginning to see *some* detail: but again, they weren't looking up, all their attention was on the gangway, awaiting their turn to move.

None of them looked anything like Frank. She admitted it to herself quite brutally, in the hope – *belief*, almost – that in a moment she'd be able suddenly to contradict herself – flat contradiction and a shriek of joy, there he *is*! Not yet, he wasn't. No Frank, no Tom. She hadn't seen *any* child, Oh, well – contradict that, all right, a small girl was being lifted out at this moment. And another: and their stout mother following, two seamen hauling her up on to the lower platform of the gangway. They were the mother and daughters who'd been on E deck and gone up with the steward, the tail-end of that party she and Frank had followed. So it *was* possible to recognize . . .

Could see them all now. All those still in the boat. All on their feet, preparing to disembark.

No Frank. No Tom.

Shock was tempered by disbelief. Although she'd tried to prepare herself for this it was simply not possible to accept. Visions forcing their way in again: the rushing, overwhelming, crushing flood, bodies being swept away, smashed against bulkheads as the crushing weight of ocean thundered through. Telling Mrs Dalby through her tears – she'd staggered backward from the rail and those short, thick arms were around her again – gasping through tears that she must have missed seeing them, they could have come out of the boat right at the start when she'd had hardly any view at all, when it had seemed to be all women disembarking, but Frank with Tom might well have been amongst them. See – the blond stewardess, if she'd been carrying Tom, Frank sticking close to them as he would have –

'Then we'll catch 'em when they come up to the saloon, honey!'

Wiping away tears with her headscarf: and in a last look downward seeing what looked like a dead body swinging up in the rope sling. A man's body – bald head, seaman's sweater. She knew they would *not* be coming up to the saloon. Fighting hysteria, breakdown, relapse into the way she'd been when they'd gone on lowering and other women including Susan and Mrs Dalby had had to hold her in it against her frantic struggles – fighting it because it gained you nothing, only shamed you later; but then again the image of the man in carpet-slippers waving his arms and shouting 'Lower away!' Ruling out any chance Frank might have had of scooping up Tom and getting back with him: she told this – this Elizabeth Dalby, who was still gabbling about getting to the saloon – Eileen told her, 'My husband and my son have drowned. They'd have been drowning when we were listening to their cries.' She'd managed that much – putting it at its starkest, as if making the statement so plainly might cut her adrift from the reality, as it were to float clear of it; but felt herself going now – buckling at the knees, strength drained, in her fogged brain the sound she'd still be hearing on the day *she* died.

4

***

She remembered Frank saying to Tom, 'When we pass *this*, Tommy boy, 'twill be the start of a whole new life.' 'This' being the Statue of Liberty; and he'd had Tom on his knee, showing him a picture of it in some book. Frank's voice a true-to-life echo in her brain, Tom's sharp look of enquiry just as it were behind her eyes. There it was now – the statue itself, in the gloom of this wet Thursday evening, with the *Carpathia* nosing up towards the Battery and the Hudson River.

Flags at half-mast. Not only the *Carpathia*'s, but on other ships and ashore as well. Eileen thinking, *For you, Frank, and you, Tom. I'll do for him, I swear to God I will. No – swear to you, Frank – not owing him much.*

She'd sworn it in Elizabeth Dalby's cabin – two nights ago, might have been – and had it in and out of mind ever since. In every interval of wakefulness or semi-wakefulness since then. She'd been drugged, she knew that well enough. Also that she'd kill him – clear-minded enough on *that*, even in her dreams. Smiling her thanks to Mrs Dalby, dutifully taking the doctor's medicine and advice, telling herself that *somehow* she'd do for the carpet-slipper man. What else – dry your eyes, walk away, forget it? She sniffed, glanced

at her watch. Eight p.m. now – on Thursday 18th April.
A while ago there'd been trouble with pressmen trying to
board, when the ship had stopped at Quarantine and the
captain had prevented them. Eileen had only heard about
it, hadn't been on deck then. They were husbanding her
strength in order to get her to the Dalby home on her feet
– except she could cat-nap in the automobile, Elizabeth had
said – *And soon as we get you home you'll go right to bed, you
hear?* Now, Elizabeth was shepherding her across to the
starboard side – Manhattan side, Manhattan Island with
the Battery at its southern point. She'd been pointing out
all the sights – she was pointing again now: 'There – that's
it. Oh, sainted aunt—'

'What?'

'Did you ever *see* so many people?'

Eileen focusing – with some effort, she was still a little
under the influence of the stuff Dr McGhee had been giving
her – focusing on that point of land.

It *was* an enormous crowd.

But silent. That was the astounding thing. Only the thrum
of the ship's engines and the hiss of water along her sides:
there wasn't a sound coming from that vast assembly.
Elizabeth's hand on her arm again, the other one pointing:
'Battery gardens, see, and – there, that's the Aquarium. Oh,
Jesus God, Eileen . . .'

'So many of 'em, and so quiet!'

'Downright uncanny.' She'd muttered it. But nobody was
talking much. As if silence were infectious or compulsory.
When a woman sobbed, fifty feet away, you heard it.
Eileen could hear Elizabeth's hard, puffing breaths; she
was casting anxious looks at her all the time, warned
by Dr McGhee that she'd be nowhere near out of the
wood *this* soon. But all right, since she'd made such a
hullabaloo at the prospect of being taken on a stretcher to
hospital, so be it: he'd agreed grudgingly with Mrs Dalby,

If you can manage, dear lady, give her the time and care she needs . . .

These last few days Elizabeth herself had been very quiet – as well as a guardian angel and tower of strength – really noticeably quiet, in contrast to her previous and doubtless habitual ebullience. Indicative of a change in character? But as if she'd been hit as hard as Eileen had been. She'd been wonderful to her. Eileen had woken some time on Monday in a berth in a first-class double cabin into which she – Elizabeth – had transferred from her single-berth one. There'd been a re-shuffle in which Susan too had been involved; the detail of it wasn't clear – quite a few things weren't, due largely of course to the opiates administered by Dr McGhee. He'd given her an injection, apparently, when she'd been unconscious – had fainted, or whatever – and subsequently doses of some medicine which Elizabeth had sniffed at and then murmured to Susan, 'Laudanum. Can be addictive, so one's heard.' They'd kept her semi-comatose throughout that first day and the next, and she'd got up yesterday for the first time, on her own insistence and still groggy, to dine with Elizabeth in the first-class saloon, where several total strangers, friends of Elizabeth's, had spoken to her sympathetically. One in particular, a Colonel Gracey, who in fact had joined them at the end of the meal and taken coffee with them; Elizabeth had known him since the first day out from Southampton, apparently, and he'd been one of the men rescued by boat number twelve after spending five or six hours standing on the keel of the upturned collapsible.

'Impossible, my dear.' Answering Eileen's question as to whether they couldn't have got off it, turned it upright and then climbed in. He'd explained, 'Clumsy great brute of a thing. Not that I should be disparaging about it, seeing it saved me as well as about thirty others!'

He'd been washed off the roof of the officers' quarters – above the boat-deck – and sucked down with the ship to start with, but fought his way back up to the surface and encountered various floating objects to which he'd clung before spotting the overturned collapsible, floundering to it and hauling himself up on it. He hadn't at any point seen a tall, reddish-haired young man with a little boy. 'I'd like to think that if I *had*—' pausing, thinking about it, and not finishing that sentence; he'd shaken his head. 'Regrettably I did not. I'm very, *very* sorry, my dear. Tell me – I've been hearing about you from Mrs Dalby here, of course – have you any thoughts of what you'll do now?'

'Sure she has!' Elizabeth, taking over again. 'She'll be coming home with me and be put to bed and stay there until she's a lot stronger, *that*'s what!' Eileen smiling tiredly, shrugging her acceptance of *force majeure*. She certainly did have her own thoughts, but couldn't possibly have voiced any of them to Colonel Gracey. But some of it was based on things one had been told – or anyway *heard*. There'd been visitors to Elizabeth's cabin from time to time, notably of course the doctor and Susan but others too, women acquaintances of Elizabeth's, and Eileen hadn't been unconscious *all* the time, even when they'd thought she was. The dream that had turned out worst had been that Frank and Tom were alive and well, having been picked up by some other ship; the news had come through Matt McGrath, who'd had a wireless message from Frank on that other ship. She'd woken *believing* it: which had led to something like a fresh emotional eruption a minute later when she'd *really* woken. Her reactive thinking then had actually been suicidal – a line of thought which to an extent she'd developed further, in connection with other – well, the intention concerning Mr Ismay. On which she could hardly have expanded in reply to that question of Colonel Gracey's – had she any plans now. She had no others, was the truth of it, only repetitive, confusing dreams and day-dreams of which that was the nucleus. No others, partly because Elizabeth had urged her not to make any – 'Just take it easy, honey, as it comes . . .' Elizabeth had sent wireless messages to Matt McGrath in Philadelphia as well as to her husband, putting them in touch with each other and saying that Eileen could stay at the Dalby home at New Rochelle, New York as long as she liked; the McGraths would be welcome to visit her there. It might well have been where that other dream had sprung from – from Elizabeth telling her about the messages she'd been sending.

Eileen didn't think the McGraths would want her in Philadelphia. As far as they were concerned she'd have been an appendage to Frank, nothing more, and now with Frank gone they'd have no interest in her at all. Might visit them there if they insisted; could not, she felt, take advantage of Elizabeth's hospitality for more than a few days, even though *she* was insisting she'd need weeks of convalescence.

Back to Ireland, then?

She had enough money for a steerage-class passage back. *More* than enough, in fact. Even in his wilder days Frank had never been improvident, they'd saved all they could out of their joint earnings even before receiving his uncle's renewed invitation to come over. 'Like I've said how many dozen times, I'll not be working with my hands for ever, Eilie, and you'll not work at all when we can get by without it. Raising a family'll be *your* work. But no matter which way the cat jumps when it does, we'll need money for it, so.'

'Money you'll not be spending on your political ambitions, I hope to God!'

'I've *no* "political ambitions". I'm minded to help my country, that's all!'

'Sending rifles and bullets? Don't *they* cost money?'

'Collecting funds for the sending of rifles, Eilie, against

the day we'll need 'em. Why, there are thousands of our people over there now, and small contributions, if there are enough—'

'I don't want to know about it, Frank.'

She'd had that argument with him again in her sleep last night; woken thinking that if she went back to Cork now, which might turn out to be the best choice for her, she'd get word to O'Meara via the other one – Twomey – let them know they'd have to look elsewhere. For Frank's sake, what he'd have wanted. But then the thought that maybe he would *not* have had her involving herself even to that extent – since he hadn't before, hadn't wanted her to meet them, maybe because of the way she felt about all that kind of political shenanigan.

They'd get to know he'd drowned in any case. There'd be lists of names on all the newspapers, surely – including the *Cork Examiner*.

Another consideration was that your man – Ismay – would be going to England, not Ireland. White Star was run from London, and Dr McGhee had told Elizabeth that as boss of it he'd be getting back there on the first ship that was going, to deal with the crisis at that end.

'He's not looking forward to it, believe me.'

'In bad shape, you said?'

'He's getting the same medication I'm giving your young friend here. Not the same dosage, but enough to – oh, for its calming effect, you know. He's at sixes and sevens, poor fellow.'

Eileen had been listening to this with her eyes closed, breathing evenly. The doctor had checked her temperature and her pulse-rate, and told Elizabeth it would be advisable to reduce the dose now; might get her on her feet just for a little while the next evening, he hoped. Since she was so adamant in her refusal to be taken off to hospital on a stretcher, which in his view would be the right and proper thing – well, in her particular state of mind it might, he admitted, do more harm than good. She'd suffered a dreadful blow, and in her state of physical and emotional exhaustion had been in no condition to stand up to it; but since admittedly there was nothing organically wrong with her . . .

Elizabeth had put in, 'Feeling as strongly as she does, she might just walk out of any hospital. Whereas if we have her at home—'

'Precisely, dear lady!'

Eileen had heard her ask him then, 'What about Bruce Ismay?'

'Much the same, really. A nervous condition, acute anxiety . . . As I say, mild sedation is all I'm giving him. But he's a strong man, and fit.'

'They're saying he shouldn't have saved himself.'

'He's well aware it's what half the world will be saying. It worries him a great deal, it's at least half the problem. But – anyone in the position he was in – a boat ready to be lowered, and no one else there to get in it – well . . .'

Eileen, listening closely to what he was saying, had opened her eyes, and he'd happened to see it; he'd broken off, turned back to her bunk, placing a cool hand lightly on her forehead. 'A little better, Mrs Maguire? I was just saying to Mrs Dalby that we can reduce the dosage from now on. Although I'd still like you to get all the rest you can.'

She'd told Elizabeth, after the door had closed behind the surgeon, 'The man he was talking about – Ismay—'

'Oh, you heard that. D'you know who he is?'

'Yes, some people told me. Someone important in the White Star Line, isn't he?'

By about nine thirty the *Carpathia* was alongside pier 54 with her gangway down and the disembarkation of *Titanic* survivors beginning. The only people allowed to come on board, other than officials from the Immigration department – whom Elizabeth Dalby had seen on Eileen's behalf – were doctors, Red Cross nurses, stretcher-bearers and a bevy of priests; all others, friends and families of survivors numbering about a thousand, were waiting in the great hangar-like shed. The sick and injured were taken ashore first – ambulances from several hospitals were waiting on the quayside – and then the rest, starting with first-class but including Eileen, who went down behind Elizabeth – bear-like again in her fur coat, and with her felt hat jammed on tight – and Susan Harper following her. Thanks to Elizabeth, Eileen was still getting very special treatment. In the shed were a crush of people and sheer bedlam – weeping relatives, reporters bawling questions and stopping any who'd allow themselves to be stopped, emotional reunions and others lost and panicking. Many of the women from shore-side were dressed in mourning. Elizabeth led Eileen to the 'D' for Dalby section in the Customs area – Customs themselves having nothing to do, since there was no baggage being landed – and her husband, who'd climbed on to the bench for a better view, leapt down and came thrusting through to meet her. He was a man in his late forties, of medium height but no lightweight: bushy brown moustache, head shiny-bald under the overhead lighting as he swept off his Homberg and flung his arms around her.

'Liza! My precious Liza, *bless* you, and thank God! Oh, my *dearest*—'

'Swell to see you too, Bill.' Elizabeth drew Eileen up beside her. 'This is my very good friend Eileen Maguire. Eileen, my husband William K. Dalby.'

'Mrs Maguire, how do. May I say, you have *all* my deepest sympathy—'

'She's going to need a heck of a lot more than *that*, let me tell you. You did bring the motor?'

'Sure did. You wouldn't want to be standing around on any railway platform, huh?'

'Wouldn't *want*, Bill, this young lady *couldn't*. She's an invalid and the minute we get her home she's going to be tucked up and sent by-byes!'

'All right. Sure. Sorry, Eileen—'

'Actually I'm perfectly all right. Elizabeth's been caring for me so marvellously—'

'Perfectly all right, my foot!'

'All right, all right.' Dalby hushed her. 'Far as the motor's concerned though, I better warn you getting away from here may be a little slow. They have a police cordon along Eleventh Avenue right from Twelfth to Sixteenth Street, and they say there are thirty thousand people rubber-necking. In the *rain*, mark you!'

Susan had been introduced, and kissed them goodbye before – hurrying off to the 'H' for Harper section. Eileen would have liked to have caught sight of the Scottish fiancé, but there was no chance. Looking after her, she did see the Parry couple though – his over-large white cap, and the same flowered hat on her, and their arms around each other as they dodged through the crowd. Bill Dalby was asking his wife, 'How about Immigration? *Is* Eileen an immigrant?'

'She's not, she's a visitor and our guest. If she makes her mind up otherwise, then she can *become* an immigrant. It's all fine, I fixed it, we had a team of 'em on board. Press *tried* to get aboard, would you believe it, a whole boatload, Captain Rostron had to threaten he'd turn the hoses on 'em!'

'Good for him. What most of those guys need is a good hosing down. Now stay close, eh? How about one of you each side?'

'Eileen, see *there*?'

Ismay. Same suit – would have been valeted, no doubt

– and a bowler hat. And shoes, evidently, not slippers – he was walking fast, not shuffling, in the centre of a group of similar-looking men shouldering through. Bill Dalby said, 'That was Franklin – White Star vice-president here in New York. Had his photo on the *Times* front page this morning. Guy in the centre'd be Ismay, right?'

Getting away from the docks was as slow as Dalby had intimated it might be. Huge crowds everywhere, and hundreds of policemen; initially the car had been boxed in by ambulances. But once out of all that and on their way to New Rochelle there was a feeling of escape. An illusion, of course, Eileen reflected: what had happened *had* happened, wherever you went you'd take it with you. Take *them* – invisible to others but not to you – almost tangible, to you. Tommy on her lap, Frank's strong arm around her. Oh, Christ Jesus . . . Dalby telling them that ever since word had come on Monday that *something* terrible had happened to the *Titanic* there'd been conflicting newspaper reports and official statements. That the ship had been damaged but was still afloat and making her way slowly to New York had been one; another that she was being towed stern-first to Halifax. Philip A. S. Franklin, the vice-president whom they'd just seen with Ismay, had issued a statement in which he'd repeated the legend that the *Titanic* was unsinkable. And then the shattering announcement, also from him at the White Star office: 'The *Titanic* sank at 2.20 a.m.'

'Even then we were getting a lot of hogwash. All contradictory, hour by hour. For instance, word got out that White Star was reserving whole wards in certain hospitals, and the rumour was – well, they were saying *mental* illness too. Fact, I guess some *could*'ve been hit that way – not all of 'em as strong as this young lady – eh? But see, your *Carpathia* skipper wasn't answering questions they were wirelessing to him. Even a message from President Taft didn't get answered. Well, what they're saying now is Ismay was imposing this censorship. I dare say being White Star business he'd be able to – although the *Carpathia*'s a Cunarder?'

'No idea at all. Anyway, Bill, let's leave it?'

'Huh?' Peering ahead through drizzle. 'Oh – sure. I guess – yeah. I'm sorry—'

'You might like to snooze a little, Eileen. We've a way to go – and nothing to see, a night like this. Normally, we'd take the train – Bill does, most days, getting to his business. He has offices in Manhattan, a new place. Are you happy with the new location, Bill?'

'Oh, sure . . .'

Honking his horn at a cat.

'May I ask what sort of business, Mr Dalby?'

'Well – I call myself a property speculator. I deal in real-estate, and I put up buildings or take a piece of the action in buildings other guys are putting up. But I don't mind telling you, I started as a builder pure and simple.'

'What was that word – *pure*?'

'Now, Liza—'

'See, Eileen' – Elizabeth admitting – 'it's a success story, really is. He made it on his own from the ground up, so to speak, using his own muscle. *And* nerve – even now, let alone in those early days. I'm sure I don't have to tell you we're not exactly Social Register, but – we don't lack for anything we need, either.'

'*I* think you're absolutely marvellous.'

'Oh, heck—'

'Mr Dalby, it's the truth. If it hadn't been for your wife – well, right at the start I think she probably saved my life, and since then she's seen to it that I've had everything *I* need.'

'I'm glad to hear it. Doesn't surprise me, mind you. And

while on that subject, I'd like you to know that I'm *deeply* saddened by your tragic loss. Words fail me, absolutely—'

'So leave it there, Bill. You've said it twice now, I've said it a hundred times. What we want for Eileen is a chance to sort of distance herself a little from these last days. Or *start* to, just a little . . . Think you *could* sleep now, honey?'

In the dark the house looked massive: three storeys, stone-built, in a large garden which they called a yard. A coloured maid by name of Dinah told them as they entered the wide hallway that a Mr McGrath had telephoned from Philadelphia and would do so again in the morning if they didn't call him back before that.

'Well – might be a bit late now—'

'It *is*.' Dalby tossed his hat on to a coatstand and threw a macintosh after it. 'Get back to him first thing in the morning. Maybe they'd come over at the weekend. If he has a motor works he'll have a motor, I guess. Eileen, how about a little supper now, *then* hit the hay?'

It was decided they'd have soup followed by cold meats with a salad, and while Dinah was seeing to the soup – the cook had gone to bed – Elizabeth showed Eileen some of the house and the room that was to be hers; it was large and sumptuously furnished, and there was a bathroom just along the passage. Eileen told Elizabeth, 'It's beautiful! Biggest house I was ever in!'

'It's certainly the biggest we ever *owned*. We like it, I confess. Only thing is it sort of keeps telling you it's the kind of place needs to be filled with family, and that's the one thing we don't have. Can't have it *all*, I guess. Let's go see if Dinah has that soup ready. Listen, what we have to do tomorrow is some shopping. A few things I need, and a whole lot you need – right?'

'Well – *some* things—'

'You need about everything – and it'll be my pleasure.

I'm not saying let's go *mad*, but you're going to be with us quite some while, and – well, heavens . . .' Leading the way down the stairs, prattling on . . . The best shopping would of course be downtown, but for first essentials there were a couple of good stores much nearer. Eileen would need a few things in which to travel to New York, even. 'Wouldn't want to go as you are now, would you. *I* wouldn't want you to. And since nothing of mine'd come anywhere near fitting you – in any case, mourning, of course . . .' That had slipped her mind, and she was embarrassed that it should have: sniffing, changing the subject: 'Hey, that's onion soup I smell. Onion all right with you? Listen, you really up to this, wouldn't sooner have it upstairs on a tray?'

She had the dream again of Frank and Tom being safe and well and on their way. It was what Matt McGrath had telephoned about. From that beginning – the maid telling them he'd called – it was essentially the same dream with slightly altered detail: they'd been picked up by this other ship which had landed them in Halifax in Nova Scotia and they were on the train to Philadelphia: Matt McGrath had asked would Mr Dalby bring Eileen over so she'd be there to meet them on arrival. In fact they'd be changing trains at Grand Central in New York, but God only knew what time or on which day, even. She'd woken as she had the last time, in a surge of happiness, then thought that she did need to go on this shopping trip, get a *few* things – like underwear and another skirt and some shirts and maybe a jacket and a jersey – oh, and shoes, stockings – and she could *not* use that much of the money she and Frank had worked for and saved, although it would be shaming in these new circumstances – dashing off to Philadelphia – to trade to that extent on Elizabeth Dalby's generosity. For a minute or half a minute, this – and whether she might find a second-hand clothes store, at least for some items –

preoccupied her; she'd got as far as thinking maybe *borrow* what she needed from Elizabeth, when the hideous truth and the misery hit her, in the grey light of early morning and the most comfortable bed she'd ever slept in, with a dawn chorus of birdsong outside the window.

She wished she'd drowned with them.

A little while thinking about that: recognizing it as yet more truth, that if she'd been able to wave a magic wand and put back the clock to two twenty or two thirty a.m. Monday, and have drowned with them, thus be with them now wherever they were – yes, she definitely *would* have gone for that. For Tom not to have been alone, as he might have been – if Frank hadn't found him, hadn't had him in his arms when the moment came. Well – moments, plural. Minutes. Tom alone and terrified, shrieking for her or for his father, was about the most hideous picture that off and on racked her imagination. But another flash of memory then, and this one not imaginary at all but fact: when they'd been trying to put the life-jacket on him and he'd fought against it, she'd told Frank no need, you or I will be his life-jacket if there's need of it. If she hadn't interfered like that, if they'd just soothed him and made him wear it, he wouldn't have been able to have twisted out of Frank's grasp as he had, or run away: so she'd have had him in the boat with her, would have had him here *now*, in this warm bed.

Frank would still have drowned.

And the carpet-slipper man was going to pay for it. *How* was something else. The first thing being somehow to get close to him. Presumably in England: Dr McGhee had said that Ismay's intention was to take passage in the first ship that was going back there. It was not inconceivable, she thought, that White Star would give her a free trip back to Ireland; Elizabeth Dalby had said that if eventually this was her choice, it might be worth trying it on them. In fact her husband would take it up with them, if that was what she opted for: he'd know how to handle it and he wasn't a man to be easily put off. So – from there, she'd get on the ferry from Cork to Fishguard. Have to keep enough money for that – not that it would cost any vast amount, the day-and-a-half's journey as a deck passenger. Not comfortable, but – comfort was not the issue. (So enjoy *this* while you have it. And if Elizabeth really is happy to foot the bill for those essential items . . . Qualms faded when you had a purpose such as she, Eileen, had, social niceties became less significant.) But – all right, obviously she had to get to England – London – and she wouldn't be able simply to arrive there, walk up to your man and kill him and catch the next boat home; she'd need to live somewhere – a few days, a week, even several weeks. If he was approachable at all, in fact. But that would be part of it – just getting to him. Then, how to do it. A woman's simplest weapon, she'd read in some detective story, was poison; but to administer it you'd have to be living in the same house, eating at the same table – or waiting on him maybe, have a job as a servant of some kind. Which might not be posssible at all . . . So how else to do it – maybe having established where he was to be found at some particular time of day or night? He was a big man, she knew that: and strong and fit, Dr McGhee had said. So – a gun might be the answer? In which case you'd need first to get one, and then to learn how to use it.

A knife would be far easier to get. But stabbing – two drawbacks to that, one that strength came into it – or most likely would – and the other that to be sure of killing you had to know precisely where to stab, and do it fairly expertly.

A pistol, she thought. One capable of firing several shots. Revolver, in fact.

Might get one from Jack Twomey in Cork, the man who'd taken Frank to meet the politician O'Meara. If Twomey didn't have one himself, he might know who would. The cost of it was something else again, but since timing wasn't a major factor, she thought – although it would be best to get it over and done with as soon as possible – if things were tight by then she could take a job for a while and save. Her old job might still be open to her – they'd said it always would be – but if it wasn't there'd be others. She could work for a few months, save a bit and *then* go over. Having learned to use the thing by that time too – again perhaps with help from Twomey. He was an engineer, had been a colleague of Frank's at the motor-bus company; she'd never met him but he'd be easy to track down, and she'd have reason for getting in touch – what she'd been thinking earlier, telling him about Frank.

Bill Dalby called the McGraths early next morning. McGrath hadn't left his telephone number when he'd got through the evening before, but Eileen had it amongst the papers Frank had left in her keeping – which was how Elizabeth had been able to wireless them from the *Carpathia*. It was Matt who answered the phone, Dalby told him they had Eileen here at New Rochelle and invited him and his wife to come over maybe the weekend after this one and, if they cared to, spend the night. He was suggesting leaving it until then, he explained, in order to give Eileen those ten days to rest up; she was in pretty good shape, considering what she'd been through, but she *had* had a very rough time, and – well, McGrath could imagine . . . No, she hadn't made any firm plans yet, whether to remain in America and find employment – which he was sure he'd be able to help with if that was what she wanted. Anyway, how about it – Saturday or Sunday week, or come that Saturday and stay over?

Eileen and Elizabeth were breakfasting upstairs in Eileen's bedroom. She'd have come down but Elizabeth had insisted she stayed put, especially as the doctor was coming; she'd had her own breakfast brought up too.

'And from here on we'll do as Dr Barnes tells us – right?'

'Well—'

'Eileen – he's a very good doctor, and if *he* says you're to stay in bed—'

'I don't know why he should, though. Physically, I'm right as rain!'

'He might feel – as I do – that you need to lie low a while. And if he were to prescribe a sedative—'

'That's something I do *not* want. I've got to face the facts of what's happened, not just lie around drugged and—'

Tap on the door: Bill Dalby told them, 'I just spoke with McGrath. You won't like this, Liza, just wasn't any other way to play it. I suggested it the way we discussed – come the weekend after this one, but they couldn't make that, he has to be at some automobile convention in Detroit, he said, and anyhow he'd much rather see you sooner than that, so – '

'Bill, she's not fit!'

' – so he can write to his sister before she blows a fuse not hearing. Anyway they're coming Sunday – for lunch. I told him you'd like as not be in bed, Eileen, in which case he or his wife might speak with you for five minutes or something—'

'What's his sister got to do with anything?'

'Frank's mother. Kate Maguire, in Tipperary.'

'Well – if Dr Barnes tells us it's too soon for Eileen to have company—'

'Then I'll call him again and lay it on the line. Sure.'

'I'm sure I'll be perfectly all right. Honestly, Elizabeth. I am *now*. I know Dr McGhee wanted to put me in hospital, he most likely wants to put *everyone* in hospital—'

Dalby laughed. 'Wouldn't surprise me *at* all. So no matter

what, he can't be blamed and White Star taken to the cleaners!'

'You didn't meet him, Bill.' Elizabeth got up to pour Eileen more coffee. 'He's a very straightforward kind of man and been doctoring at sea Lord knows how long, he'd know all there is to know about shock and so forth. Another thing you don't have much concept of is the stress of the ordeal this poor kid's been through!'

'But—' Eileen took the cup from her. 'Thanks. Thing is – of course, let Dr Barnes have his say, but the ordeal is something I've got for life now, I've got to stand on my own feet coping with it. I'm sure those two days I was doped are what's made all the difference, I'm very grateful to you and to Dr McGhee too, but I'm sure I don't need another week of it. All right, I may burst into tears for no reason or wake up howling, but I doubt it'll be so different in a year's time either. Elizabeth dear, I'm not saying I want to run races or climb mountains – yet—'

'You surprise me. Bill, did you have breakfast yet?'

He nodded. 'Only came up to tell you – Sunday lunch, the McGraths. You said you never met them, Eileen?'

She shook her head. 'They've been in Philadelphia since before I met Frank. Frank said he was a bad-tempered man.'

'Ah. Did sound a little gruff. Asked me to extend to you his and his wife's sympathy. Not a word about having you visit *them*, I noticed.'

Elizabeth murmured charitably, 'Be saving that for Sunday, maybe.'

'They won't want me there, I'm sure.' Eileen had enjoyed a breakfast of egg, bacon and fried cornbread. 'It was Frank's mother persuaded her brother to take Frank into the business with him – and he'd have only been on trial, six months to prove himself or out. Well, Frank *would* have proved himself, but he said it wouldn't matter, it would be a jumping-off point and that was all he needed.'

Dalby nodded. 'Sounds like sense.'

'His mother – Kate – is a sweet woman, you'd like her too. She'd be horrified if she heard her brother had *not* been over. Could be why they're coming – but I'm sure they *wouldn't* want me there.'

'Suits us.' Elizabeth shrugged. 'Makes New Rochelle your base, not Philadelphia. Selfishly, I'm glad of that.'

'"Selfish" is the *last* word . . . Which makes this hard to say . . . Because – well, kind as you've been and *are* being, and lovely as it is here—'

'You haven't seen it yet, honey!'

'I mean your house, and you, and being pampered like this. The thing is – forgive me – I'm sure the answer for me is Ireland. You see—'

'You don't mean soon, I hope?'

'Well, there again – if there's a chance White Star'd give me a passage home – you were saying you thought they might?'

Dalby cut in, 'I could enquire about it, if you like. Since I'll be there in an hour or so. Get a flat "no" it'd make Liza *and* me happy, but in fact I guess that in the circumstances they'd *have* to. Shall I see them about it?'

'Could be we'll get a flat "no you don't" from Dr Barnes before you even leave the house, Bill!'

'Well, if we do—'

Eileen said, 'No harm in asking them anyway – if it's not a lot of trouble?'

'None at all. White Star's at 9 Broadway – spitting distance from where I am now. To steer me right, though, what sort of schedule would you have in mind – a week to rest up with us here? A month?'

'A month at least, Bill!'

'As long as she likes, she knows that. But I'll find out.

Speaking as a business man, I'd guess there'll be conditions, for instance they wouldn't hold out any such offer
indefinitely, might say either you want to go back or
you don't. Well – hold on, Liza – that wouldn't finish
anything, I'd have no objection to stumping up the fare,
if that helped any—'

'No. Thank you, but – there's a limit, there has to be. I
mean, if I had to leave quite soon, to take advantage of –
what you said, whatever they're offering – well, I'd *have* to.'
She looked at Elizabeth. 'You've very, *very* kindly offered to
help me get some clothes—'

'Yeah. We're going shopping, Bill. Oh, I told you. But I
was thinking next week maybe, not right away!'

'But since these folk are coming Sunday . . .' A nod to
his wife: 'With Barnes's permission of course, better make
a start today. Although I'll raise that with White Star too.
Not that I or Liza'd quibble any, Eileen, we would not,
but – a matter of principle, *they* lost all your gear for you,
didn't they? I suppose you don't have any documentation
I could take along – proof you're who I say you are,
ticket or—'

'Yes – as it happens. In the canvas roll there. Frank put
all our papers and money in it. We'd started up from the
cabin when he thought of it and went back down. God,
I thought I'd lost him *then*, he was gone so long and the
water was—'

A bell had rung downstairs. Dalby went to the window
and looked down: 'That's the doc's motor. I'll go bring
him up.'

Elizabeth stayed while Dr Barnes examined her. He was
a shortish, sturdy man with a wide head and a neatly
trimmed brown beard. He asked a lot of questions, checked
her temperature, blood-pressure and pulse-rate, tapped her
kneecaps to make her legs jump, listened to her heart and

breathing and had her focus on a pencil while he moved it to and fro.

'You're sleeping well, you say.'

'I did last night. Before that I was full of dope.'

He'd cocked an eyebrow towards Elizabeth, who told him, 'Laudanum. Dr McGhee—'

'Quite.' To Eileen then: 'You don't feel you'd benefit from further medication of that sort?'

'Not at all. Definitely not.'

'Good. There might be some danger of addiction, if it were prolonged.' Folding his stethoscope back into its case. 'I'll prescribe some other pills, which if you found you were suffering from sleeplessness – nervous anxiety, and obviously grief – but if you can do without them – well . . .'

'There's nothing wrong with me, is there, doctor?'

'Nothing organically wrong, to the best of my observation, and nothing of any other kind that time and rest won't cure. Or at least mitigate. Rest *is* important, Mrs Dalby is absolutely right. And you could well afford to put on a few pounds in weight. Otherwise, I'd say you've weathered this terrible experience extremely well.' He nodded to Elizabeth: 'All due credit to your care of her.'

'Yes. She's been wonderful. And remember, she's been through the same experience herself!'

'Not quite the same. I still have a husband.'

'You know what I mean. She's been extraordinarily kind and thoughtful, doctor. Not only to me, either – why, in the lifeboat she took off her coat to cover some children – when we were in a sea full of *ice*!'

'But listen, doctor. All right, Mrs Maguire seems strong enough right now. But she's contemplating an immediate return to ordinary life – including getting on some ship to go back to Ireland. Well, *I* say she ought to give it at least a month. *Wouldn't* that be better?'

'Well. A month's rest would be good for her – yes. And a month of home cooking and long, quiet nights. *But* – if she's fretting to get back there – you really *are*, are you, you feel you must?'

'Yes. I'm sorry. This is where Frank and I and Tom were going to make our new life – you know, *share* it, the three of us, and – I'm sorry, it's not easy to explain, and I really and truly do appreciate—'

'Yes, well.' A slow nodding, eyes on Elizabeth. 'All in all, I think we should let her go. In *all* the circumstances . . .'

You could intend shooting a man dead and still have qualms accepting charity, she was discovering. Qualms at odds with the pleasure of acquiring clothes of much better quality than those she'd lost – as well as brand new, and in the few instances where she was allowed to see a price, far more expensive than she'd ever have bought for herself. Ever *could* have bought. The predominant external colour had to be black, of course.

'One of the other things you need is a good warm coat. That garment you have—'

'It's ancient, I know. I bought it off an old-clothes stall – '

'Eileen, now *hush*!'

A salesgirl's ears flapping . . .

' – in a back-alley in Cork.'

'Those days are over, honey!'

'*Are* they?'

They could have been. She could still change her mind, elect not to go back but to stay here in this land of infinite opportunity, let Bill Dalby use his influence in finding her a job, find some place to live, put all the rest behind her – *eventually* put it all behind her. It was what Elizabeth wanted for her. She – Elizabeth – had argued quietly with her on their way down to this store in the small town's commercial centre, 'I know, you loved the guy, it's plain

you did – all right, still do. And your little boy, *that* loss
is – indescribable. Right now *you're* sort of lost, aren't you.
Anyone would be. But see, honey, pain wears off, gives way
to – oh, sadness, and respect, and – you can begin to live
again – a new life, that other was the *old* one. Keeping it on
like out of a sense of duty – all right, compassion, love, all
of it – honey, wouldn't be doing *them* no good. And going
back where you came from – I have the feeling that's how
it might go. Like wounded, crawling into cover? I'm talking
out of turn now, it's too soon, I know, a whole lot too soon
and I'm *sorry*—'

'It's all right . . .'

'Heck, how *can* it be? Honey, you may not realize, but
you have to be at least to *some* extent still in shock, try think
ahead a year or two?'

She felt like a confidence trickster. Not for the gift of
new clothes – it obviously gave Elizabeth pleasure and
satisfaction to be doing this, it was marvellous and solved
all kinds of problems but it would also have hurt Elizabeth
if she had *not* accepted it – but on the major issue, why
she had to go back, she had no option but to dissimu-
late.

At White Star they'd told Bill Dalby that a return passage to Ireland *would* be provided gratis by the company to certain categories of passenger, of which Eileen
Maguire's situation as he'd described it was typical –
bereaved widow, no home in the US, no job and no other
means of support – in a word, therefore, stranded. Addi-
tionally, a third-class passenger who'd lost all his or her
belongings was entitled to an ex gratia payment of one
hundred dollars, provided the passenger was not contemplating suing the company for any greater amount
and was ready to sign a document to that effect. These
arrangements had been agreed between Mr J. Bruce Ismay

and Vice-President Franklin – Dalby put on a prissy voice, imitative of the official who'd told him this – '". . . prior to Mr Ismay's departure – why, he's sailing about *now*, I do believe."'

Eileen was surprised. 'Gone *already*!'

'In a ship of some other line, apparently. I suppose he needs to be back in London double-quick. But listen – the provision of a buckshee passage *does* mean taking what they offer, and in your case it would mean departure this next Wednesday afternoon.'

'Wednesday. *That* soon . . .'

Glancing at Elizabeth, who was looking shocked but saying nothing. She'd already said it all, of course. Eileen shook her head. 'It's much sooner than I'd *hoped*. But—'

'Will you take it?'

'I think I have to. Elizabeth won't be pleased, but—'

'Pleased? I'm *mortified*!'

'Liza – I'd sooner keep her with us, too, but she does have to decide for herself, you know. As you told me the doc said—'

'I've a good mind to change my damn doctor. Husband too, maybe!'

'I *am* sorry, Elizabeth. I'd have loved to stay longer – I mean it, I *would* – and when you've been so hugely kind and generous—'

Scowling: 'Want to hear me scream?'

Gazing at her: small shake of the head, lips framing 'No—'

'Say that again, I will!' She looked at her husband. 'You tell 'em we'd bring her there Monday to fix it up?'

'I said maybe Monday. Might be easier by then, they've been real besieged, still were today. I said I'd give 'em a call first, let 'em know one way or the other. I'd better do that. You'll come along, will you?'

'Of course. I want to show her Macy's.'

'Oh, *no*, Elizabeth!'

'And a couple of other places. As well as see what White Star's proposing to do about the stuff *I* lost. Then you'll take us for lunch somewhere real nice – won't you, Bill?'

'Why, sure.'

He'd brought a selection of newspapers back from town, and the three of them sat around looking through them. Page after page was filled with *Titanic* facts and figures, interviews with survivors and profiles of prominent persons who had or had not survived. The latter included a number of millionaires and multi-millionaires. Approximately 1,500 people had drowned. The ship had been carrying 1,400 passengers and had had 940 crew; simple arithmetic suggested that on this basis 840 people would have been saved, although the figure given by a committee of survivors brought to New York on board the *Carpathia* was 775. The *Titanic* could have accommodated as many as 3,500 passengers, and would thus have had a total of 4,440 souls on board – or more, since they'd have needed a lot more stewards – although her lifeboats all loaded to capacity – reckoning this as 50 persons per boat – could have held only 1,000. Figures varied widely from one news-sheet to another, but that was about how it averaged out, and it matched the sober *New York Times*'s analysis. All the papers mentioned that there had been another ship closer to the *Titanic* than the *Carpathia* had been, and which had lain stopped in the ice-field all night within ten or twenty miles of the disaster scene; whereas the *Carpathia* had covered fifty-eight miles at full speed after receiving a distress call quite by chance. Her Marconi man had shut down for the night – as was customary, especially in a ship that carried only one such operator – but he happened to return to the wireless room to send 'a routine message' and to his surprise picked up the SOS call. The other ship – the one much closer to the *Titanic*, named as the *Californian* – had shut down its wireless for the night only seconds before the *Titanic's* first SOS transmission. It had in fact been 'CQD', the replacement of which by 'SOS' had come into force only in recent days, and to which the Marconi operators had switched within minutes. The *Californian's* second officer did see flares but mistook them either for private signals between ships of the same line or for a liner's firework display for its passengers' entertainment. While as to the causes of the tragedy, allegations were that the ship had been steaming much too fast, especially since she'd received numerous warnings of ice ahead of her, and that the two lookouts in the crow's nest had had no binoculars, the two pairs normally issued to them having allegedly 'gone adrift' during the vessel's stay in Southampton.

Bill Dalby had shown one article to Elizabeth – he'd folded the paper so as to expose it, and passed it to her without a word. Eileen had seen this out of the corners of her eyes while studying a breakdown in the *New York Times* of numbers saved of respectively first-, second- and third-class passengers. Glancing up again, she saw Elizabeth looking startled as she scanned whatever it was he'd given her: then re-folding it quickly and pushing it down beside her in the chair.

Eileen offered her the *Times*.

'Oh. Thank you.'

'Might I see *that* one?'

'What?'

'The paper down there beside you?'

'Honey, it's nothing, you wouldn't—'

'Please – if it concerns us – me – and it's there for all and anyone—'

'Well.' Elizabeth sighed, glancing at her husband. He frowned. 'It's not *nice* reading.'

Eileen read:

GRIM WIRELESS MESSAGE FROM SCENE OF DISASTER. From
the cable ship 'Mackay-Bennett' which was hurried to
the scene of the disaster to bring in any dead bodies
that could be found, the following wireless message
received in New York . . . *Bodies are numerous in latitude
41.35 North, longitude 48.37 West, extending many miles
both east and west. Mailships should give this region a
wide berth.*

*The medical opinion is that death has been instantaneous
in all the cases owing to the pressure when the bodies were
drawn down in the vortex. We have been drifting in a dense
fog since noon yesterday, and the total number of bodies
picked up is 205.*

*We brought away all the embalming fluid in Halifax,
which is enough for seventy. With a week's fine weather . . .*

She didn't finish it. Putting it aside, she met Elizabeth's
anxious, almost frightened gaze. Bill Dalby cleared his
throat: 'Eileen. There'll never be a *good* time to raise this,
but since it's come up . . . I asked the guy in White Star
about – you know, identification of any bodies, how they'd
notify you if they had any such information—'

'Which they wouldn't have – as yet?'

'Not so far. But when they do – have any for *anyone*, that
is – survivors or family will be notified immediately, and
whatever detail they may have they'll make available from
their offices here and in London and Ireland too – Cork, I
guess, maybe Dublin too. But you see, they'd be glad to
have any assistance *you* could provide – for identification
purposes? Descriptions, they mean – just basic points to
go on?'

'What a thing for the poor girl to have to do!'

'I know, Liza, I know, but—'

'It's all right. I'd wondered about that myself . . .'

Realizing that *most* of them would probably have no way of being identified: people woken in the night, pulling on sweaters and trousers over night-clothes: no pocket-books or papers . . . And in what condition they'd be, after how long in the water?

She got up, not looking at either of the Dalbys, managed to say as she went quickly to the door, 'I'll do it now. Excuse—'

On that Sunday morning, the Dalbys were attending their own Episcopalian church service, and they offered to drop Eileen at the Catholic church and pick her up there afterwards – if she'd like that, and felt up to it. She was on the point of declining, having thought about attending Mass prior to this but for some reason had flinched at the prospect of doing so. Second thoughts now, however, persuaded her that she should; less as a matter of religious duty than of maintaining an appearance of normal and proper behaviour, especially in Elizabeth's eyes. So she said yes, please, and they dropped her – dressed incidentally in some of her new finery including a black straw hat, black veil – at a corner near the church. She started in that direction – looking back to wave goodbye as they drove on – but at the last moment baulked, walked on past the church and around the block, veering off then into a public park where she found a bench to sit on. It was a beautiful morning. She thought about Frank and Tom and J. Bruce Ismay for forty or fifty minutes, then walked back to the corner where she had been dropped off and waited until the Dalbys came motoring up the dirt road and pulled in beside her. The car was a Delage; it had been put up for sale by a departing French diplomat, Bill Dalby had informed her; you could see from his attitude in the driving seat that he was proud of it. Eileen climbed in behind the couple; Elizabeth reached back to pat her hand. 'All right, honey?'

Shrewd, questioning gaze. Eileen nodded, glancing away as the big car rolled forward. 'Yes. Thank you . . .'

Matt McGrath was about fifty, with black hair without any grey in it, a florid complexion and what in Ireland would have been called a porter-belly. He reminded Eileen of her stepfather Dennis Burke, who'd taken an unhealthy interest in her. Very much the same type, anyway, and the similarity did nothing to endear Frank's uncle to her. Nor did his coldly artificial expressions of sympathy and regret. It was an attitude he was striking, a formal thing. He'd clearly had no intention of encouraging her to visit them in Philadelphia, barely disguised his relief at hearing that she was expecting to leave for Ireland within a few days. His wife Kathleen did bring it up: when they were alone for a few minutes, she intimated that she would have invited her if there'd been more time, although to be honest Eileen wouldn't be missing much, since Mr McGrath invariably worked a twelve-hour day and she herself was put to the pin of her collar coping with her brats.

Eileen had thought, looking at her across the conservatory – Elizabeth had gone to have a word with the cook and the men were smoking cheroots in the yard – she'd thought, staring at this buxom woman with her straight black hair and fat, pale face, that presumably it was a 'brat' she herself had had.

'Brat' name of Tom.

That steward's exclamation – Starbridge, the man pulling the oar that had struck a body: *Crikey, little kid!*

She'd shut her eyes for a moment: opening them again, found the woman's eyes on her: probing, blatantly inquisitive; Eileen remembering that one of those on the thwart behind them had only hesitantly supported Elizabeth's assertion that the body had been that of a female child – aged about seven, she'd said.

Probably hadn't seen clearly. Like as not, hadn't wanted to.

To everyone's more or less concealed relief, the visitors left quite early in the afternoon, making various excuses for so doing even though the Dalbys weren't trying to detain them. McGrath asked Eileen on the doorstep, 'Will you be seeing my sister when you're back in th'oul country?'

'I will, of course!'

Stupid question. Frank's mother: what did he think – that Frank's widow would *avoid* her?

'Give her my best, so. And commiserations, naturally.'

Naturally. Watching their Model 'T' grind away, she thought *Frank, that's something you've been spared* . . . She was bracing herself to write to Frank's mother that evening; to her own mother as well – she supposed she'd better – but it was how to tell it all to Kate Maguire that was really tormenting her.

Next day – Monday – White Star Line considerably simplified her plans for her when an official at their office on Broadway told her that the ship on which they'd booked her, departing on Wednesday at four p.m., would be sailing direct to Liverpool, not calling at any Irish port.

Bill Dalby was with her at the counter. His wife had been ushered to some inner sanctum to discuss her own claim for compensation for lost possessions; he'd be joining her when he'd made sure Eileen was getting a square deal. He exploded now: 'No, that's too bad! Darn it, just you put her in a ship that'll take her back where she started from!'

'That's difficult, Mr Dalby. For survivors who are fit to travel, that's to say not medically certified as *unfit*, we have a time-limit to observe; *and* it has to be a vessel of our own line. But if I might explain – Mrs Maguire will be supplied by us with vouchers for a railway ticket from Liverpool to

Holyhead in Wales, and for the ferry connection from there to Kingstown.'

Eileen asked him, 'And the train from there down to Cork?'

'Well – yes. That would fall within your entitlement.'

'But better still – ' a new thought surfacing – 'if you're sending me by way of England – although what I *want*, mind you, is simply to get home to Cork – see, I have relations in London and the way things are I'd be duty-bound to visit them. So not Holyhead – train from Liverpool to London.'

'I'm rather less certain about this, madam. Sir . . .'

Dalby growled. 'It's darn little difference – and considering what this lady's been put through – which I trust you *are* bearing in mind—'

'Excuse me.' She went one better. 'Rail to London, and from there later to Fishguard in the south of Wales for the ferry direct to Cork. That way I end up where I need to.'

'We'll settle for that, then. Otherwise I'd insist we wait for another steamer – and be blowed to your time-limit! There's no reason Mrs Maguire *should* accept this kind of run-around, you know there isn't!' Dalby's jaw jutting: 'Uh? Don't you think she's been caused grief enough?'

'Then there's this.' The notes she'd put down for them – guidance for the identification of Frank and Tom Maguire. *Male, aged thirty years, height six feet three inches, ginger hair, strong build, top joint of forefinger on right hand missing*; and *Male child, aged two years and nine months, ginger hair, crescent-shaped birthmark on left shoulder*. She'd written it on a sheet of the Dalbys' headed paper, and asked for any notification to be sent to her at her mother's address in Skibbereen in County Cork.

5

The night of Sunday–Monday, 28th–29th April, she spent alone at the rail on the port side of the second-class section of the promenade deck. Second class by entitlement, not trespass, since on their way into town from New Rochelle on the Wednesday Elizabeth had broken it to her that they'd upgraded her from steerage to second class. It would apply to her steamer passage from Fishguard to Cork as well, apparently.

'Only a very small difference, Eileen. Anyway you're too well dressed for steerage. Besides any of that, as I told Bill, I just couldn't have borne to let you go back that way.'

They'd both cried, while Bill gazed fixedly ahead through the windscreen of the Delage as if he wasn't hearing any of it, and they'd done it some more on board the ship, the Dalbys having boarded with her and gone below to inspect her single cabin and the second-class dining room and saloon, then come back up on deck with her again. Elizabeth damp-eyed, hugging her.

'Come back please, Eileen. So be it, you feel you have to go now, some darn reason, but when that's out of your system – honey, it's early days, I know, I'm not for a moment belittling your tragic loss but you must know that in the course of time you could have yourself a great life here!'

'I do know – yes. But . . .' She'd tried to explain: America and the 'great life' was where she'd have been with Frank and Tom, and without them, despite the astonishing kindness she'd been shown, she'd always have felt out of place. Ireland after all was where her roots were: where *somehow* she'd get herself back together again. She did actually feel this: putting the other business out of mind, it was the plain truth and nothing else – or *would have been*, had it not been for the other business. She'd met Bill's eyes momentarily over his wife's head, and he'd shrugged, grimaced slightly and put in, 'But if things change for you, my girl – due course of time and things kinda settle down – well, we'd both very much hope—'

'I feel – *awful* – when you've been so wonderful to me, both of you. But listen, if you should ever contemplate a trip to Ireland—'

'Send us your address when you have one – huh? And write – let's *really* stay in touch?'

'Well, of *course*—'

'But listen.' Elizabeth, still holding her, blinking up into her face . . . She was actually quite short, had only *seemed* enormous in the lifeboat when Eileen had been on the deck beside it and they'd been getting set to help her in, in fact more like *throw* her in: she'd seemed toweringly tall, and of course wide as well, even more immense in that ankle-length mink coat. The visual flashbacks still occurred, maybe wouldn't ever cease. In fact, one now saw detail that one hadn't remembered from the time itself, the actual memory: and the picture now of that immensity, how huge she must have looked to little Tommy – whereas she was actually quite dumpy, lecturing Eileen from down there: 'Honey, you look after yourself real good, now. Hear? I feel like you're our own daughter, you know, I'm going to be so darn worried for you! Even now you could change your mind, you know. Huh? Couldn't we just walk down that gangway?'

'Now hell, Liza . . .'

'I do have to go back, Elizabeth. Simply *do*, that's all. I *am* sorry, but—'

Then the boom of a gong – a steward was carrying it around – and a yell of 'Will all persons not travelling in this vessel kindly proceed ashore. The gangway will be removed in exactly five minutes. Will all persons not travelling . . .' The tears had sprung again, and Bill had his arm round his wife's shoulders, prising her away: 'Now, Liza, please . . .'

Eileen had noticed a small man standing nearby and looking at them a lot; meeting her glance at this moment he'd stepped closer, raising his hat. 'Excuse me, madam. Sir. Miss . . . Reginald Deacon, at your service. I have been visiting my son and his family, my grandchildren, in Cleveland, Ohio, and I'm returning to England in this ship. I'd very willingly extend my protection to the young lady, if she'd accept it and it might help to put your minds at rest? I must apologize, but I couldn't help overhearing—'

The ship's siren shrieked, either to summon a tug or to warn non-passengers. The little man's mouth still opening and closing but not a word audible. Bill Dalby shouting then as the din subsided, 'That's very civil of you, Mr – er—'

'Deacon. Reginald Deacon – of London, England.'

'If I had need of protection – ' Eileen smiled at him – 'but in any case' – to Elizabeth – 'if it *did* help put your mind at rest—'

Dalby had drawn him aside. Elizabeth smiling through her tears, murmuring, '*Looks* a perfectly decent little old guy. More like you'd protect *him* though, I'd guess. Nice anyway to have an acquaintance, honey . . .'

In the event, she and Reggie Deacon had stood side

by side waving goodbye as the ship had warped out into the river with an attendant tug, the crowd on the quayside all waving and calling goodbye; Bill waving his hat, Elizabeth with a handkerchief intermittently at her eyes. The little man had had no one else to wave goodbye to; his son Percy, he'd told Eileen within minutes, was a manufacturing chemist in a new plant near Cleveland, and was a very busy man who hadn't been able to get away. Well, Cleveland was the best part of five hundred miles from New York, after all. She herself was not American, was she? Irish, by any chance? 'But – Mrs Maguire, if I have the name correctly – Mr – that gentleman down there now—'

'Mr William Dalby.'

'Quite so. He confided to me that you and his wife were passengers on board the *Titanic*?'

There were some other former *Titanic* passengers on board, but all apparently in third class, and none of their names – which Deacon obligingly obtained for her from the purser's office – were familiar to her. There were two *Titanic* stewardesses travelling steerage – the ship having a full complement in that category there'd been no working passages available to them – but it seemed neither was blond nor young. She could have asked to see them, of course, enquired whether they'd had a colleague answering that description, or any knowledge of such a person having a small child in her care during the ship's last moments, but there was no point: enquiries had been made, instigated by Bill Dalby, and there'd been no trace, no vestige of hope at all, the only surviving 'unclaimed' children having been literally babes in arms who'd been thrust into lifeboats like small parcels and cared for by the women already in them; how so many babies had come to be deserted by their mothers was a mystery. Eileen hadn't wanted to talk about any of it anyway – except to old Deacon, for whom she was sorry and with whom she spent a lot of her time and shared every meal. Then at breakfast on Sunday, April 28th, someone having questioned absent-mindedly whether by that afternoon they'd have been two days or three out from New York, it had occurred to her that the *Carpathia* had taken three and a half days getting in, and that this ship steaming at approximately the same speed must during this next night be passing through the area of the tragedy. She'd murmured something to that effect, and later in the day, without telling her what he was doing, Deacon sought out the purser again – who'd approached the ship's captain, who'd told his second officer to attend to it. The first Eileen had known of it had been when an apprentice had come down into second class asking for Mr Deacon and Mrs Maguire; the second officer had sent him to invite them up to the charthouse, to be shown the ship's position and what would be her track during the early hours of Monday. Which was how she'd come to spend virtually all that night on deck. Between three and five a.m. would be the crucial period. The second officer's name was Morton, Charlie Morton; he'd told her, 'We're on this track – see, this line here? – a few miles to the south of that taken by the *Titanic*, as far as I've been able to ascertain. And – *here*, where we should be at 0400 – well, if you'd like to come up here, you could have that open area to yourself – with you accompanying the young lady, Mr Deacon?'

She'd thanked him, but declined. She'd be perfectly all right down there on the boat-deck – the central part, which was a second-class recreation space with in fact no boats on it, the boats in their davits being in two sections, ten or twelve at each end of the deck, none right there in the middle – and she'd surely have it all to herself in any case. Morton had himself escorted them back down, on the way asking Reggie Deacon whether he'd be staying up on deck with her. She heard this low-voiced conversation behind her as she went down the companionway from bridge level to boat deck, including Deacon's *sotto voce* reply to the effect that he thought she'd much prefer to be alone, but that otherwise he most certainly *would* be willing to keep her company. Morton's comment then had been that things often felt strange at night in the solitude of empty seascape, especially in such shatteringly dreadful circumstances and so soon after the event.

Hence, she realized, a man in the wing of the bridge on this side, visible in silhouette against the stars and – she was almost sure – with binoculars trained on her from time to time. Also Deacon's consideration and gentle probing during the earlier part of the evening, his offer to sleep on deck – well out of her way, with no intention whatsoever of intruding on her privacy, only to be there within call. He'd have been worrying, of course, suspecting – as Morton had – some suicidal intention – which in fact she wasn't contemplating for a moment. Not at any rate at *this* stage, with the other business very much in her mind. Not that she'd even mentioned Ismay to Reggie Deacon – who had said that if she had more than a day or two to wait in London before continuing to Ireland he'd be only too glad to show her around or be of any other help to her.

He was a widower, had been a printer all his life and had recently retired.

'Semi-retired, I should say. It's been intimated to me that there'll be plenty of freelance work coming my way. Proof-reading mostly, but also standing in at times for men off sick or on their holidays, that sort of thing.' He had lodgings, he'd told her, in which he'd lived for the past sixteen years, in fact since his wife had passed on.

Eileen had begged him *not* to think of spending the night on deck – not even at some distance from her in a steamer chair and under rugs, which was what he'd proposed.

'I'll be quite all right. Believe me, I've not the least intention of jumping overboard.'

'Oh, my dear girl!'

'It was in your mind and Mr Morton's, I know. Quite understandable that it should be, and I appreciate your care of me. But please accept my word . . .'

What could he have done in any case – leapt overboard after her?

The moon was only a day or two old but there was enough of it to impart a polish to the slide and heave of ocean, glisten on the white stain spreading from the ship's side. They'd be out there somewhere. In an hour's time maybe one would be as close to them as one *ever* would be; but it was all conjecture, there was no scientific accuracy about it. Like traversing a vast burial ground where no graves were marked. She remembered that report from the ship that had been trawling for bodies, the litter of them 'extending many miles both east and west'; she'd thought of it when Morton had told her 'between three and five', and discussed it with Reggie Deacon; if this ship was making twenty knots, which he thought it might be, it would cover forty nautical miles in those two hours, and given that spread of drift as well – wave- or wind-drift, whatever caused it – all you could say was they'd be out there – down there – *somewhere*. As imprecise as that: except for her private certainty that their remains would be inside the carcase of the ship. It was how she'd seen it in her nightmares and waking imagination, it was how it *felt*. She'd asked Morton in what depth of sea the *Titanic* might be lying, and after consulting small italicised figures on the chart to the north of this ship's pencilled track, he'd told her, 'Fifteen hundred fathoms, approximately. Nine or ten thousand feet, say.' Deacon had commented, 'Then she'll lie undisturbed until the very Day of Judgment'; and Morton had agreed: 'Much to the good, I'd say. If *anything* can be to the good, out of so frightful a circumstance.'

Might be Second Officer Morton up there, she wondered,

in that extremity of the bridge, with a pair of binoculars trained aft? So what would *he* have done if she'd jumped – stopped the engines and lowered a boat? In any case she didn't want to embarrass whoever it was by letting him see her seeing *him*, therefore didn't do more than glance that way occasionally. Leaning here well protected against the cold – new coat, new gloves, a felt hat such as Elizabeth Dalby had worn in the boat – and so on – with this boat-deck empty, twin funnels looming over her, masts and rigging fore and aft swaying against stars and the young moon's radiance; rumble of the ship's engines, thumping and hissing of the sea as she drove through it. Far better surroundings for remembrance of them, she thought, here in this enormous emptiness, than any church or cathedral thronged with people who'd never known them. She was here, dry-eyed now in her solitude and as close as she'd ever get to them: not necessarily to their mortal remains, to *them*.

In nomine Patris et Filii . . .

She wondered whether the drowning people's cries still rang in that man's ears, as they did in hers. As an accompaniment perhaps to his own high warbling cry of 'Lower away! Lower away!' Might *he* have seen Tom scuttling away and Frank blundering after him, heard *her* screaming while Elizabeth Dalby had just about sat on top of her to hold her down? Or might he have been blind or impervious to all that, only watching for his own chance to slip into some other boat? Eileen stooping as in a pew in church with her elbows on the rail and her face in her hands, long fingers spread around her eyes, whispering into the empty night, '*I wouldn't have got in it, didn't want to – well, you know I didn't, Wouldn't have left either of you, ever . . .*' She could see Frank smiling, shaking his head a little – *knowing* she would not have. He'd be hearing her all right; that was partly why the exact location of their physical remains wasn't of any great concern. What mattered – mattered *desperately* – was not to let them down.

'Did you sleep at all last night, Eileen?'

She shook her head. 'I'll rest during the day. Well – this morning. My cabin's all right, the bunk doesn't need making up, I'll ask them to miss it out. You slept well, I hope?'

'Not very. A little worried for you, I suppose.'

'Well.' She drank some coffee. 'No need to have been. They had a watch-dog on the bridge, keeping an eye on me. Out on the wing, surveying me with binoculars?'

He'd nodded. Small eyes blinking behind thick-lensed spectacles. 'I rather supposed they would.'

'Distrusting me to that extent?'

'Well. If a sensitive person is deprived at one stroke of everything she holds dear, I'd say she'd need to be exceptionally strong-minded not to give way to – aberrations of one kind or another?'

'*Madness* of one kind or another.'

'Let me put it this way. You told me there were women on board the *Titanic* who were urged to embark in lifeboats but refused to do so without their husbands. As it happens there was mention of it in the newspapers. Would you assert that they were behaving sanely?'

'I can only tell you that I envy them.'

'Although you claimed to have had no suicidal intentions.'

'I'm only saying I'd sooner have stayed with them.'

'You feel you were tricked into embarking. Yes, you *did* say—'

'Forced to, as much as tricked. But I've thought since that I could have hung back, not *allowed* myself to be separated from them, not even for those few seconds . . .'

She hadn't wanted to continue the discussion, talk about

it any more than they had already – had been obliged to, in response to his concern for her, his anxiety to help, ameliorate, but only out of a sense of good manners and – all right, liking him well enough too. The reality was that Frank and Tom were the only people she was really in communication with, that she knew what she was going to do – *had* to do – and this was the only answer to any of it; the rest was only a matter of form and politeness, as it were, preliminary exercises in subterfuge.

On 2nd May – a Thursday – the ship tied up in Liverpool's Gladstone Dock and she and Reggie Deacon went ashore and to the railway station together. On their way across Liverpool Bay and into the Mersey he'd remarked on how lucky they were that this wasn't August of the previous year, when Liverpool had been paralysed by strikes and riots – railwaymen, stevedores and other transport workers bringing most of the country to a standstill – the power stations in London starved of coal, two men killed in the riots, warships anchored in the Mersey, and so forth. She vaguely remembered hearing of it; but it could have been more like a decade ago rather than only a few months. Following Reggie into the Customs shed now, carrying her own suitcase although he'd argued that he should take it and she carry his, since hers was heavier and larger; it might have been tactful to have allowed it, if he could have managed, but what if he'd found he couldn't? Such a little grey shrimp of a man – grey-haired, grey-eyed, grey-skinned, in grey trousers and a grey herring-bone tweed jacket; the only things that weren't grey were his green hat and black shoes. Her own hat was dark grey, matching the discreetly chequered overcoat she and Elizabeth had acquired at Macy's – whose proprietors, incidentally, had been the old couple she'd seen hand-in-hand in adjacent steamer chairs on the *Titanic*'s boat deck. Mr and Mrs Isidor

Strauss: in a magazine article, which she'd read during this crossing, the old lady had been quoted as protesting 'We have lived forty years together, and will not part now in our old age'; while her husband, when assured that if his wife could be persuaded to get into a lifeboat, in view of his advanced years he would be permitted to go with her, had exclaimed 'Not as long as a single woman remains on board!'

Going by the published figures, quite a *lot* of women had remained on board. She wondered how the man in carpet-slippers – Ismay – might be feeling about that, having managed to save himself.

She still hadn't mentioned him to Reggie Deacon. It would have been rash to have evinced any interest in the man at this stage. Better that she should barely have heard of him – maybe show vague interest, but no more than that and certainly have no personal feelings on the subject of his having got away. It was going to be tricky enough in any case, she realized, needing to discover all she could about him and his routine comings and goings and so forth, but hardly daring to ask questions of anyone at all. Some source of information in the White Star office would be the obvious thing to try for. Former *Titanic* passenger Eileen Maguire would have to show her face there in any case, to exchange her New York voucher for rail and ferry tickets to Cork via Fishguard – and that was fine as far as it went, but if they simply issued her with the tickets or vouchers and saw her to the door it wasn't going to get her far.

Enquire about possibilities of employment, perhaps – whether there might be vacancies for shorthand-typists. London would no doubt be stuffed full of them, she guessed, but it might be a way of establishing contact anyway. Ask whether there might be vacancies *in Ireland*, even. After all, London was the Line's head office: and in view of her situation they might be sympathetic, at least be willing to discuss it with her. It would make perfectly good sense – a woman in her situation would naturally be concerned as to how she was going to make a living – and being in touch with a fair-sized organization like White Star – where people surely *ought* to be well-disposed . . .

Try it. Think about it, meanwhile.

Here in Liverpool she had a voucher to present at the railway ticket office, where it was exchanged for a third-class ticket without query or hesitation, the clerk not even glancing up as he went through the motions. Maybe it would be like that when it came to boarding the ferry – she hoped. (If she got as far as boarding any ferry: if she ever got out of London, even.) Reggie, who paid for his own ticket in English shillings and pence, said he thought passengers were quite routinely issued with such vouchers, depending on ports of arrival and their destinations. 'Over there it so happened that the date of our ship's departure suited me, rather than having to spend an expensive week or more in New York. I *chose* to come by way of Liverpool.' Consequently he was now out of pocket by four shillings and sevenpence, Eileen had noticed. He was careful with his money, keeping it in a leather purse in an inside pocket. Eileen herself was rather well off at this stage; the Dalbys hadn't allowed her to spend any of her own and Frank's savings in America, she'd collected the White Star handout of one hundred dollars, and Elizabeth had insisted on giving her a present of about thirty pounds sterling which she'd happened to have in the house at New Rochelle. She'd demanded, 'What use is it to me, here in New York?'

'Couldn't you change it at a bank?'

'So I could, and *they*'d keep about half of it! *Bankers*, my foot! You ask my husband what he thinks of bankers! Any case, why would I? Why, that funny money'd still be lying there in the drawer ten years from now, if you didn't oblige me by taking it!'

*   *   *

In order to stop over in London for whatever period of time was necessary she'd evolved a story that differed slightly from the one she'd given White Star in New York: it was not her own relations she'd be looking for, but cousins of Frank's; she'd be in trouble with his family back in Ireland if she passed through London and made no effort to find them. She had no address for them, but knew of people who she felt sure would have. They were Maguires, but anglicized to a degree which, with his political views, Frank might have found unacceptable but to her surprise had not. Elaborating on this to Reggie – practising it on him – she remembered having teased Frank by suggesting that maybe *they* represented the Irish occupation of England.

'Was he strong in his politics, then?'

'He'd got into a circle of acquaintances who talked that kind of hot air. To do him justice, though, he had a questing mind as well as a great love of Ireland. I don't know about them, the truth is I never met them, but *he* felt a duty, you might say.'

'But was prepared to wash his hands of it, in taking you off with him to America?'

'Well, yes.' She'd shrugged. 'Because making a new life for the three of us was what mattered to him more than anything!'

It was Frank's business anyway, not Reggie Deacon's. She'd amazed herself with her ability to tell lies with such facility – almost to the extent of believing in them herself. But lying was especially easy when it was on a subject that was now of no consequence whatsoever – as *well* as being none of this little man's business. Little man still probing, though . . .

'In your own case though, Eileen – your father having spent his boyhood and youth here – did he not become anglicized – making for problems between you and Frank?'

'*Not* at all. In any case he was dead, God rest his soul, years before I met Frank. But no, he was an Irishman to the very marrow of his bones. Just as I'm an Irishwoman. How I might sound sometimes – if that's what you're getting at – Reggie, I've been talking this past week with no one but yourself – *and* been concerned to make myself understood – and vice versa?'

A smile, movement of the hands: 'I can assure you, *I've* had no problems!'

'But if you were to put me down amongst Irish again now, why, you might *not* follow it so easy!'

'It's a very pretty accent, Eileen. A great deal more so than my London one, I'm sure!'

He didn't actually believe that, she could see. Probably thought he had *no* accent. She told him, 'I've been very glad of your company and conversation, I may as well tell you. When I write to Mrs Dalby I'll tell *her* the same. But listen to me now – we'll have a decent meal on this train, so we will, and *I* shall pay for it, d'you hear?'

'Why? Heavens, Eileen—'

'I came away from New York with more money than I ever had in my life all at one time. I never spent even a penny on the ship, and I *want* to do this, please. We'll not be getting to London until after midnight, what's more. We'll have a decent meal, Reggie, and it'll be my treat!'

She'd dozed in the train, after a meal that had been acceptable but nowhere near up to the standard of White Star Line's second class: brown soup, fish pie, ice cream, cheese and biscuits. Reggie wouldn't have had the cheese if she hadn't insisted on it. Woken later by a jolting, noisy stop in Crewe, she'd found his eyes fixed on her, the carriage door swinging open, other passengers alighting into steam and smoke and a guard's raucous shouts. The other passengers had left behind a *Daily Sketch*, in which Reggie now showed her a headline: 'What would your husband's view have been of *this*, Eileen?'

She read the caption: IRISH HOME RULE BILL PROVOKES STORM IN ULSTER. The roar of escaping steam meanwhile reminded her of that truly thunderous gushing from the *Titanic*'s boilers. And the mention of Frank switched *him* suddenly into mental focus, with the recollection that when she'd first become aware of that deafening racket she'd little dreamed that neither he nor Tom, who at that time had been cradled in her arms, had more than – what, two hours to live. There and then the only fly in the ointment, as she'd seen it, had been Frank's determination to work for the gun-runners over there, either raising funds or helping to organize the cargoes, whatever 'they' wanted him to do, after he was settled and knew his way around. That had been the one and only cloud on the horizon; she'd prayed that with the passing of time and in new surroundings and the preoccupations of a whole new life it might fade away. Wouldn't have, she thought now. Knowing Frank, he'd have kept his word to them, no matter what *she* thought about it.

But that headline. She looked at it again, told Reggie, 'A swindle, Frank was calling it.'

'*Was* he. But it's been forced on Asquith by the Irish MPs, as I understand it. Would your husband have said Redmond and his parliamentary colleagues were swindling *themselves*?'

'Your man's forced to it, Frank said, by the Liberal majority falling so low he must have the Nationalists' support in other legislation. Oh, for the budget, of course. to get *that* through. Frank said the powers to be transferred weren't more than a parish council's – only Irish internal affairs and so forth – and anyhow it'll be thrown out in the Lords. So your man knows—'

'Asquith—'

'Asquith, sure – knows he has two years he can spend wriggling out of it in any case. Isn't that the truth of it?'

A wry smile, and a shrug: 'Just a *little* unfair, perhaps, but – consequent to last year's Parliament Act, yes. Although what *really* knocks it for six is the fact the Unionists will fight it to a standstill. Or worse – there's even talk of their importing arms – rifles – in which case the other side will do the same – and where are you then? Well – civil war! See, it says right here – a number of Orange Lodges already drilling and studying military tactics. And Sir Edward Carson is *not* a man to back down, you know. Why military drill, one might ask, if they aren't expecting to have guns before much longer?'

'Frank would have agreed with you, I'm sure.'

'Well, I'm not arguing the case for either side. I fear for the future of Ireland, that's all. And I'm sure Asquith—'

'Up you get, girl!' The door had flung open again: a whistle shrilled out there. A large man in what looked like his Sunday best – blue serge, and a frayed collar so tight it cut into his neck – was pushing a young woman up and now heaving himself up behind her. No luggage. And on closer inspection she wasn't all *that* young. Reggie allowed her a formal smile and returned the man's grunt of 'Good evening'. The train lurched, was rolling, the newcomers inspecting Reggie and Eileen guardedly. Eileen thought the woman looked scared. Reggie asked the big man, 'Do you happen to know whether there are any more stops before London?'

'Hope so. Coventry's where *we*'re gettin' off.'

'Ah, Coventry . . .'

'Northampton too, wouldn't be surprised.'

Coventry came, and they were alone again. Eileen trying to reconcile the need to save money, or at least spend as little as possible, with the fact that by the time they got to

London there'd be no buses running. Reggie had mentioned that getting to Clerkenwell after the buses stopped would mean hoofing it for a mile or more. 'Carrying our stuff, at that . . .'

She told him now, giving up on that good intention, 'So we'll take a cab. I'll pay. Supper cost less than I expected, and I really do have quite enough.'

The point being that she wasn't going to need even a quarter of it, if all went well. Wouldn't need money *after* doing what she had to. Only a second bullet. Assuming that the most suitable weapon *would* be a pistol – revolver – and that she'd be able to get hold of one. Money would obviously be needed for that, maybe not in a small way either. It must be illegal, she guessed, to possess or carry a lethal weapon for any reason other than sporting purposes; therefore the purchase of it would be an illegal transaction. Alternatively, to get one legally you'd presumably need a licence, which would mean going to the police and explaining why you needed such a thing.

Purposes of self-protection?

Newly widowed, travelling on one's own, men taking advantage or trying to? There had been one, on the ship – two in fact if you included the rather pompous-looking married man who'd kept sneaking glances at her across the dining saloon, until she'd drawn Reggie's attention to him and Reggie had turned to stare at *him* – which must have alerted his Gorgon-like wife to what he'd been up to. Reggie's had been a careful, deliberate stare, after first polishing his spectacles on a corner of his napkin; he'd done that well. She *had* been glad of his company – even more so in regard to the other one, a 'lounge-lizard' type who'd twice tried to engage her in conversation on the subject of her escape from the *Titanic*. On both occasions she'd been on her own; she'd seen him hanging around often enough when she'd had Reggie with her, but at those times he'd only watched her covertly from a distance – which had spoken volumes about *him*, she'd thought.

Her mind drifting, circled back on itself, jumped from one image to another. Focusing, she saw that Reggie's eyes were open again.

'Reggie, would someone like me, travelling by herself – as I will be, when I leave London – for purposes of self-protection might she ever carry a weapon, would you think?'

'A weapon . . .'

'Pistol, say?'

Shake of the narrow head. 'Never heard of such a thing. Perhaps in a play or a novel – if she were the kind of heroine Mr Conan Doyle might invent.' He was suppressing a smile, she saw. 'A young woman in flight from the hound of the Baskervilles for instance?'

'You're joking, but I'm serious. That man on the ship most certainly *would* have pursued me, if I'd not had you with me. For which incidentally—'

'Blaze away at him with a six-shooter, would you?' Chuckling at his own humour. 'Eileen Maguire, fastest gun on the boat-deck?'

'Very amusing – but just think. Tonight, if I was on my own, with – what did you say, at least a mile on foot through London back-streets?'

'No, that I would *not* recommend.'

'So – might one not be justified in carrying some kind of weapon?'

'I'd say not. Unless you were fully competent and experienced in its use. Even then . . . Better to stay *off* streets at night. Were you having second thoughts about taking a cab, is that it?'

'No. That was only what started me thinking on these lines. No, we certainly *will* get a cab. But when in due course I need to get about on my own – in London or elsewhere—'

'In London, I am at your service. As long as I'm not immediately innundated with work, of course. I'm afraid that if I *am*—'

'In any case I won't impose on you, Reggie. I'm sure you 'll be very busy, and I will be too. I really must find these people as soon as possible – then get on over to Ireland and get *myself* a job – because heaven knows—'

'But we'll see each other? You won't just dash off—'

'Without saying goodbye? Of course not! But I won't be – round your neck, either . . .'

He'd told her on the ship that he thought his landlady, a Mrs Craven, might be persuaded to put her up for one night, especially as they'd be arriving rather late – she was a kindly soul – and to direct her to some other reputable boarding-house in the morning. He was drawing her a map now, on the back page of that newspaper where there was a vacant white space headed STOP PRESS . . . 'Here, Euston. And Euston Road which becomes Pentonville Road. We pass King's Cross station, and forking right here – this is King's Cross Road, which down here becomes Farringdon Road. This area here is Clerkenwell, and Mrs Craven's house is about – here. It fronts on to a connecting lane called Coldbath Passage, leading from a small square here, of the same name. Not all *that* far – if you wanted to save the cab fare?'

'Far enough, by the looks of it – with bags to carry, too. No, we must definitely take a cab. But while you're at the map-making, give me some notion how I'll get to White Star in the morning?'

She had no intention of seeing any more of him than she had to while in London. In some ways she would have preferred now to have been on her own – simply take pot luck, look for a 'rooms to let' sign – or whatever they had, in London – and get on with it, with a high degree of anonymity. Whereas Reggie would now know where she was living – whatever place his landlady found for her tomorrow – and while there was no *immediate* reason that he shouldn't, in connection with what came next, what she was here for, she'd have preferred not to have had him or anyone else knowing it – or her background, anything at all about her.

Too bad – or rather, too late. But it would have been impossible to have parted company at any earlier stage.

6

―――•◦•――

May 3rd, Friday, mid-morning: from Cyrus Lane in Islington, to which she'd been escorted by Mrs Craven to be introduced to her friend and fellow boarding-house proprietress Elsie Whitten, Eileen had walked back to Farringdon Street in order to catch the bus recommended by Reggie. She was to get off it at Ludgate Circus and take another penny ride westward through Fleet Street and the Strand to Trafalgar Square. But at the Ludgate Circus stop she could see no other bus coming, and the traffic was so slow-moving that the only thing was to walk the rest of the way – saving a penny and almost certainly getting there a lot sooner. Her destination – the White Star Line's office – was Cockspur Street, the other side of Trafalgar Square.

She was wearing an ankle-length black skirt and a pearl-grey blouse with a high ruffled collar pinned with a blue-and-white cameo brooch, yet another gift from Elizabeth Dalby, and her chequered coat and the grey hat with a darker band around it, and black gloves, and carrying a reticule as well as an umbrella lent to her by Mrs Craven. There'd been some drizzle earlier but the clouds

had mostly cleared, she wasn't going to need it. She'd
found that she was a celebrity in both Mrs Craven's house
and Mrs Whitten's. Mrs Craven had practically fainted
from excitement at becoming personally acquainted with
a survivor-victim of the disaster which had electrified the
nation and was on the front pages again – the Board of Trade
Inquiry being now into its second day; she'd provided
Eileen with bed and breakfast without charge, and had
been *privileged* to take her along and place her in the care
of Mrs Whitten.

'Such tragic, devastating loss, poor lamb! So young and
yet so brave, so *steady*!'

How they talked about you, even in your own hearing.
With no real understanding of the realities: obviously not
guessing for a moment that one fell asleep every night
thinking of Frank and Tom, dreamed of them all night,
woke crying for them in every dawn.

Smiles and surface sympathy: they might have thought
it was more than that, but you could tell that was all it was.
She'd told them about her anxiety to find her late husband's
cousins.

This was Fleet Street – which at some point became the
Strand. It had to be less than a mile, Reggie had told her,
from Ludgate to Charing Cross, which she'd find on her
left shortly before Trafalgar Square. She *was* getting along
faster than the westbound traffic, most of the time. A lot
of it was still horse-drawn, she was surprised to see. The
horse-powered cabs were nippy enough, but the carts and
heavy drays were something else.

Glancing in a pawnshop window as she passed, she saw
the pistol.

Horse-pistol – an antiquity, the sort of thing you might
see in a museum. Obviously of no practical use, but still a
firearm of a kind, so perhaps a pawnshop was the sort of
place you might find one. In fact she'd only taken a sidelong

glance at the window to check on her own reflection – in particular the angle of her hat.

Ask inside?

Happened to notice that old pistol, and wondered, do you ever have more modern ones brought in . . .

They'd want to know why she was asking. Maybe suspect she had plans to shoot a husband or a lover. Then – maybe – police brought into it. But surely there'd be some kind of reason she could give, some convincing lie – out of her newly found inventiveness? She put her mind to it, while scanning the items in the display window – several cigarette and cigar cases, a necklace of amber beads with what looked like a gold clasp, and a fob-watch on a gold chain. If one had been looking for a present . . .

Might be the answer? Looking for a present for a man. But a *pistol*? Well – a man on his way to foreign parts might find use for some sort of weapon. If he was going to Africa, for instance – setting out on his own, facing heaven only knew what hazards. Your own younger brother, say – taking his life in his hands in pursuit of fame and fortune: what more appropriate gift could you imagine?

She looked at the shop's door – dark glass, or plain glass with dark material behind it – and hesitated. Thinking that even if the pawnbroker's answer was a flat 'no' he might be able to suggest where she could get one: and whether she'd need a licence – which might be a snag. She'd turned away, continuing westward but still thinking about it. This was the Strand now. The road divided around some kind of church and there were narrow streets running down to the left. The river would be down there, with what they called the Embankment this side of it.

She *should* have gone into that shop and asked: having

the horse-pistol there as an excuse, which was supposed to have put the idea in her mind.

So why hadn't she?

Because her priority was to see them in the White Star office. Which would be clear cut, straightforward, could be settled quickly, whereas the pistol business might be difficult and take some time.

Making excuses to herself for dithering, she realized. Pausing, checking on how far she'd come and looking back towards the approximate location of the pawnshop: telling herself she'd come back later. Pausing again now before crossing a fairly major road which led down to a stone bridge spanning the Thames. A fair width of river, from as much as she could see. Even if the pawnbroker didn't have a pistol to offer her he might have some idea of what one might cost. Even to know that would be a help. That and the legality or illegality of it.

She'd have it in her coat pocket or the reticule – as long as it wasn't too large. Then at close quarters point it at his head, and –

The mind reeled. To get to close quarters in the first place: then to muster the nerve . . .

How else face them again, talk to Frank – as she did so often – without shame?

Crossing the road. Others surging forward, taking her with them. Point it at his head and pull the trigger, obviously, and then – well, the question 'And then what?' didn't need answering, what mattered was simply to *do* it – make the plan, steel the nerve and get it over. To kill oneself immediately then would be the obvious thing: and to do it quickly. Otherwise – visualizing it – Ismay falling dead, bystanders snatching the pistol, grappling with *her* . . .

Nearing the far kerb, people close all round her and others coming the other way, a newsboy somewhere ahead was yelling, '*Titanic* Inquiry! *Titanic* Inquiry!', and looking through the shifting crowd she saw him and his poster:

TITANIC

50 CHILDREN

DROWNED

Passers-by looking aghast, exchanging shocked glances. But to her it was old hat. Those fifty – actually more than fifty – had all been in steerage class. The figures had been published in New York; this inquiry's findings would only be reiteration of what was already known, she guessed. There'd been five children in first class, and five saved, twenty-four in second class and twenty-four saved, but seventy-six in steerage and only twenty-three saved. Meaning fifty-three drowned, not fifty. Even if fifty *was* a nice round number.

Fifty-two *and Tom*, one might say.

How many steerage-class passengers might be giving evidence at the inquiry? she wondered.

Expert witnesses would be the requirement. Engineers, ship-builders, ships' officers and so forth. The *Titanic*'s wireless operators and lookouts too, probably. She'd stopped again, at another side-street.

'Crossing or not, madam?'

It was a man behind her – tall and burly in a bowler, dark suit, no topcoat. She glanced at his middle-aged, disapprovingly set face as he pushed past her, shaking his head and muttering 'Excuse *me* . . .'

She'd stumbled, and choked off a cry of alarm: in that moment startled, under a quick and false impression that it was the man himself – only not in carpet-slippers . . . It was not him, of course. She knew *his* face all right, having seen it with traumatic clarity on board the *Carpathia* and later in New Rochelle in at least a dozen newspapers – wavy hair that was dark in the photos but in real life greying, and rather pleased with himself, she'd thought, and with his moustache with its tips curled up; whereas this one lumbering by had a bovine, stupid look, glaring more than glancing back at her, as if she'd been a nuisance to him in some way.

Skirting around the southern side of Trafalgar Square, recognizing the lions and Nelson's column from photographs she'd seen, and from there so to speak out of its top left-hand corner, finding herself first in Cockspur Street and then suddenly – no, that was Cunard: but *there*, really very similar – White Star. On a corner – actually more of a curve, which broadened the pavement outside it – and with a White Star flag drooping at half-mast above it. Having to cross over to that side, waiting for a motor-bus and several cars to pass, she saw stone pilasters framing a central doorway, and ground-floor windows stencilled with the names of other shipping lines as well as White Star: Red Star and Holland-America were emblazoned on this nearer one. People were standing about on the wide curve of pavement, two smartly dressed women in conversation with a man in a top-hat, one of them looking round at her as if wondering what the cat had brought in *this* time – while a few other pedestrians skirted around them, passing yet another newsboy – the same gull-like screech, same poster about drowned children.

If one found a gunsmith's shop – the sort that sold sporting guns – they might deal in pistols and revolvers too. Giving them the story about a young brother going to Africa: told convincingly, they could hardly fault it. But – in the interests of economy, try the pawnshop first in any case . . . She was in the White Star office: looking around. To her left, the curved end of a counter which extended the full width of the office: customers in hats and coats on this side of it, others in chairs around a table in a

window recess. No women, that she could see. Odour
of cigars. Behind the counter three or four bare-headed
men were dealing with enquiries or bookings or whatever.
The floor was marble-tiled, chessboard fashion in black and
white; there were electric candelabra overhead and a glow
of polished mahogany in the sweep of the counter and other
furniture.

'May I help you, madam?'

A young man in a chalk-stripe suit with lapels on its
waistcoat: shiny back-swept dark hair, dark eyes. He was
shorter than she was, and maybe younger; he'd left a group
– there *was* a woman with them – who were at that round
table, on which lay a book of plans of ships' cabin layouts. A
white-bearded, important-looking man in a frock-coat was
glaring round as if affronted at having been left unattended.
Eileen told the young man, 'I have a letter here from your
office in New York, saying you'll give me rail and ferry
tickets for my return to Cork. I'm Mrs Frank Maguire – I
was on the *Titanic*.'

Heads had turned; a dozen pairs of eyes were on her. The
name *Titanic* had a way of stopping other conversations. A
thick-set bald man had got up from a desk at the back and
was coming this way, one of the others lifting a flap in the
counter to let him out. Having exchanged glances with him,
the young one ushered her towards a door further back on
the right: 'Through here, please – if you wouldn't mind?'

First thought – her heart jumping as it hit her – *Ismay*,
behind that door?

He was not, though – it was *not* the sanctum of the Line's
managing director. The degree of her relief surprised her.
Simply not ready for him yet, she told herself. And for that
matter he would hardly have been receiving former steerage-
class passengers anyway. In fact it was an unoccupied office
they'd shown her into; and at that they were treating her far
more courteously than a steerage passenger would normally

have expected. Her clothes might have had something to do with it, she guessed; although having survived the stares out there and being now under the scrutiny of these two she was conscious that in terms of etiquette she should have been veiled and dressed in black from head to foot.

Not that Frank would have given a damn. Which was all that mattered.

'If I might see the letter?'

The bald man had introduced himself as Bernard Fawcett. Dark coat, grey waistcoat, striped trousers, patent-leather boots and a lot of facial hair. They'd given her a chair and he'd now gone round behind the desk, taking the New York letter with him and putting on glasses. The young one meanwhile leafing through a file of documents, finding what he was looking for and placing the file, open at that page, in front of him.

There'd be some note there about Frank and Tom, she realized.

'Allow me to express my most sincere condolences, Mrs Maguire. These have been heart-rending days for all of us, and in your own case words simply can't express the depth of our concern and—'

The door jerked open, and again she'd started: but it was only another of them putting his head in, glancing around and withdrawing again with a muttered, 'Beg your pardon . . .'

She'd nodded in reply to Fawcett's speech of condolence. Glancing up then to acknowledge the younger man's quiet, '*So* sorry, Mrs Maguire.'

Fawcett cleared his throat. 'Might one assume you'd like to continue to Cork by the first available connections?'

'No. I explained in New York, there are relations here whom I'm bound to try to see, and getting in touch with them's likely to take at least a few days. Even a week or so. In the circumstances – 'I mean my husband and son's deaths – if I didn't at least make the effort—'

'Well – that's understandable, of course . . . I see here there are twice-weekly sailings in each direction, between Fishguard and Cork. And of course a daily railway service, so—'

'What I'm saying is I'd like you to give me undated tickets or vouchers so I can leave when I'm ready to. The point is, they weren't able to provide me with a passage directly to Ireland, which is what I wanted – and having been forced to come this long way round—'

'Yes, Yes . . . I see that our New York office did tentatively agree to this.' Sighing; removing his glasses. 'Oncarriage *should* be immediate and by the most direct route available, but – since they did accept this – which I dare say in all the circumstances . . .' Smoothing his moustache, and glancing up at the younger man, who was standing at his elbow. 'You can see to it, Napier. Vouchers for Fishguard by rail and for the Fishguard–Queenstown ferry. Dates to be put in later, but I'll sign the vouchers right away. Then if Mrs Maguire should complete her business sooner than she expects and decide to set off during the weekend—'

'I certainly couldn't leave *this* weekend!'

'None the less . . . We prefer to insert the dates of travel ourselves, I should explain, since a copy goes to the other carrier, d'you see. So if you *could* come in again before departure – literally for just a minute?'

'Of course. But one other matter – your advice, really—'

'Yes?'

'I am a shorthand-typist. I worked in a business in Cork for several years, and I have a letter of reference from my employers there – which you can see, if it would help – but they'll have filled the post by now, and I wouldn't care to displace some person who'd just settled in. But – well, being now thrown back entirely on my own resources – and this being your company's head office – would you have anything to do with the engagement of staff in Ireland?'

'In *Ireland* . . . Hardly, I'm afraid. Very much their own business, you see. No, I'm sorry—'

'We might provide Mrs Maguire with a letter of introduction, Mr Fawcett, against the chance there *should* be a vacancy?'

'No harm in that, I suppose.' A shrug of his heavy shoulders. 'An introductory note to our manager in Cork – why not?' He nodded to her. 'Mr Napier will attend to it – as well as to your travel documents.' He got up, came round the desk and took her hand. 'Once again, Mrs Maguire, my deepest sympathy.'

The vouchers would be ready in about half an hour, Napier said. But they'd need Fawcett's signature on them and by that time he'd probably be out at lunch. He did usually go early. So, if it wasn't shockingly inconvenient, might she be able to call in at some time after two p.m.?

'Certainly. Not inconvenient at all.'

He escorted her through the general office, and out on to the corner. She thanked him. 'Say two thirty, then.' She took her eyes off the placard about drowned children. 'I'll – wander around, meanwhile.'

'Did I gather that you're a stranger in London?'

She nodded: sensing the opportunity, the moment, his quick interest in her, and responding to it. A small smile, shrug of helplessness: 'I could as well be on the moon!'

'Well – *you'll* be needing some lunch?'

'A snack, perhaps. Is there some place nearby that you'd recommend – preferably not at all expensive?'

Glancing round, he lowered his voice: this wasn't orthodox White Star behaviour, she guessed. The young man telling her, 'There's a luncheon room that I patronize – just a short step up Charing Cross Road and off to the right, in

Cecil Court. I'll be there myself just after one o'clock; I'd be honoured and delighted if you were able to join me. Forgive me if I'm being presumptuous—'

'Not at all—'

'Really? You mean you *might*—'

'Except I'd insist on paying for my own meal.'

'Well – we might discuss that when the time comes. But – oh, capital! Mind you it's not a *smart* place . . .'

He'd told her how to find it – from here down to Trafalgar Square and across the top of it, then left into Charing Cross Road and over to its other side. Five minutes' walk, no more. They'd agreed to meet in Cecil Court at five or ten past one.

Big Ben struck noon while they were talking; she hadn't even known what Big Ben was, until he mentioned it. But she had an hour – ample time to get to the pawnshop and back again. She wondered – heading back towards the Strand but passing around the northern side of the square this time, to check where Charing Cross Road began – about Mr Napier's motive. Kindness of heart for the bereaved young widow? Or seeing her as an easy mark?

Elizabeth Dalby's admonition came to mind: *There's one under every stone* . . .

And thank God for it – for a gift horse definitely *not* to be looked at in the mouth. Although even without this she'd established several excellent reasons for going back to the White Star office anyway – for the letter of introduction to White Star in Ireland, and for the vouchers of course, and later to have them dated – then if necessary re-dated . . .

Traffic was thicker than it had been earlier. At this point anyway, with the number of cabs thronging in an out of the yard at Charing Cross. Being slowed down there anyway she bought a *Daily Mail* – although the vendor's screeched

headline was incomprehensible. Might have meant something to English ears, she supposed. The news placard had
been changed, now read:

US SHIP

MINED

165 MISSING

Another maritime disaster statistic. The report on the *Titanic*
inquiry had been moved to a lower position on the front
page, she saw. Might have time to peruse that before
meeting Mr Napier: as a guide to possible conversational
openings. One would need to be careful not to question
him overtly, about Ismay. She wondered why an American
ship should have been mined, or where. There'd been
some problem building up between the US and Cuba,
she recalled. Or had it been Mexico? Somewhere down
that way, perhaps. She was crossing the road where she'd
seen the man who had, for a split second or so, looked to her
like Ismay – because of his size and the dark suit and the fact
she'd had Ismay in mind as she'd been making for his office.
That and of course her jumpy nerves. In the White Star office
too: nervous of a first meeting with him because he *was* an
ogre-like figure, *had* haunted her thoughts and dreams ever
since that night and then his startling reappearance in that
icy dawn . . .

The pawnshop was on the next corner. Time – twelve-
twenty. Allowing another twenty for getting back, she
had a quarter of an hour in hand. Waiting for traffic to
pass, and still thinking of the need to control her own
nervous reactions. Partly through being so much alone, she
supposed – *totally* alone now in every way, not only physically. It was Frank's support, of course, that she needed . . .
Crossing now: and even from the roadway she could see
the horse-pistol was still there. Her young brother's name
might as well be Reggie, she thought – easy to remember,

rather than referring to him as Peter one day and George the next. Which could happen – to a bag of nerves. Younger brother, name of Reggie. Not that the pawnbroker need know even her own name, let alone her brother's; it was only that once one got talking – *if* one did . . . She pushed open the glass door – a bell clanged somewhere overhead – and found herself in a reek of Macassar oil in a room about ten feet square with a short, high counter, a man – customer, presumably – lounging against it, glancing round at the clang of the bell, now straightening and staring. She was conscious of the unpleasantness of his stare – and of the smell – while herself focusing on the squat, unshaven, disreputable-looking proprietor.

She didn't like the look of the customer either. Raffish, as one imagined a racecourse tout might look. Tight-fitting checked trousers, a cut-away jacket and a striped shirt – shiny cravat, pearl tie-pin. Brown hair slicked back: it was the source of that stink, and the hat at an angle on the back of his head looked stained with it. Narrow face, patches of brown fuzz on the cheekbones, thin moustache: she caught all that in a single glance as he shifted, making way for her at the counter and muttering to the creature behind it, 'I'll 'ang on, Lev. Don't mind me, miss.'

She told them, 'Please finish your business. I'll wait.'

'See, goin' to take us a while yet, this is.' She saw a scattering of rings and brooches on the counter, and in front of the proprietor a grubby piece of paper with pencilled figures on it. He'd thrown down the stub of pencil. 'Help you, lady?'

'I don't know. You may be able to.' The last thing she'd have wanted was an audience: she *had* one, that was all. She half-turned away, putting him behind her right shoulder.

'I happened to notice the old horse-pistol in your window.'

'Ah, well now. Very much in demand, these days, is 'orse-pistols. Might you be a collector, lady?'

'No. It gave me an idea, that's all. I'm looking for a present for my brother.'

'And you're right, you couldn't do better!'

'You misunderstand me. It so happens he's leaving shortly for Africa. I've been trying to think of some useful gift, and the sight of that pistol made me think perhaps a modern one – a revolver?'

'Revolver!'

'Do you ever have such things brought in?'

'No, miss, can't say I do. And if I did I'd want to know where it come from like, how it come to be in the gent's possession, so forth. *Revolver . . .'*

His stare had shifted to the other customer. Might have been getting some sign – a headshake maybe? Back to her now: 'A licensed firearms dealer, you might try?'

'Would *I* need a licence to make such a purchase, do you know? Or would my brother need one, since it would be his, not mine?'

'Well . . .'

'Not if he was taking it out of the country, I can't see he would.' The customer, offering *his* opinion. 'But a rozzer could tell you, right off the bat. *Or*, as my friend here proposed, a regular firearms dealer. Though where you'd find one as sold revolvers I'm sure I don't know. Rozzers might be your best bet, by an' large. Might enquire at New Scotland Yard, Lev, mightn't she? Victoria Embankment, lady – would you know where that is?'

'Perhaps I won't bother. It *seemed* a good idea, but—'

'What might you expect to pay, then?'

The customer seemed to have taken over, but Eileen told the pawnbroker, not *him*, 'I was going to ask you that. But if you don't ever have them brought in—'

'Nothing less 'n a fiver, I'd guess.' The customer again.

She glanced at him: 'If a fiver's *all*—'

'A good 'un, in good repair and with six chambers – the gent'd want *that* – price might run a little 'igher. Tenner at the outside, I'd say.' She was halfway to the door, but looking round at him and catching another glance, might have been a wink he'd given the proprietor. Adding, 'Specially with no questions asked, see. I mean, if the gent's takin' it off to darkest Africa – where you're right, it *might* come in quite 'andy like—'

'I think I'll leave it.' She nodded to the pawnbroker. 'Thank you.'

'I got a very 'andsome crocodile-skin cigar case as 'd make a nice present for a gentleman – if you got a minute, lady?'

'I'm sorry, I have not.'

'Allow me.' Smart-Alec pulled open the door for her; the bell clanged again. 'Allow *me*, miss.'

She stepped out on to the pavement: thankful to be out of that fetid atmosphere. It was time to get along, in any case. After luncheon, she thought, find a shop selling sporting guns.

'Oh, miss—'

She looked round: he was coming after her. She waited, frowning. 'Well?'

'Didn't want to say much in front of old Lev in there. Bit of a stickler, he is, though you mightn't think it. But if you was still set on getting – you know – and you could go as 'igh as a tenner say – might be less, but say *up to* a tenner—'

'There'd have to be bullets with it.'

'Six chambers, six bullets. No use *without*, eh?'

'And not too big or heavy. To fit in a coat pocket, say.'

'Yeah, well.' Nodding. 'You'd want *that*.' He'd glanced at *her* coat pocket. His eyes were pale, and shifty, never meeting hers for more than a second or two. Not the sort

of person she'd want to have dealings of any kind with;
on the other hand if he *could* provide her with exactly what
she wanted, and at that sort of price . . . He added slyly,
'There'd be no licence problem, see. But it came to me all
of a sudden where I believe I *could* lay 'ands on one.'

Pausing, tipping his hat to a passer-by . . . Then: 'Interested, are you?'

'I'd have to see it before I agreed to buy it.'

'Course you would! Stands to reason!'

'Would you be able to show me how to use it?'

'Show *you*?'

'So I can show my brother. He's not the sort of person who
would know anything about firearms, and I know *nothing*
of them.'

'Well, you wouldn't. Course you wouldn't. But where'll
I find you, miss? Live hereabouts, do you?'

'No. We'd better meet somewhere.'

'What about here, then, this corner?'

'I'd have thought somewhere more private—'

'Just *meet* here, see – then—'

'All right.' She'd glanced the way he'd gestured. 'When?'

'Tomorrow? Evening? Nine o'clock, that suit?'

She was in Cecil Court by one o'clock, glancing at some
books on a barrow opposite the luncheon room. She wasn't
too happy with the arrangement she'd made for the following evening – with a man who was clearly some kind
of crook, whose name incidentally she didn't know – all
right, he didn't know hers either, and he probably wouldn't
have given his real name anyway – and whom she'd
found decidedly unprepossessing. There was satisfaction,
on the other hand, in having struck lucky twice in the
space of an hour – first in having made the acquaintance
of this Napier person, who from the little she'd seen of
him *was* decent and personable enough – and second in

having moved significantly closer towards the acquisition of a pistol.

Even if he *was* a dealer in stolen goods. If she'd backed off, she'd have been kicking herself now for missing the chance.

Turning her back on the barrow, she unfolded her newspaper and scanned its front page. The US ship that had been mined was a warship, the *Texas*, and it had happened off Smyrna.

Smyrna. In the Mediterranean somewhere. Vicinity of the Holy Land? Why there should have been either an American warship *or* mines there she couldn't imagine. Skimming down to the report of the *Titanic* Inquiry, her eye was caught by the sub-heading LOSS OF LIFE DUE TO INSUFFICIENCY OF BOATS. Which *she* could have told them; anyone could have. As a rider to this, however, a witness from the Board of Trade was quoted as saying that a week before the ship had left Belfast for Southampton an instruction to increase the number of lifeboats had been written but not despatched. He hadn't been able to say why.

'Mrs Maguire.' Napier, smiling at her. 'You beat me to it. And bought one of that lad's news-rags, I see.'

'I got this down near the station.'

'*Our* boy was holding out for a shilling to move to the other end of the street, drat him!'

'Did he get it?'

'Not from me, he didn't. No, he was still there when I left. Shall we go in? I'm sorry to have kept you waiting. I have your travel warrants with me though – save you having to come back to the office.'

'Well, that's—'

'What I've not managed yet is the letter about possible employment in Ireland. The fact is, *our* ladies at their typewriters are fairly snowed under at the moment, there's a tremendous amount of correspondence. But if I get it done on Monday, say – could you call in perhaps Tuesday or Wednesday?'

'Very easily. I'm only sorry to give you so much trouble.'

He'd be about twenty-one or twenty-two, she guessed. Entering the restaurant – luncheon room as it called itself – with him holding the door back for her, she was uncomfortable with the sense of her own duplicity. Liking him – so far – and wishing she did *not* have to deceive him, make use of him, in pursuit of an aim that would have horrified him.

If one thought about it too deeply, horrified her too. But the sense of horror – *dread* might be a better word for it – seeing that one had no choice or option, had to be – put up with. *She* hadn't caused Frank and Tom to drown.

They sat down at the end of a long, narrow table. There were no other diners at it – yet – and with luck when any did come they'd sit at its other end. Napier was saying, 'I did warn you it's not the Ritz exactly. There's a set meal each day – usually soup followed by a main course – a plateful of simple but perfectly good food, either meat or fish, and then a pudding.'

'And the charge for this?'

'You'd be surprised how little. That's one of the attractions. Won't you *please* be my guest?'

'I'd sooner not. To have accepted at all, on such very slight acquaintance—'

'Awful cheek on my part, forcing my company on you!'

'I'm grateful anyway, but—'

'Must be lonely in a place like London, not knowing anyone. Even in happy circumstances – and as it is – well, heavens . . . Have you found a place to stay, that suits you?'

'Oh, yes.' She told him about the passage from New York, and that, kind Americans having taken pity on her, she'd had the luck to travel second class, and about old

Reggie Deacon – and his landlady, and the other one. A middle-aged waitress brought plates of pea soup and bread. She asked him, 'Can you explain why an American warship should have been mined off Smyrna? Or for that matter where Smyrna is, even?'

'It's a port in Turkey not far south of the Dardanelles. The Turks have been at war with Italy since last year, you know. They've gone so far as to close the Dardanelles to shipping – which hasn't exactly pleased the Russians. Highly dangerous, really, so many sabres rattling. There's no reason it should involve America directly, of course; the mines must have been laid to sink Italians.'

'I suppose as a shipping man you'd *have* to know all about it.'

'We don't operate in those waters, luckily for us. And I'm only an apprentice, actually. Sort of doing the rounds, working in different areas of the business – in ship-management generally, and currently doing this stint in head office – passenger bookings and schedules, all that. All of which as you can imagine has been in a state of considerable upheaval – I'm talking in practical terms, quite apart from the misery of it, the appalling cost in human lives. Does it upset you to talk about it? Stupid question, I suppose, obviously it must. I'm clumsy, I'm sorry—'

'It's happened, and one has to face it. In my own case it's difficult to grasp that it's for the rest of my life, not a *passing* thing. I know that's a statement of the obvious, but' – shaking her head – 'how it *feels*, I mean it won't *ever* pass. Not easy to explain – but answering your question, no, I *don't* mind talking about it – and I wouldn't say you were in the least clumsy, don't worry—'

The waitress paused beside them. 'Cottage pie is the dish today, sir – miss – will that be all right?'

Napier cocked an eyebrow at her: 'Cottage pie?'

'Please.'

He nodded to the waitress, added in a murmur, 'It's that or nothing, anyway.' Her glanced at the folded newspaper: 'You've been reading about the Inquiry I suppose.'

'Not that much seems to be coming out of it.'

'Will be, though. There'll be new Board of Trade regulations about having enough lifeboats to accommodate every soul on board every ship afloat – to start with. Frankly, on reflection one's surprised there's never been anything of the kind before this. But a few other things too, no doubt. Carrying enough wireless operators for ships to stay switched on day and night, should be another. And perhaps regulations about reducing speed in dangerous waters. This *has* been the greatest tragedy in all our peacetime maritime history, you know.' Napier took a precautionary glance around, and dropped his voice to a murmur. 'Looking on our own side of the fence, meanwhile, the tragic figure in our own head office here is our managing director, of course – of whom no doubt you've read screeds in the daily papers. Those questions in the Commons yesterday were quite devastating for the poor chap. Did you see the *Times* today?'

'I did not. But – questions in parliament, you mean?'

'Not *half*, as they say in the vernacular. How did the managing director of White Star get himself away in a lifeboat when only twenty of a hundred and eighty Irish passengers survived?' Napier shrugged, watching the cottage pie on its way over. 'I'm told the answer – my chief's – is simply that a boat was being lowered with space in it, no-one else was coming forward so he got into it. Natural enough, but I honestly think he's wishing now he hadn't.'

The pie looked all right. There were carrots with it. The woman put the plates in front of them, and withdrew. Eileen asked hesitantly, 'Managing director – I forget the name, although it was in all the papers in New York—'

'Ismay. Joseph Bruce Ismay.'

'Oh yes, there *was* a lot about him. I suppose he'll be at the Inquiry answering *their* questions now?'

'I think he has been, but – I don't know. He's certainly not showing his face in public more than he has to. Of course I'm not in his confidence, exactly – to put it mildly – but I do run into him occasionally.'

'Coming and going from your office, I imagine.'

'Well – from *the* office – meaning the building. Not from mine, exactly. Our lords and masters are quartered upstairs – the holy of holies, some call it – and there's an entrance at the side, along a narrow passage from the street. He can arrive and leave just as he chooses, of course – as early or as late as he prefers, be dropped or picked up by cab or by some colleague with a motorcar – just dash in or out. But definitely *not* sweeping up in his Silver Ghost these days, d'you see!'

'Silver Ghost?'

'Rolls-Royce – a forty/fifty, last year's model. Absolute beauty, I can tell you.' Wag of the dark head . . . 'When I think that his father started life like me, a lowly apprentice – hope springs eternal, eh?'

'Was his father head of White Star too, then?'

Not that she cared much about Ismay's origins, or his father's. The fact was that without having shown anything more than polite or general interest, she already knew that his times of arrival and departure were erratic and that he used a staff door at the end of some side passage from the street, and was likely to arrive either by motorcar – but not in his own – or cab. It was dawning on her that she didn't really need to know much more. Certainly couldn't very well ask him whether the side door was kept locked or guarded, or where he'd be coming from or taken back to – his home, presumably, wherever it was – or whether he'd go out for lunch. Napier was telling her quietly, 'His father was T.H. Ismay, not just the head of the Line, but its founder. He served his apprenticeship with shipowners in Liverpool, then set up on his own and somehow managed to buy the White Star Line of Australian wool clippers, in – oh, the eighteen-sixties. He had a partner called William Imrie – *Lord* Imrie, the Line's chairman? – and the power behind it all is International Mercantile Marine – IMM, a hugely rich combine with a great deal of American money in it. In fact American money built the *Titanic*. Bruce Ismay's a director of IMM, I might say – as well as of LMS – London, Midland and Scottish Railway – and a number of other concerns. But – that particular question in the House – if you truly don't find it painful to discuss this – only twenty out of a hundred and eighty Irish saved – you must have been one of that very small minority, obviously!'

She glanced round for flapping ears – there weren't any – and told him, 'Thanks only to my husband. They were trying to keep us shut down below, but he pushed his arm through this sort of gateway, got a steward by the throat and made him unlock it, let us through.'

'My *God* . . .' He looked shocked. Whispering, 'So those stories are true? *Not* just malicious rumour?'

'Plain truth. Stewards and others were only doing as they'd been told . . . But he – my husband – and our son—'

'I know – and I'm *dreadfully* sorry. One feels – shame. Even to speak of it – and with you, of all people!'

'It's happened – like I said.' She put down her fork. 'Talking can't make it worse. I'm thinking of them all the time, thinking out loud's no different. Questions in parliament – well, what's *that* . . . The fact is a lot of men wanted to get in boats and weren't allowed, then women refused to leave their husbands so they drowned too. I wish *I* had. Sure, I can imagine your man wishing *he'd* stayed.'

7

✦

Early Saturday morning now, still dark; she was in the open window of her room in Cyrus Lane, on her knees, eyes and ears tuned to the surprising stillness of the London dawn. Wondering whether she'd been too outspoken, with Charles Napier. Although it had been a relief to let it out – perhaps with her guard down anyway, for the first time in weeks finding herself in the company of someone roughly her own age. And if at some later time he was to be brought into it as a witness he might give them the gist of what she'd told him – by way of explanation, to some degree mitigation maybe. There'd be some solace in having people understand.

If they got her alive, of course, she'd still hang.

He'd said over his cottage pie, 'If you were at the Inquiry now and described that sequence of events – golly, there'd be headlines then!'

'I wonder, *would* there? Isn't it taken for granted, the way it was? And besides, it's not what they'd be seeking, is it? Isn't it more what caused the ship to crash into the iceberg, and then being unsinkable why it couldn't stay afloat – and the other things you mentioned?'

He'd shrugged. 'Still . . .'

'Besides, who'd bother with headlines on such a tale. In

New York they didn't. It was the millionaires who interested them, famous names they'd recognize. Like Astor, and Benjamin Guggenheim. Dare say it was in the papers here too, how Guggenheim went to his cabin and changed into full evening dress, saying that if he had to drown he'd go like a gentleman?'

'Yes. There was a lot about the great J.J. Astor, too.'

'I read that they turned *him* away from a boat. You could say it was not a "class" business therefore – only not letting the steerage crowd up in a rush that would crowd the decks and swamp the boats . . . Tell me, though – were you ever in Ireland, yourself?'

In point of fact, she thought she'd handled it quite well. The only other reference to the *Titanic's* sinking that she could remember was a reference *he'd* made to the ghastliness of the experience and how well she was able to comport herself now in spite of it, and she'd told him she had it locked in, was all, that she knew she had to put it behind her, remember *them* but not the horror of that night.

Which was about as phony as anything she'd ever said. Horror *every* night was still nearer the truth of it. For every moment of a dream in which you were happy you paid dearly within seconds of waking. As now, in this window on the top floor of Mrs Whitten's house – there was a breeze rustling over the rooftops and now and again the rumble of a train, but it was the Atlantic she was listening to, that streaky sky was an Atlantic dawn; crouching with her chin resting on her forearms on the wooden sill she was seeing the littered ice-field and telling them in her heart, *I'm getting close, my darlings, it won't be long now* . . .

She'd explored a zigzag route between Cyrus Lane and the Strand, during the Friday afternoon, and planned to go that way on foot to her meeting with the crook this evening. Whether 'hoofing it', as Reggie Deacon called it, might cost more in shoe-leather than one would otherwise spend on bus fares might be arguable, but it took up time, of which she had plenty, and taught one the geography of the place. As well, anyway, not to have to rely entirely on bus routes and schedules. If her meeting with the man this evening was straightforward and didn't take too long she might spoil herself with a ride home after, she thought.

Mrs Whitten's *Daily Herald* carried the headline SECOND DAY OF THE INQUIRY FARCE, and the theme of its leader was encapsulated in:

> It had 2,206 people on board and boats for only 1,167. The two organizations responsible for this are the Board of Trade and White Star Line. We must go for them both, whatever happens at the Inquiry.

The Inquiry was taking place at the Scottish Drill Hall, apparently. Wherever that might be. In any case she had no inclination at all to attend – despite having a day to kill now, before her assignation with the pawnbroker's slimy friend. In preparation for which she took as much money as she needed out of the canvas roll and gave the roll itself to Mrs Whitten to safeguard for her. Mrs W had told her she had an iron-bound, double-locking silver chest, which had been her late husband's and which she used for the storage of valuables, and that she'd be 'happy to oblige'. Eileen told her now, 'If I should happen to fall under a bus, Mrs Whitten—'

'Oh, *mercy*!'

'If anything like that did happen, I'd like you to ask Mr Deacon to accept it, with my thanks for his kindness to me. Mr Reggie Deacon, who lodges at Mrs Craven's?'

The major part of it was an Irish bank draft in US dollars, which presumably he'd be able to negotiate. That would be *his* problem, anyway.

* * *

Supper in Cyrus Lane on Saturdays was at six o'clock, and having had only a sandwich for lunch she was more than ready for it: especially having covered quite a few miles on foot during the day, and expecting to cover a few more that evening. It wasn't exactly a heavy meal, anyway – clear soup, macaroni cheese and an apple flan. After it, she went back up to her room and wrote some letters – first one of several pages to Elizabeth Dalby, describing the voyage and Reggie Deacon's kindness, and telling them she expected to be crossing to Ireland in a few days; she'd write again when she had an address in Cork to give her. The other two were follow-ups to those she'd sent from America to her own mother and Frank's, letting them know she'd got this far, would be back in Cork before long and would be in touch.

Past eight o'clock now: time to get moving. Half an hour's walk, say, or forty minutes'; she'd decided not to start too early because she didn't aim to dawdle, appear to be loitering – on a Saturday night especially, with revellers in the streets. On the other hand it might be a good idea to have the pawnbroker's corner in sight before he got there – see from which direction he arrived, and whether alone or in company. For exactly what ends she wasn't sure, except that it would be better than hanging around on that corner herself, perhaps under *his* covert observation.

She'd told Mrs Whitten that she'd arranged to meet some people at Charing Cross, in connection with her hunt for missing relatives, and Mrs Whitten had given her a key to let herself in with if they were late and delayed her. In fact she hoped to be back by about ten, and Mrs Whitten had told her the buses would be running until about midnight.

'Much better to take a bus than walk, dear.'

'Yes, I'm sure . . .'

She let herself out, and set off westward by way of
Clerkenwell Green into Farringdon Road, then after some
distance southward branched right to Holborn Circus. The
streets weren't all that busy with traffic but the pavements
were crowded, especially in the vicinity of pubs and other
places of entertainment. She kept to the better lit sides as far
as possible, and walked purposefully, avoiding eye-contact
with wandering males.

Out of Charterhouse Street to Holborn Circus. Buses
seemed to run in small droves, she'd noticed, often two or
three together almost nose to tail and then maybe twenty
minutes without sight of one at all. Southward from the
Holborn corner now: Fetter Lane narrower and gloomier,
at this moment with no wheeled traffic in it. On a corner
outside a pub called the Plough she passed some women
who unquestionably *were* loitering with a purpose; she'd
have thought they'd frequent the busier thoroughfares, but
maybe their customers knew where to find them.

'Hullo there, love!'

A large man lurching out of a side-street. She told him,
'It's not me you want. Back there by the Plough.'

'Who knows what I want?'

'Who cares?'

Drunken laughter. One might not have been so lucky;
she knew from experiences in Cork that they weren't all
jolly when they were drunk. She had Fleet Street in sight
ahead anyway. Time by her watch as she passed under a
lamp, eight fifty. Deciding she'd stay on the north side of
Fleet Street and then the Strand, past the church that she
now knew was called St Clement Danes, so as then to have
a view of the pawnshop corner from this side of the road.

Ten pounds, she promised herself, not a penny more; and
no conversation other than on the subject of the pistol.

Fleet Street. She turned right. On a corner soon afterwards
the torn remnants of a poster fluttered on its otherwise

deserted news-stand: SUFFRAGETTES . . . DOWNING STREET WINDOWS. The missing word had started with an S, might be SMASH. There'd been talk about suffragettes over supper this evening; only a day or two ago, apparently, Piccadilly too had been strewn with broken glass from the shop-fronts they'd smashed. And suffragettes on hunger-strike in prisons were being force-fed; there'd been questions asked about it in the House.

What if he hadn't brought the pistol, said he needed more time or more money?

Leave it. Forget him, find a sporting-gun shop and visit it on Monday. If necessary, see about cashing the bank draft. She was skirting St Clement Danes now; it was five minutes to nine and she could see the pawnbroker's corner, street-light shining on the golden balls. No one waiting there that she could see: people were passing, but not pausing. She'd have a clearer view from farther along, though, looking directly across and into the side-street.

No. Nobody.

Maybe he'd simply not bothered. Maybe whoever he'd been hoping to get it from had already sold it.

A pair of very large policemen, slow-marching ponderously eastward, gave her a stern once-over. She frowned, looked away, thinking *Damn cheek* . . . She knew that she did *not* look like a tart. A suffragette though? They'd come in all shapes and sizes, she imagined. And if they were running riot and smashing windows all over the country, you'd hardly blame the peelers for keeping a watchful eye. She paused, glancing back. Mistake: at the same moment one of them had looked back *this* way. The pawnshop corner meanwhile still empty except for a dog lifting its leg. Carry on this way for another thirty or fifty yards, she thought, put that much more distance and a few more people between herself and those two guardians of the Law, *then* turn back. Otherwise seeming to be patrolling up and down *might* be classifiable as 'loitering with intent'. She was getting too far from that corner though: didn't want it out of her sight or to have the pistol-man think *she* wasn't coming. So, cross over, go back on that side. If he still wasn't there, continue past and maybe cross again. She paused at the kerb just short of yet another church – St Mary-le-Strand. Quite a lot of traffic on the move down here: she chose her moment and nipped across, turned back eastward, passing a pub from the upper windows of which came a loud jangling of music and raucous conversation.

'*Hello*, dear!'

Was *every* woman on her own accosted in this town? Accosted or suspected? If not, what was so singular about *her*? Waft of beer and shag tobacco: he (or another) hawked and spat, muttered something derogatory. She thought, with her eyes averted, give me Cork *any* day. She had the pawnshop in sight – corner still empty. Looking further along on the other side, couldn't see anything of the policemen either – which was something. But if this person wasn't going to show up, what a waste of – well, virtually two whole days . . .

There!

She'd seen a flash of reflected light as the shop door had opened, a dark shadow slipping out and another flash as it shut again. Now there he was: it definitely was him. Oddly, she hadn't thought of him appearing from inside. His link to the pawnbroker must be closer than she'd realized. One a thief and the other a fence, she guessed. He was standing with his hands on his hips, looking around – he *liked* himself all right, you could see that – and he spotted her now as she stepped off the kerb and started over towards him; he had the cheek to spread his arms as if greeting a dear friend.

Same clothes. Same hat flat-aback, same oily smell.

'Did you get it?'

A reproving stare: as if her lack of caution had displeased

him. Then a nod, and a cautionary movement of the head towards people passing. He put a hand on her elbow: 'Come on.' Another slant of the head indicated this side-street – as he had the day before. She'd pulled her arm free.

'Why not in there?'

'What, Lev's place?

'Which you just came out of.'

A nod. 'Looked in to say hello. Ain't none of old Lev's business, this.'

'So where do we go?'

'Short step down here.' She avoided his hand again, and he shrugged. 'Have it your own way . . .'

'You did get it, did you?'

'Got it right here on me – which you wouldn't't've credited, would you. The bee's knees, this little item is!'

'And ten pounds – or less.'

'Well – when I show it to you – for which we need some elbow-room and no busy-bodies—'

'Not a penny more. I haven't *brought* a penny more.'

He'd halted, was looking round at her. Pedestrians crossing at the top, black cut-outs against the street-lighting, but down here the two of them on their own. There was a side-alley off to the right – where it looked as if he might be taking her, in fact – which was unlit and stank of – well, urine. Staring at her . . . 'Ten's all you've brought, eh?'

'It's what we agreed and I made clear. Maybe less than ten, but certainly not more.'

'Well, like I say, it's something special, is this. You'll see – by far a better object, and that's no malarkey. Along 'ere now, a little way – basement flat, property of a friend of mine, I got the key.' The alleyway separated the backs of decrepit houses. Deep shadows: glimpses of moonglow high up past eaves and jutting attic windows but it didn't get a look-in down here, the only light came feebly from the street they'd turned out of. She avoided yet another groping hand; he muttered, 'All right – if you can see your way . . . Talk business when we're inside – all right?'

'The only business I'll talk is ten pounds. I don't know I'll buy it at all, but believe me I won't shift on that.'

'You got an eye-opener coming, though. And here we are. Like I said, this isn't my own place, it's a mate's – I borrowed the key off him, is all. Steps here – on your left. Catch 'old o' the rail 'ere, love.' He grabbed one of her hands and put it on an iron railing – such as would surround a basement area, she supposed.

Black as pitch . . .

'All right?'

'This is almost certainly a waste of time.'

'Watch your step, Irish . . .'

Iron steps, like a fire-escape. He was going down ahead of her but reaching back with a hand up to steady her.

'All right? I'm at the bottom now. You got two more steps. Hang on a mo' . . .'

He'd left her, was fiddling a key into a lock, or trying to.

'Why are there no lights here?'

'Will be in a sec. Ah, Gawd—'

A light had come on behind the door, which had a single pane of glass in the top of it. He'd laughed, called back, 'Light you ask for, hey presto, light you get!' A bolt was being withdrawn on the inside: he'd stopped poking around with the key and stepped back, bumping backwards into Eileen as a woman's voice squawked shrilly from the doorway, ''Oo's that there?'

'Why, Daisy!'

'Tony? *You*, Tony?'

'The one an' only. How come you got a key? Lev said *Judy*—'

'I borrowed it off her like. Don't tell Lev? Be a real love? See, we're off – only dropped in for a minute, like.'

Laughing . . . 'We' being herself and a man behind her in
the doorway – or kitchen, whatever. Dark trilby, coat collar
turned up. From the little she could see, Eileen thought he
might be the girl's father: she could see white hair at his
temples. She was wishing she'd left 'Tony' at the corner as
soon as he'd demurred about the price he wanted. The girl
in the doorway was tugging the man out into the area; there
wasn't much room for the four of them, with only the width
of the iron steps and two or three feet of concrete. 'Come
on, darlin'!' She was a tart of course, a prostitute, and the
man was clearly *not* her father. She'd seen Eileen now and
was peering up at her; she had a lot of bright yellow hair
over which she was arranging a scarf; her overcoat was fur
with bare patches in it, and her scent competed with Tony's
Macassar oil. Tony and she had embraced furtively, edging
past each other: she asked him, gesturing towards Eileen,
'New blood then, Tony?'

'You mind yours, I'll mind mine – all right?'

'Where'd he get you from, dear?'

'He didn't get me, hasn't got me, and I doubt very much
he'll be seeing me again. Good night.'

'Well, pardon me, I'm sure. Irish, eh?' She sniggered.
'Bitten off more'n you can chew *there*, Tony!'

'Reckon so, do you?'

'Well, I mean, an Irish duchess—'

'Oh, *funny*. But that'll do now. Daisy – next week, I'll
see you – I swear it. I been away – you ask old Lev, he'll
tell you—'

'Tell you anything, that old sod would. Come on now,
love – excuse us, Molly Malone—'

Tony pulled her inside with him, banged the door shut
and bolted it. They were in a very small, foul kitchen.
Scarred and stained table, ancient sink full of dishes, muck
and litter everywhere. The odour was slightly lavatorial.
Small door on the left and another – ajar – in front of them.

'Sorry about this. Lev's had the wrong sort in 'ere, I can see. Pete being away, like.'

'Show me the pistol, then I'll go.'

'Parlour's through 'ere. That door there's the convenience.'

The 'parlour' was as foul and airless a room as she'd ever been in. She didn't want even to guess at what the 'convenience' might be like. She'd stopped in the parlour doorway, holding her handkerchief to her nose. It was obvious, having met Daisy and her customer, what the place was used for, only surprising that any kind of customer would even step inside it.

But *she* had. Mistakes all coming home to roost, she realized: entering the pawnshop in the first place, listening to this Tony creature and then allowing him to bring her here now.

There was a table with kitchen chairs at it, and an unshaded overhead light, its flex festooned with cobwebs. An old, stained, saggy-looking couch. A tin lid on the table had cigar and cigarette ends in it. Tony was using the toe of his boot to push what looked like a balled-up, soaked handkerchief out of her sight under the couch; she'd turned back towards the kitchen.

'Come on, Irish – want to see it, don't you?'

'I've seen enough. You should not have brought me here. In any case, more than ten pounds – even if it's made of pure gold . . .'

He tossed his hat on to the table and dropped the key on top of it, and now produced this object from his pocket.

'See?'

It was very small. Covered the flat of his hand, no more. *It* was flat – the handle part brown and the rest black. He tossed it up, caught it again . . . 'Weighs next to nothing, see. But seven shots, it holds. And see this?'

Between the forefinger and thumb of the other hand he

was showing her a coppery-sheathed bullet. The business-end of it looked like shiny steel.

'Known as a point three two, Irish. Kill an ox with it, if you wanted to. It's a automatic, see, not a revolver. Bullets go into this – the magazine, they call it – and that goes in 'ere.' In the handle. He pulled it out again, clicked that bullet into the bottom of it, pushed the magazine back in and tapped it home with the heel of the other hand.

'All you do now is cock it. See – pull this part back, let it slide forward again. Listen to it now. Hear that? That's your topmost bullet being slid out of the mag into your actual breech, what it's fired out of when you pull the trigger. Only you can't pull the trigger yet, on account there's what they call a safety-catch – here. On, off – see? On that way – that's safe, can't fire – or down that way, the red spot, see? That's the safety off, pull the trigger and he's dead. Here, take it, feel how light it is. And how neat, eh? Fit in *any* pocket, that would!'

'Where did you get it?'

'Now that's *my* business. A Browning, it's called. The latest thing, neatest I ever saw, and yours for twenty quid.'

'As I said, highest I'll go is ten.'

'But you hadn't seen this then, had you. For this, honest, twenty's *cheap*!'

She handed it back to him. 'Ten's my limit, though.' Glancing round disbelievingly again at this wretchedly squalid apartment. Sofa, table, a few kitchen chairs: nothing else, except the smell. He saw her expression as she looked round, and shrugged. 'You're right – it's 'orrible. But then again—'

'It *is* horrible.'

'Bedroom in there. Tell you what, Irish – pay me the ten, the rest at a sovereign a week, Saturdays maybe at Lev's?'

'Not a *penny* a week. My brother wouldn't want anything as small as this anyway, a revolver'd be more his style.'

'I thought he didn't know nothing about guns?'

'I'm sure he doesn't. I'm saying a revolver would be better for him.'

'Want me to try again, then?'

'No, I do not – and I'm going now, so—'

'My guess is it's for you, not for your brother.'

'Guess away, so. Would you open the door for the light until I'm up those awful steps?'

'You wouldn't've come this far if you was straight, Irish.'

'I don't know what you mean – and my name's *not* "Irish"!'

'So what is it? You know mine—'

'I never wanted to, and I'll now forget it. Look – I want to *go!*'

'All right. All *right*.' He held the little pistol out towards her. 'Ten quid. It's yours.'

'You mean that?'

'We'd make good partners, Irish, you an' me. Your looks, and the way you put it on like, and my – experience, an' that. I mean, I know my way around, like. And – look, speakin' frankly, that's a most elegant figure you got on you, and you dress like a lady, and – my oath, them *eyes!*'

'Take your hand off me!'

'Take the pistol, then. Look, I'm doing you a good turn – right? No profit to me – nothing. All right? Listen – you want it as a *gift*?'

'No. Ten pounds. As we agreed.'

'You don't give in easy, do you, Irish. Me neither – so listen to this now. No matter what the job is you want this for, *I'll* do it. How about that? Show you the sort of bloke I am. Like I said, I'd be glad to 'ave you with me – your looks, your classy ways an' all . . . So you get what *you're* after, an'—'

'You must be raving mad!'

'Not such a bad-looking cove, am I? And I'm a good bloke to 'ave on your side, I'll tell you that! See, no matter what it is you're contemplating like—'

'Let me go – please?'

'I'll tell you, I go for you. First minute I saw you I thought – could be *right* between us – you know? Oh, I seen that ring, clear through your glove, but you've no 'usband, you're a loner, I'll swear to *that*!'

'I did have—'

'What 'd he do, run off?'

'He'd've broken you like a matchstick – with one hand!'

'My good luck he ain't here, then. Hey, easy with that now, that's—'

'Let me go! Take your hands *off* me, *damn* you!'

'Garn, *silly*—'

He'd grabbed for the pistol in her hand, only a second after his fingers had slid caressingly down the side of her face and throat. His left hand was clamped on her right elbow, and now the other was on the little gun between them at chest level. Her forefinger must have been inside the curve of the trigger-guard – the way she'd been holding it, that was all, not for any other reason or purpose – and she had no notion of how he'd left the safety-catch. *She* hadn't touched it – wouldn't have been able to find it without a close examination – but in any case wasn't thinking about the weapon as such: at that stage she was more immediately conscious of his left arm sliding round to clamp her body against his – and the reek of him, his breath in her face, his urgent 'Let go of it, Irish! Careful, Christ's *sake*!'

'*You* let go of *me*! Get *away*—'

It was louder than she'd have expected. Shockingly loud, totally surprising. She'd only been concerned to get free of him, pushing at him with both hands jammed up there between them. Then – ear-splitting, stunning. For a second or two she *was* stunned. Feeling his body fold, its weight against her and his head back, eyes rolling back. His knees buckled as *she* stepped back, pushing him clear – his hands had left her, falling loose. He was at her feet, momentarily on his knees but crumpling, toppling sideways; she still had the pistol in her gloved hand. It must have been against his rib-cage and pointing upwards – into his heart or throat or both, she guessed. All scarlet spreading now – the front of the striped shirt, and beginning to dribble from his open mouth.

Still dazed: gazing down at herself and at him and at the pistol, its explosion still ringing in her ears or brain – beginning to wonder who'd come running and pounding on the door, who'd have heard the shot. Nothing stirring *yet*. The smell of gunpowder or whatever was comparatively pleasant. Her brain was beginning to work again: breath short and heart thumping, but she had to *make* it work. He'd bolted the outer door, she thought. But the house above this stinking basement would surely have people living in it – it probably fronted on to some lane or alley closer to the river – but whether the shot would have been audible inside it one couldn't guess. Or, if it had been, whether they'd take notice anyway. If the inhabitants or users of this basement and the alleyway out there were all Tonys, Daisies and clients of the Daisies, who'd come running?

She had blood on her coat, shoes and stockings. None on her gloves: or on the pistol. There was a lot of it down there now but it had mostly welled out of him since he'd fallen. Since when he hadn't moved even an eyelash or a fraction of an inch. She had no doubt at all that he was dead. Or that technically speaking she'd killed him.

She felt weak: physically drained and mentally still stunned. Pulling a chair from the table, turning it so she could sit, before her legs gave way. Various things occurred to her, although it was still like thinking through a fog. For instance, that perhaps no one *would* come at least for some time. Unless some Daisy with a customer . . . But in any case it would be a relief as well as sensible to get away quickly, immediately. If one could find the strength . . . A thought of staying put, even calling for assistance and telling them it had been an accident or self-defence did occur to her but lasted no more than seconds. Who would one call and where from? Who might one *get*? This was the unspeakably and probably notoriously squalid haunt of highly unsavoury characters, and it might prove difficult if not impossible to convince anyone that she wasn't just another of them.

Only came here to buy a pistol from him . . .

That was *quite* a thought. Try *that* on whoever came!

But what other reason could one give for being here?

She was careful to keep her distance from him – from it – while cleaning herself up. Her stockings were thoroughly bloodied, also – she discovered now – the hem of her skirt. And her shoes. She removed the shoes and then also the stockings, using the unstained upper part of one of them to wipe the shoes, and the other to rub as much as was possible off her skirt and coat, especially the latter. She'd use soap and water later, in Cyrus Lane – *if* she got there. But not now, since any such efforts might only make things worse; not only were cleaning materials limited, but her hands were unsteady and any physical exertion brought on the sick feeling. Had to do as much as she could, though . . . While remembering that Daisy had had a close look at her and had recognized her voice as Irish. Daisy's companion – client – had seen and heard her too, although less clearly – he'd have been concerned mainly for his own anonymity, would *not* be likely to come forward.

Would a prostitute? If a description was circulated and police were asking questions?

Probably not. Immaterial anyway, since the description could only have come from her in the first place. She'd probably only come into it if the police roped her in and somehow got the information out of her. Via Lev maybe; they'd all be hand-in-glove and the police probably knew them all. But Lev especially might be a danger. He had something to do with this basement: Daisy had asked Tony not to tell him she had a key. And the Irishwoman who'd wanted to buy a pistol – Lev would be able to describe her, all right. And if his friend Tony had told him he was meeting her this evening – chances were he *would* have, she thought – he might be a lot more dangerous than Daisy.

Every reason therefore to clear out, and quick. Locking the place behind her, of course. Nodding to that – as if conferring with herself, approving her own wisdom. Still feeling ill; but fresh air might help. The coat was about as good as she'd get it, for the moment. The stockings she balled together with their cleaner areas outward and pushed the ball into a coat pocket. The pistol fitted easily in the inside pocket in which she'd previously carried Frank's canvas roll; as the late Tony had pointed out, it didn't weigh much. All she'd done to it, rather gingerly, was to apply the safety-catch, turning it so that it no longer arrowed the red spot. It was Tony who'd flicked it to and fro, demonstrating it to her, therefore he who'd caused it to fire – and then squeezed her hand on it. She most certainly had *not* done this deliberately – although if she'd thought of it, in that state of desperation . . . Shaking her head, feeling only this – fright, and urgency, especially since her innocence would be extremely difficult to prove, and both Lev and Daisy not only *could* put the police on her trail but might well see it as being in their own interests to do so. Looking down at Tony: the body was more or less on its side but tilted with its left arm thrown backward. Blood all over the chin and neck, the cravat and shirt darkly soaked, and one shoulder and that lapel of the jacket smothered in it too. He'd been right about the effectiveness of that calibre or type of bullet.

She wondered what he could really have wanted of her.

We'd make good partners, Irish, you an' me!

Partners in what, for God's sake? Crime of some sort. Maybe *any* sort . . .

The key of the outside door was on the table, on his hat. She picked it up; also her reticule from the floor where it had fallen when he'd grappled with her. It had fallen clear and there were no bloodstains on it. Dump the key somewhere later, she thought – down some drain. And the stockings anywhere. In a dustbin. She turned off the light – having taken a final look around to ensure she wasn't overlooking anything of importance – and went out into the kitchen, pulling shut the flimsy door behind her. Tony *had* bolted the outer door, she'd remembered that correctly. Through the glass panel at the top of it, having switched off the kitchen light, she could see nothing except vaguely and indirectly moon-washed darkness and the outline of the railings at the top. She withdrew the door-bolt as quietly as she could, then eased open the door by about an inch and put her ear to it.

Nothing, except distant traffic noise. She put on the light again, opened the door far enough to reach round and insert the key in the outside. Light off, then; she slipped out, shut and locked the door and removed the key. The night air *was* good, despite unpleasant odours. Nothing moving out here, and no lights or voices anywhere close. Traffic hum, snatches of music. She moved cautiously, groping for the railings and the steps; thinking that with a bit of real luck it might be days before any of them came and found Tony's corpse.

Except for Lev, who'd be minus *two* keys now and might come investigating. Especially when Tony didn't show up.

Climbing to the alleyway, wondering again whether Tony could really have thought of her as a potential partner. Or might it have been a duplicitous way of recruiting her to the Daisy and Judy brigade? Forcing her into it through blackmail over the pistol? If she'd accepted his offer to kill some unknown person for her: that could have been a ploy aimed simply at identifying that person. Blackmail might *well* have followed.

If he'd had that sort of hold over her, she thought, he'd have been merciless.

This was Milford Street now: she'd noticed the street-sign on the corner facing Lev's. Heading up that way, she wondered about taking a bus – whether it might be rather dangerous. Close proximity to other passengers – under lights, with her coat stained as it was, and her Irish intonation . . . Then in the course of a police investigation, someone recalling where she'd got off, so the search would then be concentrated on that area.

But even in the streets one had to pass under lights. Pass prowling policemen too: including that pair who'd been plodding eastward and might be coming back this way, who'd stared at her suspiciously even then – *before* she'd killed a man and got his blood all over her. It was a matter of weighing chances: best of all though not to have to speak to anyone at all, with her Irish accent.

Tall, with dark hair and yellow eyes: and she's Irish . . .

All right, so chance it – get on a bus and not speak to anyone, just hand over the penny. Decision made, cease dithering, just *do* that. She was on Lev's corner now: waiting while a cab clattered past. The horse-drawn variety. Reggie Deacon had said that in London in recent years hundreds of horses had been consigned to the knackers and hundreds of cabmen and their dependants to the poorhouses, and that the only benefit he was aware of was that the streets were cleaner. Crossing, now. Henceforth this was one part of London she'd take care to avoid. All right – she was over, less conspicuous again. By no means home and dry yet, but at least feeling a little safer. By and large she'd be more sensible to ride than walk, she thought. Once on a bus with the fare paid, nose against the window and coat arranged so the stained area didn't show, if anyone spoke to her she'd just shake her head. Off at Ludgate Circus, and another bus up Farringdon to Clerkenwell; then ten minutes' walk, and please God no policemen.

Yet another hansom cab – its trot easing to a walk as the cabbie reined in to the kerb only yards ahead of her. Providential, maybe – and suddenly *very* tempting. A cab being one thing she hadn't thought of. Just to flop into it and be taken right to the door. Giving nothing but the address 'Cyrus Lane' would hardly betray one's Irishness. Better still, just say 'Clerkenwell', and walk the last few hundred yards. As for the extravagance – having just saved ten pounds . . .

'Thanks, pal!'

Young girl jumping lithely down: evidently didn't have to pay the cabman – only a wave and a cry of 'Nighty-night!'

Eileen called, 'Cab?'

The girl, turning to face her, was Daisy. She was in the course of pulling the scarf off her mop of dyed-blond hair, shaking it and throwing it back over, fingers on the lower corners ready to knot them but static suddenly, eyes widening at recognizing Eileen: 'Why, *'ullo*, Duchess!'

Eileen, aghast, tried to smile. Cursing herself for not having reacted more quickly, turned away instantly and avoided this – as she *could* have . . .

'Where's my 'andsome Tony, then?'

'God knows. Look – excuse me—'

'Where to, miss?'

'Drive on, I'll show you. Night—'

She *should* have fainted, but instead had climbed aboard. Managing a good-night wave to Daisy: not uttering even one inessential word, make things even worse than they'd so suddenly become. Daisy knew she was Irish but the cabbie didn't and didn't have to. He was grumbling that *he* wanted to be off home too, and so did his nag, they'd had a hard day of it. She called up – with Daisie out of earshot – 'Clerkenwell. The Green'll do.' She didn't think that much could have sounded Irish.

Daisy on her way back down there *now*?

8

She didn't sleep that night. Mostly, agonized. She'd got into the Cyrus Lane house without seeing anyone or, as far as she knew, being seen, and having dragged herself up to her room, utterly exhausted, had made herself get down immediately to the task of cleansing her coat and skirt. She'd wanted only to lie down, pass out, *escape* this new horror now possessing her; but the urge to some-how come to terms with it – make it less awful than it was, maybe – wasn't resistible. Re-runs, guesswork, at times plain disbelief- hadn't she *had* her nightmares, wasn't she living one already? Waves of hopelessness were semi-salvaged at intervals by the practicalities of possible cover-up, evasion.

Frank's murmur in her head: 'You want to get away, go *now*, girl!'

'And my promise to you?'

'*You* I'm thinking of!'

It was the truth – he always *had*. And making a run for it now would be easy: tell them she'd given up on the family business, and get on the first train for Fishguard, be out of it long before Daisy's description could lead to recognition and arrest.

Hang by the neck for that Tony object?

Daisy, and Lev. Daisy might *not* have been on her way back to the basement flat. Not until or unless she'd picked up another customer, and even then might not have used that place. Where had she been for instance in the cab? Almost certainly she'd have been working – if that was the word for it – elsewhere. It was about evens therefore that Tony's corpse would be lying there undiscovered, might even remain so all weekend.

Depending perhaps on whether prostitutes worked on Sundays.

If it was Daisy who found the body, she'd run to Lev. Or to the police, but more likely to Lev. Lev, who it seemed had control of the keys and had been a close colleague of Tony's, could hardly not be brought into it, and from the way Daisy'd spoken of him to Tony he had some degree of authority in her eyes; she hadn't wanted him to know that she'd got in with a key borrowed or purloined from someone – another tart, presumably – name of – Judy.

Which might stop her going back to the basement flat at all, since she could only do so using the key that shouldn't have been in her possession and which she'd now get back to Judy, not wanting Lev to know she'd ever had it.

But others might use the place. Most likely did. And Lev might go round there when Tony didn't bring back *his* key. Within say twenty-four or at most forty-eight hours therefore the police would be alerted, and shortly after that they'd have Daisy's story about the Irishwoman. Even if she'd not been on her way back there when they'd bumped into each other in the Strand, Daisy's evidence would be fairly damning – however hard one tried to avoid that conclusion. Facing it squarely, perhaps one ought not to count on having more than about twenty-four hours. *Maybe* forty-eight . . . After all they had to find and identify the body, then get hold of Daisy. After which she, Eileen, would do well not to show her face in any public place. But how *not*? Well – stay well clear of the Strand and Fleet Street, anyway. The nearest she'd have to go was the White Star office; so work out an approach from the north. Down the Haymarket, she thought, visualizing those streets. From Clerkenwell westward and then south – as distinct from southward and then west.

Think about changing some details of one's appearance, too. A change of hairstyle might be as good an idea as any. The weather was getting warmer, which would justify shorter hair. Also perhaps some different clothes; certainly a new hat. Straw perhaps, light coloured. Put away the mourning blacks and greys. The saved ten sovereigns mightn't cover it all, but brighter, lighter clothes, and an entirely different hairstyle could make a lot of difference.

Then, get on with it – and quickly. Having the pistol now – also knowing she could handle it, no problem there *at all* – the problem was simply how to get at him.

Hang around that corner, then when he showed his face with its little curled-up moustaches follow him into the passageway, close right up to him – a girl in a rush, arriving late – and kill him.

The 'hanging around' might be tricky. She wondered whether there might be nearby premises she could make use of. Ideally a restaurant or café. On Friday she'd been interested only in White Star, not its neighbours, she hadn't been taking much notice of the surroundings. But there might be something of the sort. A window to watch from: see him arriving, and hurry out . . .

White Star's own window – where the table was, where those people had been sitting, including the codger in the frock-coat who'd seemed angry when Charles Napier had left him? With Charles's connivance perhaps, sit *there*?

Imagining it: *Charles, I'm feeling faint, I must sit down – d'you mind?*

Crazy, really. You might say, bloody cheek. But – conceivable? Not merely the desperation of a reeling brain?

Or with even a rough idea of what time he'd come or go, one might hide in the passageway itself. Hadn't even seen it yet, only knew from Charles that it existed, but if one *could* linger unobtrusively in it: especially if it led not only to the staff door, if for instance it continued through to the back of the building. Napier had said the letter would be ready for her to collect on Tuesday or Wednesday, but she'd try for it on Monday while at the same time checking on these other aspects. A reason to be there, making a reconaissance: and with any luck saving a day, maybe two days. It would be a mistake to ask Napier about Ismay's likely times of arrival or departure, but he might say something about it, give some indication. Spend time with him, therefore, maybe lunch with him again. Then simply *be* there, take the chance when it was offered. And – back to this now – even to *hope* for one's own survival and escape was unrealistic – might only complicate or confuse the issue: the issue being Ismay's death, nothing else. Thinking about it now – and the little pistol and its effectiveness – Tony's corpse in her visual memory was how she now envisaged leaving Ismay – except for seeing it as sprawled on paving-stones instead of floorboards – and *she'*d end up the same way. This was clear thinking now, and not a gruesome picture in her mind at all, it was – well, it really *did not matter*. No more than the location or condition of *their* remains did. It would be a great deal easier for her than it could have been for them, too: a split second of pain maybe, or maybe even none at all – she remembered that Tony hadn't cried out, for instance, he'd been alive one moment and dead the next. Why fear *that*?

Elsie Whitten asked her at breakfast how she'd got on last evening, whether she'd met her friends. Eileen told her yes, but only friends of friends in fact, the meeting hadn't achieved what she'd hoped it might.

Her hand was unsteady, scattering milk as she spooned up porridge. Nervous exhaustion, she told herself. Not fear: there wasn't anything to be frightened of. Nervous exhaustion was something Dr McGhee had mentioned once or twice. Anyway, Mrs Whitten had been looking away at that moment, hadn't seen it. Turning back to her again now: 'You look tired, dear.'

'It was rather a muggy night, didn't you find?'

Some of the other lodgers agreed – they'd definitely found it muggy. The weather was warming up, and no mistake. Young Mr Odgers, whose wife looked as if she might be his mother, said he wouldn't be surprised if there wasn't a full-blown heatwave coming. Eileen asked Mrs Whitten whether there was a hairdresser in this neighbourhood whom she could recommend; with the summer coming early she'd like to have her hair re-styled – shortened and thinned, primarily.

'Shame to cut off *any* of that lovely hair!'

'Too long and thick by half. And it grows so fast . . .'

'As it happens, there's an establishment in Clerkenwell I've sent quite a few of my ladies to, over the years. The proprietor is in fact a gentleman, a Monsieur Maurice – French, you know, but he has young ladies in his employ, of course. It's easy to find, I'll tell you—'

'I'll see where it is, and do something about it tomorrow.'

'Nothing *too* drastic, I hope!'

A different hair arrangement might change her appearance quite a bit, she thought, and since the warm weather provided an excuse for it – well, a page-boy bob, even. That and the light straw hat she'd thought of – and a lighter coat, and the lowest-heeled shoes she could find. And instead of the ladylike reticule which Elizabeth Dalby had chosen for her, a cloth bag on a cord that could be slung casually from one shoulder: she'd seen one or two recently and liked the effect, and there'd be practical advantages too. Several such small changes might cumulatively quite disguise her, she hoped – at least make it less likely she'd be recognized at a glance in the street. By Daisy, for instance: Daisy who was after all a street-girl and might be encountered anywhere. See to it all on Monday, *before* going down to prospect around White Star. Time was of the essence: there *would* be a description circulated, there was bound to be.

Thank God, anyway, that there was no way the police could connect Daisy's or Lev's tall, dark Irishwoman with the White Star Line or the *Titanic*. Also for the fact that there were thousands of Irish in London, a fair number of them female and dark-haired.

Literally, thousands.

Not so many yellow-eyed, admittedly. And not many of them noticeably tall.

Mrs Whitten asked her, after some general conversation, 'Will you be going to church, dear?'

'Mass. I expect so.'

'Mass – of course . . .'

In fact she'd more or less decided against it. Although London was enormous it was essentially a conglomeration of villages – Reggie had explained this to her – in which the residents tended to know each other as well as they might in villages in the country. Regular church-goers attending their local places of worship would know each other's faces and in many cases their names. The priests certainly would. A stranger therefore would stand out and be noticed, at least by *some*, and if a day or two later they read in their newspapers that police were anxious to interview a tall, dark, yellow-eyed Irishwoman in her mid-twenties – *in pursuance of their enquiries into the recent murder in a basement flat off Milford Street, Strand* . . .

She dressed appropriately for Mass, located the hair-dresser's shop and continued to Coldbath Passage. Mrs Craven was out – had gone to church – but the young son of another resident obligingly went up to tell Mr Deacon he had a visitor. Waiting for him, she glanced through Saturday's *Daily Express*, which she'd already seen – the Odgers took it – and had noticed a half-page advertisement for a GREAT SALE at the emporium of Messrs Jones and Higgins: and here it was – High-class Cloth Coats were priced between 23/11d and 49/6d, and Blouses had been reduced from 2/11d to 1/11 3/4d.

Monday, first thing. Or first thing after the hairdresser.

The boy came back to tell her that Mr Deacon seemed to have gone out. 'To church, I expect. Could have sworn I'd heard him up there!'

'Well, never mind. I only just happened to be passing, thought I'd see how he was. Would you tell him? I'm Mrs Maguire.'

'Why, Mrs *Maguire*! You was on the *Titanic*!'

Fame, she thought, ruffling his hair. But nothing to the fame she very soon *would* have.

Lev locked the door of his shop behind him and started down Milford Street. He was spruced up for a Bar Mitzvah which he'd be attending later in the day – dark suit, stiff white collar, blue tie, striped shirt with frayed cuffs, black boots and for the moment a soft hat. Face only slightly stubbled; he'd shaved Friday evening.

Humming some music-hall ditty, a third of the way down Milford Street he turned right into the alleyway and approached the railed iron steps leading down to Pete Bailey-Johnston's basement flat. Checking as he went down that he had the door-key in his pocket – in case neither of them *was* here. That bitch Judy had had her key a whole damn week: and as for Tony not bothering to bring *his* back last night, despite knowing damn well that Lev would have been waiting up, expecting him and curious to know how that business had gone . . .

He banged on the door with the heel of his hand, thinking – about Judy – *Give 'em the chance, they'll rob you blind.*

No reaction from inside. He kicked at a cat that had begun rubbing itself against his leg, and banged on the door again.

Not a peep. Except for the cat's miaowing.

He was confident that Tony *would* be in there, that he'd hardly have left the place without returning the key. If it had been very late, even, he'd have just shoved it through the letterbox. But – past midday now, for God's sake . . .

He'd got the key in – surprised there hadn't been one in the inside, to prevent this – and now pushed open the door.

'Tony? You in there, lad?'

The cat slid in past him as he felt for the light-switch. Nobody had done any tidying up recently, he noted. The dirty-water smell came from the WC door not fitting properly: you might as well have had the pan right here in the kitchen.

'Tony?'

He clumped to the inner door and shoved *that* one open.

Semi-darkness, airless warmth, sickly-sweet odour . . . And – a dark shadow. Peering, stooping towards it, he saw that it was actually a hump – on the floor this side of the table. He straightened and reached to the light-switch.

Body . . .

Buzzing of flies around it: the cat had darted to it and they'd all taken off. Settling again already. Lev stock-still, with his mouth open, gasping: a sharp and noisy intake of breath then, a squawk of shock and fright. He knew even in those first seconds that the corpse would turn out to be Tony's. The dapper Tony Henshaw humped in a sticky mess of dried or drying blood. His front – lower part of his face, neck, torso – black with it: where the cat was licking, not black but blood-red. Lev, semi-stunned, staggering back, came up hard against the door-jamb and stayed there propped against it – winded, vision blurred, heart pounding.

Believe this? *Tony*?

On his back, and twisted sideways: he'd been either stabbed or shot in the chest. Dead as bloody mutton. Operative word *bloody*. Lev off the door-jamb now, shaking his head as if to deny the evidence before him: and looking round for a key that might have been dropped. But it wouldn't be here, obviously. Whoever'd done this and then scarpered had locked the place up – *course* they had, *that* was where the key'd have gone. Wasn't Tony's fault he hadn't returned it last night. Use your wits now, Lev old son. Tony had been shot, not stabbed: well, *would*'ve, wouldn't he, he'd got a pistol for her, he'd said – little beauty, just the job. Lev had asked him, 'What job'd that be, then?' and Tony had tapped the side of his nose: *Nice question, Lev, very nice – one I dare say I'll be putting to her, what's more – bet your life there ain't no brother on his way to bleeding Africa!*

That Irish female. Eyes like a – what, a leopard's, Lev remembered. He was thinking hard, standing stiff and still, only his hands moving to light a gasper while gazing down at Tony's pale, wide-open eyes. Flies all round them and *on* them; the cat licking at his neck now. Lev remembered having asked Tony after the Irish girl's visit to the shop, 'You see her *eyes*?' She'd be the one, all right. No reason the rozzers shouldn't hear about it either – especially since it would put him and certain others in the clear . . . But see Judy first – sort *her* out, get the key off her: *then* come back here and find *this*, and scream for the boys in blue.

*   *   *

Eileen had only called on Reggie out of a sense of social obligation: he *had* been good to her, after all. She remembered particularly his kindness in making those arrangements for her night on deck.

But also having time on her hands: and maybe needing someone to talk to. She'd had a vague idea of taking him up on his offer to show her the London parks and so forth; he was an easy, undemanding companion, and she could hardly go strolling in a park on her own.

Lunch, therefore, then an afternoon's rest. Rest, but probably not sleep – what with thoughts whirling around in her head, and the frustration of this being Sunday and the White Star office shut. It might even have been as well that Reggie had been out, with her nerves as jumpy as they were: he was an observant little man, and she couldn't have borne being questioned. The small-talk at lunch was bad enough – the Odgers for instance on about the weather, as always, and the old man – name of Gerard – ranting about suffragettes: while in her own skull the waves of anxiety came and went, the pictures too – mental pictures of Daisy telling policemen, 'She's Irish, about five foot ten, thick black hair – must be long, she's got it fixed back like this . . .'

And the eyes – she'd tell them about the yellow eyes, damn sure she would.

'If I may say so, you're not looking very well, Mrs Maguire. I know you were tired – and it's not surprising, after all you've—'

'Tell you the truth, I've a slight headache. In fact I think I'll go up and lie down, if you don't mind . . .'

'I'd say that's an excellent idea!'

They were *all* saying it, then. Eileen leaving her roast beef hardly touched, telling Mrs Whitten that Mr Deacon might call in: 'If he does, would you be very kind, tell him – I mean not alarm him, it's only a little headache . . .'

*　　*　　*

Lev had been to where Judy lived in Southwark, to get the basement-flat key back from her – and warn her to keep her mouth buttoned – before going to the police. But he'd drawn blank; the man who paid the rent for the shabby little house she shared with him had dragged himself grumbling to the door and said he didn't know where she might be. Off with her friend Daisy, like as not; anyway she hadn't been home last night. He had a gammy leg and bloodshot eyes and was supposed to be her father – might have been, for all Lev knew, except for the fact he was called Smithers and Judy's surname was Simpson. Well – stepfather, might have been. Lev had asked him to tell her to contact him as soon as she could, and to return the key she'd borrowed, but that if there were strangers around when she called, better not let on what she'd come about.

The pink-rimmed eyes blinking: 'P'lice, d'you mean?'

Lev shrugged. The man wasn't *completely* witless. 'Could be.'

'This key. Big 'un, with a blue tag on it?'

'That'd be it.'

'Stay there, I'll get it. Is yours, I s'pose?'

Lev went back to the flat, 'found' Tony's body, went at a shambling run to the bookmaker's shop next door to his own and rang the bell of the living-quarters above it. The bookie had a telephone, and allowed Lev to come in and use it, to call New Scotland Yard.

At six p.m. he was in the flat again, being questioned by an Inspector Tait and a Sergeant Collindale. Tate was a thin, stooped man with a pendulous lower lip not unlike a camel's, while Collindale was younger and more heavily built, with a reddish-brown moustache and sideburns. Tait in a shabby grey suit, the sergeant sweating in flannel trousers and a tweed jacket. Other police had removed the body, and two in plain clothes were searching for fingerprints – in the bedroom, at this stage. Newspaper reporters had been refused either entry or information, and a uniformed constable was on guard outside in the alley.

These three – Tait, Collindale and Lev – were sitting on kitchen-type chairs at the table. Tait observing, 'You rent this place out by the hour to whores – correct?'

'I *beg* your pardon?'

Exactly the impresssion he was anxious to avoid: and why he'd wanted the key back from Judy, and for her and her friends to keep their mouths shut. The sergeant growled at him, 'Well, don't you?'

'I'm doin' a favour to a friend – keepin' an eye on the place, that's all. Why I 'appened to look in this afternoon. Weekdays I'm busy in me shop, see.'

'And evenings, the tarts are busy in *here* – right?'

'Look – Sergeant—'

'The friend in question – owner of the place – ' the inspector, chipping in – 'might he be Peter Bailey-Johnston?'

'Well, there – you *know*—'

'On the Moor – four years' hard labour?'

'My information is he was framed. I'd bet on it, what's more. A very nice fellow in all respects – *and* a toff—'

'Delightful little *pied-à-terre* he has here, too.' Sergeant Collindale murmured it, glancing around. 'Bright and airy, immaculately furnished—'

'This Tony – ' the inspector flipped a page over in his notebook – 'Anthony Henshaw, deceased . . . He came to you for the key, you told us – last evening?'

'About nine, must've been.'

'He wanted to bring some woman here – right?'

'Yeah – but—'

'For a game of chess, would that have been?'

'It was a matter of business, Inspector.'

'Isn't it always?'

'Not what you're makin' it out to be. I told the sergeant

– this woman – Irish – comes into the shop Friday, says she wants to purchase a revolver—'

Collindale put in, 'Which we're to assume was the murder weapon.'

'*Very* handy!'

'There's a antique 'orse-pistol in my display window, see. Her eye 'appened to fall on it, she says, and it give her the idea, maybe I'd 'ave a *modern* firearm brought in on occasion like. I tells her no, never 'ave 'ad, an' if I was offered any such object I'd want to know where it come from *and* notify the appropriate authority – meanin' your good selves of course—'

'So where did she get it from – if not from you?'

'*He* got it for her.' Lev pointed down at bloodstained floorboards. 'Tony did. 'Appened to be in the shop when she come in, didn't say nothin' to me but he slipped out after her, then he comes back inside and tells me he reckons he knows where he might lay 'ands on one. Well – none o' *my* business—'

'He came in at about nine, you say. Do you always stay open that late on a Saturday?'

'Rang me doorbell. I live over the shop.'

'Ah, yes.' Camel-profile nodding. 'And he's a close friend, so – well, he *was* – and he wanted a key from you. What for? So this woman could try the weapon out on him?'

'They was to meet on the corner at nine, he said. He had the pistol, wanted to show it to her private, not on the street like, and I may have mentioned as I was keepin' an eye on this place for Pete. But it was his own business with the Irish person, I didn't know even what he'd be asking her for it or—' Raising a hand, forefinger vertical: 'No, I tell a lie. When she was in the shop, I'd said I don't know nothing about firearms, then Tony come in on it and tells her maybe a fiver, maybe a tenner.'

'Describe the woman again, would you?'

'Tall – *for* a woman, that is. Not much under six foot maybe.'

'Go on – what else? Describe her!'

'Well – black hair—'

'Age, roughly?'

'Twenties. Middle twenties, maybe.'

'Pretty?'

'Well.' Frowning. 'Yeah. Some might say so.'

'What sort of clothes?'

'Ah, *smart*. Ladylike. No street-walker, I tell you *that*.'

'You'd know one, wouldn't you.'

'I was about to say, Inspector – her eyes – like *yellow*?'

'Yellow? Like a cat's?'

'Cat-like, you might say. That was the very thought I 'ad – some kind of animal. And I mean, yellow eyes – you don't see 'em, do you. And what with being so tall—'

'Distinctive appearance.' A nod. 'And Irish, you said.'

'I *thought* so. Mind you, I wouldn't *swear* to it – if you said Scotch – or Welsh even . . . But listen, what she said to me, about the revolver she was wanting—'

'Revolver?'

'Pistol. Whatever – I don't know . . . She said she had a brother on his way to Africa, she was thinking she'd give 'im a goodbye present, and a revolver's what she thought of after she saw the 'orse-pistol. Seeing as in them wild parts he might need one, see.'

'Did you believe her?'

'No reason not to. Didn't think about it. But Tony, *he* didn't!'

'Told you he didn't, did he?'

'Saturday – when he come and asked might he borrow this flat for 'alf an hour. He told me then he reckoned she was up to something.'

'*Something*.'

'Yeah – I don't know . . .'

'Did he give any reason for disbelieving her?'

'Didn't say, an' I didn't ask.'

'But – ' the sergeant broke in – 'do you think now he might have had any particular interest in discovering what she *really* wanted a pistol for?'

'He'd be curious, I suppose. Anyone might.'

'Perhaps Henshaw more than most?'

'Why?'

'If he saw something in it for himself?'

'I wouldn't know what – or how . . .'

'If as it does *appear* she ended up shooting him dead, there'd have had to have been something between them – I mean, something more than just the sale to her of a pistol. Agree?'

'Maybe – but—'

'Tell me.' The inspector took over again. 'You've been letting keys out to these tarts. We *know* you have. Henshaw'd have known all about it too, obviously. And you let him have a key for his tryst with this allegedly Irish person. Were any other keys out at the same time?'

'What d'you mean, *out*?'

'What d'you think I mean? On loan, or hire, whatever.'

'You got me wrong, Inspector.'

'No, I think I've got you dead to rights. But what I'm putting to you now is the possibility that someone other than Henshaw and his companion might have had access to this dump last night.'

'Not as I'd know of. Definitely not.'

'You, for instance. You certainly had one key – the one you got in here with this afternoon. How many are there altogether?'

'*Now*, I got two, and—'

'Wrong – you haven't, those are ours now. But there was also the one you gave Henshaw, which whoever shot him must have taken away, after locking up of course. Might've chucked it in the river, since. Same with the pistol. On the other hand – ' murmuring this to the sergeant, seemingly thinking aloud – 'since she was only here in the first place because – *allegedly* because she wanted to get hold of such a weapon – and then Henshaw must have pushed too hard in some other direction, isn't that a reasonable guess?'

'Yup.' The sergeant nodded towards the stains where the body had lain. 'Whoever did it, shot him at very close quarters, didn't they. *She* – maybe. Shirt-front scorched, as the doctor pointed out, before the blood soaked through . . . But what you're saying, sir, is she'd have hung on to the pistol – having some presumably homicidal intention as yet unfulfilled?'

'Yes. So she'd be out there now, and armed. Whoever she may be, and whoever her intended victim might be.' The inspector looked back at Lev. 'But then again this could be a load of codswallop, couldn't it. Why, hell – nine feet tall and yellow eyes—'

On the Monday morning Eileen woke early – as in fact she'd done *every* morning here in London – but having spent a lot of the night at least half-awake as well, seeing in her semi-dreams the basement flat still locked up and dark, unvisited, hiding its grisly secret. But also remembering a thought she'd had in the night – that since she *had* to be out and about, what she had to do was put the flat and Tony and Daisy right out of mind: *not* try to hide herself away, or worry about her Irish accent, simply get on with it. It would surely take a day or two, or more, for them to get a description of her into the papers: so assume that, and just not waste time. Two days' grace, say – *use* it. To kick off with, visit White Star – Charles Napier – this afternoon, rather than wait until Tuesday or Wednesday as he'd suggested, to collect the letter to their manager in Cork. Then haunt that place: Ismay was going to have to show up *some* time between now and the weekend, surely.

She'd taken Frank's money-roll back from Mrs Whitten last night – no worry to Mrs W, since a week's rent had been settled in advance last Friday – and she'd mentioned as a reason for this that she was thinking of visiting Messrs Jones and Higgins's sale, after the hairdresser's. Or before it, if Monsieur Maurice couldn't fix her up right away. She wanted to have the money and papers with her anyway, in case she found herself face to face with Ismay suddenly, with a chance to do it – bang – and then just walk away. However unlikely it was, it was also *possible*, and if it turned out that way she'd need to get out quick. The train connecting with the Fishguard ferry on the days when it was running left Paddington at 0845, but there were plenty of others every day – might get on one to Cardiff for instance, and continue from there later – even a couple of days later, depending of course on the ferry connection.

If she *had* got away with it – had not been seen, identified – there'd be no reason they'd have the ferries watched, surely?

Monsieur Maurice wasn't there and wouldn't be until Tuesday, but the rather jolly Scottish girl of about Eileen's own age who told her this added that owing to a cancellation she could fit her in right away. She showed her an album of photos of different hairstyles, and agreed that what Eileen called a 'page-boy bob' might suit her very well.

'Although it's a shame – such lovely hair and so – abundant—'

'You could stuff a sofa with it, couldn't you?'

The girl's name was Caroline McSomething, and she did a good job, Eileen thought. Examining herself from all angles in the triple mirror: 'You wouldn't know me, would you?'

'As the lady who walked in here an hour ago I dare say not. But whether your husband will say it's an improvement—'

'I think it is.' Husband. Glancing down at her wedding ring. She shrugged. 'Cooler – that's the main thing.'

There'd been a *Daily Mail* on the arm of a chair in the customers' waiting area, but she'd ignored it. And passing news vendors on her way to Messrs Jones and Higgins she managed not even to see a headline. Safer not to, better to know nothing at all about it. There were reports of crimes every day in every newspaper in the land, why bother with yet another – when it had absolutely nothing to do with her?

At Jones and Higgins she found everything she wanted, although the hat, shoes and handbag weren't in the sale. She still came out on the right side of the ten pounds she hadn't used to pay for the Browning automatic – which she'd left hidden amongst her other things, in Cyrus Lane. On her way back there now: to change, disencumber herself of parcels, and transfer that and the money-roll into this new bag.

She was delighted with the hat she'd bought. Straw-coloured with a wide, floppy brim, it was very light and with a slightly forward tilt the brim shaded and partly hid her eyes. Keeping her lashes lowered would help too. And her shorter hair, no more than a neatly fitting black helmet now, exposed the length and slimnesss of her neck, imparting – she thought and hoped – a certain elegance. Low-heeled shoes took an inch or so off her height, and the very light, pale blue summer coat went perfectly with the rest of it. She did look – felt, anyway – like a different person.

Downstairs, before starting out for Cockspur Street, she made herself skim through Mrs Whitten's *Daily Herald*. She'd seen it each day, this far. A front-page caption read

FLAT THIEF CHECKMATED: Girl's Presence of Mind at Critical Moment . . . And below it, *TITANIC* DISASTER INEVITABLE, Board of Trade Warned Years Ago. She wondered, swiftly turning pages, how they could have foreseen anything of the sort, when the *Titanic* hadn't then existed. *Titanic*-type disaster, maybe. In which case why hadn't the Board of Trade insisted 'years ago' on introducing such regulations as might have averted the disaster – such as the provision of adequate lifeboat space for all on board? If they had, she, Frank and Tom would now have been together in Philadelphia with no worse enemies than the McGraths; the world would have been an entirely different place and she'd have been a different woman in it.

Frank's woman.

Which I still am, my darling. I only look a little different.

White Star, she read on the leader page, was having serious problems – labour problems, a strike by sections of the crew – in getting the *Titanic*'s sister-ship the *Olympic* out of Southampton, New York-bound. Departure had already been twice postponed; the *Herald*'s sympathies were with the strikers, naturally. Eileen couldn't be bothered to read it all; the *Titanic* was at the bottom of the Atlantic, had taken Frank and Tom down with her, these people could spend the next hundred years writing articles, it wouldn't change *that*. She was more interested in – for instance – WEST END TRAGEDY: Divorced Woman Fatally Stabbed by Husband. What she was looking for of course was Brutal Murder in Basement Flat – Police Seek Tall Irishwoman with Yellow Eyes.

Not yet, though. Not in *this* rag, anyway.

9

The pistol, small as it was, was too heavy to be carried in a pocket of her flimsy summer coat. She was keeping it in the new bag, which was slung on a plaited silk cord over her left shoulder. Might not be easy to get at in a hurry, she thought – the bag's mouth being closed by an elasticised drawstring. She'd have to hold it open with her left hand while delving in for the pistol with the other: and at an awkward angle. Might shorten the cord, she thought, have it waist-high rather the hip-high. Pausing before crossing Pall Mall to the White Star corner; noticing that the flag on the roof was still at half-mast. Traffic continuous in all directions, and the pavements crowded with people returning from their lunch-breaks. She'd had no lunch yet, and it would be too late for Charles Napier's luncheon room. Hadn't in fact organized it very well, would have to get a bun or something and a cup of coffee later.

She spotted the entrance to the passageway Charles had told her about. It would, for sure, lead through to the rear of the building. They'd have bins for rubbish at the back there, maybe a fuel-store for their office fireplaces, that sort of thing. She'd passed it now – hadn't seen into it, there'd been people in the way – continuing down towards Trafalgar Square.

On the far side of which was Charing Cross and the Strand and Milford Street, *that* alleyway – where the door might *still* be shut and locked? Well – hardly . . . Because although Judy had been able to keep her key for a week, which didn't suggest *frequent* usage of the place, the plain fact was that Lev would want to know what had happened to his friend and that key, and must have gone looking for him by this time.

Recalling that good resolution, though: wrenching her thoughts back to what mattered. Ismay: *all* that mattered, here and now. Stopping at the bottom of Cockspur Street, looking into Trafalgar Square for a minute, then turning in the straggle of other pedestrians to walk back the way she'd come. The new shoes were fine, still comfortable after her trek from Islington, and the hat was feather-light as well as shady. Walked quite slowly now, pausing to study brass plates beside doorways, here and there an inscription on a window – as if looking for a number or a name, a business – in order to justify stopping for a look into that passageway. Although this couldn't be the best of times – staff returning from lunch, the door in frequent use. The passageway was coming up on her right *now*. She paused, craned her head back to gaze up under the hat's wide brim at the half-masted house flag. She was a stranger here, a visitor to London – rubber-necking, Bill Dalby had called it. Looking around apparently aimlessly . . . No newsboys here today. She could see the staff doorway on the left about fifteen or twenty paces along that narrow slot. A ledge protruded, roofing it, and there was what looked like a single step up to it, the passage then continuing to a timber gateway and a patch of sunlight – at the back of the building, as she'd guessed, a yard.

See Charles Napier now, she decided, ask about the letter and spend some time in there, keeping an eye out through that window. She'd had her back to the traffic at that moment, was startled as a motorcar swerved sharply out of the stream of it and stopped within a few feet of her, with a squeal of brakes. She was facing it as the door swung open: her right hand inside the bag and on the pistol, left arm crooked to hold up the bag and those fingers holding its mouth open. But – striped trousers, dark jacket, a bowler topping a shortish, stout but youngish, jolly-looking man . . .

'Usual time, Thompson!' An instruction to the chauffeur: then, turning, almost cannoning into her. 'I beg your pardon—'

He'd raised his hat, continued across the pavement, and the car was pulling away. Chauffeur in a dark suit and peaked cap: looking to her right again she saw the tubby man pausing to glance back at her before vanishing into the passage. One of Ismay's colleagues, no doubt. She'd started up towards Pall Mall by then – hand *out* of the bag, bag swinging against her hip. Dress-rehearsal, she thought, rather pleased although nothing had been achieved – vaguely pleased on *two* counts, especially with her own quick and perhaps even quite deft reaction. She'd been startled, certainly – taken by surprise, the motorcar sweeping in so suddenly and quite possibly containing Ismay – but if it had been him she'd have coped, she hadn't panicked.

The stout man had found her attractive, was the other thing. There'd been no query or suspicion in that glance back, just normal male interest. From an individual of *his* stamp: conclusion being that she might get a similar reaction from Ismay, confronting *him*.

Cars, vans, buses growling on by. Look in that passage later, she thought; for instance, whether one might be able to pass right through and wait at the corner of the backyard – or thereabouts. And whether there might be an exit that way – back entrance to the building. She was still keeping an eye

on the passing traffic, looking back occasionally. Thinking
again of her swift reaction to that last one: the fact that if it
had been Ismay, by this time he'd have been dead.

She would have been dead too, of course: that would not
have been the kind of situation from which one could have
walked or run away. But the whole thing would have been
done with. No pain, either physical or spiritual, simply back
with *them*.

'You should have looked in earlier. I've only been back from
lunch about ten minutes. Yes, heavens, you should have
been, the "dish of the day" was Irish stew, begorrah!'

She was at that table in the window, and he'd come from
behind the counter to join her. She'd just stopped there with
a hand on the back of a chair, *expecting* him to come out to
her, and he had. Her own coolness a few minutes ago, her
new clothes and the chubby man's interest in her, had given
her a certain confidence. Telling Napier, 'D'you know, that's
a word I never heard used by any Irish person?'

'Begorrah?'

'That's the one. It's English music-hall Irish, not *my*
language.'

'Well – anyway – the stew was excellent. Tell me, did
you enjoy your first weekend in London?'

'I've been busy, anyway. All sorts of things. Letters to
write – yes, by and large—'

'You're looking most elegant, I must say!'

'Why, thank you.'

'Your hair – if I may mention one aspect alone—'

'I decided there was too much of it, for this warm
weather. But, Charles, I'm not here to waste your time –
I happened to be nearby, thought I'd enquire whether that
letter had been typed yet – the one to your man in Cork?'

'Regrettably, I can tell you it has not. Or it would have
been in my in-tray. Look – I'll find out—'

'No, don't. It's not urgent at all, and you did say Tuesday or Wednesday.'

'Ridiculous that it should take so long. One short letter. Fact is, things were upside-down last week, with the girls all up to their eyes in work, and now it's worse – *everything* at sixes and sevens!'

'Why? Still the *Titanic* aftermath?'

'Still a lot of that, of course, but most of it's stemming from upstairs. All sorts of comings and goings, and conferences up there, the girls are being worked like galley-slaves they say – oh, and the chairman's been in this morning!'

'Is that unusual?'

'Well – yes . . . A Monday, after all – and rumour has it the Board's been at it all weekend. Of course this strike isn't exactly helpful. The *Olympic* hasn't been able to sail yet – I dare say you'll have read about it. Although since Bruce Ismay's down there now—'

'Down where?'

'Well – Southampton—'

'He's gone down to Southampton?'

'Where the strike's holding up the *Olympic*. With him on the spot I'd guess it'll be settled quickly now. He does have a way of getting things done. And mark you, with the things they've been saying about him lately – he's dashed brave, in *my* opinion . . .'

Ismay had gone down there by train, apparently. Napier thought, but wasn't certain, that he'd be returning to London this evening. The strike *had* to be settled quickly; having that great ship held up was costing White Star thousands of pounds a day – and as for the inconvenience to passengers . . . 'But look here – tomorrow, how about lunch? Could you put up with Cecil Court again – at one? As my guest, though – please – and I'll have the letter for you, I swear I will!'

'Seems to me you need one or two more shorthaand-typists that you've got, Charles.'

'You've a point there, all right.'

'But if I came by rather earlier – even in mid-morning, say – might I wait here?'

Meaning at this table in the bay window. She added that she thought she'd have to be down this way quite early, to meet someone who'd be arriving through Charing Cross – so this might be handy . . .

'There's a hotel right on the station. Best place, surely. The problem *here* is that blighter Fawcett. *Such* a stuffed shirt. If it was up to me – why, of *course*—'

'I may just wander around a bit out there, then. Really, I only have to say hello to this person, then I'll be at a loose end. Anyway – Cecil Court at one – thank you—'

'I'll be counting the minutes, Eileen!'

He'd looked as if he meant it, too, his eyes fairly glowing at her. She attributed his enthusiasm to her new hairstyle; she'd noticed him looking at her neck and throat a lot. First the stout party, and now him. And the stout one had *not* been the first today, although she'd affected not to notice any of them . . . The Ismay news was, to say the least, depressing; the whole day to get through now, and nothing useful to be done with it. Just when the incident with the tubby man had given her new confidence . . . She could *see* it – her own quick dart across the pavement, and before he'd know what was happening the Browning in her gloved hand pressed against his chest . . .

In Pall Mall now, turning west. Thinking that the passage-way mightn't be such a good bet after all. With the chance of being seen and recognized, as well – by Fatty, for instance, who'd taken a good look at her and would know her if he saw her again, might well wonder why she was haunting the place.

Same applied to hanging around on the pavement, though. Possibly with *hours* to wait.

The answer dawned on her at Waterloo Place, when she was about to cross the road to the steps leading up to the statue of the Duke of Wellington. Since it was Waterloo Place, that equestrian statue *had* to be of Wellington – although she'd never heard of its existence or passed this way before. Brain beginning to stir a little, maybe? Anyway the idea struck her just as she was about to cross the road, and by the time she was climbing the stone steps – being eyed by two men in top hats passing close on their way down into Pall Mall – she was certain it *was* the answer.

One – be sure he was there, actually in his office.

Two, present herself at the staff door with a sealed envelope with his name on it, and insist on being taken to him, in order to give it to him personally. It was something he'd very much want to see, she'd assure them – or him, or her – and her instructions would have been explicit: not to put it into any hands but his.

'Instructions from whom?'

'That hardly matters. What does matter is that he'll *want* this.'

'And you are – if I may ask—'

'That doesn't matter either. Please . . .'

So then they'd take her to him and she'd shoot him.

This *was* Arthur Wellesley, 1st Duke of Wellington. Dublin-born, God bless him. Fine statue too. The horse was magnificent, she thought. She'd have the sealed envelope in her bag, show it at the door but hold on to it, not let anyone snatch it from her, in fact replace it in the bag until she was in Ismay's close presence.

She wondered whether it might be possible to fire the pistol effectively *through* the bag, from inside it. That way he'd get no warning at all: nor would anyone else who might be with them. But the real beauty of it was that there'd be no waiting, hanging around, waiting with no certainty at all hour after hour – even day after day, for God's sake – while Daisie's description of her was being prepared and then circulated to the newspapers: coming to the attention then, incidentally, of Reggie Deacon, Charles Napier, Mrs Craven, Mrs Whitten and half a dozen other residents of the house in Cyrus Lane. Oh, and the hairdresser girl, *she*'d see it.

It wasn't any stretch of the imagination, it was *real*. Would *happen*. In a few days at most, and would inevitably be followed by arrest, trial, conviction and death by hanging – for the accidental killing of an extremely unpleasant person in particularly sordid surroundings.

The most frightful ordeal imaginable, she thought. Truly *hellish*. And avoidable only by killing Ismay first, forestalling all that. Kill him, then oneself. Or rather *and* oneself, since it would be virtually simultaneous. And one could choose the time, initiate it oneself instead of all the hanging around and depressing lack of certainty. One thing she did have to take into account of course – and *not* in her control – was that Ismay had to be there, in the building, that she'd have to know for certain that he was, before she started.

Charles Napier was the answer to it, of course. He'd tell her tomorrow. Touch wood, she'd *do* it tomorrow. While one thing to be done today was to prepare the letter that she'd be bringing him. It would have to look like something important – not just some scribble, from an admirer or a detractor. He might well be wary of those, by now. From St James's Square she made her way up to Jermyn Street, where amongst a number of smart shops she found a stationer and bought half a dozen sheets of white cartridge paper and two similarly thick, crinked envelopes – about nine inches long, and two of them in case she made a mess of one – and in the evening in her bedroom, having borrowed pen and ink from Elsie Whitten, she wrote in a large, clear script on one of the sheets of thick, crinkled paper *In Loving Memory of Frank and Tom Maguire*, and addressed one of the envelopes similarly to *Joseph Bruce Ismay Esquire – By Hand*.

That was it. Direct and to the point and on the right lines at last – after three weeks that felt more like centuries. He wouldn't get to read these words, he'd be dead before he had time to open the envelope – and so would she – but others would read them and some of them would understand. It would make headlines, she guessed – unless White Star managed to hush it up. She sealed the long white envelope and put it in her shoulder-bag.

The pistol now. She took it out, and checked that the safety-catch was set to 'safe', *not* to the small red dot. She'd need to re-set it of course before presenting herself at the staff door. She was aware that there might be other points on which she should have been checking – the number of bullets in the magazine for instance, but she didn't remember how Tony had extracted it, and thought it would be safer to leave well alone. If she got it out for instance and then couldn't get it back in properly . . .

Safety-catch to the red dot, then point it – *push* it at him – and pull the trigger. Tony had said it held seven shots – she remembered thinking seven was an odd number – and one had been fired, so she had six in there now. That was, if he'd been straight with her, hadn't told her seven and actually put in only that one.

Knowing him – slightly . . .

She turned the pistol in her hand, to look into the end of the barrel. Angling it then so light could penetrate. There *was* a silvery gleam – like silver-plate, the colour of the nose of the bullet he'd shown her. So all right, count on having six. Shoot him, then step back, pointing the pistol at anyone else to ward them off, then putting it to to her head.

*   *   *

Tuesday 7th May, 1912. Elsie Whitten's *Daily Herald* reported
that a wax effigy of Captain Edward J. Smith of the *Titanic*
had been added to Madame Tussaud's collection, while the
Odgers' *Daily Express* headline was TURKEY AND THE WAR.
We Shall Fight to the Finish – Turkish War Minister on the
War with Italy. Also on the front page was SINISTER ASPECTS
OF THE IRISH HOME RULE QUESTION.

'Would you care to peruse this, Mrs Maguire?'

Mrs Odgers had seen her peeking at it across the breakfast
table. She added, 'You'd be welcome, I don't find much of
interest in it.'

'Well – thank you—'

'Irish Home Rule must matter a great deal more to you
than it does to us, I'm sure.'

Eileen looked quickly through that report. The Bill was
to be brought back to the Commons for its second reading
on Thursday. She skimmed over other pages. Nothing
here. Maybe they hadn't found it yet . . . But – *here* –
UNDERWORLD KILLING . . .

That didn't ring any bells either. But the ensuing report
did. By the second line of it she was reading intently, her
eyes racing down that column.

> Police are investigating the death by shooting in a base-
> ment flat off the Strand in central London of an indi-
> vidual identified as Anthony Henshaw, aged 30, from
> Bermondsey. Although no clear motive has yet been
> established the crime is being linked to Henshaw's
> alleged involvement in organized prostitution. He has
> also had convictions for other offences, and the flat in
> which his body was found on Sunday is owned by a
> former asssociate currently serving a 4-year sentence
> for larceny.

So *that* was – had been – Tony's name. Henshaw . . . And
they'd found him on Sunday. A straw to grasp at was that

the accent was on the so-called underworld – no mention of anyone else being sought. She folded the paper, smiled at Mrs Odgers: 'Thanks very much. I'm afraid poor Ireland's in for trouble.'

She'd come down Shaftsbury Avenue to Cambridge Circus and then down Charing Cross Road, was in Cecil Court just before one o'clock. She was poking through the books on that barrow when Napier hailed her: 'Mrs Maguire – Eileen!' Then: 'My word, Eileen, how fine you look!'

She put down a copy of M.R. James's *Ghost Stories of an Antiquary*. 'Summer clothes and a change of hairstyle, that's all.'

'Are you addicted to ghost stories?'

'I wouldn't say *addicted*—'

'But you *do* look splendid. I wasn't devising compliments, Eileen, you really *do*, it's plain and simple fact. *Especially* your hair now.'

'Well – as I said – it was simply that there was far too much of it. Thank you for the kind words anyway. How's your strike going?'

'Oh, it's over! Or virtually so. Word is that the *Olympic* will be sailing either tonight or in the morning. Which I may say is a huge relief. Think of it – that enormous ship full of passengers all getting angrier and angrier—'

'So your man fixed it, and now he's back with you?'

'Fixed it, but whether he's back with us yet – I haven't seen him today, that's all. But why—'

'Only wondering whether all the hoo-hah you mentioned might be over yet. You know, you said – sixes and sevens—'

'But I still don't know what it was about. Anyway – shall we go in, see what's on offer?'

The end of the long table where they'd sat on Friday was unoccupied; he gestured towards it. 'There again?'

'As good as anywhere.' It was frustrating that one couldn't be more certain, about Ismay. His presence being the first essential, and Charles Napier her one and only source of information.

'Very smart shoulder-bag, Eileen.'

She'd just moved it to her other side, not wanting to leave it between them where his hand might fall on it and feel the solidity of the pistol through the material. The letter addressed to Ismay was in there too. As well as Frank's money-roll with her White Star travel warrants and everything else of value. She pulled it closer still. 'It's a useful size, especially when one's on the move as I am at the moment.'

'How's the search for long-lost relatives getting on?'

'You may well ask. The answer is, it's not. I think I may as well give up.'

'Back to Ireland, then?'

'Where else? Find a job and start earning a living!'

The waitress told them, 'Beef stew with dumplings, carrots and mashed potatoes.'

'How does that sound to you, Eileen?'

'Well.' She smiled at the waitress. 'Sustaining?'

'It's that all right, missus.' Sad, spaniel's eyes on her wedding ring. Might she be assuming that Charles was her husband? Or did he *not* look several years younger than she thought *she* did? Alternatively, what might the woman think she was up to?

She'd nodded. 'Beef stew and dumplings would be splendid.'

'And for you, sir?'

'Yes, please.' A nod to Eileen. 'Just the thing, on a day as warm as this. But *faute de mieux*—'

'*Faute de* anything else, you might say.'

'I really do enjoy your company, Eileen. I hope you aren't thinking of dashing off to Ireland right away?'

'Well – fairly soon . . . Need a job, you know – I really *do* – and the sooner I start looking—'

'But – listen, I've two things to say. One, re the need for a job, I must confess I have *not* brought the letter of introduction with me. It's typed, signed and sealed, no-one's fault but mine I haven't brought it, I happened to be in a rush and left it on my desk. The solution of course is for you come back to the office with me, so I can give it to you.'

'All right, I will.'

'You don't mind?'

'Not at all.' Might get confirmation of Ismay's presence. Or absence. Presence, please God.

Charles was looking at her reprovingly. 'You haven't yet asked me what's the second matter of grave import to us both.'

'Heavens – is there another?'

'I did say two things—'

'Two beef stews.'

The waitress, delivering them – along with dumplings, carrots, mashed potatoes. Plus other essentials such as mustard and glasses of water. Finally they were on their own again: except that a newcomer had dumped himself at the table rather close to them, definitely in earshot. He was wearing flannel trousers and a heavy-looking tweed jacket: a burly man probably in his mid-thirties, with a chestnut-brown moustache and sideburns. He'd nodded pleasantly and muttered 'Good afternoon', and was now surreptitiously glancing at their plates of stew.

Nodding to the waitress, 'Yup. Do for me very well.'

'All right, sergeant . . .'

Eileen *thought* that was what she'd called him. Unless it had been some name that had only sounded like 'sergeant'. She supposed the woman would get to know her regulars pretty well. She asked Charles, 'I dare say some people come here day in, day out – for years, even . . .'

'*I'm* a day-in, day-out customer, more or less. But please God not for *years*.' He dropped his voice: 'About you and your plans, though. This is the other thing – will you at least still be in London at the weekend?'

'I'm not sure. It's only this morning I've begun to think I might call it a day.' Like him, she was speaking very quietly. 'Why, what's—'

'I have two tickets for a theatre on Saturday evening and I'd love it if you could come. A friend let me have them – he's been invited elsewhere, can't use them, but they're good seats and I'm told it's a capital show – a play by John Galsworthy entitled *The Pigeon*, starring Gladys Cooper – who really is stupendous, in my opinion – with Whitford Kane in the lead playing her father. It's at the Royalty. Kane's an artist and all the down-and-outs latch on to him because he's a soft touch – the "pigeon" of the title, I suppose . . . Anyway it's been running since the end of January and it's still getting full houses. Do say you'll come?'

'I'd love to – I *think*—'

She'd surprised him, with that lack of certainty. He asked after a few seconds, 'Does the decision – well, I suppose your departure – hinge on some particular development?'

'Not really, no. But I need time to think it out. Main thing is – well, just spending money, not earning any – and until I land some job no *prospect* of earning any—'

'How about resolving out of sheer kindness to stay for this next weekend at least?'

'Well.' For an instant she'd met the hairy-faced man's eyes: brown eyes, fixed on her. She'd looked down at her plate. Aware of being utterly duplicitous. She shook her head: 'May I decide tomorrow? Tomorrow morning?'

'Lunchtime. *Here*, again!'

'Charles – now *look*—'

'And don't imagine that your departure from London is going to stop *me* in my tracks either!'

He'd said that quite loudly, and she saw the whiskered man react to it – smiling to himself, glancing at Charles and away again. Charles's tone being so importunate, she supposed, his expression so ardent. The waitress arrived then, bringing the man his stew. He was telling her something while she set things down around him; Eileen heard him chuckle, then the woman's comment, 'You're a cynic, Sergeant, that's what *you* are.' Then she'd gone, and he began to eat – very purposefully. He wasn't going to eavesdrop much from now on, she guessed. Forking stew in with one hand, pulling a watch out of his pocket with the other, to check the time. Re-doubling his efforts then, swallowing the lumps of beef almost whole; evidently a race *against* time. She whispered to Napier, 'I'll decide tonight and tell you tomorrow. I'd love to accept and I hope it may be possible – and it's sweet of you to ask me. *Thank* you, Charles.'

She meant it, and felt sad that after she'd done what she had to do this afternoon – or tomorrow, if it had to be delayed – he'd never *believe* she'd meant it. He'd think back to this conversation, think something like *Perfidious bitch* . . .

Too bad. She liked him; in other circumstances they might have become good friends.

'Jam roll, missus?'

'Well, heavens . . .'

The man in the tweed jacket had glanced this way in sudden interest – like some animal distracted momentarily from its efforts at the trough. Napier told the waitress, 'Yes. Two, please.' He added quietly, 'You must, Eileen!'

'But I'll have no room at all for supper!'

'Oh, hours ahead!'

She thought, *Hours – or an eternity* . . .

*   *   *

Arnold Collindale had saved a halfpenny by showing the bus conductor his warrant card. He was still regretting having had to pass up that jam roll. In fact for having started his lunch so late. If it had been only the old tart whom he'd arranged to see here at two p.m. – at New Scotland Yard, on the Embankment – he'd have let her damn well put up with it, but he was due to see Willy Tait right after that, and Willy didn't like to be kept waiting.

He lumbered in through the linoleum-floored hallway and asked the constable at the desk, 'Female by name of Lane?'

'In the small interview room, Sarge.'

Birdie Lane: still a tart but well past it, more than ready to pick up a bob or two any other way. She was smoking, and there was already one fag-end in the ash-tray.

'Birdie Lane? We met, didn't we?'

'*Didn't* we.' Stubbing that one out – wet and squishy beside the other. 'When you was a new boy on the beat in Battersea. Green as grass, as I fondly recall!'

He'd removed his jacket; was sitting now, facing her across the table. Wet patches under the arms of his shirt.

'Battersea. A while ago, *that* was.'

'Put a bit on since then – eh, Arnold?'

'It's Sergeant Collindale now, Birdie.'

'But something I got, you'd like to 'ave, they told me. Cheap at ten bob, Arnold. I mean, Sergeant. Since you won't get it nowhere else, *and* it's the name you want?'

'Five bob's still the jackpot.'

'Mean as ever, still.' She shrugged. 'All right, five bob. But strewth—'

He'd nodded, reaching to unstick his shirt from his back and shoulders. 'I'm all ears, Birdie.'

'Judy, they call her. Judy Simpson. Little rat of a thing.

Lives in Southwark – Plastermill Street, next to the green-grocer's. She 'ad a key to that basement and she took another person of my acquaintance along with her one afternoon.'

'Which afternoon?'

'Tuesday or Wednesday last week.'

'Another female?'

'Yeah. Foursome or threesome—'

'Go on.'

'Well – Judy's dad give the key back to Lev sometime Sunday. Judy lent it to another girl, and she'd only brought it back Sunday morning. *That's* the one you oughter be asking questions of – right?'

'*She* got a name?'

'Best ask Judy. But she give the key to Donny – Donny Smithers, Judy's dad – on account Judy wasn't 'ome, Sunday.'

'Smithers, and his daughter's Judy Simpson?'

'Must've been married, mustn't she?'

'When did the one whose name you don't know get the key from Judy?'

'Could've been Saturday, could've been Thursday or Friday. *Must*'ve 'ad it Saturday though – else how'd she've brought it back Sunday?'

'And how do you know this?'

'From my friend – the one was there with Judy. Sunday she sees Judy, says oy, you still got that key, what about it?'

'What about what?'

'Lettin' her 'ave it. Don't ask me for what, I'd 'ave to guess. See, this was in Plastermill Street Sunday night. Judy says all right, goes to get it for her, and Smithers tells 'er Lev come for it earlier.'

'Quite a rigmarole.'

'Whatever that is, when it's at 'ome . . .'

Collindale knocked on Inspector Tait's office door, and went in. Tait stubbed out a cigarette, simultaneously sucked up the dregs of a cup of tea or coffee, wiped his droopy lower lip with his fingers as he glanced at the clock on his mantelshelf.

'Kept you, did she? Overwhelmed you with her charm and sparkling wit?'

'They all do, don't they?'

'What else did she have for you?'

Collindale told him, 'Another prostitute, name of Judy Simpson, from Plastermill Street in Southwark—'

'I know her. *And* her father. What about her, though?'

'She had a key – from Lev – to Bailey-Johnston's place – had it all last week but she lent it – *lent* was the word – to another female of that ilk as yet un-named. This one had it Saturday and took it back to Judy – well, to her address, she gave it to the father – Sunday morning.'

'Ah, *well* . . .'

'Want to talk to that one, don't we. And Judy'll talk to *me* all right, Lev wouldn't like to hear she was letting his key out on her own account. I'll get along there right away – if there's nothing else now?'

'Who knows, you might wind up talking to an Irish whore nine feet tall with yellow eyes.'

'Well – *might* . . .'

'Be a nice surprise, wouldn't it. Reckon it would be to Lev, an' all. But what we've got *here* meantime, is this.' A printed form with some spaces filled in in ink and others ruled through. 'The report on our spent cartridge-case.'

'Three-two, eh?'

'Right – and from an automatic, not a revolver. Best bet is it might've been a Browning. My guess is we can believe Lev's yarn about Tony getting it for this tall woman who might or might not be Irish. If the one Judy puts you on to happens to even halfway fit the picture, bring her in. Wouldn't want her vanishing into the woodwork, would we.'

'Or to bloody Ireland.'

'North London, Sergeant, is where the Irish live.'

Charles had been gone a long time. Not that she minded; but he should have been about ten seconds, and he'd already been ten minutes. Eileen was sitting at the round table in White Star's bay window, wouldn't even have bothered to sit down except that Charles had been showing off his good manners, pulling out this chair for her and so forth, and as there was such a good view from here of the wide curve of pavement outside, and Ismay *might* have come bowling up in a taxi in the course of this half-minute or whatever, right under her nose: although if he *had* appeared out of a taxi now, this minute, she wouldn't have gone rushing out. She'd have known he was here, that was all.

A taxi *was* just pulling up.

'Eileen – so sorry . . .'

Charles had the letter in his hand. He'd had only to retrieve it from his desk, he'd said, and he'd been away long enough to have written it from scratch. And now instead of just giving it to her he was turning another chair around, as if to join her. Two women in flowery bonnets meanwhile descending from that taxi . . . 'I'm frightfully sorry to have kept you—'

'Doesn't matter in the least.' She took the letter from him. 'Thank you. But what did keep you – the Big White Chief's return from Southampton, was it?'

'By no means. That's very much the point, in fact . . . While I think of it, though – ' he gestured towards the letter – 'that envelope's not stuck down – so you can see how it's worded. But listen – the thing is, *I'm* off to Southampton now. Now, literally this minute. The strike *is* settled, but the

Big White Chief as you call him is still down there, holding court apparently on board the *Olympic*, and our chairman wants these papers delivered to him right away. So—'

'Will you be coming back tonight?'

'Can't say. Maybe in the morning – milk train. Anyway, I'll be back in time for lunch, so Cecil Court at one, as agreed – all right?'

'Will you be bringing the great man back with you?'

'Heck, no.' Quick shake of the head, short laugh. 'Actually – well, there's a lot going on, but – none of it concerns *us*. I only just wanted to confirm lunch tomorrow and I very much hope the theatre on Saturday.'

'I don't know about that, Charles.'

'But you'll tell me tomorrow.'

'I may drop by here during the morning, to see if you're back. Otherwise—'

'Mr Napier?'

Fawcett's voice. Charles got up. 'Coming! Eileen, sorry about this. See you tomorrow. 'Bye.'

Why, she wondered, if the strike had been settled, would Ismay be staying down there? And – to her, the most crucial question – *for how long*?

10

She went on out, and turned up towards Pall Mall. Wishing she'd had her great idea a day or two sooner, and thinking that since Ismay wouldn't be back tomorrow, Wednesday, Thursday was the earliest she could hope for. And if not then – well, give it just one more day and you'd be into the weekend – still waiting, more and more nervously scouring newspapers.

If indeed they gave one *that* long.

Collindale checked at the greengrocer's first, then went to the next house along and banged on the door with its horseshoe-shaped knocker. He stood back then, watching the first-floor window until the girl appeared – or what he guessed must be her. Just a reflective change of pattern – *something*, at the edge of the rectangle of dirty glass. He waved to her – or it might have been her father – and she pushed the window up, asked him what he wanted.

'Miss Simpson? *Judy* Simpson?'

'Who wants to know?'

He took out his warrant card, held it up. 'New Scotland Yard. Spare me a few minutes, please?'

'For what?'

'Better inside, Judy. Don't worry, it's nothing *you've* done.'

The window banged down. The sergeant ran a thick forefinger around inside his collar. In this weather you'd have thought they'd have kept them open, at least upstairs ones. It had to be like an oven in there. Returning to the door, he heard her wrench the bolt back – then a key turning, and the rattle of a chain, and the door jerked open, inward – a little way. Pale, narrow face, small eyes. 'Little rat of a thing' Birdie Lane had called her, and she hadn't been far off the mark. 'Lemme see the card?'

He obliged. She was in a blue house-coat, bare feet showing under it – none too clean, and with lacquered toenails. She studied the card with an expert eye: would have been shown dozens and dozens no doubt, in the course of her professional career. She'd be about thirty, he guessed, looked nearer forty without her war-paint on.

A mean look, he decided. Probably the secret of her success.

'Sergeant Collindale.'

'Sharp eyes, you have. Your dad in?'

'What's 'e been up to?'

'I dread to think. But he and my governor knew each other, one time. Matter of fact, he knew you too – don't ask me how. Name of Tait – inspector. Dad in, did you say?'

'Resting. Like I was. Yeah, I know Willy Tait.'

'He'll be flattered that you remember him, I'm sure. I interrupted your hard-won repose, did I? Anyway – now you're up, may I come in? It's an inquiry we think you might help us with, that's all. Five minutes'd likely do it.' He glanced round at the greengrocer's boy, who was watching and listening with a shoulder against a lamp-post. 'Preferable to airing your doubtless profound knowledge for the entire neighbourhood's edification, eh?'

Backing in, still clutching the door. 'Talk funny for a copper, don't you?'

'I might say you *look* funny for a *femme fatale*, love.' Passing her, smiling indulgently. 'But I won't. Takes all sorts, and beauty is in the eye of the beholder, so they say. Once the beholder's paid his whack, you're home and dry – right? Go in here, do we?'

She shut the door, and followed him into the front room. 'Five minutes, you said.'

'If you're quick with the answers, that should about do it. Don't mind if I take the weight off, meanwhile?' He sat down at a small, square table with a maroon-baize cover and a round lace doily in the centre. There was a pervading smell of mothballs. 'I should mention, while I'm at it – ' he'd opened his notebook on the table, was writing the date and time, and her name and address – 'should acquaint you with the fact, my dear, that this is a murder inquiry – '

'*Murder?*'

' – and that failure to reply truthfully and fully to questions would constitute a very serious misdemeanour. Not that I'm implying that either you or your father could have been implicated in any way in the crime itself.'

'Tony, you're on about.' She sat down, facing him across the table. 'Tony Henshaw. Someone shot him, we 'eard.'

'Heard where – who from?'

'Well – common knowledge. Who *exactly* told me—'

'Your friend Lev perhaps?'

'Lev?'

He began tapping with the pencil. 'Judy, you are bearing in mind the extreme seriousness of this inquiry, are you?'

'Might've been 'im told me, I s'pose.'

'You had one of his keys to the flat, Judy. You are one of the people who had access to that stinking hole at the relevant time. You had the key from – oh, Tuesday or Wednesday last week, and you certainly had it on Saturday and Saturday night, which was when your friend Tony got knocked off.'

'No.' Shaking her head. 'I never.'

'But you did, Judy. You obtained the key from Lev earlier in the week, and he collected it here from your father on Sunday.'

'*He* tell you that?'

'No. Because if he did he'd be admitting his involvement in prostitution. No – the person who told us was with me in an interview room in New Scotland Yard only an hour ago. *Now* what do you say?'

She might call his bluff, of course. But he didn't think she was that sure of herself – or of her friends, probably. They were all rats, when you came down to it.

She'd shrugged. 'I lent the key to another girl. She brung it back Sunday.'

'Good. I knew that, as it happens. Except you say you lent it, what you mean is you *rented* it to her. Lev of course doesn't know you were doing that. So it's just as well from the point of view of your close friendship with old Lev that this other girl *did* bring it back here before he came for it. Right?'

'Not really. I was out meself, could've 'ad it with me. *Would*'ve, if I 'adn't done her the favour.'

'Can you guess what I'm after, Judy?'

'You want her name.'

He poised the pencil: 'And address, while we're at it.'

'Don't know her name *nor* her address. She's a person I met in the street, like. Oh, I don't mean just the once, seen her *often* – passing the time of day like, not—'

'You're lying now, Judy. You wouldn't have trusted her with the key if you hadn't known her. Hand out a key belonging to Lev to some female you didn't even know the name of? Then again, you wouldn't have seen anyone that often and *not* got to know her name, would you. At least *a* name. And she knew *your* address – brought the key back here, remember?'

'I can't explain that no more'n I can give you a name I don't 'ave – *Sergeant*.'

'I hate to say it, Judy, but you're still lying – also withholding information pertinent to my inquiries into a case of murder. I did warn you, didn't I. Apart from which—'

'Daisy couldn't've 'ad nothing to do with it. They was *friends*, she and Tony!'

'So you're saying now—'

'I'm not giving out names, I'm tellin' you she wouldn't *never*—'

'We'll take that as read. Daisy, though. Surname?'

'No, that I *don't*—'

'Surname of this Daisy?'

A long breath, shake of the ratty head: 'Look – Sergeant—'

'Want to come along to the Yard, Judy? You *and* your daddy?'

'Adams.'

'Daisy Adams. Address?'

'That I definitely *do not* know.'

'Put it this way, then. If she still had the key, or owed you for it, where would you go looking for her?'

'St Clement Danes. Round there. Evenings, that is. Other times, no idea.'

'How come she had this address and you don't have hers?'

'Told 'er where to bring it back, o'course.'

'Next to the greengrocer's, Plastermill Road. Easier than remembering numbers, I suppose. But one more thing I want, Judy – and let's see if we can manage it without a fight. What does Daisy look like?'

'Blonde. Well – artificial blond. About my height, or – yeah, couple of inches taller.'

'Five-five, say?'

A nod. 'And full-figured, you might call her.'

'All bum and bosom, you mean. Pretty?'

A shrug. 'Wears a lot of rouge an' that.'

'Age?'

'Same as me, near enough.'

He wrote, 30+. Glancing at her again: 'But you definitely wouldn't describe her as *tall*.'

'No. I *said*—'

'Has she always been dyed blonde?'

'Far as *I* know – remember—'

'And *still* is?'

'Yeah. *Course* . . .'

Eileen had a cup of tea with Reggie, but she didn't stay long. He was amazed at the change in her appearance, especially her new hairstyle, but despite his compliments she had the impression that he didn't entirely approve, perhaps felt she'd distanced herself from him somehow. Which she supposed was the truth. He had plenty of work on hand, apparently. He hadn't called round on Sunday when she'd been lying down, but he'd sent a note regretting that he hadn't been at home when she'd dropped in that morning; this was the reason for her own visit to him now. She told him what she'd told Napier – that she was thinking of giving up her current efforts, and getting back to Ireland to start looking for a job, and promised him she wouldn't leave without saying goodbye.

Crossing fingers mentally: thinking that it would depend on the manner of her departure. Ismay's absence, and having no idea at all when he'd be back – or what might or might not be happening elsewhere – wasn't exactly making for peace of mind. She was tense and distracted at supper, and Mrs Whitten was sensitive to it, overly solicitous. To Mrs W of course she was the stricken young widow: who after such dreadful experiences *wouldn't* be a bag of nerves? Which was valid enough, except that the worst of *those* memories really only returned in sleep now, the nightmare sessions; in waking hours they were buried under more immediate concerns. She went to bed telling herself – trying to convince herself – that Ismay *might* return sooner than Charles Napier had thought he would. If for instance it had been a meeting of some kind that he'd needed those papers for – then it would be over by tomorrow, surely. Again – fingers crossed. It wasn't the sort of thing you could *pray* for.

The *Daily Express* on Wednesday morning carried another report of the continuing *Titanic* Inquiry. TITANIC'S BOATS: STRANGE EVIDENCE Crewmen Not Knowing Where Their Boat Stations Were . . .

She skimmed the account rapidly, under the eyes of Mrs Odgers. On her own she would hardly have bothered to read it; she was expected to show a burning interest, though, had to play the part. As with Reggie. One was dissimulating, in fact, virtually all the time. Simply because it had *happened* – Frank and Tom had drowned. Or *had been* drowned, was closer to the truth. The papers could have splashed that across their front pages in banner headlines, and thereafter dropped the subject altogether.

'Yes.' She nodded to some comment from the Odgers. They looked like two cats, she thought. Nothing to do with their eyes – but their cosiness, complacency. She confirmed, 'There *was* a lot of – well, confusion . . .'

'I dare say you'd sooner not be shown—'

'Oh, no – thank you, you're very – considerate . . . If I might just skim through . . .'

'Of course – *please* do.'

And there it was: MURDER IN LONDON BASEMENT FLAT.

Police investigating the shooting at the weekend of Anthony Henshaw are believed to be pursuing a line of enquiry from which an arrest may be expected soon. Henshaw, who had convictions for involvement in prostitution 'rackets' and for common theft, was found shot through the heart in a flat owned by a former associate of his who is currently serving a hard-labour sentence on Dartmoor. He had been shot at such close range that his clothing had been scorched by the discharge of the pistol. His killer is believed to have been female and to be known to others in the circles in which he conducted his loathsome business.

She turned the rest of the pages – pausing at the Fashion section – then handed the paper back to the Odgers. She thought the tone of that report was encouraging – if it *was* the way the police were thinking. Clutching at straws? she wondered. But there was Elsie Whitten's *Daily Herald* to look at then, with yet another *Titanic* Inquiry report. A Dockers' Union legal representative had questioned witnesses, and a lawyer by name of Harbison, said to be representing 'a number of third-class passengers', had stated that he could find no trace of any discrimination. He, Eileen thought, ought to have been on the wrong side of one of those locked gates. She turned the page; breakfast was over by this time and she was on her own, could study the crime reports at her leisure. Could have – but there was no mention of the Henshaw killing.

Daisy Adams lit yet another cigarette. 'Keepin' it quiet, are you? Next to nothin' in any paper *I* seen.'

Collindale's brown eyes rested on her pudgy, sulky face. This was the same small room in which he'd interviewed the other one. He told Daisy, 'There's been mention of it. They'd like more than we're ready to give them yet, that's all. Softly, softly, catchee monkey's the policy on this one.' He was toying with a pipe which he'd filled but hadn't lit. 'But if you're going to pretend you didn't bloody know about it—'

'*Course* I knew about it!'

'Just from street gossip?'

She'd been picked up near St Clement Danes at midnight and given a cell for the night, and breakfast. Collindale had explained that since she hadn't come forward voluntarily, despite knowing of the crime and having had access to the scene of it on the night in question, Inspector Tait had been concerned that if left loose she might make herself difficult to find, and had therefore arranged for her temporary detention.

'*Only* street gossip, no *other* way of knowing?'

'Not until now from you lot!'

'But none of us would have told you anything you didn't already know. The fact is, I have good reason to believe you know as much as anyone. If I'm right, that means that from the moment you learned Tony Henshaw'd been murdered you've been holding out on us. It's called withholding evidence – alternatively, accessory after the fact. Even *before* the fact maybe?'

Shaking her blond head – blond with dark roots. She'd been combing it when he'd arrived to interrogate her, and the comb with peroxided hair in it was lying on the table beside her paper packet of Woodbines and a box of lucifers. Shaking her head, expelling a plume of smoke . . . 'Don't know what you mean.'

'For a start, we know you were in the flat yourself that evening.'

'I was *what*?'

'You had a key in your possession and you used it. You

returned the key to Judy Simpson next morning. Not in point of fact to *her*, she wasn't there, you gave it to her father, old Donny Smithers. Thought you'd better get it back to Judy quick – in view of what had happened – right?'

'I didn't know *nothin'* 'ad 'appened!'

'You'd had the key since Thursday?'

'Might 'ave.'

'You *did* have. How much did Judy charge you for it?'

'*Charge* me?'

'Repeating bits of questions isn't answering them, Daisy. Answer this one now: are you denying you had the key on Saturday?'

'You know I 'ad it Thursday and took it back Sunday, so – yeah—'

'What happened Saturday night, Daisy?'

'What d'you mean? Oh – they *say* Tony got shot, but—'

'What made you so keen to hurry the key back to Judy on Sunday morning?'

'Trying to make out because I 'ad a bloody key I must've killed 'im?'

'We know you were in that flat Saturday night. How do we know? Well, say a little bird told us. And you denying it makes it twice as interesting that you went tripping off early Sunday to Plastermill Street when any other Sunday you'd be having a nice long lie-in. Daisy – unlike you, this little bird came of her own accord, and what she had to tell us fits in very nicely with the rest of it. See – main points, the kind of stuff that'd make a judge and jury sit up and take notice – number one, you were in the flat Saturday night and took care to get shot of the key bright and early Sunday – and as we both know – as will the said judge and jury also know – point two, a man with whom you are known to have been closely acquainted and to have had certain, shall we say, underhand dealings with happened to get murdered there that night – oh, by a female, we're very near certain—'

'You *can* be bloody certain!'

'Say that again?'

'Tony wouldn't've been there with a *man* friend, would he!'

'Come on, now. Wasn't what you started saying, was it. And what I was pointing out was you had a key – which you would not have had if you didn't intend making use of it, after all it was costing you money – and we've got this person who'll swear you *were* there that night. Well, Tony got himself shot by *some* female—'

'She was there with Tony. I'd *been* there, I was on me way out.'

'*Who* was there with Tony?'

'Irish bitch. Never seen her before. Hoity-toity.'

'Now maybe we're getting somewhere . . .'

'Why I took the key back Sunday was I met Tony there – with this Irish thing – so he knew I had Judy's key, and seeing as he's thick with Lev—'

'Daisy – hang on. Tell me about the Irish woman – where and when, exactly?'

'We was leaving the flat—'

'We?'

'Me and this old bloke – well, he was lonely, I'd said I'd keep him company a little while—'

'You're telling me – ' Collindale glanced up from his note-taking – 'that he was a friend of yours – or perhaps of your father's, if he was so old – you'd happened to run into him, and being a sweet, caring little creature you took pity—'

'All that, yeah. And we was just leaving when Tony comes – an' this Irish object with 'im—'

'What makes you so sure she's Irish?'

'Way she talks – what else? Like I said, la-de-da, an'—'

'Did you meet inside the flat?'

'In the area. I said – we was leavin', Tony shows up with this bitch—'

'Did you see her clearly?'

'Not so clear *there*, but later – well, clear*er* like—'

'You saw her a second time the same night, are you saying?'

'Yeah, I'll tell you—'

'Describe her, first?'

'Tall. Black hair – a lot of it. Eyes like a fucking cat's. You wouldn't miss 'er eyes, tell you straight—'

'You mean their shape?'

'No – colour. Well, shape too maybe, I dunno. But with that door open an' the light shining in 'er face – couldn't've been more than seconds, but – *yellow* eyes, I'll swear to *that*!'

'What time was this?'

'After nine. Not *much* after.'

'When you say "tall", *how* tall?'

'Six foot?'

'*Really.*' Scribbling away . . . 'You're doing well now, Daisy . . . What about her clothes?'

'Sort of a grey coat, patterned, an' a grey 'at. Grey or black. Little shiny 'andbag – it caught the light.'

'All right. All *right* . . .' Finishing, and glancing up, pencil momentarily at rest. 'You and your client were leaving the flat, and they went into it. Lucky timing for the change-around, one might say. Sure it wasn't pre-arranged, you hadn't been allotted times?'

'No, we 'ad not!'

'By Lev, for instance?'

'Lev didn't even know I 'ad a key!'

'No, that's right. He knew Judy had one, though . . . Anyway – did you actually see them go inside and shut the door?'

A nod. 'Then it was dark, there's no light outside.'

'What did you do then?'

'Took this geezer up into the Strand and got 'im a taxi. Then I took a walk like.'

'Feeling the need for fresh air and exercise.'

'Yeah. But this other feller in an 'ansom stops and asks would I fancy a ride. So – why not – nice evenin' and early still—'

'Was this another old one?'

'No, but I knew who he was. So would you.'

'But you aren't *saying* who he was.'

'Course not. Why should I, what's—'

'You gave him his half-crown's worth on the hoof, so to speak.'

'You got a nasty mind, Sergeant.'

'I'd call it a vivid imagination. Go on, what next?'

'Come back to where he picked me up, didn't I. St Clements, thereabouts. He'd paid the cabbie, see. Well, out *I* get – and who should come 'urrying, screechin' "Cab!" but the bloody duchess!'

'Duchess?'

'What I called her – on account of her high an' mighty manner. Irish, all right, but – superior with it, know what I mean?'

'Same one who'd been with Tony – you're certain?'

'*Course* I'm certain!'

'You got a clearer sight of her this time, you said?'

'Yeah. It's well enough lit there – must've been a street-lamp close—'

'And she took over the cab in which you'd so assiduously been earning your daily crust?'

'She got in the 'ansom, if that's what—'

'In and out of flats, in and out of cabs. Amazing. She didn't have Henshaw with her by this time, though?'

'Might've looked funny if she 'ad 'ad, mightn't it?'

Collindale blinked at her for a moment, then shook his head. 'You're assuming she'd killed him by then.'

'Stands to reason, I'd've thought.'

'Not entirely. Obviously it's on the cards. Did you have

any *reason* to think so – I mean, looking back on it now, how she looked or sounded – as if there'd been any rough stuff?'

'She wasn't 'anging about, I'll tell you that. Wasn't too glad to see me, neither.'

'She did recognize you?'

'Oh, yeah—'

'Did you speak to her?'

'I said 'ullo, and "Where's Tony, then?" an' – yeah, I remember, she just says, "God knows" and tells the cabbie, "Drive on, my man, I'll show you where to put me down" like.'

'Must have been cursing her bad luck, eh?'

'Serve 'er bloody right!''

'Would you know the cabbie again if you saw him?'

'Might. I dunno. *If* I saw 'im. But they're all alike, miserable sods. Them on the Embankment's the worst.'

'He could have been one of that lot. You've no idea which cab-rank he worked from?' She'd shaken her head. Collindale added, 'He didn't object to you plying your trade in his hansom, eh?'

'That was your idea, not mine.'

'You wouldn't want to identify the client either. Someone we'd all know, you said – an MP, or somesuch?'

She was stubbing out her cigarette. 'Somesuch.'

'And he'd be part of the reason you haven't come and told us all this before. But Henshaw having been your friend a long time, I'd have thought you'd *want*—'

'Didn't want to fetch up in court again, did I. Still don't.'

'Well.' A shrug of the heavy shoulders. 'Oddly enough, it *may* well not be necessary. Faced with this evidence – circumstantial though it may be—'

'Leave me out of it, could you?'

'Chances are she'd come clean. In which case, why not?

We'll talk again in any case, Daisy. I'll have this lot drawn up as a statement for you to sign, and—'

'Reckon you'll catch her?'

'If we find the cabbie. Any case, with that description – crikey . . .'

Eileen got to Cecil Court at one o'clock, and to her surprise and relief found Charles Napier already there. He looked delighted to see her too, and she realized that in a way she'd been missing him. But then a second thought – that what she'd been suffering from had been a sense of isolation, being cut off less from him than from Ismay. But either way she must have shown pleasure – relief – seemingly matching Charles's; he'd grasped both her hands in his, beaming . . .

'Heart grown fonder?'

'Go on with you. You haven't been away all *that* long. How did it go?'

'Oh, very well. He's a nice chap, when you get to know him. Poor fellow, I feel sorry for him, I really do. But come on, let's eat!'

'No breakfast?'

'Oh, yes. But a late night and it's a heck of a long way, slow train too. I confess I slept like a log, on the way back.'

'Big White Chief wasn't with you, then?'

'No. No . . . Actually it's an extraordinary situation.' He shook his head, pre-empting her next question. 'Company business, I won't bore you with it. The strike's finished, anyway, the *Olympic*'ll be on her way by now, everyone in the office is highly relieved, I can tell you. But what I want to know now is are you coming to the theatre with me, on Saturday?'

'Charles, it's awful of me and I'm sorry, but – I *still* don't know . . .'

Didn't know whether Ismay would be back tomorrow or Friday, was the crux of it. If he stayed out of reach she'd still be here but very much lying low, that was the point. Theatres were such public places: and by then God knew what might have been in the papers. All right, if he did show up and she got it done, it wouldn't matter a fig if she *had* accepted . . . Glancing at him again as he put the obvious question: when *would* she make up her mind?

'I'd better, hadn't I. But I don't want to say yes and then let you down.'

'Couldn't you simply decide you're going to, no matter what?'

'Well.' She sighed. 'All right, Charles. Just as long as I don't have to go out of London.'

'Out of London?'

'Well, to *meet* these people! If the mountain won't come to Mohammed?'

Frowning at her. 'But is that likely?'

'Probably not, but—'

'Then I'm going to assume you'll be with me. All right?'

'All right, Charles.'

'Well – hurrah! And come on inside now, nosebags on!'

'Our sergeant friend should be provided with a nosebag, don't you think?'

'Should indeed . . . Oh, our table's already crowded, darn it. How about over there? It's rather near the kitchen, but—'

'We'd be on our own, in any case. Nowhere else anyway, is there?'

'Maybe a bit warm, but – as you say.' A hand on her arm. 'But this is capital, Eileen! Except that it's sausages today, look. Can you stand sausages?'

'Sausages and mash?'

'Looks like it. And what's – oh, red cabbage . . . All right?'

'Absolutely!'

He'd signalled to the waitress that they'd have it. Murmuring as they settled down, 'I do wish we had a job for you here in London, Eileen. Awful to think I'll be lunching on my own again. Eileen, I *adore* your golden eyes!'

'Golden?'

'I dare say you'd tell me they're light brown – but when there's light in them – sunshine, whatever – or when you're laughing or excited—'

'They're just ordinary. Brownish. Anyone's eyes shine in bright light, don't they? Tell me about the *Olympic*, Charles. She's about the same size as the *Titanic* was, isn't she?'

'Near enough. The *Titanic* was forty-six thousand tons and the *Olympic*'s forty-five. Same overall length and beam exactly. The main difference, what had everyone so impressed, was the internal décor – furnishings, carpeting, cabin fittings and so forth. Mind you, the *Olympic* compares well with any other liner afloat today. *And* she's the biggest now.'

'You went aboard her last evening, did you?'

'Sausage and mash for two.' The waitress, with her loaded tray. 'Good afternoon, missus. The sausages is pork, they're all saying they're very tasty.'

'I'm sure they are . . .'

'Tell me.' Charles hesitated: 'No – never mind, I can see you're much busier than usual—'

'Not all *that* busy—'

'Well – our neighbour yesterday at the table over there – you called him "Sergeant" and he ate like – well, we wondered, might he have just got back from the South Pole with Captain Scott?'

She laughed. 'Not *quite* his style, that wouldn't be. Likes his comfort, that one does.' Leaning closer, she told him quietly, 'He's a bobby. Sergeant – New Scotland Yard – *murder* squad. Would you credit it?'

'Good Lord . . .'

Eileen was filling her glass with water from the jug. Eyes lowered, and shielded from the light – she hoped – by their dark lashes. The waitress telling them, 'Arnold Collindale's his name, old friend of my 'ubbie. It's my 'ubbie does the cooking here, see. He cooks, I wait. He does the buying too, mostly.'

'Was he a bobby too?'

'Well, he *was*, one time!'

'And this place is yours?'

'The business is. The premises is rented.'

'You give excellent value for money, I must say.'

'Why, thank you, sir . . .'

Charles muttered, 'Murder squad, indeed . . .'

'What you were saying about the *Olympic*, Charles – Big White Chief was living on board, was he – so you went on board to see him?'

'I did indeed. Ship's full of passengers, of course, all grousing like mad, but there was a suite available and he'd ensconced himself in it. He was greatly relieved at getting the papers I took down, made me very welcome.'

'To do with the strike, were they?'

'Well, the business generally . . .'

'So what's he doing now – if as you say the ship's gone by now?'

'She'll have steamed out on the morning tide. About eleven. What Bruce Ismay's doing – that's not my business, really.'

'How d'you mean?'

'Scrumptiously spicy sausages, don't you think?'

'Delicious. But how is it not your business, if it's company business? Sorry, I'm just curious – but you work for the company—'

'Not really for me to discuss, I should have said. Things have been really darned unpleasant for him, you know. While one can well understand that to someone like your-self—' He'd checked himself: looking over towards the door. 'I say . . .'

She'd seen him too: the murder squad sergeant. There were two other men with him: but it seemed no room at any of the tables. The waitress/proprietress had gone over: they were looking round for vacant places, or places that might soon become vacant . . .

Eileen was concentrating on her second sausage.

'These *are* good.'

'Our sergeant's leaving. He *and* his posse . . . Poor chap, he'll be famished – and imagine what *that*'ll look like! What I was saying – Bruce Ismay's taken it all on the chin, but—'

'Speak of the devil, eh?' The waitress. On her way to or from the kitchen she had to pass this way.

Charles asked her, 'Weren't you frightened he might arrest you?'

She pointed with her head. 'They'll go up the road a ways – place up there at the circus with a licence, little bit more of a walk, that's all.'

'Wouldn't it be worth your while to get a licence?'

'Might be, might not. "Keep it simple" is our motto. So we can handle it on our own – as we *can*, like this. Enjoying your meal, dear?'

'*Very* much . . .'

Napier murmured, 'You've been promoted. "Dear" instead of "missus". That's a significant advance. You've *arrived*, you might say.'

'What were you starting to say just then, about the Big White Chief?'

'I don't know . . . Oh, about the poison-pen letters . . .'

'Is he still getting them?'

'Not from now on, anyway. At least, one might hope

not. Look – Eileen – I *will* tell you. If you can keep a
secret? There'll be an announcement before long, but in
the meantime—'

'Yes?'

'Fact is, I mentioned you to him, anyway.'

'Mentioned *me*?'

'I had a meal on board with him, you see, and we were
just chatting. I told him about the frightful time you had,
and – frankly, how brave and level-headed you are. We
were talking quite personally – despite the fact that he's
senior enough to be my father – but being on our own, and
the situation – as I said, no sort of *formality*, d'you see—'

'I don't, really.'

'Well – the mention of you was I suppose *partly* to do
with the business – the letter of introduction we've given
you – you going back to Cork, looking for a secretarial job
and so forth – and, as I say, all you've been through – my
point being I suppose that not everyone spends their time
writing poisonous accusations and so forth. To which his
reaction was something like "My dear Napier, you should
have sent her to *me*! Except – well, in practical terms, no,
I'm going to be the deuce of a long way from Cork!"' He
saw her continuing mystification, shook his head. 'Sorry –
I should have explained to start with—'

'I wish you would!'

A nod. '*Strictly* under your hat, mind.' Leaning closer,
and speaking *very* quietly. 'He's thrown in the towel.
Resigned. Buying a place in the west of Ireland. How do
you like *that*?'

Staring at him. Struggling to comprehend, believe this . . .

'*Where* in the west of Ireland?'

11

The train rocking, drumming westward, Eileen avoiding eye-contact with other passengers – with anyone at all, that she could help. On the platform at Paddington she'd sat huddled on a bench, doing her best to look small – easier sitting down, it was her length of leg that contributed most of the extra inches – while covertly looking out for policemen, uniformed or otherwise, even for the sergeant from the luncheon-room. Ridiculous, paranoiac, she suspected; that individual probably had nothing at all to do with any Henshaw investigation, he'd certainly taken no noticeable interest in her the other day. Had seemed amused by Charles's ardour, that was all, listening to *him*. No earthly reason they'd have been watching train departures from Paddington anyway; only Charles, Reggie and Mrs Whitten had known she was leaving London, as far as she knew no one else would have the least interest in her movements.

It was how one *felt*, that was all. Those news reports having referred to police inquiries being in progress, and the fact that Daisy, the blond prostitute, had made so much of her being Irish, and this railway line one might say the highway to Ireland. But then again, they'd also know that if she was making a run for it she could have left days ago:

and could have travelled by routes other than this. As Bruce Ismay had: he'd left in the *Olympic* yesterday mid-morning, and would have landed at Queenstown soon after dawn today. There'd been a few dozen passengers to embark there, Charles had told her, despite the majority of those who'd embarked there in the *Titanic* exactly four weeks ago having perished.

'We could have shipped *you* to Cork in her, if you'd been ready to leave and anyone had thought of it. Nice fast trip – and what, just a short rail hop from Queenstown into Cork?'

She'd nodded. Thinking of that short rail journey which she'd taken southbound so happily with Frank and Tom a month earlier: a month more like a lifetime. She'd asked Napier, 'Where is this place Costelloe?'

'Galway, he said. Out to the west from Galway town. Or should I say city?'

'City, yes. Costelloe Lodge, you said.'

'A fishing lodge, he explained. It's owned at the moment by a syndicate of which he's a member, but the others have agreed in principle to sell out to him. It's the best sea-trout fishing in the world, he said.'

'That'd be in Connemara, so.'

'Would it?'

'Out to the west from Galway, sure. Not that I've set foot up that way. He'll find it a benighted spot in winter I should say. What'll he do when he's not fishing, would he have thought of that?'

'He'll have quite a lot on his hands still. He's to be available for consultation on White Star affairs, and he's still a director of certain other enterprises. That's the reason he pricked up his ears about secretarial assistance. I suppose in Galway itself – it's a fair-sized place, isn't it?'

'There are several bigger. Cork, Dublin of course, and

Waterford, and – oh, Limerick too, up in the west there. Will your man be taking his family with him?'

'Yes, of course, but not right away. They've a biggish house here in London – fourteen servants, he mentioned – '

'Fourteen!'

' – and he hopes a dozen of them will make the move as well.'

'So the lodge must be of a fair size too, but the local people won't be so pleased. They'd be hoping for work themselves, I'd guess. There'd not be so much employment in those parts.'

'He's also taking a White Star steward with him, as his – well, steward, I suppose. Chauffeur, anyway – driving one of the cars over – by way of Holyhead and Kingstown, does that make sense?'

'It might, I suppose. Landing at Kingstown he'd have the road straight across to Galway right under his nose before him. Is it the luxurious contraption you spoke of that he's taking?'

She'd considered taking a train up to Holyhead herself, and crossing from there to Kingstown, thereby evading them if they had any way of knowing she'd had the White Star vouchers for *this* route. But to start with it would have cost her the fares – she couldn't have asked White Star – Charles – to have changed the documentation at this stage – couldn't have explained why she'd want it, especially as doing so would have meant revealing that she now had no reason or wish to go to Cork – and in any case she didn't see – on calm, logical reflection – how the police could have any notion of her connection with White Star.

Touch wood.

But they could *not* have. If they had, they'd have been there asking about her. But that yellow-headed prostitute could have given them nothing but a description – tall, dark, Irish accent, yellow eyes. A freakish-sounding figure of a woman indeed: and no longer, thank God, to be seen on the streets of London. Not that they'd know it until they'd searched for a month or two maybe. On the other hand if they did put it in the papers – for Reggie and Charles Napier and Mrs Whitten to see – and doubtless jump out of their skins – *that* might lead them to White Star.

Reggie wouldn't volunteer information, but Charles Napier one might feel less sure of. If they did somehow find tracks leading to White Star – through one of the landladies for instance, and the *Titanic* background which had so intrigued them all – and Napier was faced with the straight question 'Might this resemble anyone you've seen or dealt with recently?', would he find it in himself to say 'No, never'?

She doubted it. Not only because she'd let him down – telephoned him at White Star from Mrs Craven's house to say, 'I'm so sorry, Charles, but I have absolutely *got* to go down to Dorset – tomorrow, and I'll have to stay down there a day or two – over Saturday for sure . . . What? Well, there was a letter waiting for me here, d'you see, the one I've been waiting for all week . . .'

He hadn't sounded too pleased. And within a few days, by which time the railway and the Fishguard–Cork steamship company would have sent in their invoices with detached portions of the White Star warrants, he might be even less so. On top of which the other passenger clerks – including the stuffed shirt – would have seen her with him more than once; he might not be able to lie about her even if he wanted to. Which she thought he would *not*. By then, after all, he'd be conscious that she'd not only let him down over the theatre, but had actually lied to him and scuttled off. She could imagine him answering the man, across that White Star counter: 'Yes. Yes, indeed. She's back in Ireland now, though.'

In Cork, he'd say: and White Star had her mother's address in Skibbereen. She'd given it to them in New York and they had it in her file in London too. Which was most of the reason she'd no intention of going anywhere near Skibbereen or her mother. They'd try the Skib address sooner or later, for sure. And run into a dead-end. Mama would say her daughter couldn't be back in Ireland yet or she *would* have been in touch. But another thing she might mention was that Frank's mother Kate might have heard from her; so they'd get the Maguire address in Nenagh and check there. In which case it might be prudent not to visit Kate either – as she'd definitely been intending, up to this moment.

Think about it. Nenagh would have been a diversion *en route* from Cork to Galway; she'd have changed trains in Limerick. She really did want to see Kate: tell her everything, cry on each other's shoulders. In a way, cry on *Frank's* shoulder: Frank being of Kate's flesh and blood, with a great warmth of affection between them.

Eyes shut again as the train clattered westward: whispering in her mind I *will* go see her, Frank . . .

Reading, Swindon, Bristol, then under the Severn. In the dining car she had fish cakes with bread and butter and a pot of tea, and returning to her carriage she found that a fellow passenger, who judging by his bag of tools had to be a carpenter, and who must have got out at Newport, had left behind a copy of the *Daily Herald* – which, having left Mrs Whitten's house so early that morning, she hadn't as yet seen. The carpenter had left it folded small at the racing fixtures; returning it to its proper shape, her eye was caught and held by headlines standing out blackly on page 2: yet more of the *Titanic* Inquiry, she realized.

PUSHED OFF!
Startling Charges at Inquiry
'Tried to Rush the Boats'

Passenger Thomas McCormack alleged that 'after jumping from the *Titanic* and while swimming in the sea
he was struck on the head and hands by members
of the crew in a boat, and pushed off, in an effort to
drown him'.

Then, lower down:

Lord Mersey said he didn't think such a case came
within his jurisdiction.

There was no mention that she could see of the basement-
flat murder. The paper stank of the carpenter's shag tobacco,
though, and she only flipped through it quickly before
discarding it. Head back then, eyes shut, recalling this
train's route as shown to her by Reggie last evening when
she'd called at Mrs Craven's house to tell him she'd be
leaving in the morning, and he'd produced an atlas. After
Cardiff – Swansea, then Carmarthen. He'd told her, 'Might
pay you a visit myself one of these days. When I've saved
a bit. Keep your eyes open for a place where I could stay –
decent, but not expensive?'

'Oh, I'll know someone by then who'd put you up. But
there's an express train to Fishguard that might suit you
better. Starts later and links up with the boat to Kingstown
– the "Dublin Express" they call it. Must overtake my train
somewhere, maybe when we're stopped in one of those
places it'll rush through – Cardiff maybe.'

She'd taken this train, the 0845 from Padddington, because
she'd wanted to be out of London as soon as possible. This
being a Thursday too, and the Fishguard–Cork steamer
making one of its twice-weekly departures this evening –
so she'd be in Cork tomorrow, Friday, in the afternoon.

Ismay was about two days ahead of her, therefore.

She'd looked for Costelloe in Reggie's atlas, and not found it. There was the thinnest hairline of a road marked along that north shore of Galway Bay, and where it turned up northward and touched the head of a small inlet was where she *thought* Costelloe had to be, going by Charles Napier's recollection of what Ismay had told him.

At Carmarthen a fat woman got in with a heavy suitcase, and Eileen helped her push it up on to the rack beside her own. Sweating and gasping from her own share of the effort, the woman offered her a *Daily Express* to look at.

'Oh, well – thanks, but—' She'd indicated the crumpled heap of the *Daily Herald*, implying that she'd already absorbed as much of the day's news as she needed. In point of fact it was the *Express* that had carried all the reports of Henshaw's murder that she'd seen thus far: and more specifically than 'head-in-sand' Eileen felt that the last thing she wanted was any *bad* news now, that she was better off believing that if they were working on the case at all they'd be concentrating on that 'underworld' background, looking for some kind of *crook* answering to the blond prostitute's description.

'See this 'ere?' The woman slapped the back of her hand against the newspaper's front page. 'Huh? See *this*?'

PASSENGERS ALLEGE THEY
WERE LEFT TO DROWN

She'd glanced at it, and nodded.

'Dreadful.'

The woman glared as if she felt she'd been insulted. Taking that comment as sarcasm, perhaps.

'Ye don't care, is that it?'

'Why, not at *all*—'

'*Disgusting*, is what *I* says it is!'

Glaring at her. Angry, piggy eyes in the fat, sweaty face. Eileen nodded, agreeing with her: 'It is, so.' She could have added, 'And it *was*.' Then all about it. But Pig-face looked as if she wouldn't have been mollified; more as if she didn't hate you for one thing she'd loathe you for another. And if she was to be a fellow Fishguard–Cork passenger, you could guess she'd enjoy telling all and sundry on the steamer 'That one there was on the *Titanic*, would ye believe it!' One wanted neither to look like a fugitive nor to have oneself singled out for any other kind of attention. Glancing again at the woman, offering a small, placatory smile and meeting the same ferocious glare, she thought the creature was probably demented.

The sun was easing itself down somewhere over Ireland – but hidden by the high western promontory here – when the train chuffed slowly into the Fishguard harbour station. Passengers embarking in the steamer had only to cross the platform and the railway lines the other side of it, where there was a footway over with a slope for porters' trolleys and a guard on duty with a furled red flag; the fat, angry woman had stumbled on over, dragging her heavy case, and Eileen followed now in a general straggle of people but in company for the time being with a grey-haired Englishwoman, who was as tall as she was and had told her she was crossing to visit her daughter and son-in-law at Youghal.

Youghal being a seaside resort about twenty miles east of Cork – on the near-side of Dungarvan, Frank's trawler base when she'd first known him.

Up the slope now to a gap in a picket fence. There were sheds along this side of the quay, also the steamship company's harbour office. Eileen pointed with her head: 'That's where I go.'

'Perhaps I'll see you on board, then.'

'You will so. If they'll let me on.' A smile to tell her this had been a joke. The son-in-law worked in a whiskey distillery at Youghal, the woman had said, was an engineer of some kind. Eileen had just noticed that there were two policemen at the double-doorway entrance to the office where she was going to have to present her White Star document, dated 3rd May, in exchange for a ticket to Queenstown.

She had the Browning, loaded and set to 'safe', in her shoulder-bag, and was sorry to have lost the other woman's company. If they were on the lookout for anyone answering to her description they'd surely be looking for a loner, not for one of any group or pair; also, the other woman's height might have made her own less noticeable.

Why *two* policemen?

In fact, why *any*?

She murmured in passing the nearer one, 'Good evening.'

'Evening, miss!'

He'd shown surprise – maybe *pleased* surprise – at her having spoken to him. They'd been eye to eye in that moment: now she'd passed between the two of them. Tall, dark, yellow-eyed and Irish, but remembering her resolve – Eileen Maguire, widow of Frank and distressed mother of Tom, who'd never heard of any Tony Henshaw, never infringed any law, let alone committed murder. This was one of the moments in her transition from London to Connemara that she'd remember: as it were the deliberate insistence on her own identity and background but with the past week excised, as if it had never been. She was as she had been on arrival in Liverpool with old Reggie. All right, she'd had then and still had now the *intention* of killing, but – locked in her own brain, accessible to no one until it happened. The intervening week had gone – truly *had* – and she was conscious of an immediate and significant lightening of the spirit as she reached the boxwood counter and met the quizzical stare of the clerk behind it.

'Good evening, I have this document from White Star in London.'

He'd taken it from her, was studying it. A balding, thick-set man in a striped waistcoat and with his shirt-sleeves held back from his wrists by elastic bands – baring thick, very hairy wrists and forearms. More suitable for driving in fenceposts, she thought, than for fiddling with slips of paper.

'May the third.' An eyebrow raised: he'd glanced past her, at the doorway where the policemen were. 'And this is the ninth.'

'Yes. They spoke of re-dating it, but I was breaking my journey in Cardiff, you see, so—'

'It's of no great consequence, I dare say.'

'I'd hoped it wouldn't be.'

She'd said Cardiff because she'd felt he'd be more inclined to approve a stop-over in Wales than anywhere outside it. Counting on *his* blind eye. He'd found the flimsy duplicate of the voucher that would have come to him through the post, applied a rubber stamp to both and pushed them into a wooden tray behind him. Looking up at her again: 'A berth in a second-class cabin is your entitlement. The ship's about full, you *will* be sharing, see.'

'All right.'

As long as they weren't putting her in with the dotty one. He was making out the ticket: now applying a different rubber stamp to it – he had a whole battery of them – and scribbling on the counterfoil in the book he'd torn it out of.

'There now.' A friendly smile. 'Pleasant journey, Mrs Maguire.'

'Thank you—'

'You'll have a smooth one, by the looks of it.' He turned to his next customer, a clergyman. 'Yes, padre?'

Only the policemen she'd spoken to was there now. Maybe he'd been taking over from his colleague, who'd now have gone home to his wife and children. All routine, this, no trap for any murderess on the run. Over the roof of a cargo shed she saw the steam-packet's twin funnels and masts black against a peach-coloured sunset sky; also the head of a crane turning slowly. She passed through on to the quayside – there were still a few stragglers coming from the train – and saw they were loading motorcars, one dangling from that crane – being lowered now, plumbing the ship's well-deck – and two others standing ready. Reminding her of Ismay's being shipped from Holyhead to be driven across Ireland to Galway. Ismay himself on the train from Cork to Limerick by now maybe. Escaping his notoriety, public hostility. In essence, ashamed to be alive? She was at the gangway's foot, showing her ticket; a sailor snatched up her suitcase and the peak-capped official told her, 'Follow him, Mrs Maguire, he'll show you to your cabin.' She was still thinking about Ismay – that she'd be relieving him of *that* shame, all right. Using the letter of introduction from White Star, she supposed: at this Costelloe Lodge. Show the letter to whoever answers the door and ask to see him? From what Charles Napier had said, there should be no problem about that. In London there might well have been – getting past other White Star employees, but there'd be nothing of that kind, by the sound of it he might even be *glad* to see her.

'Here you are, missus.'

The sailor put down her case and stood back, indicating a cabin door, one of several in a small offshoot from the corridor they'd been following. He'd led her into the ship, down a stairway or two and round corners – she'd followed him barely noticing which way at all, thinking about – all that . . . She thanked him, knocked on that door and thought – hoped – she recognized the voice that called 'Yes?' and then 'Come in!' She was right – it was the tall woman with the daughter in Youghal.

'I'm so glad! They told me there'd be someone else – oh, but I've taken the lower bunk, if you don't mind—'

'Not at all. I'm glad too. That small, stout woman who glares at you – I had a dread—'

'Me too!'

'Well, *some* poor soul has got her!'

'She's probably quite harmless. I was just going up on deck – we should be sailing quite soon.'

'As soon as they get those motors stowed and lashed down, I imagine. Yes, I'll come up too.'

She wasn't mentioning the *Titanic*. When this Mrs Harrison enquired as to the circumstances of her journey she told her only that she had a mother living in West Cork, had been in England for a while but was returning now either to take up her old job again or to find a new one. Yes, *had* been married, was now a widow; she made it obvious that she'd prefer not to talk about it. The two of them moved about the deck as the ship manoeuvred to leave harbour: it was a lovely evening and the coastline and headlands were beautiful, but darkness was coming on and there was nothing to stay up there for. Nor did either of them want much to eat, in case of seasickness, but they went down to the dining room where they had ham with salad followed by cheese and biscuits, and the clergyman who'd been in the steamship office asked if he might join them. He and Mrs Harrison had met on the train, apparently. He was Church of Ireland, with his parish at Macroom in County Cork; he'd been talking with the ship's purser, who'd told him that according to a wireless broadcast that evening that the Irish Home Rule Bill had passed its second reading in the Commons with a majority of 94; 360 votes in favour, 266 against. In the course of the debate the Prime Minister, Asquith, had attacked the Ulster Unionists' threats of violent opposition, arguing that the British people were by nature just and generous and were not to be frightened out of doing what they knew to be right by 'the language of intimidation'.

'Mr Asquith said something very similar only the other day, I seem to remember.'

'Indeed. Indeed.' The parson agreed. 'Endeavouring to avert catastrophe, no doubt. And of course addressing himself primarily to Sir Edward Carson – whose recent utterances truly *have* been threatening.'

'That speech of his a few months ago in Omagh – eh?'

Eileen remembered Frank's angry reaction to it, but not precisely what Carson had said; one didn't really need to know, in detail, one knew the type of rhetoric. There'd been a great rally of Unionists who'd flocked there – to Omagh – from all over the North, in pouring rain, in carts and charabancs and marching on foot behind standard-bearers and beating drums, to listen to inflammatory anti-Home Rule speeches.

'What exactly your man said, I don't recall . . .'

'Well.' The parson grimaced. 'Much the same as he's been repeating since, I fear. That if the political system is not left precisely as it is, he and his supporters will *take matters into their own hands*. Those very words – which, coupled with the fact that the Orange Order has indeed embarked on a programme of military training, amounts to an explicit threat of violence. Of civil war, in fact – rebellion!'

'But you – ' Mrs Harrison had finished eating – 'you yourself, Rector, as a minister of the Protestant church in Ireland, surely—'

'No. I know what you're about to suggest, but I won't have that at all. The fact that the Ulster Unionists are all Protestants does not for one moment mean that all Protestants should be ready to defy the best intentions of the British Government and the wishes of the vast majority of the Irish people. That would be akin to saying that since all cats are animals, all animals must be cats.'

'I heard the Unionists were bringing in guns.' Eileen asked the parson, 'Do you think it's true?'

'Alas, it would not surprise me. It would logically accompany the Ulstermen's threatening stance. And you may be sure that if they do, so will the others!'

'Yes. I'm sure.' Eileen thinking of course of Frank; also of Reggie Deacon's discourse in the train from Liverpool to London a week earlier. She nodded. 'The person who was telling me – oh, just the other day, what you were saying yourself, about the Orange Order going in for military training – a very nice, quiet, elderly gentleman, an Englishman – *he* said why military drills, unless guns were coming? And exactly what you said then, that it might end in civil war!'

'But surely – ' Mrs Harrison – somewhat incredulously – 'simply because of drum-beating by the few in Ulster, would the Roman Catholic majority in the rest of Ireland actually take up arms?'

'Wouldn't you *think* they would?'

Eileen had said it. The parson nodding, mumbling to Mrs Harrison yes, yes, he feared that this was very much the shape of it. Eileen added, 'But for Home Rule as it's being proposed only as a *start*. My husband for instance – my late husband—'

'Your *late*—'

The parson quizzing her. She nodded. 'He maintained that the bill was a swindle – home rule only in domestic matters, not even a whiff of any move beyond that, *real* home rule. And why should Ireland be in the control of anyone but the Irish?'

'Ah, well.' The padre wagged his head. 'I don't believe I could argue a case for *that* degree of home rule. Perhaps in gradual stages *eventually* – a long, long time ahead, dear lady . . .'

'There are many who may not be so keen to wait "a long, long time", padre.'

'You say so? As a Catholic – am I right? And speaking from a depth of knowledge of your co-religionists—'

'As an Irishwoman, speaking of my fellow Irish.' She glanced at Mrs Harrison, who was looking startled. Then to the padre: 'Or you might say speaking as a cat who *is* an animal?'

Later, alone on deck, asking herself what on earth she'd meant by that, she came to realize that whereas when Frank had been alive his political notions and involvement had seemed to her a potential threat to their future well-being, now with no such future to be endangered she could afford to accept as her own view whatever *he*'d believed in.

Why not, when it was part of him?

She was on the ship's starboard side, which was the more sheltered side, the wind being from the south or southwest and the course westward, plugging out into St George's Channel. She'd told Mrs Harrison that she wanted a few lungfuls of fresh air, would be as quiet as a mouse when she came down later, do her best to get herself undressed and into that top bunk without disturbing her at all.

The ship was moving around a bit, but not excessively. It was what Frank would have called a flat calm: and *was*, she supposed, a very moderate sea.

Correction: a swell, was what it was. A low swell, at that.

But no argument, Frank, none at all. Although if I could wake up in your arms now and find this had all been nightmare and we were on course for New York and Philadelphia and the McGraths, I'd most likely feel as I did then. I admit – because you could read it in me anyway – it's still less my own conviction than it was yours, but I'd go along with it all right. And I'd know you were right when you swore you'd never been simply under those others' influence – that it was because you believed in it that you came to know them in the first place, not the other way about. And you said later – although I had no recollection of it then and to tell you the truth still haven't – that it was right at the beginning you first let me know of it – that early morning in the trawler in the harbour at Dungarvan, the weekend you'd got me down there from Cork with the Monday a holiday so I'd have that time off from work. And the first time ever – but not just your idea, mine too; it was in my mind within half a minute or even less from hearing you ask me, 'Want to see what the old boat's like inside, then? See, she's tied up not a quarter-hour's stroll from here, and only the boy aboard to watch the ropes, and I'll send him off for a beer or two or three. He won't hang about, believe me!' As no more he did. So we had the creaky old trawler to ourselves, and the oil lamp and that hard narrow bunk and us naked and your hands on me, the first time a man's hands ever and I cried, but not from hurt, from loving you, Frank love – loving us the way we were together – and wasn't it that night or the one after that Tommy was begun?

Frank's voice in the second dawn, she remembered, telling of his shame at how little he had to offer a wife and especially one like her, like he'd never met before or dreamed would give him a second look or as much as a minute of her time, but that it wouldn't always be so meagre, by God it would not, he'd make something of himself, make money and get somewhere, he'd had the urge in him ever since he and his father had split brass rags – *before* that, in fact, it had been at the roots of the row they'd had – but now he had ten times as much reason for it – meaning it would be for *her* he'd do it, he'd sewn all his wild oats and – *now*, see, I can't tell you how exactly, this fishing and sailoring is all I have open to me at the moment but from here on I'll use whatever skills I can pretend to or acquire like, use and build on and go from to something better – move on until I'm damn well *there* – and you with me, Eilie darling . . .

But the first mention of the politics that she did remember came in another, much later dawn – after they were married. According to her mother, she had defied her, shamefully rejected her advice and warnings and married grossly and wickedly beneath her – but there'd been a bit of a hooly at the place she'd lived at along with Betsy O'Flaherty – why, Betsy's twenty-first, of course – Frank with a skinful and a half and Eileen sure it was the drink talking, although she knew now it had been more just the drink loosening his tongue, to the extent he'd told her things which, sober, he'd have said weren't women's business, not even *his* woman's. He'd been rambling back over the other stuff, how by hook or by crook he *would* make it big, for himself and her – and the child that was by this time visible to them all: he'd make it to an extent that would *stun* that woman in Skibbereen. Meaning of course her mother. He'd finished, 'But listen now, Eilie, best you should know this too: what plagues me is to do my living best not only for myself and you and this small object here, but for my country, for the sweet love of Ireland and the freedom she and we ourselves have a right and a duty to – you know?'

Her first inkling of it, that had been. Pre-Toomey and pre-O'Meara. Frank's own reflections, conceived on bucking salt-washed decks in the black wind-torn Atlantic nights.

She'd turned her back on the ship's rail, tipping her head back to gaze up at the last quarter of the post-*Titanic* moon. Remembering that when he'd blurted all that out – there'd been more but she remembered only the gist of it, at the time she'd been concerned mainly to get him home to the two rooms they'd had then over a saddler's shop, and she'd nagged him into explaining it more lucidly later in the day

– what had forced up the subject in the first place had been that they'd just effectively turned down Matt McGrath's first invitation to Frank to join him in the business in Philadelphia – accepting with enthusiasm but asking for a few months' postponement because of Eileen's desire to have the child born in Ireland. Frank, for all his keenness to grab at the chance right away – the kind of opportunity he'd been praying for – had for her sake accepted what she now saw as a foolish and tragic whim. Foolish because they'd known Matt Maguire to be a hard man, whose response – turning them down flat, if they wouldn't come now, the hell with them – might have been anticipated, and tragic because if they *had* grabbed the chance there and then they would never have been on board the *Titanic*.

The last-quarter moon streaked the ebbing Thames. The cabbie had got down, leaned against the body of his hansom like a sagging scarecrow, stuffing his pipe with tobacco from the pouch Collindale had offered him. Black figures and cab-shape in silhouette against the river's soft reflected light, but with a street-lamp this side high-lighting the man's gaunt features and bony hands and the bulk of the constable who was standing near the horse's head.

'Remember her because I'd a mind to pack up by then, but she was aboard before you could'a said "knife". I'd dropped this young 'ore, see—'

'Sure she was a whore?'

'Huh.' Rolling the leather pouch and handing it back. 'You get to know 'em. Yellow 'air, this one 'ad.'

'And you let 'em thrash around in there. Good business, is it?'

'Business? I *never*—'

'You'd dropped her, you say – the client had paid you to bring her back to where the two of you had picked her up.'

'Wasn't like that, Sergeant.'

'Who told you I'm a sergeant?'

'Why, *'e* did!'

The constable who'd been waiting with him, while the other one had gone to a telephone to call the Yard and hadn't yet returned. Collindale said, 'Tell me about the one who took over from the blonde, now.'

'She wasn't no 'ore, I'll swear to that.'

'But you wanted to knock off, and before you knew it she'd jumped in. Would you know her again if you saw her?'

'Dunno. Might. The yeller-'aired one knew 'er, called 'er "duchess".'

'Despite which, you don't think she was a whore too.'

'Never.'

'Clothes – accent—'

'None I could 'ear, she didn't say much. Posh, though. 'Ow she'd've known Blondie I couldn't say.'

'Short or tall, dark or fair?'

'Not *short*. I'd say dark.'

'Any particular distinguishing features?'

'What d'you mean?'

'Tallish and dark, you've said. But – did she have a long nose, or noticeably large teeth, for instance?'

'Not as I seen, no.'

'Colour of eyes?'

'Dunno.' A cloud of smoke and a shake of the head. 'Sorry.'

'So where did you take her?'

'Tell you that, yeah – Clerkenwell.'

'Street? House number?'

'The Green. She says "Clerkenwell", then "The Green'd do."'

'So you dropped her there, and she paid, and – she say anything else?'

'Might 've said good night.'

'See which way she went, from the Green?'

'I was off 'ome, no reason I'd—'

'The time then being about – ten o'clock?'

'More like ten thirty.'

'And this was on Saturday – *last* Saturday, May the fourth.'

'Well, yeah—'

'I got all that, Sarge.' The constable held up his notebook. He winked, on Collindale's side, that side of his face under the street-lamp. 'Worked that out between us like.'

'Good. We'll need it in *our* files, of course. But you, – er—'

'He's Godfrey Brown, Sarge.'

'If we need you again, Godfrey Brown – to identify her maybe, or it might be give evidence in court – '

'*Gerraway!*'

' – you'll hear from us. But you can take me back to the Yard now, if you'd be so kind. Night, Hawkins.'

Clerkenwell, he thought, climbing in. Starting at the Green, radiating outwards. A dozen bobbies, maybe . . .

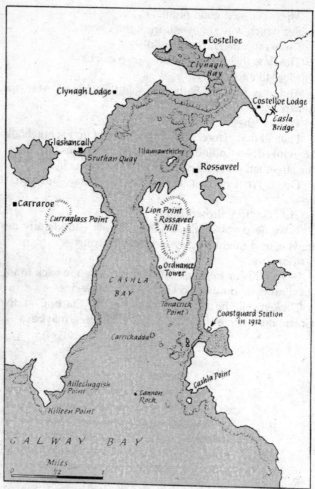

Costelloe

Clynagh
Bay

Clynagh Lodge ■

Costelloe Lodge
Casla
Bridge

Glashancally
Sruthan Quay
Illaunawehichy
Rossaveel ■

■ Carraroe
Curraglass Point
Lion Point
Rossaveel
Hill
○ Ordnance
Tower

CASHLA
BAY
Tonacrick
Point
Coastguard Station
in 1912

Carrickadda
Cashla Point

Ailleclaggish
Point
Cannon
Rock
Killeen Point

G A L W A Y   B A Y

Miles
0   ½   1

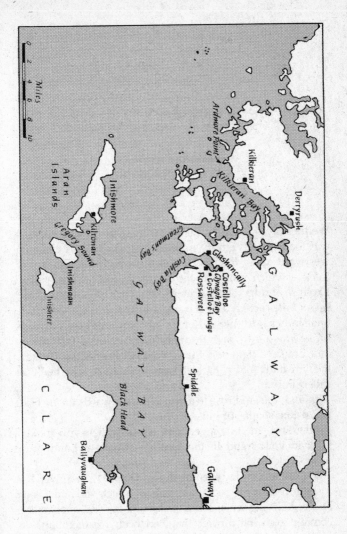

12

Wednesday, 15th May: Eileen swaying at the tail-end of a cart loaded with empty milk churns, jolting and clanging westward along the road – so-called, but more of a rocky track – which followed the north shore of Galway Bay. Expanse of ridged blue-grey water on her left – it was about seven miles across at this point, and that was County Clare on its other side – while here on the land side rock outcrops broke like a grey rash through rough grazing land. Sheep and donkeys here and there, very occasionally a cottage, half an hour ago a hamlet which her map told her was called Barna.

Inland, the land rose in a bluish haze towards the distant, cloud-like shapes of hills.

Beautiful, in its rugged emptiness. When you looked back in your mind to the teeming streets of London: or even Cork . . .

In Cork last Friday evening Betsy O'Flaherty had given her a spare bed in the rooming-house in which she and Eileen had been living when Frank had made his first appearance, coming from his trawler that had been weatherbound in Unionhall. All of it was entirely different now, of course. The house, that district, Cork City itself. Nowhere that

Frank had been with her would ever be the same, to *her*. It wasn't like that with Betsy, no reason it should have been; and Betsy herself was quite unchanged – except cock-a-hoop from having become engaged. Anyway, on Saturday, from the post office in Oliver Plunkett Street, Eileen had sent Frank's mother a telegram asking if she'd meet her in Nenagh, between trains, maybe on the Monday; her thought had been to spend just a few hours there, returning to Limerick in the evening and continuing to Galway probably next day, but Kate Maguire's answer, received on the Sunday afternoon, was insistent that she should stop there at least two or three days; Kate's sister, Mary Duggan, would be happy to have her stay in her house in Abbey Street, in easy walking distance of the station. The thinking behind this was that Eileen wouldn't then have to meet Frank's father, which would surely have been an embarrassment to them both – never having met, Frank having left home after the fist-fight in which he'd thrashed his father. Eileen guessed that Kate wouldn't tell her husband she was coming, so she answered by wire to Mary Duggan – whom she knew, Mary had come down for her and Frank's wedding – so she could pass the word privately to Kate.

Betsy, red-haired and bouncy, was in great form, and despite the sadness underlying it all they had a good couple of days together. Betsy's fiancé, who'd taken his law exams but hadn't yet had the results and was working meanwhile as an articled clerk in Bandon, took them to Sunday lunch at the hotel there, the Munster Arms – which was chancing it a bit, as Eileen had been acutely aware, not wanting to meet any others of her own and Frank's friends in and around Cork, then have them *all* know she'd been here, word of it sooner or later reaching her damn mother. She'd explained to Betsy that at this stage she didn't intend going anywhere near Skibbereen, didn't want her mother knowing she'd arrived back in Ireland. For the time being, anyway, it was only Frank's mother she wanted to see.

Betsy had asked her whether she'd see Frank's father too, when she was in Nenagh.

'If Kate wanted me to, I would. But Frank would not have.'

'Didn't know what was going to happen to him though, did he. I'm sure the oul' feller'd be terrible sad now – half out of his mind I wouldn't wonder – that they parted as they did.'

'It'll be for Kate to say. But, Betsy, would you keep it to yourself entirely that I was here at all? Even though people might come asking?'

'Is it your mother you're on about again?'

'Or anyone else. *Anyone.*'

'So how long will you be away now?'

'I don't know. Don't know *at all*. Honestly, Betsy, I do not.'

'Is it at Nenagh you'd be though, this unpredictable length of time?'

'No, that's not likely. Look, I'm sorry, but—'

'Oh, keep your secrets. Although I must say I don't like it much – having to tell lies—'

'White lies, Betsy—'

'Whatever damn colour—'

'No mention of Nenagh either?'

'God's sake, since I'm not telling 'em you was here in the first place, *eejit*—'

'You're right, I'm sorry. It's important, that's all. I'm thin air, the last you saw of me was me and Frank together, the night before we left.'

'What if someone you know spotted us in Bandon and us not seeing them?'

'They'd have been mistaken. Someone they might have *thought* was me.'

A sigh. 'All right, Eilie . . .'

She'd have liked to have told her everything; it would have been a relief if she could have. But she couldn't have told any of it without saying what she'd wanted the pistol for and still had it for – in her shoulder-bag with the six bullets in it – seven minus one, *if* there'd been seven in it to start with, for which she had only the word of that crook. But Betsy would not have countenanced another killing, once given prior knowledge of it. She'd have said no, this is where you draw the line now Eilie, where you *stop*.

She'd have run to her priest. Would have believed she had no other choice – just as Eileen knew *she* had none.

Must be getting towards Spiddle now, she guessed. How she'd come to be riding in this cart was that on the advice of the woman in whose lodging-house in Galway she'd spent last night, she'd gone bright and early to the depot off the Salthill Road, where carts and lorries brought in milk from farms out to the west here – there being no railway along this shoreline – and asked here and there whether any of them would be starting back soon and have room for a passenger, and this pink-faced farmer's son had told her sure, he'd take her as far as Spiddle and be glad of her company. His auntie, who'd been visiting in Galway, had been due to come back out to the farm with him but must have changed her mind or overslept, and he had work to do, his father wouldn't thank him if he spent the day kicking his heels around here. He'd told her all this in the Irish, which she could follow all right but found less easy to use herself, needing time in which to think the words out before she uttered them. Anyway, Spiddle – which he called *An Spidéal* – was on her route to Costelloe, and she'd accepted the offer gladly; then within the minute, while the boy was obviously in a rush to get the churns stowed and start off, the aunt had appeared, so instead of sitting on the short bench beside him Eileen had moved into the back-end here

– the boy looking fed up, shaking his head and muttering to himself, bundling a heap of sacking into a cushion for her to sit on with her back against the tail-board. The cart had iron-rimmed wheels and it wasn't comfortable, but it was going in the right direction, a lot better than walking; and sitting here instead of nearer the front at least she wasn't having to converse.

Getting a *free* ride, anyway – which was as well, since her money had to be conserved – future needs being unpredictable, and not wanting to cash Frank's bank draft at *any* time – in her present circumstances – at least for as long as she could avoid doing so. Being a US dollar draft there'd surely be some elaborate procedure – she'd obviously have to identify herself, and by that time there'd as likely as not be a hue and cry for this Maguire woman who'd shot and killed the Englishman at Costelloe.

Thinking of which – it was in her mind a lot of the time – you'd imagine that out here in the wilds you'd be able to do it and then get away – circumstances being so different to how they'd been in London. But then again – when you really put your mind to it – get away *how*?

Shanks's mare, she supposed. Wouldn't be safe by then to cadge rides in farm carts. A horse, maybe: or a bicycle? Hardly – with the suitcase. But not Shanks's mare either. She'd have to ditch the case. Would be a vagabond then entirely, a solitary creature travelling without possessions – moving by night and hiding by day, maybe. But going where? Dublin? Easier to hide in crowded places. She did have a map, had bought it in Galway last evening, hesitating before parting with the sixpence for it but knowing it might be her last chance of getting one.

To escape in any of those ways after killing him was hardly a practical proposition though. Not for *her*. For some hardened criminal maybe, but – Frank, she thought, would have told her this, was telling her now maybe, inside her skull: *You'd run into worse trouble still, Eilie. Better keep it the way you've been thinking all along, have it over with entirely.*

It was mostly just speculation though, when you hadn't even seen the place, had no notion what other people might be there or close by. But in principle that plan – the second shot – having killed him, *finish* – was probably the best one.

Joining him and Tom, then.

Leaving the other envelope in her bag: *In Loving Memory . . .*

So they'd all know, understand. The people here, and others reading about it in their newspapers: Kate, Betsy, Reggie Deacon. Elizabeth Dalby even, if the ripples spread that far. Which of course they would, Bruce Ismay being a well-known name now on that side as well.

Dome of cloudless sky, sun well up and hot now. There was a breeze from the west riffling the bay's surface but you didn't feel it here on shore. Trundling, jolting iron-shod wheels, crunching the rock-strewn track. The noise as well as her distance from the driver and his aunt made it impractical even to attempt conversation – which would have been in the Irish and she guessed exclusively in the form of questions from the aunt – a diminutive, gnarled crone who plainly hadn't liked the look of the passenger her nephew had picked up. They'd presumably live somewhere near Spiddle: which was about halfway from Galway to where the track turned northward on this side of an inlet shown on the map as Cashla Bay. About ten miles on from Spiddle, that would be, and from that point there'd still be four or five miles to go, to Costelloe. *Might* walk it, she supposed – if she had to. Not as the day was now, but later, in the cool of evening – maybe. But it *should* be possible to get another lift. Crossing fingers – Frank's ring glinting in the sunshine . . . She spread out the map again. Costelloe village was at the head of that inlet – Cashla Bay – and Costelloe Lodge – it was marked – came some way before that. A mile or so, roughly. There was a bridge over a river and then the Lodge would be on her left, between the road and the water.

Grinding and thumping on: and no sign of Spiddle yet. It was *too* hot; even the timber of the cart was hot. Ireland had no business to be like this, ought to be cool, damp and green. She felt sorry for the horse. Flies, and all. The green of trees she could see now, north and northwestward where the land rose towards hills – and behind them, further still, what might be mountains. Connemara, she knew, was mountainous, and that *would* be Connemara over there. The amount of rock here, even – she'd never seen so much of it. Not even in westernmost Cork and Kerry, where rock was very much a feature of the landscape.

In Nenagh she felt she'd done *some* good. She'd got there on the Monday afternoon, made her way to Abbey Street and Frank's aunt's terraced house easily enough, and found her – Mary Duggan – welcoming and warm-hearted. There were floods of tears of course, and then more when Kate arrived in her pony-trap, more again from time to time as Eileen told her story – about the sinking and the lifeboats and her own rescue in the *Carpathia* and so forth, and how kind the Dalbys had been to her in New York, nothing about London. She'd let them think she'd spent longer recuperating in New York than in fact she had, to fill in what they might otherwise have noticed as a void in time, but apart from that she'd told it exactly as it had been, including the sight of Ismay taking part in the lowering of boats, stopping men from joining their wives in them but then getting away in one himself.

Kate was indignant: 'Wouldn't ye think he'd want to shoot himself!'

Eileen staring at her . . .

Mary Duggan damp-eyed, shaking her head: 'Would ye *not*, so . . .'

Crossing themselves. Bewildered, as much as indignant. Eileen in the telling of it seeing it again in its scarcely believable reality: that man shuffling in his slippers, asking for the use of the doctor's cabin – presumably there'd been no other cabins available for male occupation without sharing, and company – according to what Dr McGhee had intimated, being precisely what Ismay hadn't wanted – and Frank and Tom *gone*, sharing by that time God alone knew what and with whom. The black gulf: visually, a bottomless gulf of black water and through it the howling of the damned: and that one up there with the seamen at the boats doing what had come to look like a shuffling, sidling dance, arms circling and that howl of 'Lower aw-a-a-y!'

Whether he'd *want* to be shot or wouldn't, even by that time – on the *Carpathia* – he'd have been deep in shame.

Kate had asked her, to her surprise, 'Would ye visit us on the farm, Eileen – tomorrow or the day after?'

To see Frank's father, of course. As Betsy in her natural wisdom and kindness of heart had suggested she might do. Eileen had gone out there the next day, Kate sending Frank's brother Padraig for her with the trap, and she'd been welcomed shyly by the other brother and one sister – the elder girl had a job in Limerick now and boarded there – and received shakily inside the house by Frank's father, who'd put on his Sunday suit for the occasion. Induced to do so by Kate, no doubt. He was a big man, in whom Eileen could see traces of Frank but not the strength of character, the spirit; this was only the husk of the man he had been, Kate had told her, and it was Frank's death that had reduced him so. He'd always been one for the whiskey, but now he lived on it almost entirely, and when he was drunk she said he wept a lot. He did so when Eileen was there too, although apart from the reek of the stuff that hung about him he'd seemed sober enough. She'd agreed to making this visit primarily for Frank's sake, although she knew that Frank himself would not have; she was doing it for Kate as well because she'd asked her to; and she took it to the lengths of lying to the man, telling him that Frank had been deeply saddened by their having fallen out as they had, that she knew he'd have wanted her to come and tell him so.

'Your son was as fine a man as ever came out of Ireland, Mr Maguire.'

'I know it. I've always known it.'

This was when he'd wept. Kate had too – hugging her. But Eileen and the old man had only shaken hands, not embraced or kissed, and at no time had she implied that Frank would have apologized for any aspect of his own behaviour. That *it* had happened at all, he'd regretted sadly, but not his own part in it: it had been his father's action in attempting to thrash *him* – which he'd in no way been obliged to submit to.

In fact which he'd regarded as an insult, she remembered.

She'd told Kate, 'It's like we were one person, Frank and I. With Tom then like a piece of the two of us. So, *three* in one. It's a fact, I'm just sort of a fragment that's left over now. With him still there, mind you – ten times a day I'm asking him for his advice, should I do this or that.'

'Won't you give me even a hint of what you'll be after doing now, dear?'

'The truth is, I don't know. Except I must find a job of course – the shorthand and typing again, it ought not to be difficult. But, Kate, I've no wish at the moment to see my mother, in fact I'd sooner she didn't know I'm back in Ireland. If anyone at all should come asking was I here or do you know where I might be, would you please tell a lie for me?'

'You think there might be such enquiries?'

'It's possible. From whatever quarter . . . Would you

forget I was ever here, Kate – and ask the others to do the same?'

'But to stay away from your own mother . . .'

'You know why, mostly – the man she married. But in any case—'

'I know. She didn't want you and Frank to marry, did she. She told *me* so, would you believe it. But – poor woman—'

'She's content enough. What she wanted, she's got. Kate – when I'm settled somewhere, I'll write. I doubt it'll be in Cork – places I was with Frank and Tom I don't believe I could live in now.'

She'd taken the train back to Limerick that afternoon, and from there another up to Galway. With everything said that had needed saying, and – she hoped – her tracks all covered.

She was gazing out to her left at the distant grey shapes of the Aran Islands humped across the wide exit from this bay. The nearest of them would be a dozen or fifteen miles from this point. The map showed three islands – Inishmore, Inishmaan and Inisheer – but if she'd not had it to refer to she'd have thought more than that, and smaller, since the low-lying parts weren't visible and the higher ground on them looked like separate islands.

And beyond them the whole width of the Atlantic. Three thousand miles of it, for God's sake, and according to that ship's officer – Morton, the one who'd let her stay on deck that night – some of it as much as four miles deep. Such a *huge* mass of ocean, she thought. Such vastness: really unimaginable. But in which the three of us should now be together. That's the *real* default.

The cart had stopped. The young driver twisting on his seat to look back at her, and pointing at a narrower, rougher track leading northward off this one.

'We have to leave you here. *An Spidéal*'s two steps ahead. D'you want a hand down with that bag?'

'No.' She gave him a smile. 'Thank you.'

The aunt was telling him anyway: of course she didn't need his help – big strapping creature that she was! She, the aunt, being such a mean little old scrap of a thing, of course. Eileen climbed out over the tail-board, then reached back in for the suitcase. The boy, she noticed, was now scarlet in the face, instead of pink. She came up level with them on the aunt's side, told him across her in careful Irish, 'I am much obliged.'

'Where might you be making for, girl?'

'Oh.' Nodding towards the road ahead. 'Some way, yet.' If the boy had been on his own she knew he'd have taken her into the village: would have helped her down with the case as well. Poor lad, he'd been doing his best to get going before that ratty old thing showed up. He'd flipped the reins, and the horse lurched forward, the cart tilting as its offside wheels rode over a heap of stones. Eileen crouching then to open the suitcase and fold her smart summer coat into it. It had been cool enough earlier on, but a coat was definitely superfluous now; this one was also too elegant for these surroundings and her circumstances. Just blouse and skirt now therefore, and the straw hat. Even the hat might be a bit smart, on the head of a woman trudging through the wilds of nowhere, but it was entirely practical with its wide brim and its lightness. *Too* light, maybe: she could feel the sun scorching through it.

The road bridged a river here: and the sea was closer on her left than it had been all morning. On the right, over a low stone wall, a donkey grazed in a miniature green valley between rock outcrops.

But there – that wasn't rock. A building – cottage or farmhouse . . .

Spiddle – this close?

If it was, that lad had told the truth, it *hadn't* been more than two steps. For whatever good it was going to do her – the name 'Spiddle' was hardly alluring. Trudging on, round a slight bend, that side of the bridge. Ready for the worst but hoping for the best. Several houses in sight now; and – glory be! – along on the right there, an inn. The sight of which *was* alluring . . .

She was very thirsty: could acknowledge that to herself now. Peckish too: having had no supper last night and only a light breakfast very early this morning. Although the question of money surfaced again, at the thought of buying a meal. She did have *some* money, but – well, would be needing a bed tonight – somewhere or other – *and* a meal . . .

It was *extremely* hot. She rested for a moment: put down the case and sat on it. Feeling dizzy, somewhat: and aware she should get out of the sun, not sit here baking. A glass of water would cost nothing, anyway. There was activity around the doorway of the inn, and a trap had just drawn up there. Easier to let that lot disperse. Sun scorching hot on the back of her neck, despite the hat's wide brim. She put one hand up, shielding it. But – *should* have cashed the bank draft – or at least enquired as to the procedure. Heaven knew what might be done with it if she still had it with her when she came to the end of this – finally, to Ismay, and then killed herself – which however drastic it might sound – and at certain times *feel* – surely must be the ideal solution. Over in a second, and with luck painless – if one did it right – as compared to weeks or even months of discomfort and opprobrium and then the final, climactic ordeal – the rope.

Which, all right, one *might* have to face, if one messed up on the other.

The smaller detail did have to be thought out, meanwhile. Detail for instance such as how long the small amount of cash remaining might have to be made to last.

Possibly only hours? Finish it all *today*? Arrive at the Costelloe place this afternoon – or evening, maybe – knock on the door and ask for him, have the White Star letter ready . . .

'Mr Bruce Ismay?'

Would he smile? Or sense danger and show fear?

Either way, that cracking, deafening explosion. Then another.

I'd have done it then, Frank . . .

Just get there, that was all. And a first step might be to get out of this damn sun. Looking around, then pushing herself up and seeing that in front of the inn some men and a young boy were grouped around that trap, which had a sturdy, lively looking pony between its shafts. A Connemara, she guessed it might be. And that would be a really splendid way to travel. They were loading various items – a basket, fishing-rods; a wolf-like dog meanwhile relieving itself against the wheel on this near side. She was up and on the move again – towards them, towards the inn's open door. The dizziness still affecting her. In the cart all morning under this broiling sun – she hadn't realized. Couldn't have done much about it if she had, for that matter. The three men were in breeches and boots, shirts with rolled-up sleeves, and caps; the boy in short trousers and a grey shirt, grey felt hat. Bright-eyed, pink-faced: there was a mood of jollity – an outing of some kind, she supposed. Well – fishing, of course.

The boy had drawn the men's attention to her. A tall one with a moustache rather like Bruce Ismay's turning, smiling, raising his hat.

'Looks deuced heavy, that!'

'It is, rather.' She put it down, smiled at the child. 'Hello, there. Going fishing, is it?'

'Oh, we've *been* – last night we were after white trout, and—'

'George, be quiet a moment.' The tall one again. Anglo-Irish. Eileen's height, roughly – good-looking and conscious of it, using his smile on her: glancing away now though at a heavy-set, grey-haired individual who'd emerged shading his eyes against the sun and looking at her – as they all were now – and who by his dress and bearing was almost certainly the inn-keeper.

The tall man asked her, 'Are you stopping here, my dear?'

My dear . . .

She guessed that if she said 'no' he'd offer her a lift, which a minute ago she'd have jumped at but now wouldn't have accepted for all the tea in China. Recalling Elizabeth Dalby's warning *There's one under every stone . . .* No warning needed, though, she simply didn't *like* this person. Turning away from him, she picked up the suitcase again and started towards the inn door, the grey-haired man at once offering to take the case from her – he clearly *was* the inn-keeper – and she let him take it. Hearing one of the others growl, 'Lay off it, Jack, we'd best get moving. Lot of ground to cover, you know. Besides—'

Something about the boy. Then the tall one's mutter of 'Spoil-sport . . .' She told the inn-keeper, 'I'd like a glass of water, please.' Adding quickly – having forgotten what she'd decided when she'd been pondering it all out there – 'And something to eat – but just a snack – if that's possible?'

'It is of course.' He let her enter ahead of him, then put her case down inside and went back to see off the fishing party. 'Please come by again, sirs . . .' Eileen finding herself in a hallway with chairs and a few small tables in it, and hearing from an inner room voices that sounded English, both male and female. There was a smell of beer and, she guessed, roast chicken. It was pleasantly cool, she thought, subsiding into a chair, *Just what the doctor ordered* . . . It was all right about the money, she remembered: this might even be the last she'd ever spend. The inn-keeper came back: 'For the "something to eat", would cold cuts suit you?'

It would suit very well, of course. And shouldn't cost much either. Meanwhile if she'd care to refresh herself, he was saying, the bathroom and WC was up the stairs on the half-landing there. He'd be a minute of two getting her lunch, which he'd serve to her at that table there – if that would suit? He had a party of five inside – English folk touring; the ladies were painters, artists, apparently.

'Cold cuts' meant cold mutton with onions and boiled potatoes. She drank the water, and asked for more. The mutton was perfectly edible, though rather tough. No, no tea, thank you. The coolth was attributable to the building's thick walls and surprisingly high ceilings. There were sporting pictures on the walls and a very large fish in a glass case. She was feeling a lot better, really herself again. The inn-keeper brought a whole jug of water and asked whether she had far to go yet.

'Costelloe. Not all that far.'

'Costelloe, is it.' Gazing at her, rubbing the back of his head. He'd pronounced it *Cost*elloe, not Cost*ell*oe as Charles Napier had and consequently she had too. 'A sight *too* far if you was thinking of getting there on foot. And Lord save us, with that portmanteau too! Fifteen mile, if it's a yard!'

'I've not been walking. I came from Galway this morning on a milk cart.' Pointing with her head: 'It turned off just back there. Might be some other conveyance passing through that might take me on?'

'You'd have folks at Costelloe expecting you, I dare say?'

'Well – I hope so.'

A silence, gazing at her. He'd know everything about

everyone for miles around, she realized. He'd want to, would be expected to by other locals. Loud talk was continuing from the inner room meanwhile. He turned his head, listening to it for a moment; one of the women had a laugh like a parakeet's screech. The inn-keeper suggested, 'I could ask these English, if you like.'

'Are they going that way?'

'Oh, they are. Making for Clifden but even in a motorcar it's a long way, that coast road the way it winds, you know. Likely they'll stop for the night at Kilkieran, their driver tells me. It's a big old yoke he has, kind of a charabanc – he's from Galway, but it's his cousin has the inn at Kilkieran, see.'

'I don't know the area at all. But I've a map here—'

'From what part of Ireland might you be, then?'

'From Cork City.'

'Ah, well, Cork. A fine city indeed. Costelloe's so small you'd barely see it, if you passed by at more than a walking pace. But you'd have kin nearby, no doubt—'

'Do you think those people *might* have room for me?'

They did have, and agreed to take her – after eliciting that Costelloe was as far as she wanted to go and being shown it on the map. There were two men and three women, the men's wives and one wife's sister; all three were painters, or aspired to be, would be painting the coastal scenery while the men did some fishing. It was the older wife who screeched. They had plenty of room in their hired vehicle and would be pleased to take Eileen as far as Costelloe.

The inn-keeper, whose name it transpired was Donelly, asked her whether it was in Costelloe village she'd want to be set down.

'Well – yes . . .'

'Else ye might've been looking for the Lodge. That's before the village. I'd only wondered might that be it because we've heard the place is changing hands. I was told the feller's name but I forget it. An Englishman, he is. 'Twas a fishing syndicate had it – oh, still does, I suppose—'

'The village would suit me best, in any case.'

'There's no inn, d'you see. Only Lorna O'Neill's shop – which is the post office as well – but she might put you up if she had a room spare. She would, I'm sure. But you have your own arrangements made, of course . . .'

The car was in front of the inn by this time, parked in the middle of the road with a trio of cows being driven past it by an old woman with a stick. The car was a long tourer with three rows of transverse seats, charabanc-style as Donelly had said, and the driver a short, stout man, clean-shaven, in a crumpled, dusty suit. Apparently there was another inn where he'd been having his lunch, which judging by the aroma surrounding him might have been mostly liquid. One husband got in the front beside him, the other put himself in the middle of the second row with a female on each side, and the unmarried sister shared the third bench-seat with Eileen. The ladies were wearing hats similar to hers but were securing them now with scarves which they knotted under their chins; she followed suit, Donelly having put the suitcase in beside her. The space behind was already full of luggage and painting and fishing gear.

'I can't tell you all how grateful I am. Really it's very kind of you.'

'We could hardly have driven off and left you to *walk*, my dear!'

The screecher, that had been. The husband beside her exclaiming loudly, 'Good Lord, no!'

'Are ye all set then?'

'By all means, driver!'

He had goggles on now. Donelly stooped to crank the starting handle and the engine clattered uncertainly into action. Donelly coming round to the side of the vehicle then with both hands raised, either in triumph or conferring a blessing: leaning over towards Eileen, shouting, 'The Englishman that's after purchasing Costelloe Lodge goes by the name of Ismay, I recall!'

'Oh . . .'

'Heard that name somewhere recently – haven't we?' The man in the front, turning to address the row behind him; the inn-keeper continuing, 'What he's gettin' with the house would be no more than a hundred acres, but all up-river, both banks and the lakes above, the greatest fishing in Ireland, so it is!'

Engine revving. A jar as the driver pushed it into gear and reached over the side on his right to release the handbrake: stones rattled like bullets under the mudguards as the tyres span before they gripped. The man in front shouting to his friend, 'A rich man's water, by the sound of it!'

'Well, Harry, *you*'re rich—'

'But that name *is* familiar, can't think why . . .'

It was the girl beside Eileen who came up with it. They were out of the village by then, the road as it had been before – straight, narrow and rocky – but diverging somewhat from the shoreline. There was a small steamer out there, plugging in eastward from the south side of the Arans. The girl said suddenly, tapping the shoulder of the man in front of them, '*Titanic*.'

'What?'

'She thinks that's the *Titanic*.'

Screech, screech. The others waiting, straight-faced, for the noise to subside. Then the man in front caught on, and snapped his fingers: 'You're right, Helen! *Bruce* Ismay – managing director of White Star, chap they've been kicking up such a fuss about – should have gone down with the ship, all that!'

'Well *done*, Helen!'

'I don't see why he shouldn't have saved himself, though.'

'Well – same as the captain of a ship, isn't it?'

'No, it isn't – he was *not* the captain, not crew at all.'

'Similar position, though – head of the company that owned it?'

'Exactly. And hadn't provided enough life boats, consequently a lot of passengers were left to drown. This fellow none the less making sure of saving his *own* skin.'

'That's the point they've been making, of course, but—'

'Anyway it wouldn't be *this* Ismay, would it. I mean, bit of a dashed coincidence – what?'

'How, coincidence?'

Helen asked Eileen, 'Do you come from this part of Ireland?'

'No. From Cork.'

'Oh. It's lovely down there, I've heard.'

'It is. West Cork especially, I'd say.'

'So what are you doing up here? Just visiting, or—'

'Believe it or not, I'm seeing a man about a job.'

'Up here – a *job*?'

That had set the screecher off again. Eileen said to the girl as it faded, 'It would take a lot of explaining. If you don't mind . . .'

'Of course—'

'Shocking business, though. Appalling loss of life – among the steerage-class passengers especially. I saw a summary of it in *The Times* – and honestly, if *I'd* been that Ismay chap—'

'A point *I* saw made – may have been in the *Morning Post*, I think probably a letter from a reader – yes, it was – man who'd been in another White Star liner that went down three or four years ago – forget its name – this chap remembered the captain telling passengers, "Look here, it's women and children first, then first class, then the rest." Simply reminding them what the form was – absolutely normal and customary – *accepted*.'

'Then it shouldn't be.'

The girl – Helen – had said it, not as a participant in the conversation, only throwing it in as it were *en passant*. She was studying the Aran Islands and referring to the map which Eileen had spread out between them. 'I wonder if there's any way of getting out there. A fisherman who might take us, for instance.'

'A high proportion of the Irish passengers went down with her, mind you.'

'Only because they happened to be travelling steerage, old chap. I dare say an even higher proportion of *Dutch* may have drowned too.'

'And are you postulating that that makes it all right?'

'I'm saying that harping on the question of nationality is simply playing politics. Which is precisely what those blackguards in the House were doing – ostensibly going for White Star and Ismay, but *actually*—'

'Yes – ' the wife on the right – 'I think you're right—'

'I'll tell you one thing.' Harry, again. 'The Ismay who's buying the place our friend there was talking about can't possibly be the *Titanic* wallah. Simple reason that having drowned all those Paddies he'd be a bloody fool ever to set a *toe* in Ireland. What?'

That set the screeches going again. The other wife meanwhile grasping her husband from behind and talking into his ear. Telling him, Eileen guessed, not to refer to Irishmen as 'Paddies' in the presence of their Irish passenger. Or in the driver's hearing either, maybe. Harry chuckling, telling her 'Stuff and nonsense, Dolly! Aren't I right, Charlie, *wouldn't* he be a damned idiot?'

At the crossroads they turned right. There were fresh-water loughs on both sides then. Costelloe about three miles ahead, the driver told them. They could have gone straight on over and then up the shore of Cashla Bay, but it would have added several miles to this stage of the trip and would hardly have been worthwhile; they'd get all the coastal views they wanted later on. Cashla Bay was only a small inlet: beyond it was Greaterman's Bay and then Kilkieran Bay, and to reach Kilkieran itself, as they'd said they wanted, you had to drive clear around the whole of that lot – 'd'see, sorr . . .'

'Well, we're in your hands!'

'The ladies'd find all they'd want to paint around the coast there by Kilkieran, I'd say.'

The discussion turned to where else they might stop, if anywhere, before reaching Clifden. Eileen acutely aware that Costelloe Lodge, and Ismay, couldn't be much more than a mile ahead now, since it was on this side of the village. But village first: not to arrive at the house with a suitcase, and not to arrive with this crowd of witnesses to her getting there as a total stranger, unexpected. Well – witnesses *at all*, to *whatever* . . . Feeling her shoulder-bag from the outside, the shape of the pistol in it. They'd just passed over a narrow causeway between two loughs: and those far-off mountains had harder edges to them now. The map told her they were the Maumturks. A couple of thousand feet high, she guessed – massive, in contrast to this low-lying, gently shelving landscape. Low-lying except for a hill off to the left now. Consulting the map again – Rossaveel Hill. Rossaveel, or in the Irish *Ros an Mhil* – was also the name of a village of sorts right on the bay's edge, the narrows there.

Glancing up from the map she found Helen watching her. She nodded. 'Not far now.'

'D'you really think you'll get a job here?'

'Yes. I do.'

'Wouldn't you rather live in Cork?'

'I did live and work there, but – recently I lost my husband – and our little boy as well – and—'

'My *dear*.' A hand light on her forearm . . . 'How perfectly frightful. How – no, you wouldn't want to talk about it—'

'Nor to live in Cork again.'

'No, I understand . . .'

Shouldn't have told her even that much, she thought. But you felt shut out, at times – lonely, *needed* to. While there was still *time*, for God's sake, to talk normally to anyone at all . . . Focusing somewhat distractedly on a sign that pointed left to Rossaveel. Straight over: then a bridge – as her map showed, the River Casla, no 'h' in it although it emptied into Cashla Bay. Ismay's river, she thought, the car rattling over it. Then a fork away to the left, into a stand of trees, and a sign saying COSTELLOE LODGE. Ismay's *house*, in there. She was looking into that small side-road almost fearfully as they trundled past it; but there was nothing to be seen except the trees, the track slanting away into them. Harry shouting back, 'The house that Ismay chap's supposed to have bought, eh?'

'Eh, driver?'

'So they're sayin', sorr, so they're sayin'.'

It had been more of an entrance drive than a side-road, Eileen realized. It rejoined this road fifty or sixty yards further along. No gates at either end, just a way in and a way out, with the spinney shutting off any view of the house – unless one *had* turned in, presumably. The road had swung around it and was now straight again, leading northwest across the top end of the bay, which – at this time anyway, low tide she supposed – was all exposed rock, certainly more rock and weed than water, just a pool or a bit of a channel here and there. There was a stone jetty though – and some boats on a bit of a stony beach there. She was looking back to see if there might be a view of the house from this angle, but there wasn't.

Seaweed growing up to a certain height on rocks and on the jetty too showed that the tide *would* flood in here.

'Costelloe village, ladies an' gen'lemen . . .'

'Stop long enough to drop off our passenger, that's all.'

'Right y'are, sorr.' Slowing, into a cluster of five or six dwellings, all quite close to the rocky basin. She saw the shop then: and a weather-worn sign over the front of it: DENNIS O'NEILL, in blue lettering on a maroon background.

Donelly at Spiddle had said *Lorna* O'Neill. The driver was braking to stop outside it.

'Give the young lady a hand with her baggage, driver, will you?'

'No – please.' She was already half-out, dragging out her suitcase. Helen murmuring to her 'Goodbye – and good luck with the job and everything', and more privately, 'I'm *so* sorry about – you know . . .'

'Yes. Thank you.' Thanking them all: 'You were very kind to bring me.'

'Oh, rubbish, my dear!'

The driver was pointing – beyond the shop, where a track of some sort ran up between it and the next-door cottage. 'Who might that belong to now, I'm wondering?' Eileen looked round over her shoulder, but from where she was couldn't see what he was talking about. She turned back to the others: 'I hope your holiday goes well.'

'Well, thank you—'

'A Morris, is it?'

'A Siddeley, I'd say. Y'man from the Lodge, it could be. There's a solicitor here from Galway at times has a Morris, but that's not—'

'I say, Harry, shouldn't we push along?'

'Yes. Driver—'

'Of course. Of course . . .'

'Goodbye!'

Brake off, clutch engaged, throttle opening; a few hands waving. Eileen stooped to pick up her suitcase; wondering what she'd do now if Lorna O'Neill could *not* give her a room.

Ask if she could leave the suitcase here, walk back to the Lodge, and –

No. Not right away, drop of a hat like this. You'd need time to get your wits together, so you would. Thinking Irish now, she realized. The shop door opening and a man coming out, hurrying: quite smartly dressed, not a local – but certainly not Ismay either. Standing aside now with an arm out holdng the door for her: 'Beg your pardon—'

'*Not* at all . . .'

He'd looked at her as if wondering who she might be: then to his right, to where the tourists' car, emitting bluish exhaust, was taking a right fork – northwards, away from this bay altogether. It occurred to her that he might well be the owner of the other motor: the tourists' driver had speculated that it might belong to 'your man from the Lodge', meaning presumably Ismay, but until now that hadn't really sunk in. The door had swung shut behind her, she was in the shop's mixture of light and shadow and an aroma – oh, an amalgam – ham, beer, oats perhaps – and she'd stopped abruptly.

She knew him.

Titanic's E deck. The great vessel shuddering in the early stages of its death throes. Frank had rejoined her and Tom after risking his life and her sanity going back down there for the money. This first-class steward appearing then in his white jacket, on his way up, heading for the staircase that was barred to third class; she'd asked him wouldn't he unlock the gate for them, and he'd exclaimed, 'Great heavens, you'd have me *shot*!'

13

That Wednesday morning, Reggie had been visited in Coldbath Passage by an Inspector Tait from New Scotland Yard.

'Taking the liberty of assuming you'd want to assist us with certain inquiries we're making, Mr Deacon.'

A man in his forties: thin, stooped, with sparse hair mostly grey; brown suit with a chalk-stripe in it, brown boots. Reggie had agreed: 'If I'm in a position to, of course . . .'

It had then transpired that the inquiries concerned Eileen Maguire: that the inspector had been talking to Mrs Whitten, knew of the *Titanic* background and that Reggie had accompanied her from New York, and that she'd now left for Ireland.

'Is she supposed to have committed some misdemeanour?'

'Well – if under that heading you'd include shooting a man dead, sir . . .'

He was silent for a moment, staring at him. A shake of the narrow, grey head. 'This is quite positively ridiculous, Inspector!'

'That reaction does not surprise me, sir. Having interviewed Mrs Whitten and had much the same from her. We were led to that address, incidentally, by information received from a hairdresser here in Clerkenwell. Mrs Maguire had her hair "re-styled" there, on the morning of May the sixth – a Monday – and in the hairdresser's opinion the "re-styling" substantially changed the young lady's appearance.'

'And what bearing might that have on—'

'Just a moment, sir, and I'll tell you. On the night of Saturday, May the fourth, a person named Anthony Henshaw was shot dead in a basement flat just off the Strand, and a woman answering Mrs Maguire's description was seen at the place of the killing a short time before it was committed and again an hour later, getting into a hansom cab in the same vicinity. We were able to trace the cabman, and our description of her was good enough for him to recall having taken her to Clerkenwell Green. From there she'd have had only a short walk to Cyrus Lane, of course. And on the Monday morning she set about changing her appearance – in various ways . . . Mr Deacon, you'll tell me this evidence is circumstantial – and to an extent it may be – and another line might be that the killing was in self-defence. It might have been, too – the victim was – well, far from respectable. Mrs Maguire had gone to meet him, I might add, in order to purchase the pistol with which he was killed. But what would she have wanted the weapon for in the first place? Not to kill *him* – he was a means to an end, not the end itself – d'you follow?'

'Follow, but—'

'Another question, then. Is it possible that her experiences on the *Titanic* could have affected her mentally? That under a seemingly normal demeanour she could be deranged?'

'In my view she was and is absolutely sane and normal. "Level-headed" was a congratulatory term I used to her myself, I remember.'

'Another question, then: did she at any time mention any

person for whom she might have felt hatred – desire for revenge, say?'

'Never. It would have been utterly out of character. She's a particularly calm, sweet-natured girl. *Really*, Inspector!'

'But suppose – as in the event does seem quite probable – under that calm surface there *was* some such homicidal intention—'

'So *im*probable I'd dismiss the notion altogether!'

'Well.' A slight shrug, and consulting his notebook. 'One or two less speculative questions now . . . She left on Thursday, I gather. Do you know whether Cork – Cork City? – was her ultimate destination?'

'No, I don't.'

'Then – do you know whether she has any family in Ireland?'

'A mother, somewhere in West Cork. She did name the place but I don't recall it. And the mother has re-married, since the death of Eileen's father. So even if one knew Mrs Maguire's maiden name—'

'We don't know her stepfather's.'

'Quite.'

Tait made another note. Then: 'If I may ask this, Mr Deacon – for our records – how did it happen you were accompanying Mrs Maguire from America?'

'I'd been over to see my son and his family at Cleveland, Ohio, and I met her on board ship – at sailing-time, as it happens. She'd been looked after by some well-to-do Americans – whose name escapes me for the moment – they were seeing her off, and this good woman – also a *Titanic* survivor – was obviously distressed and worried for her, so I offered myself as – *in loco parentis*, if you follow me.'

'Were White Star paying for her repatriation?'

'I believe so. They'd have had to, wouldn't they?'

'So they may have an address in Ireland for her.'

'Well – since at the time of her departure *she* didn't have one—'

'If he did not offer me the job, might you want help here in your shop?'

There'd been a telephone call. Mrs O'Neill had sounded as if with Eileen present she hadn't wanted to say any more than she had to. Eileen remembered: *Yes, they are, of course. And now yet another. No, no – here.* (Referring to herself, Eileen Maguire the new arrival?) Then: *Why no, happens I cannot, at this moment.* (Can't speak plainly, because of this person's presence?) *But I believe – no, such – as far as we know. Of course. Of course. Thursday, the evening. Very well. Goodbye, Mr O'Bry—'*

Surname O'Brian or O'Bryen, obviously, but she'd broken it off short. Was back at her ledger now, totting up columns of figures. She had an oil lamp there beside it on the bar. A woman of about fifty, fifty-five: brisk, robust-looking: not tall, but sturdy, large-bosomed and with a squarish face, firm chin, dark hair streaked with grey, alert blue eyes and deft, swift movements. As matter of fact and natural in her manner as if she'd been expecting Eileen, or someone like her, although that guarded telephone conversation had seemed to contradict this, make an actress of her. Caught on the hop by the man's call, embarrassed then, she showed none now, was continuing as if it simply had not occurred. That was the bar, on which she had the ledger – a drinkers' bar, the pub side of the shop, herself on a high stool on its far side, bar-tender's side. It was on the right as you entered from the street, while on the left was the shop counter, with a weighing-machine and a side of bacon on it, and at its far end a railed-off post office section – telegram forms on a spike and the telephone on the wall behind. Across the back wall of the shop were shelves packed with provender of all kinds – jars, tins, bottles and packets – while overhead the ceiling was festooned with everything from clothing to shovels and cooking-pots, slung on hooks. There was a door at the back here in the middle and another at the post-office end, but the only natural light came from the glass-topped shop doorway and farther along a sash window.

Mrs O'Neill had laid down her pen, to answer Eileen's question – about working in the shop – with a question of her own: 'Why should he not give you the job?'

'No reason especially. I hope very much he will. But he mightn't need me now.' Short laugh: 'Might not like the look of me. Could be too soon for him, if he's only been here since – Friday, did you say?'

'Last Friday evening, yes. The pair of 'em. The one you're after working for and that fellow you saw just now – Lloyd, his name is. Master and servant but acting like they was brothers, almost. How they'll be gettin' on in that place I *don't* know. A fair old mess it's in, more than ready for a woman's hands on it, I'd say.'

'Not mine, however. I work at a typewriter, not—'

'In any case 'twould be more a builder's hands, an engineer's it needs. It leaks something terrible, they say. But you'd know shop work, would you?'

'I worked in a big store in Cork more than a year. Sold hats and dresses while evenings I was studying the shorthand and typing.'

'There's not many hats and dresses sold here, I'll tell you. It's more oilskins and seaboots they want when they've the money for them. They've always money for the drink, mind you.'

Eileen had mentioned her hope of working for Ismay in practically her first breath, partly to explain what she was here for – this Lorna O'Neill's son having looked at her initially as if she might have been something from Outer Space – and partly because her expectation of being gainfully employed was obviously linked to her affording board and lodging here. The place, and Mrs O'Neill herself, were too basic, down-to-earth, to risk any misunderstanding. She'd asked was there a room available for a night or maybe two, and at what price – with supper and breakfast, say. The son, Michael, had been there at the time but only for a minute, careering out through the shop, coming from the doorway at the back and barking at his mother that he was going to see about some boat or other, hurrying because that former *Titanic* steward – 'Mr Lloyd' – had been giving him a lift to wherever it might be – the Lodge, presumably. The car's engine audible then when he'd had the shop door open, pausing to look back at Eileen for a moment with that same startled look: a tallish, slim, fit-looking man about her own age with curly dark hair, a beak of a nose, tanned skin and blue eyes. The ex-steward had been getting petrol apparently, there being a tank of it and a hand-pump up the side there, so Mrs O'Neill had explained. 'Not just for the few motorcars that come by, there's boats too has petrol engines now, the lads fill their cans from that pump. It's why I keep a padlock on it and the key in here, d'ye see.' All this much of an introduction in no more than about twenty minutes: Eileen had been shown the room she could sleep in, and the lavatory outside that you could see from the window – could also see a donkey which had happened to be braying at that moment, in a small paddock with a lot of nettles in it; she'd left her suitcase and her shoulder-bag on the narrow iron bed and come back downstairs – out through that potato-patch to the privy, a quick word to the donkey and then back into the living-room cum kitchen and through it into the shop again just as the telephone had rung.

Mrs O'Neill was leaning on the bar-counter now, on her stubby, strong-looking forearms, watching Eileen who was wandering about inspecting the items hanging from the ceiling: wondering who O'Brian might be and why her arrival here should have been of presumably covert interest to him.

Or why his name should have been withheld from her, for that matter.

'Two things I'll put you right on, girl. One is the Englishman's not yet at Costelloe Lodge as you seem to be imagining. The Lodge is taken as it always is this time of year – there's half a dozen of 'em in the syndicate, they have it however they arrange it between theirselves. By this time they'd have settled who'd have it week by week *next* summer, see – only since the Englishman's buying it for himself now he'll have it all year to himself – and his family no doubt, if he has any – but not yet, because of these others in it, see?'

'But he and Lloyd – got here Friday, you said—'

'At Glashnacally is where they are. Sure it's a wreck of a place but it's big enough. Where Michael's gone now. It's the house those English are in, but it's the name of the village too, such as it is – fishing village, a cottage or two with a pier the boats use. Struthan Quay, they call it.'

'Is it far from here?'

'Two miles maybe. Less. You'd walk it easy. That west side of Cashla Bay, across from Rossaveel, which is a place the trawlers berth, betimes. Glashnacally was a coastguard barrack at one time – long ago, coastguard's the other side now, down by Keeraunnagark. Then it was used for houses – Glashnacally, I'm telling you about—'

''So there'd be room in it for me, if he did give me the job?'

'A *room*, is it?'

'To work in. The office work I'd be doing if he did take me on – despite the fact he's not yet in the house he's buying—'

'Bless you, you'd stable a dozen *horses* in that place if you had a mind to!'

It mightn't improve her chances, she thought, that he wasn't yet in his own house. And the lines she'd been thinking on – since talking to that girl Helen, telling her she was here looking for a job – had changed somehow to the extent that it was what maybe she *would* be doing. Genuinely, for all Ismay would know. If he was ready to take her on – which maybe he would not be, now, while he was at Glashnacally – if he *did* want her to start right away – well, all right. Giving herself *time* . . . The talk with Helen having coincided with their passing close to Costelloe Lodge, herself suddenly aghast at the prospect of knocking on that door, having it opened to her perhaps by the man himself: this suddenly, this soon – face to face, and the pistol in her hand, no time to draw breath or think or—

'The other matter I'd be inclined to put you right on, girl—'

'Oh, yes.' Cowardly thinking – what *else* was it? – shelved, for the moment . . . 'Oh, yes – sorry—'

'Don't be forever apologizing now. You want to look round, look round all you like, you'll not see anything you shouldn't. Please God you'll not.' Cackle of laughter, Eileen not making sense of it – of anything much – at that moment. 'No, girl, what I'm saying is you thought Michael was my son, did you not – but he's my nephew. Raised in Dublin so he was, but his mother was a poor weak thing, and when she run off with some blackguard and my brother-in-law was not able to look after him – see, we sent for Michael to live with us here. My husband Patrick was a fisherman, and young Mike took to the sea like he'd been born and bred to it. That's what he does, it's the lobsters and the fishing off the islands there beyond. He'd help me when I'd need help, all right, but that's not often. But – there y'are, my *nephew*, see.'

'I'll remember. But your husband – Patrick, you said—'

'Drowned.' Pointing with her head. 'Out there where so

many have. Fourteen year ago, come Saint Stephen's Day. I
was hired labour then for Pat's brother Dennis – and when
he passed on having no wife or children of his own he left
me the business. He died above here, in his own bed. Now
there's my history and Michael's for you, girl, or most of it
– though why I should be drivelling it all out, and you a
stranger, a blow-in from the Lord knows where—'

'Would you like to hear my story?'

'Well, I would, but you might save it until Michael's with
us to hear it too?'

'If you like.'

'A good story, is it?'

'Good . . .' She shrugged. 'I don't know about *good*.' She
was at the bar now, facing Mrs O'Neill across it, with the
ledger open between them, to her own eye all upside-down
spikey entries and the figures in neat columns between the
red-ruled verticals. Mrs O'Neill checked that the ink was
dry, then closed it: a great big thing, heavy-looking. Eileen
pulled a stool closer and got on it, her hands together on
the edge of the counter as on the back of a pew in church
– or as on a ship's rail in the middle of the night with a
man in the open wing of the bridge watching through
binoculars: the memories still came and went, triggered
by God knew what. Mrs O'Neill's eyes steady on her now
though, glinting bright blue with the lamplight in them:
'When will you speak with the Englishman then?'

'The morning would be soon enough. I suppose you
know *his* story?'

'To do with the *Titanic*, sure. Head man at her owners,
wasn't he. For years he's been coming here to fish, but what
they say is he's crossing the water now for good an' all on
account of the hullabaloo it's caused.'

'That much is true, I believe.'

'It would be, seeing it was George Henry O'Bryen himself
was tellin' us.'

'Who's George Henry O'Bryen?'

'Oh, what is he *not*, you might ask. Solicitor – he has places of business in Galway and in Clifden too, and residences in both towns, but Clynagh Lodge here as well. He's one of the six that has Costelloe Lodge as well, he's acting for them all now with the selling of it to your Englishman. And look here, now – if your man did not come up to his promises to you, George Henry'd be the one to advise you about work of that kind in Galway.'

'There was no promise made. Only someone else told Mr Ismay I'd be looking for employment, and he showed interest.'

'It's a peculiar thing, or seems so, all of you descending on us now at just this time.'

'All of us . . . But I'm on my own – all right, so I heard *he* was coming here—'

'To us here, you'd understand, 'tis a crowd of blow-ins coming all at once, and picking this time for it . . . You yourself now would not be wholly Irish, would ye?'

'But I would – I *am*! My father had most of his education in England, that's all. He and I were close, and the way he sounded – some of it comes through at times, so I've been told.'

'What did he do, and where?'

'He was a doctor – in West Cork, where I was born and brought up. Then he died, and my mother got married to a man I don't like at all, so—'

'So you skedaddled and married some lad by name of Maguire.' Mrs O'Neill's eyes had flickered towards Eileen's wedding ring. 'Where might *he* be now?'

'He drowned.' Yellow eyes on the blue ones. 'As *your* man did. Only Frank was in the *Titanic*. So was I and our little boy, and I was the one got away – more's the pity. You're getting my story now after all, you see. I'd sooner be there with them now than sitting here – than alive at all. They wouldn't let Frank in the lifeboat, and Tom broke free and ran off into the ship somewhere when Frank was trying to pass him to me in the boat. I was struggling to get out then, with other women stopping me, weighing me down. I've understood this since, from pieces out of the Inquiry – a boat slung seventy feet or more above the sea wouldn't want tipping up. But Frank had gone haring after Tommy, and in that crowd, the deck packed as it was—'

'How old, your Tommy?'

'Not three. Two and three-quarters. But you see – you see – Christ Jesus, the three of us – then in the lifeboat – me, *only* me, and—'

Head in her arms: struggling to hold back the tears, the wail. For the first time in – oh, except once or twice at night, the early hours . . . Hearing herself now telling about – about Tommy, Christ's sake – while in her brain the body in the water they'd said wasn't his but *might* have been, which she'd spared herself even looking at – spared *herself* . . . Mrs O'Neill reaching to her across the bar, her voice a crooning from way outside, from *miles* away: 'Poor creature, you – poor dear girl, oh, my poor dear . . .'

She'd moved out to the kitchen not long after that – just as well since there'd been customers in the shop, including two old women wanting pints of porter with whiskey chasers – and then up to her little closet of a room, transferring the contents of her suitcase to a chest of drawers. Even if this did turn out to be for only one night – and she didn't see how that might come about, since there was nowhere else she could go except to the place Ismay and his man were in – Glashnacally – where *she* certainly would not want to stop – not alone with those two, in any case.

Get the job – if it was offered – which it might well *not* be; Charles Napier could have misconstrued Ismay's reaction. But stay here. For the time being – but here in any case,

where to her surprise and despite that peculiar telephone
call – from George Henry O'Bryen? – she felt at home. For
no good reason at all that she could think of.

Kind of a refuge?

A good distance from London, sure. Not that one could
afford to forget London and its threat: or stay here *too*
long.

Two or three days?

The job, though – she was lying flat – or as flat as she
could – on the narrow bed with its hard edges and central
sag: thinking that two or three days might be safe enough,
taking the job if he offered it and when the time came –
facing him, actually speaking with him – if she found she
could tolerate that prospect say for long enough to see a
way to do it that would give her a chance to get away . . .

Dublin, she thought. Hide out in Dublin.

Not just funking it Frank. *Not* losing my nerve. Did for a
moment, that's all. But not killing myself as well as him if
there's some way I needn't: not sending a shriek of 'Here I
am!' to the police in England either.

Michael O'Neill got back later than his aunt had expected
so they'd already had their meal – fish pie, predominantly
mackerel – and were drinking tea by the time he did breeze
in. He came in through a side door, not through the shop;
they were in the living-room cum kitchen, a long room
extending across almost the full width of the house, behind
the shop.

He was in an open-necked shirt and salt-stained rough
cotton trousers. He was brown from the sun – and from
the sea, the way Frank had been as a trawlerman in the
summer, when as he'd explained you got the sun off the
sea as well as from above. In a really fine month he'd go
almost black sometimes.

Michael crouching at the stove, getting the pie out. There

were carrots to have with it. He was slighter than Frank had been, smaller boned.

'Would you believe it, Sergeant Donovan and that new one from the coastguard was there?'

'At Glashnacally?'

'So they were. My God, they say 'tis a free country.' He laughed, glancing at Eileen as he set the pie down, and a plate and the carrots. 'A joke in the first place, if you're easy to amuse, but a strange circumstance that no matter where I tie up a boat them creatures can be counted on to show their ugly faces.'

'Was it at the house they were? Talking to the Englishman?'

'Some of the time, sure. And easy enough to guess what they'd be after saying. "Any boat you see on the move at night, *sorr*, be sure to give us a call."' He'd put on a whining tone and mimed a tug at his forelock. Then again in the same voice: '"And should you ever suspect there's goods being brought ashore over that quay, *sorr* . . ."'

Shaking his head, mouth already full of mackerel, onion and potato, his eyes on Eileen, their whites brilliant in the half-light and his tanned skin. Mrs O'Neill asking him, 'You did not in reality hear such things spoken?'

'I said, it's what they *would*'ve—'

'I had a call from George Henry, earlier.'

'And?'

'He'll be here Friday. Nothing much else.' She glanced at Eileen before switching the subject back, telling her, 'Michael has been accused of landing a package or two, once in a while.'

'*Falsely* accused. Suspicioned is all – for no good reason, no proof at all!'

He'd smiled at her. She asked him, 'Packages of what – what would it have been, if you had?'

'Who'd know? Tobacco or drink or both, I'd guess, but it's

them guessing, not my affair at all. What *I* land is lobsters. Are ye stayin' here with us then?'

'A night or two. All right?'

'It was just for the one night you said, when you walked in here. Now, one or two, is it. And what then – *where* then?'

'She's hoping the Englishman will want her to work for him type-writing letters and that. Then she might want to stay here permanent. Your man was told by some other feller she'd be wanting such work and he let on he'd be interested.'

'Typing letters, is it . . .'

'And business documents, and filing them and so forth. He has a lot of business to attend to, and secretarial work is what I've done before, so—'

'So.' Nodding, chewing, watching her. Glancing at his aunt then. 'Like we were saying, only this is one more now, just at this time all flocking in like crows?'

The same as *she*'d said, roughly. Eileen gave him the same answer: 'If you mean those two Englishmen and myself – the only connection is I want a job from him – and *he's* here because he's after buying Costelloe Lodge – as you must know—'

'Paying six thousand for it, so he is.'

'As much as *that*?'

'It's the fishing, see, more than the house.'

'I've heard about that. Best fishing in the world, so forth. But the other one was a steward – in that same White Star Line—'

'That same *Titanic*. Didn't he rush to tell us. Why, scores of lives he saved. Irish lives too, would you believe it. But his boss is here not only because he likes to fish, it's more because his name stinks, over.'

'Over' meaning in England – over the water. She challenged him, 'You know it all, so why do you find it strange them and myself coming here as you say *at this time*?'

'Mrs Maguire was on the *Titanic* too, Michael.'

Knife and fork descending slowly. Michael staring at her, swallowing.

'Tell me.'

'Her husband and child was drowned. They'd pushed her into a lifeboat then wouldn't let her husband into it, and the little boy ran off in a fright, so her husband starts after him—'

'I never saw either of them again. I'd never have got into the boat without them if I'd known – but they were letting it down then and I couldn't get out although I tried, there was other women sitting *on* me, and – ' Shaking her head. 'I was screaming mad for a while, so they told me later.'

'You would be still, I'd have thought, and I for one wouldn't blame you for it.'

'I'd have stayed with them in the ship if I could have, They were saying women and children first and I'd told him I wasn't going without him. Then I was tricked into it – and they wouldn't let Frank come – although men *did* get away—'

'Same as the feller here at Glashnacally.'

'He was helping with the boat-lowering, shouting orders – when they were keeping men *out* – would you believe it?'

'And him the boss of it all – and your man and child drowned – and you're here hoping he'll let you write bloody *letters* for him?'

Staring incredulously from her to his aunt and back again . . .

'It's not quite like that.' Eileen returned his glare defensively. Then – 'Wait, I'll show you. A letter I have upstairs.'

She fetched the White Star letter. Meaningless, but she was putting a lot of faith in it. She took it out of its envelope and handed it to Lorna. There were only a couple of paragraphs of it – introducing her as someone worthy of employment by White Star in the event of there being a suitable vacancy.

'So?'

'They gave me a passage from New York to England, with the steamer crossing then to Cork, because no White Star sailing was due to call at Queenstown at that time. Well, in Cork I had a good job before I gave it up to go with Frank and Tom to America, but they'd have replaced me by that time, so at White Star's office in London I asked was there a hope of working for them back here in Ireland. In Cork was what I had in mind, that's what the letter was for. But then just this last week one of the White Star people said Mr Ismay was coming here, and he'd told him about me, and *he'd* said oh, he'd need that kind of help all right, but what use if I was down there in Cork, for God's sake? The truth of it is I've come to realize now I wouldn't *want* to be in Cork – where I was happy with my husband, and had Tommy, and—'

'I'd have thought you'd want to kill the bastard.'

In a silence, the eyes steady and hard on hers. She couldn't answer. It was a jumble in her mind now. Too much of it. *And* the fear of that loss of nerve. Suppose for instance he said no, he had no work for her? *Then* what?

Mrs O'Neill said, 'With what he has on his conscience, wouldn't he kill *himself*, the blackguard?'

'No.' Michael shook his head. 'He's the fellow that *saves* himself. So *you* . . .'

With his eyes still on her he'd reached to help himself to tea: but had seemingly frozen in that position. The hand moving from the pot then, finger pointing: 'You *did* come here to kill him.'

'No, I—'

'Wanting only one night here – right?'

'Because—'

'Because after that you'd be legging it. Or maybe you'd have—'

'No – *no*—'

'You were a thought ahead of me saying it then, girl. But what *other* reason?'

Shaking her head: 'Because I simply did not know—'

'There's no other answer to it. I'm right, I know I am.' Looking at his aunt: then getting up. 'I'll be a minute. Hold on now.'

On his feet, heading for the door at the end. Mrs O'Neill seemingly unsurprised: 'More tea?'

'No, thank you.' She heard his boots on the stairs. No call of nature, therefore, for that he'd have gone outside. She was looking up at the cracked ceiling, wondering. His aunt telling her, 'Michael never did sit still more than five minutes when he could help it. And the ideas in his head you wouldn't *believe*. But I'll admit to you, girl – not that it's to your discredit at all – on this business about yourself he has *me* in two minds as well.'

'What – that I might—'

'Have come to kill him. Mind you, I hope you have *not*.' A jerk of the grey-streaked head: 'Here he comes now.'

Boots on the timber stairs again; then he came bursting in. Looking – triumphant, she thought.

'So what would *this* little yoke be for?'

The Browning – on the flat of his hand, as it had been the first time she'd seen it, on Henshaw's. She'd pushed back her chair, was rising. 'You've been into my room and rummaging—'

'I shan't need to again though, don't worry.' Tilting his hand to allow his aunt a better sight of the pistol. 'We know her *now*, so we do!'

'It's for my own protection, nothing else. Alone in London as I was—'

'A smart little weapon if I ever saw one. A *woman's* weapon. Easy to hide an' carry, and – close range, deadly enough. A thirty-two, I'd say. What – six, seven shots in it?' Sitting again, sliding out the magazine and thumbing out the little gleaming shells. Five of them. Joggling them in his palm like dice. He murmured, 'And one up the spout, maybe.' Working the cocking mechanism, jerking the upper part of it back: a sixth round flew out, was caught in mid-air in his left hand – like swiping at a wasp. 'There, now.'

'You're more familiar than I am with such things.'

'Not with this little article, I never saw the like before.' He was reloading the magazine, pressing in the six rounds. Counting: 'And – six.' Feeling the spring then. 'You'd get another in all right – if you had another. Fired one off for practice, maybe?'

Smiling up at her. Lorna O'Neill murmuring, 'Sit down, girl. Don't mind Mister Know-all.' To Michael, 'Give it back to her now.'

'I'm not sure I will. See, Mrs Maguire, no matter what I said a minute past, we wouldn't want you killing him, and especially not just now. No matter that you might want to – and you *would* – t'would be the wrong thing entirely.'

'Why? I *could* wait a day or two – I was thinking I would in any case, see how the land lies before I just – you know – wade in and—'

Surprisingly, Mrs O'Neill's hand had moved to cover hers. 'Hanging'd be no fun now, would it?'

'It would not, so.' Michael agreed. 'In any event I'd ask you at the very least to hold on a while.'

'For how long? Two or three days maybe, but – there's a good reason – private reason, I won't go into it—'

'Another thing I'll tell you – if you're interested. It'd suit *us* well, having you there with them. If you have the chance to. The job type-writing, I mean. But a good friend of ours, a person of importance to us what's more, would be fairly destroyed if any such outrage should be inflicted on your Mr Ismay – and with us having prior knowledge of it, even more so!'

'Tell me why in any case you wouldn't want me doing it right away?'

He looked queryingly at his aunt, and she nodded. 'You might say it's because we'd sooner have the place stay quiet. Not have the police all sniffing round more than they're bound to do no matter what. They'd be glad of the excuse I wouldn't be surprised. Suppose there was boats on the move at night, my dear – the way Michael was saying. There *could* be. Unbeknown to ourselves, of course. Or known, even – say by chance it was Michael's boat was being made use of. You heard him say what he was guessing Donovan or the coastguard would be asking those English – should they see a landing there. The pier's open to all, of course – and directly below the house – which has views both ways along the shore, besides. And the house itself with its barns an' that, and a good enough road from it. The owner's a man by name of Donal Cleary – a Wicklow gentleman, his business is horses but he's another of the syndicate here. George Henry O'Bryen had no hand in the letting of it, he might have taken steps to prevent it had he known a deal was in the making, but unfortunately he did not because your man moved in on it so quick – being himself a close friend of Cleary's, d'ye see?'

'My head's buzzing.'

'Ah, well, you're tired. The travelling's tiring, and in the heat of the day as well.'

'No need for her to know it all, besides.'

'Tired or not, there are still questions in my mind. Why, for instance, would it suit you to have me at Glashnacally?'

'Because if there was constabulary or soldiers around there much we'd be glad to hear of it. Whatever they was saying to the English, too.'

'Out of interest in the boats, landings—'

'Because they're more than enough interested in the place and us already. We wouldn't want to go blundering in where they might be expecting us.'

'Likely to happen soon, is it?'

'Ah, well, who'd know *that*?'

'I'd *need* to know. I told you, I can't wait many days. *Can't*.'

'We can trust her, Michael. Knowing what we do now.'

'If that's all gospel – sure.'

Mrs O'Neill poked at the pistol. 'This is real enough, is it not? She didn't show it to us either, remember?'

Michael told her, 'How soon it may or may not be is something I can't say. What comes, if it does, comes a long way, so . . .' A shake of the head. 'A fortnight, maybe?'

'I must be gone long before that.'

'Ten days, say?'

'A week at the outside. I'd thought two, three days at most. Look, I'll tell you – to me it could be life or death, staying too long.'

'But 'tis not in my power to change what's afoot already!'

'Then we can only hope it's sooner than you expect.'

'It might be, so.' Lorna O'Neill's tone was reassuring. 'But, Michael, she should know *something* of what it's about, at least. The importance of it, like. See, girl, you might say it's not so much whatever we're doing, it's what others believe we *might* be. Like – ' she'd dropped her voice to a murmur – 'what they say is going on up there in Ulster – the talk about landing guns and drilling, all that? So, there's others thinking then "Sure won't they be bringing in rifles here in Galway too?"'

'And will they be?'

'Maybe all over.' Michael shrugged. 'Wouldn't you guess?'

'*Guess* . . . You say you *know* me – ' a nod towards the pistol – 'because of that. But you don't trust me, Michael, do you. So you'll only drop hints. Why not come right out and say it? You ask me to spy for you, but—'

'*Spy*? Who said—'

'*And* you'd have me stay longer than is safe for me at all . . . Listen, I'll tell you a bit more of my story – what Frank and I would have been doing in America. He had a job to go to – an uncle with a motor repair business he was joining. He was clever with his hands, with everything mechanical. He was a trawlerman too – that might interest you, uh? When I first met him he was working out of Dungarvan, in Waterford. But as well as that he had his own ideas thought out – political notions, and friends in Cork who were – oh, you'd call them politicals, I suppose—'

'What kind of politics?'

'A free Ireland was their dream. Not "Home Rule" free, *truly* free. That was a point he made often enough. I'm reminded of it through your hints about landing guns. As if that's not the way your thoughts are running too? Well – in America when we'd got settled Frank was going to help in the raising of funds for it. Organizing shipments too, he said – whatever was asked of him.'

Both of them were watching and listening quite intently. Michael with an expression on his face she wasn't sure of. Suspicion lingering, maybe: of herself with this yarn so ready to trot out, having jumped to conclusions he and his aunt hadn't been entirely ready to confirm – although they'd let out enough. Thinking they could say a thing and at the same time *not* say it. But when the time came – *her* time – she might need their help. She told them, 'If you wanted proof of us there's the name of a man in Cork I could give you. I wasn't taking part in it myself then, I had a baby to look after, but for Frank now I would.' She nodded. 'I'll spy for you, don't worry.'

14

She'd passed a wretched night. Michael had left the house before she heard the aunt receiving a telephone call downstairs in the shop, and got up herself: realizing that she *had* slept a few hours, then – since he was gone and she hadn't heard him leave. Over a breakfast of porridge and tea she received then a whole stream of information from Lorna: the telephone call for instance had been an incoming telegram, and most calls were of that nature. There were only a few telephones in private houses in the district – yes, one at Glashnacally all right, Donal Cleary needing to be in touch with his studfarm in Kildare even when on fishing jaunts; he'd pulled strings in high places to get it installed. Costelloe Lodge had one too, on much the same basis – as had Clynagh, George Henry O'Bryen's place, which Eileen would be passing on her way to Glashnacally. Clynagh Lodge, that was: and this rocky basin here at this end of Cashla Bay was called Clynagh Bay – like the bent tip of a finger as it might be, at the top of Cashla. With the tide on it the boats could get in and out easy enough – the way Michael had gone at first light this morning, him and another lad rowing themselves down to Glashnacally where he was keeping his motor-launch – where he had it now, at any rate. He had another boat – a pulling-boat – in the pool of the river below Costelloe Lodge, keeping it there for when he did ghillie work for the salmon fishers, as he did for one or two of them when he was asked, especially when conditions weren't right for the fishing outside. Not that just ordinary bad weather would keep him in – it would have to be a blow and a half to do that – although when it was at its worst from the southwest his best lobster ground wasn't worth the risk. Risk to the pots, she meant by that, having them taken up and smashed among the rocks and then whole days and more to be spent repairing them and making new ones. That lobster ground was just to the west and south of the coastguard station, would you believe it: from Carrickadda all the way down to Foal Island and Coddu Rock, where in good times the shiny-blue creatures fairly teemed. There was other good spots too, of course, but that was where Michael had always done best – he and a friend, Mick McGurk from Rossaveel, sharing the best of it and mostly keeping others out.

A pause then, and a hard glance: 'Would you be after leaving that weapon of yours here in the house, Eileen?'

'You'd sooner I did not.'

'I would, and that's a fact.'

'I'll take it with me, then.'

'But not to be making use of it, uh?'

Looking at her, thinking about it. She'd done a *lot* of thinking, in the night. A shake of the head: 'Probably not.'

'*Probably*, is it now?'

'If he's giving me the job, don't worry, it'll be as I agreed.'

'But if he's not?'

'Well, listen. First – it's what I came here for. If I'm to be working there I'll have chances day after day. If I'm not, however – well, this morning I'll be there with him and *that* will be my chance – which I'd be bound to take. No –

wait, listen to this, please. If it goes that way, there'll be no doubt who's done it, or why. I'll be dead myself if I have the courage and I'm quick – it's that fellow Lloyd I'm scared of, if he should be close by. But my point is this, Lorna – I'd be either dead or running like a headless chicken, there'd be no reason for police searching or routing round, either alive or dead they'll have me – end of story and no bother to yourselves, d'you see?'

'But there's the other reason Michael gave you.'

'You mean your friend who'd be upset.'

'*Upset*, is it! Jesus God, girl—'

'Upset you too. I know. There's still a limit how long I can stay here.'

'Tell me why that is?'

'It has nothing to do with anything that's happened here. In Ireland even.' She slid her chair back. 'Now if it's two miles I have to walk, I'd best start out. Just smarten myself up a bit first—'

'But while I'm thinking of it – tell me the name of the man in Cork?'

'The man—'

'You said – your husband—'

'You want to check on me?'

'Not if you don't want us to – but you offered—'

'All right, so. O'Meara. I think *Doctor* O'Meara, and first name Eddie. He's important in politics down there and he spends time in Dublin too. As I said though, I myself never met him, it's only Frank he'd know of. And he met him through someone called Twomey – Jack Twomey.'

'All right. I know who'd know of him, d'you see. If he counts for anything much, he would . . . But this fellow Ismay now, Eileen – you don't think he'll guess what's in your mind – as Michael did?'

'He may do. I don't remember exactly how much the other White Star person said he'd told him. I suppose telling him anything at all about me would include that Frank and Tommy drowned. If he didn't know that, I'd be safe enough.'

'When you've come this far to seek him out – and with no halo hanging over you at least that's visible—'

'The rest of the circumstances, though – that I was looking for employment, which is natural enough – and got them to write that letter for me, and only after *that* was told about him?'

'But with the outcry they say there's been – him you might say sort of a fugitive already —'

'Yes. It's one of the things that's been filling my skull all night. But I believe, as I say, those other circumstances . . .'

Lorna had surprised her with her incisive tone, in that exchange about O'Meara. And even that she'd have wanted the name. She surprised her again now, to a lesser extent, by offering to lend her an old bicycle she had out there.

'It's a fair trudge, otherwise: and you in good clothes, and another hot day coming. Mind you, we have the donkey out there, and a cart, but ye wouldn't want the bother of it. It's Michael employs that yoke most, when he has pots to bring up an' that. But wait now while I show you – this old chart my husband had, show you where you'll be making for. Here, see . . .'

She pointed out the main features – on a much larger scale than her own map. Here, Costelloe village on the north shore of Clynagh Bay and Costelloe Lodge to the east with the river passing close; the tide would flood in there past the house and to a sharp elbow where it turned up under the road-bridge they'd come over yesterday. While the other way, where she'd be going now on the bicycle, passing around the top of this small bay and a few more cottages, then what looked to be a dead-straight mile of road, before long passing Clynagh Lodge on the right, and a couple of little hills, and straight on to a fork in the road at Glashnacally: 'If you wanted to leave the bay there, this way'd take you to Carraroe where there's a constabulary post, d'you see—'

'That close to Glashnacally?'

'When the post is manned – which often enough it is not.'

Across the bay from Glashnacally was Rossaveel – with a fairly substantial pier, by the looks of it. Trawler berths, maybe. Well – *would* be. Deepish water, there. She'd picked up enough from Frank to recognize features of that kind. And thinking of the talk last night, vague as it had been, about Michael's or other boats on the move: from there, might be? A trawler in from sea and berthing, boats then transporting illicit cargo from it across the bay to Glashnacally? Distance – to Struthan Quay, where the road curved closest – not much more than half a mile. Before moonrise or after moonset, or with the moon hidden on a cloudy night, maybe?

Opposite Clynagh Lodge, she noticed, not only was the road a lot further from the foreshore, the fringe of rock along the coastline stretched much further out. Hence, obviously, any smuggler's preference for Glashnacally and its quay.

There'd been a new moon the night before last, she thought.

'Where's the coastguard station?'

'Here.' Touching it with the tip of a knife. It was a mile or more below the narrows. She could see the offshore rocks Lorna had mentioned, Michael's lobster-catching ground. Cashla Point there, inside Foal Island, and on the other side of the entrance to the bay, Killeen Point. The length of the whole inlet, Cashla plus Clynagh, from there up to Costelloe was about three miles.

The shop door from the street had banged open, and there were voices – Irish-speaking. Customers this early in the day. Eileen murmured, 'I'll go out the back way.'

'You may need to move the saddle higher, with the legs you have on you. There'd be a spanner on the bench there.' From the doorway into the shop she called to them in Irish that she'd be with them directly, but came back then to Eileen: 'You have that object with you?'

'Oh, yes.' She was putting on her sun-hat. The day wasn't hot yet but it was going to be. 'When I get back I'll hide it somewhere outside.'

'Good luck, so.'

She rode out down the lane at the side where the petrol pump was and Ismay's motorcar had been parked the day before. Then into the road right-handed. Like yesterday's, it wasn't so much a road as a stony, juddery track. She'd raised the saddle but could have done with another inch or two. Managing, however – though not having ridden a bicycle for years – and passing the right-hand turn which the English tour party had taken and led seemingly for ever into a haze topped by the Connemara mountains. Then on her left were some men building yet another pier: although even with a high tide, she guessed, you wouldn't float anything bigger than a rowing boat in here. A man leaning on his long-handled spade waved to her: an *old* man, and other old men with him. She'd risked a quick wave back – the bike wobbling, and the shoulder-bag, the plaited cord of which was slung diagonally like a bandolier across her chest, bumping against her lower ribs. She had Frank's money-roll in there as well as the pistol. And she'd checked the pistol earlier – that the top round was out of the magazine and in the chamber, and the safety-catch set to 'safe'.

If he began 'No, I'm sorry but until I can move into the Lodge . . .'

Do it? Get it over?

Recent habit of thought – her promise to Frank, and all the exertions and emotions of the past month urged her *yes*.

To get rid of the doubt too – the fear of it, fear and shame of losing her nerve. Also – this was a thought she'd had in the night – that if he said yes, start work at once, and she did start and then Michael O'Neill's business was concluded – the rifles landed – so she'd have no reason to wait longer – mightn't it be more difficult when you knew the man?

Wasn't it impossible *already*?

She saw what had to be Clynagh Lodge off to the right. She'd have taken it for a farmhouse, with its barn behind it. And the small hill, flat-topped and neatly rounded: could have been man-made. A motte: man-made no less than six or seven hundred years ago, that would mean. And another, after only a few hundred yards, on the left. From the road, from just this angle and looking past that ancient hump of a fortification, there was a view straight down Cashla Bay to the open sea – well, out into Galway Bay, its wide entrance. After some burning off of the sea-mist you'd be looking at the Arans down there, she supposed. But the view was already closed off by the bulge of the bay's western shore thrusting in towards the narrows – Curraglass Point that would be, she remembered from the chart.

Buildings ahead now, though. Glashnacally, no doubt. A farmstead on the right, and a scattering of dwellings farther off and to the left; a track led off in that direction – to the north shore of the little Glashnacally inlet, of course. Then the fork which she'd expected – right to Carraroe and beyond, or left – this way, and around the head of the inlet then straight on southward to villages further down the peninsula, but she was branching away left again, free-wheeling down to the big old stone structure with a square lookout tower in the centre, and whole batteries of chimneys; and the quay down there below it, a pier jutting out beyond that to the left. On the level again, pedalling towards the back of it – what would be the front-door entrance maybe, but was still the back of the house, surely, its *face* would be the side that looked out across the water. Back of the house on her left now, therefore – and a timber barn on her right, with its doors standing open, and a larger, stone-built barn beyond.

Neglected, untidy yard. Nettles growing tall in patches, ivy clinging thickly to the walls and roofing of that other barn. Which in fact – getting a better sight of it – was the end of a line of stabling, with a multiplicity of doors. The house was greyish; she could imagine it as a barrack building – functional, austere, the row of windows on its upper floor as regular as a rank of soldiers – except for missing or broken panes of glass. Mr Donal Cleary wasn't bothering with this place much, even if he *had* installed a telephone.

'Good morning!'

Lloyd – emerging from the barn. The motor was in there, behind him, she could see the gleam of a brass-rimmed headlamp. The former steward was in overalls, with rolled-up shirtsleeves. She propped the bicycle against a stone mounting-block and lifted the bag's silk cord from over her head to her left shoulder. Left hand resting on the bag then, with its fingers inside the mouth of it, that draw-string closure, as she turned towards him: Lloyd was coming across the yard, wiping his hands on a rag.

'Help you?'

Narrow brown moustache: she remembered that: and the slicked-back hair. She reminded him, 'I saw you yesterday, did I not, in Costelloe?'

'Oh, yes, of course. At the O'Neills' shop – as I was leaving—'

'Mrs O'Neill told me your name is Lloyd.'

'And that I am in the service of Mr Bruce Ismay, no doubt.' A quick smile . . . 'We've been here only a few days but everyone knows everything about us, it seems – while we as yet know nothing about anyone. Except that I know you are not a local person – because Michael O'Neill didn't know who you were.'

She remembered having thought, at that first encounter, that he was noticeably well-spoken, for a steward. She told him, 'Michael knows now – I've taken a room in his aunt's house. It's Mr Ismay I've come to see. I'm Mrs Maguire.'

'Is Mr Ismay expecting you?'

'No. But he knows *of* me.'

Staring. A hand up to shield his eyes: the sun was getting to him over the southern end of the house, while Eileen was in its shade. Recalling that on E deck in the sinking ship she'd been in that ratty old coat that she'd bought from off a second-hand clothes barrow in a back-street of Cork, and her hair loose, unkempt – in fact both she and Frank would have been looking fairly desperate. Frank dripping wet from his expedition to their cabin: she thought there was a good chance the man wouldn't recognize her now.

No point reminding him, either.

'Ask Mr Ismay would he see me, please?'

'But may I ask in what connection?' He'd moved past her – ostensibly out of the sun's blinding effect but in the process putting himself between her and the house. Bodyguard, she thought: remembering Charles Napier's mention of poison-pen letters – which might well have included death threats. Lloyd explaining – somewhat apologetically – 'Part of my job, you see, is to protect Mr Ismay's privacy. You say he knows of you?'

'In connection with a job. I'm a secretary, shorthand-typist. I enquired of the White Star Line whether there might be prospects of employment – here in Ireland – and Mr Charles Napier of White Star mentioned me to Mr Ismay, and told me he'd expressed some interest. So—'

Lloyd had come closer. 'Mrs – Maguire – this may seem to be an impertinent request, but may I ask you to show me what's in that bag?'

'Show you – my *bag*?'

'I'm sorry, but – there have been threats, d'you see.'

'*Threats*? To – good heavens, you mean to – ' She'd turned, looking at the house. Back to him then: 'All right, then. Although it's – barmy—'

'World's full of barmies, Mrs Maguire.'

'But – how awful.' Moving as if to comply, but then stopping: 'Oh. Oh, look here.' Turning away slightly so he couldn't easily have grabbed it, while fumbling inside it for those letters: pushing the *In Loving Memory* one back in then, and handing him the White Star introduction. 'This would set your mind at rest.'

Bruce Ismay rose from a hard chair at what looked like a kitchen table piled deep with documents and files, and came towards her across the large, plank-floored room. This was on the first floor and at the left-hand end of the building as she'd entered it from the yard – the northern end, in fact. Lloyd had left her in the yard and taken the letter up to Ismay, then come back down and brought her up here, was hovering somewhere behind her now as Ismay strode forward with his hand out. He was wearing flannel trousers and a white shirt with a blue-spotted cravat at the neck.

'Mrs Maguire.' Not just shaking her hand, holding on to it. A crucial moment if there'd ever been one: she was aware of it even then, but retrospectively yet another that would stand out as a turning point. Her hand *had* been on the drawstring access to her bag: had moved virtually of its own accord to meet his. The moment in which if she'd been going to do it she'd have done it: and that moment gone now – without any truly conscious *decision* on her part, gone for ever. They were about eye to eye: she in her flat shoes, at that. His brown eyes wide apart and concerned, sympathetic. The curve of his moustache with its up-turned ends gave him a smiling look although there was no smile on the full lips below it. He let her hand go: 'Young Napier did tell me about you, but I must say I never dreamed you'd turn up here.'

'I didn't expect to either, Mr Ismay. But I found that Cork had become – uncongenial. Having been happy there before – '

'I understand. I do indeed. And Mrs Maguire, I am so *very* sorry—'

' – and since Charles Napier had told me this was where you were coming and that you might need secretarial assistance—'

'*Might*, indeed!' Turning and waving a hand towards that table . . . 'Look at that – just to kick off with. Some of it's going straight back to Cockspur Street with Bob Lloyd tomorrow, that's what I'm sorting out this morning. Now please, sit down.' He indicated an old rattan chair lined with worn brown cushioning; he drew up another for himself. 'Napier told you, I suppose, that I'm buying Costelloe Lodge.'

'Where I'd thought you'd be. Does it mean you couldn't employ me in the meantime? I do need a job, you see. I'm sorry, coming right down to it so abruptly, but even to pay for my board and lodging at Mrs O'Neill's—'

' – would be the least of our problems, I assure you. Accommodation of a more permanent nature would have to be arranged for you later, but in the interim if that suited you well enough – well, capital! Although we *are* going to be pigging it here rather, I may say . . . No – you want the work, and you'd be the answer to my prayers. Terms of employment we can agree easily, I'm sure.'

'I do have a letter of reference from the company I worked for in Cork until as recently as – oh, six weeks ago—'

'That's splendid. Matter of fact I was going to ask – well, he's a lawyer, name of O'Bryen, about finding someone in Galway perhaps, or even Dublin. He's expected here today or tomorrow, I believe. And to be spared all that – interviewing, and so forth – well, a Godsend. But – there's one very important aspect of it we must talk over, Mrs Maguire. It strikes me immediately and forcibly: the *Titanic* factor, you might call it – which in a way we share. That is to say it's the reason you're here and the reason *I'm* here – but it *could* make a working relationship pretty near impossible. If it did I wouldn't blame you – or be in the least surprised. After all you've been through – and who and what I am, and how you must feel – if one can even begin to guess at that . . . I repeat, I am so very, *very* sorry. Words are – inadequate, I'm afraid. Putting it at its simplest, the doubt is whether you might have – shall we say reservations, about working for me – with me – considering that, as has been pointed out and argued *ad nauseam* by this time – I have to bear primary responsibility for that disaster – including how it's turned out for you?'

She held his gaze. Telling herself *No, I would not.* But scared that the intensity of his gaze might draw the truth out of her. What had *seemed* to be the truth, although whether that had been never-never land, or *this* was . . .

She took a long breath. Either way, she was stuck with playing *this* part now.

'You say you bear the responsibility, but surely once a ship's at sea the responsibility's the captain's and the engineers' – or the ship's designers'?'

'The question of lifeboats, though. The loss of life – yet saving one's own. Mrs Maguire, if this is too sickening for you—'

'I wouldn't say so – and I'd agree with you it might be best to talk it out.'

'From *my* point of view, certainly. If you can bear it – I could well understand it if you couldn't. It's my own weakness, essentially, that makes me want to – improve – or at least ascertain – my standing in others' eyes, I suppose.

In this case, of course, in yours. Not exactly justify myself, more to *explain* – after all, if we're to work together, see each other practically every day—'

'Yes – I agree.'

'You're very kind, then.'

'I need a job – sir.'

'But there must be dozens of jobs going for experienced stenographers. Not this side of Galway, necessarily, but . . .' He shook his head: 'You're pulling my leg. You wouldn't dissemble to that extent, I'm sure. Napier told me – no, never mind that . . . Would you mind if I smoked a cigarette?'

'Not in the least.'

If she'd stuck to her original resolve, she realized, watching him cross to the chimney-piece and get himself a cigarette, he'd have been dead by now. Five minutes ago. She too – necessarily, because of Lloyd; he was still with them – at the far end of the room, a quick look round revealing that he was unpacking a tea-chest, carefully removing objects – glassware, by the look of it – wrapped in newspaper. An excuse to remain up here? she wondered.

The room was three or four times as long as it was broad, must have been made by knocking out at least two – no, three – internal walls. No less than four windows looked out on the bay, admitting a blaze of sunshine. All the windows were in need of cleaning, and the furnishings – well, a miscellany of junk. Behind her a match flared: Ismay was coming back, bringing an ashtray and a scent of Turkish tobacco with him. 'As I was saying – confessing – my own weakness. Since the event I've been through it a bit, one way and another. Nothing like as bad a time as you've had, I know – and must still be having, and I'm appalled to recognize will have for ever . . . My own experiences though – obviously of quite a different kind – frankly, they've put me to flight. Partly I may say for the sake of White Star, which in some ways will be better off without me now. It's a complicated move, of course – affecting family, friends, other businesses with which I'm connected, and so forth.'

'Will your wife and family be joining you here soon?'

'Not here, no. After I get occupation of Costelloe Lodge – and have certain alterations made. There's plenty to be done – and a cottage to be built behind the house. That's why I needed somewhere to live within easy reach – one really has to be on the spot. But we – my wife and I – have two sons and two daughters – still of school and Varsity age – and a fairly large house in London – anyway, I won't bore you with domestic detail. What's vital to establish between you and me is whether you're certain you could take this on, *not* be riven by – oh, attribution of blame, even feelings of disloyalty to those who were dear to you and for whom you'd not unreasonably hold me responsible. Understand me, please – well, as I've said, I couldn't posssibly blame you if you did. The very worst of it, of course, being that I was able to save myself – and the truth there – the *absolute* truth – is that if it were to happen all over again I would *not*.'

'But nor would I.'

He was gazing at her through a haze of pale blue smoke: with the sun behind it, an ectoplasmic aura surrounding him. If she'd been pointing the pistol at him he'd hardly have looked more riveted. The pistol in the bag, under her hand. Ismay nodding: 'I believe you mean it.'

'I've never been clearer about anything in my life. I was tricked into embarking. If I'd known my husband wasn't going to be allowed to come – let alone what happened with our son—'

Both looked round as Lloyd left the room. Eileen heard him going downstairs then, rattling down the stone stair-case – stone treads all slightly hollowed, she'd noticed on the way up, doubtless by the hobnailed boots of coast-guards, a century or two of them. The stairs were in the centre of the building, under the tower, might well form part of its support. Ismay resumed: 'Sadly there's no palliative, let alone cure. For you, that is – I'm not speaking of myself. But if we could – if you'd hear my explanation of the events, the degree of my responsibility for them – as I see it, of course, I can only give you my own view – and you could *then* decide whether you could work for me?'

She'd nodded. 'Certainly.'

'The last thing I want is to put you off. As I've – indicated, I'd like it very much if you felt you could – from several points of view – but if on reflection you decide against it, if you like I'd have a word with this solicitor I'm dealing with – local man, O'Bryen, I've fished with him and know him well, he's as sound as a bell – well, he'd know of any other openings there might be for you – in Galway, for instance.'

'Mrs O'Neill did mention him. The same way – in case you weren't in a position to take me on.'

'Did she, indeed. But what *I'm* getting at is that you should not feel pressured by the need of work in purely financial terms. I'm sure there'd be such alternatives, and – what help you might need, you'll get. But now let's get started. An obvious starting point being – taking it head-on now – lifeboats. Of which, well, I hardly need tell you there weren't enough of them – and as managing director of the Line I can't evade responsibility for that fatal deficiency. I *was* responsible for it – as the head man, I *was*. And you could see it as a very simple issue requiring no depth of technical knowledge at all – so many souls on board, so many places in each boat, *ergo*, required number of boats is A divided by B, and that's the answer. But – one, the ship was regarded as unsinkable. It wasn't, but it was generally regarded as such. Lifeboats therefore *might* even have been thought of as superfluous altogether – and in fact there's no liner operating today that has a sufficiency of boats for its maximum number of passengers and crew. The Germans – Hamburg Amerika Line – claim that their ships do have now – but only since our own disaster. In the case of the *Titanic*, when she was fitting out in Belfast it was recommended to us – all right, to *me* – that fewer sets of davits should be installed than had been on the blueprints. The reason put forward was that the second-class recreation space on that deck would be less restricted. Passenger comfort versus passenger safety, you might say; but then again, since she was supposedly unsinkable . . . Anyway I accepted the recommendation, so it's fairly and squarely down to me . . . As to this "unsinkability", I might add – well, if you read all the Inquiry reports you know it – the effect of ramming that iceberg was to rip her open like a can of sardines – which had never been envisaged as a possibility. Perhaps it should have been, but that's an entirely technical matter – design and construction, in which area a business manager can only be guided by the advice of experts in those fields.'

Pausing. Eileen hearing Lloyd on the stairs again: and in her head re-hearing Frank on E deck, back up from his trip below, *Safe now, Tom. Home and dry*. Then a minute later, this steward: *She won't float more than another hour*. As echoey in memory as some stage voice of doom: even *then* it had seemed unreal, not really happening. Tuning to Ismay's voice again though: 'Causes of striking the iceberg, next. First and foremost – speed. Although warnings had been received of ice ahead of us. I admit, we were set on making a fast passage. I personally was calling for full speed. But I could only urge, not order – I was not the captain or chief engineer or navigating officer. If Captain Smith had said to me "No, we must reduce speed", I could have argued – *would* have, the fact is I had huge confidence in that ship, I wasn't foreseeing any danger – but I couldn't have overridden his decision.'

Lloyd had lumbered in; he set down another heavy-looking tea-chest, stood watching and listening for a few moments – or getting his breath back – then went off again. Ismay sucking in another lungful of smoke, and stubbing out the cigarette.

'Another and perhaps more direct cause – ridiculously simple as it is – is that the lookouts did not have binoculars. Consequently the 'berg was only sighted at such close range that the helm order to avoid it was given too late. How the binoculars could have been lost or stolen while the ship was in Southampton – as has been asserted – I have no idea whatsoever. In my own non-technical view it's the one quite dramatically simple cause of the disaster. Indeed, how lookouts could be sent up on watch without binoculars strikes even the landlubber as barely credible. But there it is, it happened. That great ship and all those people – for the want of two pairs of field-glasses. Good God, they might even have borrowed some from passengers!'

She was seeing it as well as hearing – anticipating the scene he'd be describing – interpreting – soon. That figure capering about, howling, 'Lower aw-a-a-y!' Not the boat *she'd* been in. At that stage she and Frank and Tom had been amongst the crowd on deck. Whereas when hers had been on its way down she'd seen nothing – she'd been fighting, screaming – *mad* . . .

With that sequence printed on her brain?

'It's kind and patient of you to put up with this dissertation, Mrs Maguire. We're coming now to what bears most directly on your own – nightmare, it must have been. If this were a report I was writing the headings would be: "Boats – women and children first – prevention of embarkation by males". And my own escape. Can you put up with hearing it?'

'It's – the whole crux, isn't it?'

'It is. It *is*. So – all right . . . You'll know that the principle of "women and children first" is an ancient one – especially at sea, and quite plainly right?'

'At least when it's known there aren't enough boats for everyone.'

'Exactly. If there *were* enough, there'd be no reason a man and wife or whole family shouldn't escape together. Unless a ship's going down so fast it's only the first away who'll be saved. In this case it was purely a shortage of boats, places in boats—'

'Not *purely*. There were a lot of people trapped below: including women and children.'

'That's true, I know. And entirely – hideous. But we could talk for a month, trying to explain that side of it. For present purposes let's concentrate on passengers who were on deck and handy to the boats, and the exclusion of men – although some were required, to handle the boats—'

'Some of them stewards who'd never touched an oar or steered a boat in their lives.'

'So I've been told.'

'While my husband had been a trawlerman, a seaman. Unfortunately he didn't say so and I didn't think of it as having relevance. Nor were we asked. I think if I *had* had that much sense it might have saved his life and Tom's.'

'Your little boy, who took fright.'

'Charles Napier did give you the whole story then. Yes. As I said, I was tricked into embarking. I'd assumed Frank *would* be allowed to come with me. We'd seen other men embarked, and boats being lowered with men in them—'

'Certain officers applied the principle more rigorously than others, I'm afraid.'

'If I'd known how it would be, I *would* have stayed on the ship with them.'

'My dear – Mrs Maguire.' Swallowing, shaking his

head . . . 'If *you* feel that – when you had every right
to embark – imagine how *I* feel, when I had none, only
succumbed to – to a momentary *aberration*—'

'Tell me how it happened?'

'Yes. On a personal level this *is* the nub of it, of course.
The crux, you called it. Simple enough – as well as shame-
ful enough. Well . . . I was on the boat-deck, trying to
help. None too successfully, at one stage. As an officer
of the company, one felt one *should* be helping. But I
was roundly ticked off by one of the young officers –
I was making a fool of myself, giving orders I had no
right to give . . . So – I stood aside for a while, then
went to another boat to help – helping women to climb
aboard and so forth. The officer in charge of this one was
calling for more women passengers to come forward and
embark, and they weren't forthcoming. I and a few other
chaps tried to rout some out of the crowd – but there
were a lot who wouldn't move. Clinging to husbands,
hiding away, insisting they were safer where they were
– scared of what they saw as the fragility of the boats and
the distance down to that icy sea . . . But we persuaded
some, and helped them over. This was boat C, by the way,
one of the four canvas-sided collapsibles. The boat that had
been on these davits – number one – had been lowered, this
one then man-handled into position and hooked on, swung
up. And two male passengers who promptly forced their
way into it were just as promptly hauled out – with the
help of other male passengers who were standing by. Men
were trying to rush boats here and there – I dare say you'd
have seen some of it. But this boat C – we'd collected all
the women we could get, and the officer – it was the chief
officer, Wilde – still shouting for more, but none coming
forward – and the lowering started. There was still room
in it, you see.'

'So you got in.'

'Yes. I got in. I saved myself while others were standing back, or – as in your husband's case, for instance—'

'He'd gone inside the ship in pursuit of Tommy. That truly is *not* relevant. You didn't take a place that anyone else might have occupied if you hadn't.'

'The bandsmen were still playing. That's one of the sounds I still hear. The other – the truly *awful*—'

'The people in the sea.'

His eyes on hers, and a slow nod. 'As you say. The people in the sea.'

Arnold Collindale checked the time as he entered the White Star office. His hand with the watch in it rising to his mouth then, covering an almost soundless belch. There were customers at the near end of the mahogany counter; he passed behind them and stopped at the other end, surveying the clerks at their desks. Napier recognized him after only a moment's hesitation: hesitated again before going to attend to him.

'Mr Fawcett . . .'

'Well?'

'That's a police sergeant from Scotland Yard. I should imagine he's here on the same business as the other one – which you dealt with?'

'How d'you know that's what he is?'

Getting up, though: having at a glance taken in the off-the-peg tweed jacket, luxuriant moustache and sideboards, meaty hands resting on the counter. In another glance showing surprise at Napier's 'I just do happen to know.' Napier went with him to the counter: 'Good morning, Sergeant. My name is Napier, but if it's about that address in Ireland, Mr Fawcett here—'

'I'm Sergeant Arnold Collindale, Mr Fawcett. This gentleman's right, it was you I was to ask for. Inspector Tait called on you yesterday, about nine thirty?'

'About then. I was able to give him *two* addresses. But if this is likely to take us long, Sergeant—'

'It is not, sir. Brief, and discreet – my word on that. No, it's just that on both addresses regrettably we've drawn blanks.' He had his notebook out. 'Here we are. One address in Cork City, the other at – Skibbereen. Some distance away, I gather.' He wetted a thumb, to flip pages over. 'Our friends the Royal Irish Constabulary have been quick enough – indeed *very* quick, twenty-four hours, not much more – they telegraphed the inspector this morning – in a nutshell, no dice.' A glance at Napier: 'You're keeping well, I trust?' Then to Fawcett, 'We patronize the same gourmet establishment of a lunchtime, not infrequently.' A nod to Napier: 'And after hearing mine hostess call me "Sergeant", you enquired of her from which regiment had I deserted. Or something on those lines. No, don't worry, sir – the enquiring mind is one of our greatest natural assets – you might say very much up my street. But these addresses now, sir.' Tapping the notebook, addressing Fawcett: 'The one that seemed most likely was that of Mrs Dennis Burke, mother of the young lady we're endeavouring to trace, at this place – Skibbereen, County Cork. However, the RIC tell us that Mrs Burke was unable to assist them. The last she'd heard of her daughter was a letter from a London address which we have already – Cyrus Lane in Islington – a letter in which Mrs Maguire said she hoped to be back in Ireland soon and would be in touch. Nor does this Mrs Burke know the address of the husband's family, although she thought it might be in Tipperary. She had no personal contact with her former son-in-law's people, apparently. But RIC inquiries are continuing, in that direction. While this other address – the town one, rooms the Maguires were renting right up to the day of their departure for America – is a complete dead-end, apparently. No forwarding address, no incoming correspondence since then, nothing.'

Fawcett asked Napier, 'She *has* returned to Ireland, has she not?'

'We issued rail and steamer warrants which you signed on May the third, and she left about a week after that.' Napier added – to the sergeant – 'Sailing from Fishguard evening ninth she'd have landed at Queenstown late afternoon tenth.'

'Could be anywhere in Ireland by now, then.' Collindale shrugged. 'Only a skip and a jump from end to end – uh?'

Fawcett asked him, 'Would your Irish Constabulary colleagues have questioned the mother as to other friends or relatives?'

'Definitely would have. But Mrs Burke was not exactly spilling over with information, I gather. You'd think she *would* know of a friend or two. Unless of course she feels she has reason not to. We might go back to them, on that.' A shrug, and shutting the notebook. 'If anything should occur to you, sir – or crop up from any other source—'

'Of course. But—'

'If I might leave you Inspector Tait's telephone number at the Yard, sir?'

'Certainly, although it's unlikely—'

Napier asked him, 'What is Mrs Maguire supposed to have done, Sergeant?'

'Oh.' A shake of the head, and a glance round towards others now at the counter. He murmured, 'That I'm not at liberty to discuss. In fact she may not have *done* anything at all. But it's a murder inquiry – '

'Murder—'

' – with which she may be able to assist us, sir, that's all.'

Ismay sat back. 'So that's settled. Napier was absolutely right about your attitude – bearing no grudge. I must say, I found it hard to believe. "Stricken but not blaming" was his phrase. Bless the boy, I'd better drop him a line.'

'No – please – may I ask you not to?' She saw his surprise: added quickly, 'I'd sooner people did not get to know I'm here. The main reason is I have a mother – here in Ireland – who's married to a man I detest, and I couldn't *bear* – see, she might hear from others, if—'

'Just as you like.' He gestured: '*Both* of us in our own ways hiding out. I won't mention your name to anyone. I have secretarial assistance here, that's all. But in all the circumstances, Mrs Maguire, I am *so* pleased . . .'

He clearly was delighted. And she'd have liked it to be real – *not* to have been wondering *For how many days?* A hand to her forehead: dizzy, suddenly. Ismay halfway to his feet, alarmed: 'Are you all right?'

'It's nothing. Just—' She shook her head: she'd felt she was about to faint. 'No, I *am* all right. Truly. I'm sorry – *stupid*—'

'Not an adjective that I'd have applied. But perhaps you need a rest. On top of that dreadful experience – and then the labour of getting yourself over here – a bit of a steeplechase, I dare say, culminating in the Becher's Brook of bearding me in my den here?'

'Quite all right now, anyway.'

'Weren't you almost fainting?'

'No, just – I don't know. Perhaps. But working would be better for one than resting. Take one's mind off – all that . . .' Glancing round, telling herself, *You've been out of your mind, Eileen. Go rattling on, he'll realize it.* Focusing then on the steward, Lloyd, who'd just come back into the room: and on the stack of papers on that scrubbed-wood table . . . 'When should I start? Can I help with *that*?'

'No. Thank you, but I'm nearly done with it – and I know exactly what I'm looking for. Mainly documents and copies of documents that shouldn't be here at all – that I don't need and in any case would more properly be in the strongroom at Cockspur Street. So – well, there'd be nothing for you to do tomorrow either – I'll be driving Lloyd to Galway, to put him on the train. More specifically, Lloyd driving, I'll bring the motor back. And on your own here, none of this would make sense. Which reminds me, we need a typewriter. One on its way, Lloyd, am I right?'

'There is indeed, sir. *Ought* to be here any day now, with the other bulky items. The same shipment as your cabin trunks. I say "any day", but by cart or lorry from Galway, I suppose—'

'We'll have to be patient.' Ismay turned back to Eileen. 'In which circumstances, are you *sure* you wouldn't like a week's rest before you start?'

'Certain, absolutely.'

'Start on Monday, then. On Saturday – if you like – I'll show you round. In the motor, I mean, our surroundings here. From my fishing jaunts I know the lie of the land fairly well. But here now – you two haven't been properly introduced, have you . . . Robert Lloyd, formerly a first-class assistant chief steward in the White Star Line – in the *Titanic*, in fact. He's given up seafaring to come and smooth my path for me here. Lloyd, Mrs Maguire will be joining us as from Monday, as my secretary. For the time being she'll continue to board at Mrs O'Neill's, and when we have the Lodge and the new cottage – well, that we'll have to work out. Lloyd will be bringing his wife and children over, in due course – for the time being they're having to do without him – and later on there'll be a number of servants moving over from London. Depend on it, you'll have some place of your own. And what else . . . Well, we do have a cook here – name of Mary Nagle, lives nearby, recommended to me by the owner of this place – so you can lunch here of course, during the working week. In the normal course of things I'd suggest you and Lloyd might mess together, but as things are for now we'll be all hugger-mugger. Oh, transport – you came this morning on a bicycle, Lloyd mentioned.'

She nodded. 'Mrs O'Neill very kindly lent it to me.'

'You'll need one of your own. We'll see to that. In foul weather Lloyd might drive you to and fro, but—'

Telephone. She'd noticed it was on the wall at the end of the room where Lloyd had been unpacking tea-chests. He – Lloyd – went to it now.

'Glashnacally – Mr Ismay's—'

Listening . . . Then: 'Yes, sir. I'll see if he's available. He was just going out, but – would you hold the line, sir?' He put his palm over the mouthpiece. 'Mr O'Bryen for you, sir.'

'Ah, capital . . .'

'Mr Ismay is just coming.' He left the receiver hanging: Ismay had to stoop slightly to the level of the mouthpiece. 'That you, O'Bryen? Yes. Yes, indeed. Come when it suits you. Tomorrow I shan't be here until fairly late, I have to leave for Galway, first thing, taking a chap to catch a train—'

Lloyd offered, 'Might show you the rest of the house, Mrs Maguire? They'll be talking for some while, probably. I might introduce Mrs Nagle, too?'

Ismay had his back to them and the receiver at his ear, Eileen asked quietly, 'Is it possible to get up to the tower?'

It was. And the view, he assured her, was stupendous. He escorted her along the passage to where the stairs came up from below, and ducked into a low, arched entrance to the spiral leading on up. Cold, damp-feeling stone, the spiral a tight corkscrew, sunlight admitted only through narrow slits. Lloyd climbing ahead of her: not a big man, but broad, filling the space above her, telling her over his shoulder that when she saw the view she'd agree it was worth the climb. She remembered having thought on E deck that he had the voice and manner of a person of some education. Hence Ismay's choice of him as general factotum, she supposed.

The top of the tower was square, with a low crenellated wall around it, and a view that was quite stunning. Sea, land, coastline, headlands, and the grey sprinklings of villages. Blaze of hot sun: already *very* hot. Behind – westward – was a large inland lough: looking over it one saw the blue of the next bay – Greatman's, she remembered. Northward lay the dusty ribbon of the road she'd come down – with those mottes and Clynagh Lodge in the near foreground and Costelloe at the head of the inlet. She was turning and turning: whichever way you looked there was so much to see: over there, Rossaveel, and southwards Cashla Bay's widening exit into Galway Bay.

Lloyd was pointing southeastward. 'If you look just over that coastline and the water beyond its southern point, that whitish building's the coastguard station that replaced this one.'

'Overlooking the entrance to the bay.'

'The bay's outer approaches too though. And southwestward, the entrance to that next bay as well. Greatman's, it's called.'

'You've only been here since Friday last, but you've absorbed a lot.'

'Yes – well . . . Mr Ismay knows it well, of course, I've some catching up to do. And as it happens we had a visit yesterday from a coastguard officer – we came up here and he was pointing out this and that feature of the seascape. They're concerned – coastguard and constabulary – that there may be an attempt to land guns here, in the very near future.'

'*Really?*'

'I think we're supposed to send up distress rockets if we see it going on. They're prophesying that it's likely to happen all over Ireland – countering threats of military action by Ulstermen, you see. Well, I shan't be here, of course.'

'As imminent as that, is it?'

'They seem to think so. They were asking might they billet soldiers here – at the south end or even in the stables, maybe.'

'When?'

'Oh – at short notice. When and if. Mr Ismay could hardly have refused. But – why *here*? one wonders . . . Mrs Maguire – may I ask you something?'

'Of course.' Taking her eyes off the narrows – Curraglass Point and the view down to and past Cashla Point, and way out there, seaward, the Arans. 'Ask anything you like.'

'Might we have met on board the *Titanic*?'

'Oh.' Pausing – as one might, if one had been wondering, but unsure. 'How strange you should ask. I think we may have. It's the timbre of your voice I seem to recognize. But—'

'And I yours. But also – if you'll forgive the personal allusion – your tallness. If it *was* you – with your husband and small child – I was on my way to go up on deck by way of the grand staircase – coming along E deck from my cabin, and I'd met a whole crowd of third-class going aft with a steward guiding them. Then – some time after that main body of them – these others. You, if it *was* you . . . I stopped and advised you to hurry, catch up with those others. You seemed to be stragglers, and I wondered for a moment or two whether I mightn't let you up through first class – but I had to decide against it. If an officer had met us, for instance . . .'

'You'd have been in trouble.'

It had been her suggestion, of course, and his response had been *Heavens, you'd have me shot!* She remembered Frank's growl then – *There's worse deaths.* The two men she remembered as standing eye to eye then – her own view of them in profile and close-up. The steward *might* have been deliberating whether to chance it and let them up: might have forgotten that it had been she who'd asked him to.

But she also remembered Michael O'Neill's caustic *Didn't he rush to tell us. Why, scores of lives he saved*! She shook her head: 'It wouldn't necessarily have got Frank into a boat, even if you had.'

'But – isn't it *amazing* that—'

'I guessed you'd be up here.' Ismay, emerging from the stairway. 'Some view, isn't it? About as fine as any . . . Lloyd, small change of plan. O'Bryen's motoring to Galway in the morning, so *he*'ll take you. Saving me the trip – and he'll be back tomorrow night, he and I can do our business over the weekend. So tomorrow, Mrs Maguire – unless you'd prefer to take it easy?'

'No—'

'A preliminary run over the scope of the work we'll be doing, then. And in the afternoon perhaps, a guided tour? Anyway, come on down now, let's see what Mrs Nagle's giving us for lunch.'

15

She asked Mrs O'Neill that evening, 'Remember Michael saying there was a policeman and a coastguard officer at Glashnacally when he was there yesterday?'

'I do, of course.'

'Well, the steward – Lloyd – told me they'd informed Mr Ismay that an attempt to land guns might be expected soon. How soon exactly he couldn't say, but he's going to England tomorrow for about ten days and he seemed to think it might happen while he's away. He also said the coastguard asked might they billet soldiers there at the house – in the south end where the roof's fallen in, or in the stables.'

'And will they?'

'I think so. Lloyd only said, "Mr Ismay could hardly refuse". I suppose he couldn't.'

'And that's all?'

'Yes. I didn't want to seem nosy.'

'Nothing said about Michael – although he was there below?'

'Nothing as far as I know. What I mean is it wouldn't do for me to ask too many questions.'

'It's interesting enough in any case, what he said.'

'The only other mention of it – I said to Mr Ismay this afternoon, "I hear there's to be landings of guns here" – that Lloyd had told me – and all he said was that he hoped they were wrong, billeting of soldiers and so forth was the last thing *he* wanted.'

'Sounds like you're getting along well with him, Eileen.'

'Yes. As a matter of fact, I am. You'll think I'm mad, I know. One minute I'm here to – ' Glancing round: but there was no one else in the shop. ' – you know – and only delaying it because *you* wanted—'

'And now are you calling it off?'

She shrugged, turning away. Thinking about Frank: and her promise to him and Tom. The days and nights of conversation with them in Mrs Dalby's cabin, and that long, reflective night she'd spent on deck during the passage back from New York. Turning back to Mrs O'Neill – who was slicing bacon, turning the cutter handle steadily and watching the slices peeling off, folding over on each other . . . 'You see – the truth of it is – he didn't kill Frank or Tom; and saving himself, which he did in a moment's loss of control of himself or whatever you might call it – doing that didn't cost anyone else's life, only saved his own. And the way it's left him now is he's like me – wishes to God he'd stayed on the ship and drowned. There's a whole tangled mess of it but you could as well say the man who killed Frank was the creature that stole the binoculars in Southampton – and if then you were to say a sneak-thief's only a sneak-thief, he'd not have the brain to see what his pilfering might lead to – then what about the man – officer, I suppose, or petty officer – who sent the lookouts to the crow's nest and not a pair of glasses between them?'

'I'm not following you, girl.' Mrs O'Neill had pushed a heap of bacon slices aside with the blunt fingers of her left hand, and was adjusting the position of the rest of the side in the steel clamp. 'Beyond me *al*together.'

'Not having binoculars, d'you see, they spotted the iceberg so late the ship wasn't turned in time. He was telling me more of it this afternoon. 'Twas too late when the rudder was put over so the ship had no more than just begun to turn, and that edge of the 'berg under water – there's a lot more below the surface than you'd see above it, you know – was like some great blade slashing through the plating down that side. If they'd stayed on course and not touched the helm at all she'd have hit it head-on and there'd have been damage done all right but only to that first – front – compartment – which could have filled with water and the ship come nowhere near to sinking. That space and the one next to it could have filled, and she'd not have sunk, but the way it was, the plating was split open so far back the entirety of her was bound to fill.'

'Tell Michael, won't you. He's a sailor, he'd be mad for all that. Tell *me* this, though – have you rid yourself of that firearm?'

'No. Not yet.'

'Ah. Have you *not*.'

'I'm keeping it with me all the time, in this bag here. Don't worry, they'll not search your house and find it.'

'And what use would you have for it now?'

The answer to that was tied up with the threat from London – which was prominent in her thinking now. In effect, that it – the Browning – might be her best way out. All right, to herself she could admit it: to Lorna O'Neill though – who wasn't telling *her* quite everything, not by any means – 'I hope you're right, I'll have no use for it. If I did have though, it would be in connection with what I told you and Michael last night – that I shan't – can't – be staying here for ever.'

'Or even many days, you gave us to understand.'

'That's probably how it is, Lorna.'

'It depends on others, then. Outsiders.'

'I've not mentioned it to Mr Ismay. He wants me working for him and I've said I will – and God's truth, Lorna, I wish I *were* free to stay, but—'

'It's something you're running from, so.'

'Running. Well—'

'Something you did when you was over, was it? Is it the police from over that's hunting you now?'

The telephone rang. Eileen staring at her: glad of the interruption, and initial surprise fading in the realization that it had been a fairly easy guess. Also realizing that if they were on her trail at all, *running* was what she'd be doing for evermore – until they caught her. Before which, of course – the Browning . . .

Mrs O'Neill having left the slicing machine was wiping her hands on her apron as she moved along into the post-office section where the 'phone was.

'Hello. O'Neill's.'

Looking round at Eileen with that question still in her eyes. Then a sudden smile: 'Ah, it's yourself, so!'

Listening – to a man's voice, Eileen could hear it. Lorna then: 'Of course. Of course. Michael's not here this minute . . . Sure, wouldn't you know it, lobstering – but only down there by Illaunawehichy. Lifting old Joe Fahy's pots for him. Ah, he'd have some for ye, sure he would. Will I give ye a call when he's home? I will, so.'

She'd hung up.

'George Henry O'Bryen, that was. Wants a lobster or two, he'll be calling in here later when Michael's back.'

'Mr O'Bryen's giving Ismay's man a lift into Galway in the morning.'

'Then he'll be giving the lobsters a lift there too, no doubt. If Michael has any for him, that is. What I said a minute ago, girl – am I right?'

'What you said . . .'

'Why you'd be dashing off although you'd sooner not?'

'Oh. Yes.' She felt instinctively that it would be a blunder to admit to having killed that creature. Despite having made no bones about admitting an *intention* of killing Ismay. Which unlike the other *would* have been murder, and premeditated. She was aware of other confusions and contradictions too: having come with that set purpose, then agreed to hold on a while – after the sudden crisis of nerves, as a result of which she'd been ready to accede to the O'Neills' urgings to lay off – on the face of it, just for a while, but in reality *grabbing* at that as a reason for inaction. Or for 'delay', as she might have called it then – twenty-four hours ago. And 'crisis of nerves' being a euphemism for blue funk – revulsion, abhorrence even . . .

Out of fright? Or *sanity*?

She unquestionably had intended to go through with it. Wouldn't be here otherwise, wouldn't have had the pistol. Had sworn to Frank – time and time again, in good faith, *intent* on it.

Now it felt as if she might have been drunk, or drugged.

So what about the statement she'd made last night – straight off the top of her head, not having thought it out, simply blurting it out – *I was not taking part in it myself . . . but for Frank now I would . . .*

Trust oneself in *that*?

Yes. Because it was what Frank had believed in, deeply and passionately enough to have kept it mostly locked in himself – as she'd known it was, only in his lifetime tried to ignore because she'd had other priorities in mind.

Make up for that now, therefore – if they gave her a chance to, and if London held off long enough – *and* having the pistol as a way out, if it came to that.

'I'll tell you this, Eileen.' Lorna O'Neill was back at her bacon-slicing: 'Whatever trouble it is you're in, you'd not find a better man than George Henry O'Bryen to help you out of it. If you did want help, that is. He's a good man and a kind man, and as clever as they come, I'll tell you.'

Michael got in at about seven. He had seven lobsters too, he told them, good ones, his share of the catch in old Joe Fahy's pots, payment for having lifted and cleaned and re-baited the pots, the old man being semi-crippled now and his son Padraigh away at sea. Michael told Eileen he'd dumped them where he always did, in the tub outside at the back, and she went out for a look at the poor things, squirming around in there, blue-black in the clear water and softening evening light. It was an old bathtub he had them in, in salt water that he pulled up in a bucket on a rope, across the road there when the tide was in.

While he was cleaning himself up, his aunt telephoned George Henry O'Bryen and invited him to come over. He wasn't there, but his cook said he'd be home shortly, and soon afterwards he called back. She told him Michael *had* got lobsters . . . 'Bring a bucket for them, so? If they're to go to the city with you in the morning?'

She'd cackled, hanging up – for having surprised him by knowing that. Although tomorrow being Friday, chances were that he would have been going to his office anyway. He'd come down today from Clifden, apparently.

There were bar customers by this time, and as they were keeping Lorna busy Eileen made herself useful in the kitchen, where a mutton stew was simmering and there were carrots and potatoes to be prepared. Michael came down while she was doing it. He'd shaved and had on a clean shirt – out of respect for 'George Henry' no doubt.

'So you are now Mr Ismay's secretary, you say.'

'I am, Michael, and the truth is I like the man.'

'So you won't now be after shooting him?'

'I'd be glad if you'd put that out of mind.'

'If *you* have, so . . .' He was close to the doorway into

the shop, keeping an eye on the customers in there and his aunt bar-tending; it was all Irish they were talking out there. Eileen was at the table, peeling potatoes. Michael glanced back at her: 'And how long may we expect to have you with us – in view of this change of your plans, and what you were telling us last night?'

'I'll work there and live here for as long as I can. There's no change of course to what I told you, that I probably won't be able to stay long. You asked me to hold on with what I *had* intended, just so as not to have the police stirred up and nosing round. That doesn't apply now – I'll simply be working at Glashnacally and residing here – if that's all right with you and your aunt. I can't say for how long because it's not in my control, but while I am here I'll help in any way I can.'

'You mean the spying.'

'I've done some of that already. But I mean what I just said – anything.'

'What spying was it you did?'

She told him. 'But there was no mention of you, Michael. You said you were suspected of this or that, but if they'd mentioned it to Mr Ismay I'm sure he would have told me – since this is where I'm living, if you'd been represented to him as a villain—'

'Warned you to keep your door locked, would he?'

'There *should* be a lock on my door, and there isn't. How about putting one on it – or a bolt even?'

'Taking me for an eejit now, is it?' He laughed. 'I'll tell you how it might be with them though, in regard to myself. Wheels within wheels, you might call it, Eileen. You don't mind, I'd call you Eileen? Look here though – your Mr Ismay and George Henry O'Bryen are bosom pals like; and didn't George Henry win a case in court on behalf of my uncle Pat one time – since when – see, he might be a godfather to me – the way he acts and the way

I think of him, he might. It was a matter of a boat this feller said was rightly his, when it wasn't, it was my uncle's, and didn't George Henry prove it fair and square . . . What I'm explaining to you though – Sergeant Donovan knows it as well as I do myself, and George Henry's a power in the land. Donovan wouldn't be after blackguarding me when he'd know it might get back to himself – d'ye see?'

'So whatever it is they have against you, they'd like to catch you in the act.'

'You're right *there*, Eileen. They'd like nothing better!'

'You'd best take care, then.'

Movement out there: customers departing. One buying a half-bottle of Paddy to take with him. Michael came to her at the table: 'What you were after saying then, Eileen – about the lock that's not on your door . . .' He glanced back towards the doorway, lowered his tone still further: 'Would a man take his life in his hands, knowing the lady to be armed and desperate?'

'Well.' This was the last of the potatoes she'd started on. Pausing for a moment, looking up at him, knife in hand . . . 'He might, I suppose – if he was fool enough to imagine it might get him anywhere.'

'Ah. If that's the way of it, then—'

'In my heart, Michael, I'm married, and I love my husband. But – no hard feelings . . .'

'Ah now, if it isn't the man himself! Michael, come here now, will you!' Lorna O'Neill – welcoming the one and only George Henry, obviously. Michael ducking his dark, curly head down close to hers for a second, murmured, 'None either way Eileen.' Louder then, as he straightened: 'Come and meet the man, won't you?'

The man was smallish, with a humorous expression, shrewd grey eyes and a tanned, out-door face. Tanned from the fishing, she supposed. Thick grey-brown eyebrows, hair only edged with grey but thinning to a tonsure-patch of which she had as it were a bird's-eye view. He was informally dressed – breeches and a fisherman's jersey which bulged somewhat around his midriff.

Shaking her hand: 'Mrs Maguire, a pleasure. I've been told a thing or two about you. Enough that I should want to express my sympathy and sorrow for the loss you've suffered. But at least – ' a glance at the O'Neills – 'you're in good hands here, believe me.'

'I told Mr O'Bryen of it.' Lorna gestured towards the telephone. 'As by now you'll have observed, except for a few fishermen we don't get many strangers here, and folk like to know who's what. They'd ask "So where's her husband?" That kind of thing, you know. You don't object, I hope.'

'But I've also heard of you from my friend Mr Bruce Ismay. I was with him earlier. He considers himself a very lucky man that you'll be working for him. So all round you're entirely welcome, Mrs Maguire.' He looked at Michael: 'You have the lobsters out there, have you?'

'I have, so. Seven, and all good ones. How many would you be wanting?'

'Well – when I've seen the size of them—'

'Come now.' Lorna took his arm. 'Let's be getting that done with . . . Eileen, would you be so kind as to watch the telephone, give me a shout if it rings at all?'

Michael patted her arm: 'We'll be no more than a minute.' She heard O'Bryen's murmur as the three of them passed through the kichen: 'The aroma is a great temptation, Lorna, but if you were thinking of asking me to join you, please don't. I'll not be staying long – I've had a long, hard day and I'll need to be starting early for the city.'

They were out there all of ten minutes. When they came back in, it was somehow obvious that they'd been discussing her. Unless it was only that she'd guessed they had. For instance the telephone hadn't needed 'watching'

– if it had rung they'd have heard it out there. And the selection of lobsters wouldn't surely have required the aunt's participation. What was more, it turned out that O'Bryen wasn't even taking the lobsters now: Michael was to keep them for him for a day or two.

'Is it whiskey for you, Mr O'Bryen?'

'Please. A small Paddy'd be just fine.'

'And for you, Eileen?'

'Oh – I don't know . . .'

'Might a smidgin of port hit the spot?'

'Why, sure – it might.' Returning O'Bryen's smile. 'Might very well.' She was intrigued by their both referring to him as 'George Henry' in his absence, but to his face calling him 'Mr O'Bryen'. Even though they'd known him when Lorna's husband Pat had been alive – however many years ago she'd said that had been.

Michael had porter, and got it for himself. His aunt had poured herself a whiskey, but a very small one, and put water in it, which O'Bryen had not.

'I'd like to propose a toast, so.' Lifting his half-glass of the golden liquid. 'To Eileen Maguire and the blessed memory of her loved ones.'

She sipped her port. Drinking to *them*. There'd been a murmuring from the others as they raised their glasses. Lorna set hers down on the counter then, went to the street door and locked it, pulled a blind down over its glass top.

'So we can converse in peace, a minute.'

'Yes.' O'Bryen checked the time on a gold half-hunter. 'A few minutes is all I have. Mrs Maguire – I know more about you now than I did when I walked in here.'

'I guessed you might.'

'I was sure you wouldn't mind.' Lorna reached to pat her hand. 'In your own interests – as you'll also have guessed.'

'As much as you know my interests.' She asked O'Bryen, 'So what is it you know now?'

'To start the ball rolling, I'll say this – it's in all *our* interests as well as your own. In other words we're on the same side of the fence. That is, as long as you *have* discarded completely an earlier intention in regard to Mr Ismay. You have, so? Yes . . . Now then: there's some reason you may not be able to stay long in Costelloe, although you'd like to. The cause of it has therefore to be outside your own control – and is not resistible, you can't look for help against it. My guess therefore is in line with Mrs O'Neill's, it's a threat posed by some authority or other.'

'I'll stay as long as I can, that's all.'

'In other words you don't know how close they may be to you.'

'And Mr Ismay has no knowledge of it. I mean that I shan't be able to stay.'

'All right. I'm no blabbermouth, I assure you. As far as you and your situation are concerned you have my assurance that none of it will be conveyed to anyone except – well, at the most three persons, who will be as careful as I am myself to let no cats out of any bags at all, and who have – will have, when I've spoken with them – your safety and well-being at heart.'

She took a few seconds absorbing that. O'Bryen watching her meanwhile: adding then, 'This has to be a mutual respect of confidence, of course. Nothing I'm saying here tonight is for the ears of anyone but yourself.'

'Of course not.'

'One of the men I'll be speaking with on the telephone tomorrow from Galway city is Eddie O'Meara – whom I have met, just once or twice, but more importantly with whom I have a particularly good friend in common. Now, you offered his name by way of establishing your bona fides, but it's not for that I'll be communicating with him. You did say to Lorna and Michael here that you'd help in any way you could?'

'I did, so.'

'I can rely on that? You wouldn't have second thoughts when you're told what kind of help is wanted?'

She shook her head. 'As long as it's in my capability.'

'Sure it would be. And in conformity with your late husband's convictions as you've described them.'

'His convictions are mine now.'

'I am – *delighted* to hear you say that, Mrs Maguire. Now forgive me, please, for plying you with so many questions in this way. Forcing the pace, you might say . . . You can't give us any estimate even as to how long it might be before this external threat is brought to bear on you directly?'

'No. It could be either – well, stalled, for the time being, or very close. But I'll hold on as long as I can. For all I know I'm as safe here as I would be anywhere. I've covered my tracks as well as I've been able, but doubtless there'd be ways they *could* – after some time, at any rate—'

'If you were obliged to leave now suddenly, where would you go?'

'The only place I've thought of is Dublin. A crowd to hide in. The opposite of such a place as this, in fact.'

'Yes. That's logical enough. Another point, however, is that you're armed, I hear. But – don't be tempted to desperate measures, Mrs Maguire. You know what I mean. It would be not only a sin and a crime, it would be a waste. If we had to, we might at a pinch put you into hiding for a while. But in the event of any such need arising – or anything at all – Michael here is the man you should go to. In emergency of *any* kind. I myself will be seeing you again, of course, but probably not as I'm speaking to you now – only as the old friend of these good people through whom I have now had the pleasure of meeting you – just socially like this, you being here when I called in to see Michael about the lobsters. I'm a busy man, and first and foremost a law and order man, an upholder of the status quo. That's well known, you'd find no one to dispute it. And I am genuinely a friend of that fellow down the road. Ismay. I *like* the man. So don't let *that* crazy idea back into your head.'

'I swear I won't.'

'Good. So taking it a step further, since you'll have no need of that thing, get rid of it now?'

'You think I should?'

'I'm a lawyer, Mrs Maguire, I *know* you should. If your pursuers were to find it in your possession – whether or not it had been used in pursuance of any misdemeanour of which you might stand accused—'

She cut in: 'It *was* so used. You might as well know this. If I'm to look to you for help – and you a lawyer. But it was an accident entirely. I'd never touched any firearm in my life before that moment, and the man's hand was enclosing mine, I suppose squeezing it—'

'What sort of man?'

'A very unpleasant one. I was buying the pistol from him. He had other ideas – I don't know exactly.'

'Was he killed?'

'He was. The thing was right between us, I think the bullet went into his heart.'

'How much can they prove against you?'

'Of the circumstances as I just described them, nothing. But nor could I in my defence – there were no witnesses. But that I was there with him at that time, and had asked him to get me a pistol—'

'That's it, then. Cashla Bay'd make a good home for it. Let Michael here toss it in for you, he has a good strong arm. But if they were to take you and found in your possession the murder weapon – well . . .'

'It's good advice, I'm sure.'

'Which by the look on your pretty face you're not over-keen to accept?'

'In principle I would, but not immediately. I don't know

how fair a deal I'd get. *You* wouldn't be my lawyer, would you, not in England.' She shook her head. 'I'm not going to hang if I can help it, Mr O'Bryen. Waste or no waste.'

Staring at her, absorbing that: a small shrug suggesting some degree of acceptance. Then reaching for his glass, downing the last of his Paddy. A nod. 'I'll be off now. Thank you, Lorna. Good night, Mrs Maguire. Michael – a word in your ear . . .'

In other words, she thought, she still wasn't being trusted: despite having told him – them – all that, effectively putting herself in their hands. When he came back in – vegetables on the stove by then, and the table more or less set for supper – Michael asked her whether she'd like to take a trip down the bay with him in his launch, on Saturday or Sunday maybe, preferably Saturday.

'I'd like it very much, Michael. Where'd we go?'

'You're not scared of going in boats, then?'

Staring at him: realizing what was in his mind. But she was not – or didn't think she would be. Scared, yes: but not of boats. It hadn't occurred to her that she might be.

She shook her head. 'Not at all.'

'That's great *al*together.' His smile was warm, congratulatory. 'See, I've my pots to look at down near the Point. While we're at it you could give me a hand with 'em?'

'Gladly. And one day perhaps a visit to the Aran Islands?'

'Ah well – if there are to be days enough—'

'Of course . . . But Ismay's man told me you'd said you'd take him one day.'

'And I will. *He'll* not be leaving us – except this week or so.'

'You think I will – so soon?'

'Going by what George Henry was saying to us?'

'To *me*, it didn't seem he said much at all.'

Lorna chipped in, from the stove, 'Only advice you won't take?'

'But also, d'you see, he's not spoken with your man O'Meara yet.'

'And until he does, no matter what he *said* I'm not trusted?'

'I don't believe that's the way of it at all. Did I not tell you – didn't my aunt here too – how you'd picked a fine time to come knocking on our door?'

'You did – but what that may have to do with it—'

'What goes up, it must come down. Wasn't it Isaac Newton discovered that? And seeing as – look, if George Henry sees a use for you – as he must be doing, catching on so quick – and you with a need of your own to match it?'

'*What* goes up that has to come down?'

He pointed – right forefinger from right to left: 'Up.' Left forefinger then in the opposite direction. 'Down.'

'You've lost me, Michael.'

'Well, I'm sorry – but since your man himself is not divulging much of it at present . . .' He shook his head, and changed the subject: 'I'll put the cart round in front tonight, so. Johnny O'Shea will be bringing the fish after I'll be gone myself. 'Twill be herring mostly.'

In the morning Michael was gone before she came down to breakfast. She'd heard a motorcar stopping before she'd been properly awake, and Lorna told her that 'George Henry', with Lloyd in the car with him, had stopped by to save Michael the walk to Rossaveel, where he'd left his launch after yesterday's lobstering and earlier line-fishing. The donkey-cart in front of the shop, and the load of fish that was to be brought on some other cart for display on it, was because this was Friday and there'd be a big demand for it.

'But they'll be in the big city – what, within the hour?'

'Hour and a half maybe. And your man Lloyd in Dublin by midday, depending what time his train leaves. The ferry-boat from Kingstown then – and didn't I hear that from what's the place – Fishguard – there's a train doesn't stop all the way into London?'

'There is, there is. It links up with that ferry.'

'Marvels of modern travel, eh?'

'Speaking of which – may I borrow your bike again?'

She was at Glashnacally by eight thirty, and found Ismay having breakfast. In Lloyd's absence and Mrs Nagle not due in until later he'd got it for himself and seemed proud of the achievement. He'd had ham and eggs and was finishing with soda bread and honey: soda bread baked by Mrs Nagle, eggs, ham and honey from Mrs O'Neill.

'The ham's first rate – and why we don't have soda bread in England, I can't think. Here, help yourself to coffee . . .'

He'd had a letter yesterday from his wife, he told her, with news of their four children – they had two sons and two daughters – and telling him that she was hoping to come over for a visit fairly soon.

> . . . Just quietly, on my own. I want to be sure that you are eating properly and not sleeping in damp sheets. Ireland is so very damp, and that old place you're in sounds to me like it's really only fit for rats . A problem in planning a visit just at this time, I might add, is complicated by the fact, reported this morning in *The Times*, that some transport unions are threatening an all-out strike 'in the near future'. This soon again, after all the furore we endured last August! The National Transport Workers' Federation is behind it, this article says, and it's because one 63-year-old who's been a member of the Mercantile Lighterage Company is refusing to join the Amalgamated Society of Lightermen. Isn't that just crazy? Sillier even than the nonsense you had with the *Olympic* . . .

His eye skimmed down the rest of that page of blue-black

slanting handwriting. Folding it then, slipping it back into its envelope. 'My wife – her name is Julia – is by birth American. New York born and bred.' A studio-portrait of her was by this time on display on the chimney-piece in the big room upstairs. Eileen said, 'She's *very* pretty. It'll be lovely for you both, having her over here.'

'She'll find it somewhat primitive. Not so bad while the weather's as it has been, but we certainly can't count on *that*. Hot water, for instance – Lloyd's been pitting his wits and strength against that boiler, but so far it's a case of minimal results from literally hours of drudgery. I must ask Mrs Nagle if she has any suggestions. Or this place's owner, Cleary – might get a call through to him in Wicklow.'

'Or Michael O'Neill? He was telling me last night he fitted a lorry's engine into the launch he uses for his fishing – and if he can do *that* – well . . .'

'Indeed.' A thoughtful look. He'd begun taking papers out of a suitcase and piling them on the table. 'Getting on all right with the O'Neills, are you?'

'They're most kind and hospitable. Yes, I am. Why – did you have some doubt—'

'Never have until now, and I've known them quite a while. And O'Bryen swears by them. No, it was our local constabulary sergeant – Donovan – who was here the other day warning me against gun-runners. He pointed down at young Michael, who was on the quay down there, and muttered that I'd be well advised to "keep my eyes on that one too". He wouldn't say more than that, but I asked O'Bryen what it might be about, and he said take no notice – Michael might have sown a few wild oats in his younger days – and presumably come up against Donovan. So please, don't say anything about it. But you might ask him for me whether he knows anything about colossal antique stoves?'

'I will. Certainly.'

'So he's a mechanic, of sorts. I didn't know. Think he'd know anything about motorcars?'

'I'd say he must do. Since he fitted that engine into his boat, and he's using it all the time. It's strange, my husband was a fisherman – as I mentioned, a trawlerman, when I first knew him – and *he* could take engines to pieces and put them together again, too. It's what he'd have been doing in America – to start with, anyway.'

'Clever chap.'

'Ah, he was – *great*.'

'I'm so sorry, Eileen.'

She was at a window, looking across the bay at Rossaveel, a trawler just casting-off and making a lot of smoke. Ismay said, 'By the way – Lloyd was telling me – extraordinary coincidence, actually met you and your husband?'

'I recognized him before he remembered me, as it happened. I wouldn't have mentioned it, if he hadn't.'

'Why? Because he'd refused to let you up that staircase?'

'Yes. He might have felt bad about it – although he was only obeying the orders they'd all had. Anyway—'

'You're quite a remarkable person, Eileen.'

'A very *ordinary* person, is the truth. But – shouldn't we be getting down to work now?'

'I suppose we should. Just look at it all . . . Incidentally, though, did George Henry O'Bryen call in at the O'Neills' last evening?'

'He did – to see Michael about some lobsters. He'd been here earlier, I think he said.'

'Yes, he had. I'm glad you had a chance to meet him, anyway. Nice fellow, don't you think?'

'Oh, very . . .'

'Yes. And that pile of stuff over there is all to do with him – documents relating to the purchase of Costelloe Lodge – which he's handling both for me as purchaser and for the syndicate – which as it happens includes both me and himself – as vendors. It's an odd arrangement, but apparently quite legal and acceptable. In any case he's a friend, as well as a lawyer of excellent repute. But we can leave that, for the moment, it's this lot here that really does need sorting. It was put together – extracted – in a bit of a rush – by *me* mostly, I take all the blame – and you see – well, while that stack at the end is all White Star business, background stuff I may need for reference when they consult me on this or that – which they're entitled to do – this mass here relates to six or seven different companies. So to start with, let's go through it and sort it, and while we do so I'll explain something of the background. Then – in due course – in greater detail, company by company. We must set up one of the other rooms as an office for you, though. We'll pick one that has a window that opens and shuts – a lot of the frames are warped. We'll get some shelves put up, that sort of thing. All in good time – especially since we don't even have a typewriter yet. And this afternoon – ah, that must be Mrs Nagle arriving – this afternoon, Eileen, the guided tour.'

The tour started at the O'Neills', to fill up with petrol. That other driver had been right, this motor was a Siddeley – whatever difference that might make. But what Ismay was really wanting to show her was the Lodge – with which she was rather disappointed, having expected a grander place – at that price of six thousand pounds, fishing or no fishing. He'd telephoned to the present occupier, a syndicate member referred to as 'the Major', who'd said he'd be out on the river of course but go ahead, look around all you want. Ismay in fact showed her only the outside, and the garden, and the site – on the other side of the approach lane – on which a new cottage was to be built. It looked to her as if it might be at least as big as the Lodge was in its present state – although that was to be enlarged, in particular with the addition of a substantial servants' wing, allowing for existing servants' quarters to be adapted and incorporated as family rooms – for the four young Ismays when they were home on holidays, she supposed. The cottage had been envisaged as guest accommodation, but that was to be reconsidered, since the Lloyd family had to be housed and she, Eileen, provided with a flat or small annexe to herself.

'I'd guess an annexe would be the thing. But I have an architect who'll come over when I'm ready for him. The place is costing so much in any case, we might as well get it right. And Julia'll have a bagful of ideas, I'm sure.'

He took her through the garden, to a door in a curve of wall on the other side of which was a pool of the river – the Casla – where one rowing boat was afloat and two others had been hauled up on the grass bank.

'That way to the eastern end of Clynagh Bay – the river's tidal here, of course – and this way under the road-bridge and two-and-a-bit miles up to Glenicmurrin Lough. Where we'll go now. Don't want to traipse round the house while it's full of the Major's things. I'll have it for a week in September anyway, you can see every inch of it then. Have you ever fished, Eileen?'

'Only as a young girl, on a boat on Roaring Water Bay – West Cork, that is. We were after mackerel and pollock and suchlike.'

'Here of course it's salmon and sea-trout. White trout as you Irish call them. We go after them at night – the sea-trout. They're nervous fish, if you're fishing in company you speak in whispers and never show a light. Wading, of course, a boat's far too noisy. Creep out to a tilly lamp under cover, to change a fly or clear a tangle. But the salmon of course are something else . . . Come on, I'll show you Glenicmurrin.'

They got in the car and he drove on out on to the 'main' road and down to the bridge – which she'd last crossed when coming northward with the English party on Wednesday. Just about *here*, she'd developed her attack of cold feet, the loss of nerve . . . Rumbling over the bridge now: remembering having thought to herself *Ismay's river* and then – without seeing it but knowing how close she'd been to it – Ismay's *house*: and to her surprise he said it then himself, pointing up to the left as they left the bridge behind: '*My* river!' Adding, 'I'm really a *very* lucky man, Eileen.' To which her response, unspoken, was *It's an ill wind* . . . Pulling herself up short then – because thinking in that way was potentially destructive and factually unjustified: the sinking and mass drowning hadn't won him this place that he was so delighted with, he probably could have bought it years ago: you might say rather that this was the beach on which he as a survivor had been washed up, and which happened to be – for him – a paradise. That was the way to see it – if one needed to think about his side of it at all – having made one's peace, and everything being entirely changed now.

Except for London, and Scotland Yard.

The threat was personified in her imagination by that sergeant from the murder squad – the hairy-faced, heartyeating creature who at any rate the woman in the luncheonroom had *said* was in the murder squad. Wondering whether if he was, he'd have had anything to do with investigations into the killing of Anthony Henshaw. Having sat within a couple of yards of her, for God's sake . . . But also what Press reports there might have been. She could still *see* that headline UNDERWORLD KILLING . . . There could have been a dozen more pieces about it by this time. One might for instance have read one morning in Mrs Whitten's *Herald* YELLOW-EYED KILLER BELIEVED TO HAVE ESCAPED TO IRELAND?

'Here we go now.' Turning left. A wave of the hand indicating the opposite direction, the right-hand turn-off. 'There's a school down there, which perhaps the Lloyd children will attend – since they're still little.' He was having to drive more slowly on this narrow, rutted track. 'River's well off to our left now of course, but after a couple of miles we'll be on that high ground – see, ahead there – Bevroughaun Hill, it's called – and from there we'll be looking down on the whole length of the Casla and across Glenicmurrin too. The other loughs as well – marvellous names they have – Vauratruffaun for instance, Loughaunweeny . . .'

Once he'd shown her the river and the lakes, she'd guessed the tour would have been finished, he'd have shown her all he'd set out to show her, but after driving back through the village he branched off to the right, the way the English tour party had gone. This road led north for perhaps about six or seven miles before a sharp turn-off westward. During the northward stretch there'd been water at times on their left, and there was a lot more of it now – and the Connemara mountains, which had been ahead of them and which she'd looked forward to seeing at close quarters, were now towering on the right. They were approaching the head of Kilkieran Bay, he told her, would be following the road around the top of it then southward down its western side. It – the bay – looked to be about ten times the area of Cashla Bay; and Kilkieran itself, she remembered, was where the English party had been destined to spend the night at an inn owned by a relation of their car's driver. It was right on the quayside, in fact – in a village no larger than Costelloe. Ismay parked near the head of the jetty, and they got out to look across the bay – which was spectacular enough, had several islands in it, might well have appealed to those women painters. She was telling him about them – though not the remarks some of them had made about *him*; then, turning away from the sea, he asked her – abruptly, as if it had been in his mind and with that small-talk finished had suddenly found its way out – 'Shall we see if they'd give us a drink and a sandwich here, Eileen?'

'Oh.' Glancing at him in surprise: flummoxed, for a moment. 'Do you – think we should?'

Looking away then: covering the moment and the slight embarrassment by checking the time on her father's watch. No startling impropriety was being proposed: but it could have seemed like a step in a certain direction – a closer association, of which they'd both have been conscious as having nothing to do with her job as his secretary. And the fact that he was a married man aged fifty, she a recent widow of less than half that age – not all *that* much older in fact than the oldest of his children. And tongues *would* wag.

'But perhaps – ' he'd obviously taken notice of her hesitation, was checking the time too – 'we ought to be getting back, rather. Or, an alternative, Eileen, what about *this* – if we were to drive on just a mile or two, we'd come to the headland, name of which is – ' a hand to his forehead, remembering – 'got it – Ardmore Point – from where one has a view right out into the Atlantic – to the west of the Arans, if you understand me. Having come so near to it, make *that* our starting-home point?'

Ridiculous, really. The man she'd come here to kill. For which original purpose, albeit now abandoned, she still had the small weight of the pistol in her shoulder-bag. And with whom in any case she'd spent the whole day virtually alone and would no doubt be spending more. Even if not *many* more – the same doubt returning yet *again* – depending on London and also now on O'Bryen – if that was going to come to anything except warnings and riddles. So much uncertainty was unnerving – which was why it slipped in and out of one's mind all the time . . . She'd climbed in, meanwhile, Ismay had cranked the engine and then got in quickly to keep it running. Out of the village then – some children waving goodbye and shouting in Irish – and within a few minutes coastline and road were curving to the right. Another five minutes and and she could see the headland – off at an angle there to the left, pointing about due south. And beyond a nearer clutter of islands, the low western end of Inishmore, the largest of the Arans. You felt the wind here, all right – felt and heard it. Ismay had slowed, but drove on for another three or four hundred yards, to stop immediately above the headland.

They both got out. The road was edged by a low dry-stone wall. Sheep grazed on its other side, and beyond that slope of grass and gorse was the jutting headland and a mass of rock to the west of it over which the ocean flung itself booming and brilliant white about twice a minute, in all its enormous weight and power. The wind had risen even more than she'd noticed until now. Clouds racing, offshore islands ringed and sluiced in a boil of white, which at intervals seemingly exploded, white water pluming vertically then shredding into streamers flying on the wind. Gulls screeched, banking and soaring.

Beyond it all, the slow heave of that vast blue-black expanse. She shut her eyes: buffeted by the wind, tasting salt, the gulls' cries and the sea's thunder filling her ears. She had an urge to kneel: if he hadn't been there, *would* have.

16

⟫◆⟪

On Saturday she was up early, woken by Michael's knock
on her door, by which time he was already dressed, had
the kettle on for breakfast tea and was making bacon
sandwiches for their lunch afloat. The quay where he had
his rowing boat was about five hundred yards east of the
village: there was enough tide on the bay at that point for
the boat to float with their combined weight in it, as long
as he kept to the channels between rocks and between
rock-masses – which he did on the face of it miraculously,
even with his back to the way they were going. From the
stern where she was sitting she had a view for a short time
of Costelloe Lodge – the upper part of it, above that wall that
had the door in it; the river leading up to it was at this stage
of the tide all rock, where it led out of the bay – you could
have waded up it but not rowed. In any case they were
past it in no time at all, although this far Michael was just
paddling, more than rowing, and entering the narrowest of
rock-bound channels now – a westward curve of it linking
Clynagh Bay to the upper part of Cashla. Once out of that,
spinning the boat – with a mutter of 'Gibraltar Rock, we
call that feller there' – to point south towards Rossaveel,
which was in plain sight across mainly clear water and

less than a mile south. He had the boat fairly speeding then, long sweeps of the oars with a lot of strength behind them sending it creaming around the large rock-island they called Illaunawehichy – which in the Irish would no doubt mean something – and then in to the quay where he'd tied up his launch last evening.

He secured this boat on the far side of the jetty, led her up stone steps across the quay and pointed down at his pride and joy below them.

'There she is, so.'

'Was a lifeboat, you said – off some ship that sank.'

'The *Columbine*. Sank off Slyne Head in a gale no one had seen the like of – her engine had broke down. In such weather she ought not to have been that close off a lee shore, but she was, and that was that – sixteen lives lost. I got this boat for next to nothing, seeing as she'd turned over and drowned all the people that was in her. But *now* look at her, would you. Thirty-two-feet long, her beam nine and a half, and carvel-built. I put a new rudder on her myself and Mick McGurk's brother and I got that engine into her. I built the shelter you see in her bow, and a step for that mast – which came out of another wreck and cost me nothing but the labour of it – and I tell you, she's all I'd wish for now. Just wait here now? I'll be a minute. I'll leave this with ye, so.'

A sailcloth bag he'd brought, containing the sandwiches and a thermos of tea. He left her, and went off towards the activity around the shack-like buildings behind the pier there; the only trawler was preparing to leave its moorings, men were moving around on its deck and on the jetty where they'd left the other boat. Eileen walked the other way, down to the end of the quay; the sun was still low, with no warmth in it yet, although looking across the bay she saw its blaze reflected in Glashnacally's windows. Placid water in between: yesterday's sudden blow having dropped away during the night as quickly as it had come up.

Michael was on his way back, carrying a very large bucket with a lid on it, and a coil of rope over his shoulder. She went back, met him above his boat again.

'Weighs a ton.' He set it down, and attached the line to its handle. 'Now I've to lower this into the boat. Maybe if you was down there to help it in, like. There between the engine and the mast – would you go down and do that for me now?'

'Climb down here?'

Iron rungs, a fixed ladder down the stone facing of the quay. He nodded; pointing then: 'Bringing *that*, are you?'

Her shoulder-bag. She nodded. 'There's nowhere I'd leave it, Michael.'

'Because of what you still have in it, eh?'

'Also papers – items I'm keeping with me.'

'The loop of string it's on would be strong enough, I hope. If on your way down it should get caught and broke?'

'I'll make sure it doesn't. It's a silk cord, not string. What's in the bucket?'

'Fish-heads and -guts – bait for the pots. Don't worry, that lid fits tight enough.'

She turned her back on the water, and climbed down, slowly and carefully, the iron rungs abrasive to her palms. And not much looking forward to wrestling with the fish-guts. Some joy-ride . . . Now into the boat – barely rocking it at all, it was a heavy old craft. Looking up, seeing him pointing to where he wanted her: he'd moved to stand directly above that point, with the heavy bucket right on the edge.

'Ready?'

Easing it over: by its handle at first, then a tense moment as his hands shifted to the rope, and the thing was on its way down. Eileen wondering what if *that* rope broke? It was within her reach then – just. Her fingers hooking into the rim of its base, bringing it towards herself, towards the centreline of the boat.

There. And no guts spilt. Stink, though . . . She moved back to the stern, while Michael was climbing down – one-handed, having that bag suspended from the other – telling her fine, she'd done just fine. How would he have managed it without her? she wondered. Maybe moved the boat round to the steps and put it in there. It was a fair-sized boat, all right. The engine, near the stern – it would have to be in his reach when he was steering, of course – was enclosed in a varnished timber box about the size of two tea-chests and with hinged access doors, which he now had open. Glancing up from whatever he was doing and pointing towards the bow and the stubby-looking mast. 'The sail's in that bag there. She sails well enough, you'll see. Not close to the wind at all, but – d'you know what I'm saying?'

'No. I don't need to, do I?' The sail-bag was bulky enough – grey canvas, with lashings on it. She told him, 'Frank – my husband – would have known it all. The mechanics of it as well as sails and such. I told you he was a trawlerman at one time – and he was the one looked after its engine. You'd have had all of that in common with him.'

'But I want *you* to have the hang of all this, Eileen. The sail, putting it up and that, and the controls on the engine here – and you can take the helm, see how she steers—'

'Why?'

'*Why?*'

'Yes – why . . . You asked me for a day out, was all!'

'And you'll be getting your day out, so. All the same . . . Look, when we come back up here – from Cashla Point almost, where we're going now – we'll put the sail up. Motor down, sail back. The wind being right for it, d'you see?'

'So you're making a crew of me?'

'Enough to be of use – sure. Suppose the engine failed on us and the sea got up – as it might, it still has it in its mind to, I suspect – would you want to be just dunnage, sitting there?'

'Would it ever get really rough though, here in the bay?'

He'd cranked the engine, had it chugging over, was adjusting its throttle and whatever else. Looking over the side then to see water spouting out from some pipe or other. Glancing round at her, pointing south: 'When it's a gale blowing straight in – which it's not so very often, the winds we get are southwest more than south, and with them there's shelter from Killeen and Aillecluggish, though even then it can be fierce enough – see, the bay's entrance is a funnel like, sends it all screaming mad up through this channel here . . . God, if you'd ever seen it you'd not ask *that*.'

'All right.' She sat down, in the stern. 'I'll go easy with the questions.'

'No. Ask away. I said, I want you to know. That article's going to be in your way though: you might put it in the locker you're sitting on?'

The seat hinged up. There was rope and stuff inside, but it looked dry. She unslung her bag and put it in there.

'Now you might go up for'ard, cast off the bow line. See the double line there? One end you unhitch there for'ard – it runs through a ring up top. Just pull it through to fall down on you like. I'm doing the same aft here. All you need do then is shove us off a bit – mind the bait bucket, while you're at it. That's the way now – shove the bow out – then if you'd come aft here – and on your way pull in that old fender . . .'

He'd shown her the engine controls – throttle, and the

upright gear-lever with its three positions of forward, astern or stop, and what he called the mixture-control, and fuel and temperature gauges, and the tap on the fuel line. 'Which if we was to go on fire you'd want to shut off, wouldn't ye?' The pump then – for when it was rough and she was shipping some: 'Or leaking, as she might be.' The pump was operated by a lever you had to work to and fro, and Eileen got a little out, dirty water that had been swirling under the bottom boards. She'd steered for a while then, finding it difficult at first then easy – passing out through the narrows between Curraglass Point and Lion Point, under the loom of Rossaveel Hill – with Michael pointing out every feature, including where shallow and deep patches were, and the anchorages for trawlers or larger vessels in mid-stream. He was still doing this, only having to yell a bit since she'd moved to the bow, to be on the windward side of the bait bucket. They were now passing what he called the Ordnance Tower. 'And that's Tonacrick Point coming up ahead, see. Amongst the islands and rocks to the south of it is where my pots are.'

She had some shelter from the wind here, as well as less stink of old fish-heads. There'd have been even less smell *without* the shelter, of course, having such wind as there was from the southwest as well as that over the bow from the boat's own few knots through the water, but most of that was deflected by the tabernacle shelter he'd built on the launch's bow – iron hoops supporting tarpaulin-covered planking. It provided only a few square feet of overhead shelter, but he'd explained that when motoring into anything like a rough sea and headwind it was worth its weight in gold, warding off seas that would otherwise be slopping in or flying in over the stem; he himself of course at the tiller and engine where he had to be, but any passenger or crew could enjoy some shelter there for'ard.

They'd been silent for a few minutes. Eileen with her eye on the Glashnacally tower, which was visible over Curraglass Point: then calling to him: 'Michael?'

He'd put a hand up to cup his ear.

'Why would anyone landing contraband choose to bring it in up there at Glashnacally?'

'D'ye think they *would*?'

'The coastguard and police seem to believe so, don't they?'

'Well, they'd know more about it than I would.' He laughed. 'Ask *them* for me, would ye, I'd like to know!' He'd pointed – ahead and to port, at the coastguard building which was also in sight now, on a line of sight across Tonacrick Point. Eileen stood up to see it, over the roof of the shelter. Turning back to him then: 'Might it be trawlers – or *a* trawler – coming in to Rossaveel, then boats – this one, for instance – having only half a mile to cross to Struthan Quay?'

Spreading his arms helplessly: he was standing with the tiller's pressure against his left hip. Dark-skinned, hook-nosed and black-haired, he could have been a Red Indian. Shrugging: 'For all I know, it might.' Another laugh . . . 'Although who'd have the cheek to be using *my* boat for it I *wouldn't* know!'

'But then again, if the trawler's bringing the stuff that far up the bay anyway, why wouldn't they put it ashore right there at Rossaveel?'

'They might, I suppose. Unless they suspected there'd be Customs or police there to meet them? And mind you, there's the barrack at Keeraunnagark only a step down the road there. But while you're at it you might ask as well – although *I* couldn't tell you, for the life of me – where might this trawler of yours have embarked such a cargo anyway?'

'Glashnacally has the barrack at Carraroe even closer, doesn't it?'

'It does, so. I tell you, I wouldn't understand why they'd have any such thing at *all* in their minds . . . But now listen, would you. The buoys on my pots are painted red and white. See the rocks ahead now? That one that's exactly ahead this moment is Coastguard Rock, so called.' Eileen was on her feet, still holding on to the side of the tabernacle, peering narrow-eyed into the wind to spot the rock he meant. There was quite a lot of movement on the launch now – because down here they were fully exposed to the southwester with no shelter from Killeen Point, she realized. Holding on and swaying to the motion, balancing against the pitch and roll and increasingly jolting progress: thinking to herself that you could get used to this, that it was quite exhilarating. Michael's voice again: 'To your right there now – ' she glanced back, saw his long arm pointing – 'that's Carrickadda. This side of it, and to the south of Coastguard, the rocks is like in a ring, and my pots is around the inside of it. In between them in some places. Would ye come back here now, Eileen?'

To explain what he wanted of her. When they reached each pot he'd go for'ard to haul it up, remove lobsters and throw back any crabs – since no one had the time for crabs and as often as not you'd end up giving them away – and re-bait the pot before lowering it to the seabed again. Her job would be to keep the launch as near as possible where it was – especially in close proximity to rocks – by shifting the tall gear-lever to ahead or astern as might be necessary, and opening or closing the throttle a little when more or less power was called for, and of course using rudder . . . 'At each buoy I'll stop her and hand over to you, and you cast your eye around, see where we are – this rock that distance, another the other side – all that, like. The manoeuvring you'll find simple. Dead easy, Eileen, I'll tell you. If you're worried at all I'll come back to help, but after the first one you'll see how easy. That feller there now . . .'

Chugging up slowly to it: he had a long pole with a wire hook on it and he brought the buoy into the boat by snagging the line just under it and pulling it in within arm's reach where he could grab it and go for'ard with it, leaving the controls to her. A few times they got a bit close to rocks and she panicked, and once he did come back to help – bringing the rope with him, the pot dangling somewhere below the boat, Michael explaining how important it was to keep the rope clear of the propeller. On some of them, in deeper patches, there was more rope than on others; with the buoy in the boat he'd haul it in hand over hand, dripping and some with weed clinging to it; it was quite exciting, she found, when each pot broke surface and he lifted it in over the gunwale, to see how many lobsters there might be in it. Sometimes none, sometimes two or even three. Then it wasn't easy getting them out – crabs especially, the way they locked their claws into the pots' mesh and wouldn't let go; sometimes they'd shake out all right, but as often as not he'd have to use the marline-spike on his knife to prise open a claw – while another claw or two clamped on. There were very large claws on some of them.

He had a dozen pots down, he'd told her, and they found eleven, took fourteen lobsters of varying sizes, and threw out numerous crabs. The lobsters were put into tarpaulin-lined lockers in the launch's bow. The missing pot might have become separated from its buoy in last night's blow, he said; he'd not have been surprised if there'd been more gone. He was taking a chance in leaving them down now, suspecting that this might be only a short break before a resumption of that blow – but having no sound reason why that should be.

'It's a feeling you get sometimes.'

'Does it it usually turn out right, or wrong?'

'Oh. It's not all always all *that* wrong.'

'So shouldn't you take notice of it?'

'There's only one thing certain – if the pots are not down there'll be no lobsters taken. If they're down and some get lost or smashed – well, it's my time and labour I'm hazarding, that's all. If I was *sure* there'd be a storm, I'd take 'em up – but *that's* time and labour too, believe me. Eileen, are you all right still, not affected by the motion?'

'I'm fine. Thought I mightn't be, but – thanks be . . .'

'Are you ready for a sandwich and a mug of tea, so? Before we put the sail on her?'

They were motoring out towards the middle of the bay by then: pitching more than rolling, but with the wind and the slight sea on the bow, rolling too. Although only about two hours ago when they'd just been starting on the pots, that trawler from Rossaveel had come steaming out keeping well to the other side and turned west around Killeen Point, and it had looked to her as steady as a rock. She wondered whether perhaps Michael's 'feeling' about the weather changing again might have been right, with this much change so soon. Still bright sunshine, however . . . Michael maintaining a desultory commentary – telling her now that that was Cannon Rock to port now – with a marker on it to warn any ship or trawler to give it a wide berth. The trawlers, he explained, used this bay and Rossaveel to spare themselves the expense and time-waste of the long haul to and from the Galway city docks, a good twenty miles each way. And Rossaveel being tucked around that corner so to speak, even a strong blow directly from the south, such as he'd been describing earlier, wouldn't inconvenience them at all, not once they were inside there.

'Fine sandwiches you made us, Michael.'

'Ah, the bacon's fine, isn't it? But tell me, are you never seasick?'

'I've not spent much time afloat at all, tell you the truth.'

'I was thinking, anyway, besides that – you asked about

Glashnacally, why they'd land rifles there – contraband, you called it?'

'Rifles, then. Yes. I'd have thought – well, the bays to the west there – I was noticing yesterday, so many little coves and beaches, often with no dwellings anywhere near—'

'What *I* was going to say – wherever they do it, they'd need a roadway close by, a good way out. If they were landing rifles, see, 'twouldn't be just a few, but whole cases of them, boxes of ammunition too. Well, Glashnacally now, there's three roads out. And from Costelloe if that was the way they went they'd have yet more choices – another three, at least. Then again, they might take it all overland to Natawnay Point and have another boat there waiting!'

'Yes. I hadn't thought of *that*.'

'I'm only guessing, mind.'

'Of course. It's only that at Glashnacally there *are* the other houses overlooking – and it's so close to the coast-guard, and—'

'Listen to this then. Suppose George Henry was not in residence at Clynagh. Which most of the time he is not. What if these foul cheating blackguards knew it and took the liberty of hiding the stuff in his barn there? You'd have the cart continuing then through Costelloe and a whole choice of roads thereafter – the police then on its tracks maybe, up from Keeraunnagark say but on the trail of an empty cart or one with a few pots or creels in it maybe. And all the time rifles galore reposing in that barn, to be moved at some later date and not a soul the wiser – least of all himself, George Henry?'

He was lighting his pipe now: crouching and with hands cupped around it to shield it from the wind. Puffing . . . Then: 'A lot more ways than one to skin a cat, isn't that what they say. And not a soul within a hundred miles doing any-thing but hold his tongue . . . I'll turn her down-wind now – would y'ever open that bag and pull the sail out, Eileen?'

* * *

They'd made it in an hour: including switching back to the engine after they were through the narrows, to get into Rossaveel across the wind and then under the lee of that hill. Except for that bit she'd sailed the boat all the way, after he'd shown her the general principles of it; from there on she'd steered and handled the sail and gradually got the hang of it, while he'd sprawled there giving her advice and at one stage breaking into song: he had a clear and attractive baritone, had sung a selection of Moore's Melodies, old songs they'd most of them had to learn at school – starting with 'Go Where Glory Waits Thee', which when he finished she clapped and told him he'd sung it beautifully but wasn't it a dreadful old dirge of a tune. He'd spread his arms: 'But the words, Eileen, the words!' Then he launched himself into 'Farewell, but Whenever You Welcome the Hour', and followed that with a powerful rendering of 'How Dear to Me the Hour When Daylight Dies'.

'Michael, you have a splendid voice!'

'Ah, bless you, ma'am, I'll be sending the hat round in a minute. But I'm thinking I'd best take over the steering an' that now. Although mind you, returning the compliment, you've a natural talent for it, so you have . . .'

They tied the launch up where it had been before, *she* unrigged the sail – to remind her, he said, of how she'd helped to rig it – and she was impressed then by his arrangements for the handling of the lobsters. The tarpaulin linings of the lockers were actually bags: he pulled up their sides, tied the lashings that were on them and took one bag at a time up the ladder with him. Then he carried them and the empty, washed-out bait-bucket over to the huddle of fishery buildings and brought the bags back empty, went down the iron ladder again to rinse them out and replace them in those lockers. The lobsters would be on their way into Galway city shortly, he told her, along with a van-load of fish.

'Will you come out with me again, Eileen?'

The confusion again. She began, 'I'd like to. But—'

'What I'm saying is I'd be glad to have you with me *any* time. If – you never know, it might work out that way?'

At the shop, Lorna O'Neill had a message for her – an invitation to Sunday lunch with Mr and Mrs O'Bryen at Clynagh Lodge. A rider to this was that Michael should not fail to take the lobsters along this evening: 'So you know what you'll be getting – uh?' George Henry had called by, not telephoned, he'd been most of the day at Glashnacally and then at Costelloe Lodge, he and Ismay going over various details of the planned sale, and he'd had Ismay with him when he'd dropped in on their way back. He'd made a point of mentioning that he'd asked Ismay's permission to invite her, so she needn't worry about that. He'd have Father Dave Murchison there to lunch, he hoped, and Dr and Mrs Murphy, people he felt she ought to know – and Mrs O'Bryen was looking forward to meeting her too – since she was after settling here, as indeed he *hoped* she would be . . .

'But he knows darned well—'

'Ah, 'tis his way, don't you know. Talking the way he will with *them*. And your man Ismay not knowing any of that other?'

'No – *that's* true . . . But one thing I'd tell you – he's not such a bad fellow at all, Ismay. In some ways I was dead wrong about him.'

'Well – we'll take notice of it. I know George Henry thinks well of him – which he does not of *many* English. But you'll go, will you?'

'Well – yes . . .'

'I said I thought you would. And then your man said if

you liked he'd call here for you in his motor, if you'd like that would you telephone him.'

'I'll walk there, I think.'

'Or you could take the old bike.'

'No, I'll walk. It's no distance – and with nothing to do all day—'

'Only Mass. Will you not come with us? The church we attend is down by Banraghbaun, and our neighbours here the McKaigs – Mrs McKaig you met in the shop, remember? – well, they've been in the habit of taking us in their trap, and sure they'd squeeze in one more – especially as there's no great bulk to you . . .'

Otherwise, she added, there was the donkey-cart, but it was a long haul for old Billy, who was not by any means in his first youth and didn't like to be hurried. But how had she enjoyed her day on the water?

Sunday morning, then, and Sunday clothes for Mass. Lorna in black as well, and Michael in a dark blue suit that had been his uncle's so the trousers were too short and the jacket a bit tight: it was heavy serge, he agreed with her he was going to bake. This was another sunny day – the McKaigs and Lorna asking each other was the heatwave ever going to end – a question which seemed to amuse them all – although there was a good breeze from the southwest and more cloud than there'd been recently.

It was the first time Eileen had attended Mass since the Sunday before she'd embarked in the *Titanic*. She felt she *had*, in a way, that night under the stars on the voyage over – in her own mind, her own thinking, it wasn't a thing you'd try to explain to others, least of all to Father Murchison, or any other priest. Which would mean – the aspect of it that she disliked most, in fact dreaded – *pretending*. The plain truth was that both in New Rochelle and London something had kept her even from going inside a church. It wasn't all to do with the *Titanic*, either, it was something that had in fact bothered her for quite some time, part of it being the fact that her stepfather Dennis Burke was outwardly a very religious man who'd have considered himself doomed to all the fires of hell if he'd missed a single Sunday at that church on the edge of Skibbereen . . .

The *Titanic* had been more of a watershed than primary cause.

'Don't you agree, Eileen?'

'I'm sorry, what – oh, yes . . .'

Small-talk, while passing Costelloe Lodge and rattling over the Casla bridge. Then, a small distance south from there, gleaning the fact that Dr Murphy, whom she was expecting to meet at lunch, was not a doctor at all but a vet. He acted as a doctor only in emergencies because there wasn't a real one this side of Galway.

In the little church she, Lorna and Mrs McKaig were crammed into a pew – in which for Eileen there was very little leg-room – while Michael and McKaig stood with the other men at the back. The Latin droned into one ear and out the other, while she concentrated her thoughts on Frank and Tom. The little bell tinkled and the familiar scent of incense drifted, mingling with that of mothballs. Father Murchison was a portly, sag-cheeked man with cold eyes and soft white hands. She thought that if she was still here in a week's time she might find some excuse not to attend: but it wouldn't be easy, in a place like this; you'd stand out as some kind of infidel if you did not conform.

Maybe she *was*. But she didn't want to stand out in any way at all.

For the luncheon party she changed into the light summer clothes she'd acquired in London – sun-hat included. She had a walk of about a mile, mile and a half. Michael said he hoped she'd enjoy the lobster: he'd delivered them to George Henry's cook last evening, in accordance with his instructions. By the time she'd smartened herself up and come downstairs and they'd had this brief conversation he'd changed back into fishing gear, and after a quick lunch would be off to Rossaveel and his launch again.

'Fishing on a Sunday, Michael?'

'Doing a thing or two to the boat. Top up fuel, clean the sparking plugs and the filters an' that. Sunday's the best day for it. Then I'll give her a run down the bay, I expect. Don't want the old dear letting us down, do we.'

'Letting *us* down?'

'Me, then.' Her pointed at the floppy-brimmed hat. 'Mind that doesn't blow off. The way the wind is, and still rising, you might not see it again this side of Claremorris. But I tell you, Eileen, you're a picture in that outfit.'

'Why, thank you. But the rising wind – will your pots be all right?'

'Oh, sure they will. Although I like you better as you was yesterday.' He winked at his aunt. 'The sight of her at the tiller and the sun in those glinty eyes she has!'

'She looks great to me as she is now. Best be getting along though, Eileen.'

A conclusion she'd come to, thinking about it in the McKaigs' trap earlier, was that the boat-handling instruction to which he'd treated her had been altogether too purposeful to have been just a whim of his own. When the night before last he'd invited her to go out with him in the launch he'd just come back in from a final chat with George Henry outside there – and she was guessing that it had been suggested by George Henry. Or ordered by him. He, George Henry O'Bryen, the lawyer of high repute and staunch maintainer of the status quo, having his mind concentrated on the imminent landing of guns, and intending somehow to involve *her* in it – in Michael's boat, somehow. Though how, or with what advantage to him or anyone else – her imagination failed, at that point. What use they'd have for a complete beginner and a female at that:

or how it could fit in with Michael's cryptic comment about George Henry seeing a use for her, and this being linked to her having a need of her own . . .

Trying her out? Seeing if she *would* back-track?

Or using her as bait, in some way. Knowing the police would be glad to get hold of her? Not a *nice* thought to entertain, from any point of view at all, and maybe very unfair, but more than enough to spoil your sleep: she'd wondered in the course of the past day and night whether she wouldn't have done better to keep the Henshaw business to herself.

Needing his help though: and he a lawyer, with connections everywhere . . .

'Hello, there! Whoa up now, whoa up . . .'

A trap had come down out of the road she and Ismay had taken yesterday: she hadn't looked round at it – had been deep in thought and also holding her hat on against the wind – but it was now pulling up beside her. A man with reddish whiskers and a billy-cock hat and wearing a black broadcloth coat with wide lapels was handling it; beside him was a fat, dark-haired girl of about half his age, dressed in a loose-fitting knitted coat over a black skirt and white blouse.

Eileen had stopped, looking up at them. 'Good day.'

'Might you be going to Clynagh Lodge, be any chance? Or even if ye're not – but that's as far as *we're* going—'

'I am, though.'

'Well, come on up then—'

'Jump in, dear. I'm Margaret Murphy – my husband Dr Murphy—'

'I'm Eileen Maguire. How d'you do. You're very kind . . .'

She was in, and he'd flipped the reins, sent the pony clopping on. Compliments then: how uncommon smart she was ('Oh, I hope not *too* smart, I have so few clothes with me') and Mrs Murphy's admission that she'd guessed who she might be, was she not the one who by God's mercy had survived that terrible shipwreck – and lost her husband and child in it? And now staying at the O'Neills'? And so on: her mewed and her husband's grunted commiserations, Eileen guessing that the *Titanic* disaster and her own personal tragedy was likely to be the raw material of the luncheon-party's conversation – unless they were sensitive to Bruce Ismay's recent castigation in the press and Parliament, and kept off it for his sake.

They didn't – initially – but Ismay took it in his stride, provided brief but lucid answers to questions and suppositions, and described the manner of his own survival quite naturally and unemotionally before himself proposing a change of subject: 'I'd point out though that for Mrs Maguire it must have been as frightful as well as tragic an experience as any of us could imagine. Do you think we might find a less harrowing topic?'

Oonagh O'Bryen – small, dark, birdlike – backed that up immediately. 'You are so *right*, Mr Ismay. Indeed, Mrs Maguire, I apologize, I'm a poor hostess to have permitted the subject to continue as long as it has.'

'My fault, I think, *my* apologies.' Dr Murphy's complexion matched that of his lobster, just about. 'What's your view of the threats from that man Carson, George Henry? Is it civil war we'll be facing before long?'

'No. That's all wild talk, Brian. Not even that crowd would be so daft as to take it to such lengths. Home Rule will be introduced and they'll back down, accept it.'

'But there's talk of rifles being landed *here*, even!'

'Just because the Ulstermen are after playing soldiers – sure there'd be *talk* of it in every corner of the land. Which on reflection I suppose *might* persuade Carson and Company to think again. All the same I'd be dead against any moves in that direction: once you have arms available, the next thing is they get used, and it's the innocent who suffer.

Incidentally, Mr Ismay here was telling me he had a visit from the constabulary – or the coastguard, was it?'

'Both.'

'Well – it was to warn him there might be some attempt to bring weapons ashore at Glashnacally, and would he kindly give 'em a shout if he saw it happening!'

Surprise, amusement. Dr Murphy cracking a large claw open in his strong hands and commenting that he'd have thought they'd be up to keeping their *own* eyes open for such shenanigans. Especially if they had sound reason to suspect some such thing was being planned . . . 'Did they give any reason?'

Ismay said no, no explanation had been forthcoming. He hadn't questioned them, really wasn't taking it too seriously. George Henry agreed with Murphy, though. 'The fact it'd be that close under their noses you'd think would make it seem less probable to them. Or so the gun-runners might expect. Consequently if they'd thought of some way to manage it there at Glashnacally—'

'But with Mr Ismay in residence, surely—'

'Oonagh, like any other mortal being, Mr Ismay must close his eyes during some of the dark hours at least. And that quay does not belong to the house or to Donal Cleary, all and sundry have the right to use it. In fact – ' George Henry was into his stride now – 'in that place of Cleary's, tower or no tower you've no better outlook on the quay or pier than have the families in the cottages there – they're on this side of the inlet, of course, but—'

'George, dear . . .'

'Yes.' He nodded to his wife. 'I'm sorry. Rambling on. Thinking it out as I go along. The fact is I can't see it happening here at all, at all. Brian – a subject closer to your heart now – the race-meeting this summer. Do you have any hot tips for us?'

He hadn't, but nearer the time he might have. It was

a three-day meeting apparently, a major event in the Galway calendar. Mrs Murphy was meanwhile asking Ismay whether he'd noticed that all the trees in Galway and especially Connemara were inclined northeastward. 'It's not the wind inclining the trunks that way though, it's the salt southwesters discouraging budding or sprouting on that side, d'ye see, so the only way the poor things can grow out is the *other* way. It's a fact, Mrs Maguire, look about you and you'll see the truth of it, so you will!'

'The wind was coming up quite strongly again when I left Glashnacally. It fairly sings through that old tower . . .'

The priest hadn't appeared at all: hadn't been expected either, there'd been no empty chair at the table. When the party was breaking up, Ismay offered Eileen a lift into Costelloe, and Murphy trumped that, pointing out that it was on their way; but Oonagh O'Bryen begged her to stay a while – they'd had so little opportunity to talk, and she and George Henry could very easily drop her off in Costelloe; they had to be back in the city this evening and would be leaving in an hour or so.

Ismay asked her, 'Nine a.m. then?'

'Earlier, if you like.'

'Nine would be perfect. The lobster, Mrs O'Bryen, was absolutely delicious . . .'

The Siddeley, cranked by George Henry, rolled away down the treeless 'avenue'. Oonagh said as they went back inside, 'It's my husband needs to talk with you, of course. I've our packing to see to, and I might rest a while, so . . .'

George Henry waved her to a chair. 'You don't mind the smell of this?' The cigar he was smoking: she shook her head. 'Not at all. I hope you're going to tell me now what's happening. And why you've had me taught to sail Michael's boat, for instance?'

'Did he not explain it?'

'Michael talks in riddles.'

A chuckle . . . 'He's a great lad, is Michael O'Neill. But I'll tell you now – I've spoken with Dr O'Meara, he was able to confirm all that about your husband. He'd had great expectations of him, too. But of you yourself all he knew was that you existed. He asked me to convey his sincere condolences.'

'I did tell you I'd had nothing to do with him, it was all Frank's—'

'Yes. May I ask a question or two though, before we go further? For instance – your aim was to settle in America – but after the sad event you took against it?'

'Because we'd planned *our* new life there. Mine on my own where the three of us would have been, and we'd talked of so much and with such excitement – it may sound to you silly, but – I felt I'd no right, on my own – I'd have felt *wrong* – d'you understand, at all?'

'Not entirely, but—'

'And the state I was in—'

'That, yes. Tell me – had you resolved there and then – ' a gesture with the cigar, in the direction of Glashnacally – 'to go after *him*?'

'I think I had. At least, it was in my head. How clearly or otherwise it's not easy to recall, but—'

'All right. You have family over there – no, I should say your husband had?'

'He had an uncle with a motor repair business in Philadelphia. Frank was going to work for him at least to start with.'

'If you found yourself there again would you go to him?'

'Found myself – in the United States?'

'That's what I'm asking. Would it be the uncle in Philadelphia you'd head for?'

'No. I didn't like them when I met them. Frank wasn't

so keen on him either, he wouldn't have stayed long. And I'm sure they wouldn't want to be bothered with me. Frank would have been of use to him, saved him money I dare say. But there's others I dare say I'd go to – in New York state, a woman and her husband who were very kind to me . . . But why – I'm beginning to guess – well, the drift of it, but—'

'Hold on a minute now. I've not finished with my own questions, yet. Before you set off in the *Titanic*, you'd have had entry papers from the Yanks – immigration papers?'

'I still have them.'

'That's good. That's *very* good. And these other people you mention – you'd be with them – or in touch with them, so you could give me an address which in any case would find you through them?'

'I could, so. But I would not involve them in any of this. If I'm right in my guess, what you're – proposing. I like them very much, but they're not Irish, I wouldn't presume to foist it on them – or even have them know *I* had any such involvement. She probably saved my life, when we were in the lifeboat together – and they were both of them so generous . . .'

'That brings me to the next question – how you'd support yourself. You'd find work, I'm sure, but do you have funds or access to any, that would tide you over?'

'I have a bank draft cashable there in American dollars. Made up of Frank's and my own savings. So – the answer is yes – and finding a job I think would be quite easy – these friends – well, the husband, who's in business and successful – they tried hard to persuade me to stay, he'd have given me introductions and—'

'Eileen, it's almost unbelievable to me how suitable you are for this. A gift from heaven fallen right in my lap. I should say *our* laps – this is a national operation, in no way local, O'Meara and others are as as much concerned in it as I am myself. But – the advantages you have, and not even to require funding!'

'It's to do the work Frank would have done, is it?'

'Are you game for it?'

'I *want* it. I'd like nothing better. But an important question – from my own point of view obviously, but yours too – would I be safe there? If the English police got to know it was where I'd gone?'

He'd nodded. 'A damn sight safer than you are here. To start with we'd hope they would *not* get to know of it, secondly they'd have to discover exactly where you were, and if they were able to accomplish that much there would then be legal procedures that could take a long, long time while you'd have our help in disappearing again. One thing worth looking into once you were settled might be a change of name – the simplest way of it for a female – this is purely an observation, Eileen, not necessarily a recommendation – being to get married. Which could in itself make for complications, unless you were very, *very* careful in your choice . . . But a sound precaution in any case would be not to correspond with anyone here or in England; it might be hard for you in some respects, but – you're potentially of great value to us, Eileen, we'd not want to lose you now. D'you see, to find people – I admit, only men is how we've thought of it until now – of the intelligence and education that you have, and who are willing and able – have the *spirit* for it – I tell you, such don't grow on trees. Also to be self-supporting – seeing as we have use for every penny we have in the kitty at this stage . . .'

'Frank's doing entirely. As a matter of fact he risked his life going back down to our cabin for the papers and the bank draft.'

'He was a fine man, no doubt of that – and your work will honour the memory of him.' George Henry crossed himself, with the cigar-hand: paused then, drawing on the cigar, then squinting at its glow. 'You'd find employment in New York to start with, I suppose. Later you might find your way into shipping circles – a freight forwarding agency maybe – in Boston rather than New York maybe?'

'I'd know better when I'd been there a while. But yes – if that was what was wanted of me. Someone will be told to get in touch with me, will they?'

He nodded. 'But in New York, even. New York, Boston, wherever, you'll work it out for yourselves. There's three main sides to it, as we see it now: the fund-raising, and the organizing – that's to say acquisition, and forwarding – and the personal contacts with ships' masters and others. Landings don't have to be in deserted coves, incidentally, illicit cargoes can be secreted amongst legal ones. But once you were settled – New York or wherever – you'd write to Oonagh. Never to me, only to her. Calling yourself let's say Bernadette McCarthy. She has McCarthy cousins. You'd write saying that life had begun to go well for you and any time she wanted you'd be happy to welcome her and show her the sights. Then after a while you'd be visited at the address you'd have put on your letter by some person asking for Bernadette McCarthy. You'd be in business then – or on the threshold of it. Now, before we take you back to Lorna's, give me the address of the friends you have in New York? I wouldn't allow it to be used unless there was an emergency of some kind.'

'All right. But I do have this one *tiny* little question.'

'How you'll be getting there.'

'Exactly. I'm not writing to White Star or Cunard for a passage. I'm not waiting here much longer either. In fact if it's going to take any time at all – you said something about hiding me?'

'Nervous, are you?'

'Of *course* I'm nervous!'

'Well, try not to show it. Before the weekend, I promise we'll have you on your way.'

'On my way . . . In five days at most, then?'

'About that – yes.'

'But "on my way" how?'

'Didn't you ask me why did Michael teach you to make yourself useful to him in his boat?'

'That launch – how far? Where to?'

'Not so far as to make you squeak like that, Eileen.' The chuckle again . . . 'Listen, I don't believe in divulging secrets sooner than I have to. But for your peace of mind I'll make an exception now.' He'd lowered his voice: as if maybe even Oonagh shouldn't hear it. 'There'll be a ship berthing in Galway docks this evening. She'll be two days discharging and two more loading, so the earliest she'll be on her way is Thursday evening – although it might extend to Friday. Depends what overtime is worked, and so forth. You don't need to know her name – I wouldn't want you in panic rushing into Galway to stow away and the ship then searched – she's a vessel they *might* be after searching – and that's why Michael will put you aboard her out there somewhere.' Pointing with the inch that was left of his cigar. 'Off the Arans, maybe.'

17

George Henry had told her he'd be back at Glynagh on Monday evening. He and Oonagh had some church function to attend that Sunday evening, and he'd be spending a few hours in his office on Monday, but the Major at Costelloe Lodge had offered him a night or two's fishing on the Casla and he, O'Bryen, was not a man to look a gift horse in the mouth. Eileen had said she was glad he'd be here, but he insisted she should put it out of mind: he'd be fishing on those nights and catching up on sleep in daylight. She'd get news from Michael when there was any. 'Mrs Nagle you can count on, by the way. I myself have nothing to do with any of it, remember. It's Oonagh you've been conversing with here – talking of your settling down here and meeting people, and how she'll rack her brains to find a husband for you, in due course?'

She'd said to Michael that evening when he came in, 'I've learned now what you meant with your "what comes up must come down". Nothing to do with Isaac Newton, is it?'

The ship, was what it was: eastward to Galway, then westward back into the Atlantic. Please God – well, by a wave of George Henry's magic wand – with her on board. And 'a vessel they might be after searching': one might suppose bringing illicit cargo – possibly right into the Galway docks, as hinted by George Henry – rumours of a landing at Glashnacally therefore being all a blind?

Michael had avoided discussion of any kind, last evening: at least, in his aunt's presence, as if even she wasn't to be apprised of detail she didn't need, only of general intentions. Maybe that was how it was: George Henry using Michael but by excluding Lorna making it easy for her to play dumb, *vis-à-vis* such folk as Donovan? Awake early this Monday morning, so early that the light was still soft, milky, the mountains to the north still shrouded, and hearing Michael leave – which might have woken her – she recalled the two instructions he *had* vouchsafed to her. She'd been out to the back and he'd come out to intercept her, told her, 'From Thursday on now, keep your bag packed. A smaller one than that portmanteau. Ask Lorna. And listen: if there's a message "the mackerel are running" it would be time for us to be doing the same – I mean running. Uh?'

In London, in the White Star office, Charles Napier replaced the telephone receiver and ticked off another name on the list in front of him. Two other clerks were similarly occupied, the list having been split into three; and telegrams were being sent to passengers who weren't on the telephone. A sailing brought forward was actually more difficult in many cases than one being delayed, and this one was being advanced to beat the threatened strike.

A door at the back of the office was opened, and Napier heard Theodore Bellamy's voice boom, 'That's him – *that* one. You can get out that way then – flap in the counter, he'll show you. Give Mr Ismay my best regards, will you?'

'I will indeed, sir.'

Theo Bellamy was an assistant general manager, quartered upstairs in the holy of holies. He'd gone back up.

Napier glancing round from his desk at this stranger in a ready-made brown suit, with a brown trilby in his hand.

'Mr Charles Napier?' Transferring the hat to his left hand, right hand extended. 'My name is Lloyd – Robert Lloyd, formerly first-class assistant chief steward on the *Titanic*, but now—'

'Heavens, yes. He told me about you. Over from the Emerald Isle, eh?'

'I am, Mr Napier. I've just delivered some documents Mr Ismay felt were better here under lock and key than lying around over there. I've a few other commissions over here of course. But he asked me to give you his regards and tell you that the arrangements you made for him – the train from Cork, and hotels there and in Galway, where I met him with the car of course – were very satisfactory.'

'I'm glad. But heavens, you haven't been there long . . . Getting settled in all right, are you?'

'At Glashnacally, we are, more or less. We shan't be in Costelloe Lodge for some months yet – can't even start the building alterations, on account of the syndicate reservations all through this season. It's a strange old place, Glashnacally – former coastguard barracks. Likely to be hellish in the winter months, I'd imagine. But marvellous views, the surroundings are quite beautiful . . . Anyway – I'll get along now. Down to Southampton this evening, for a few days with my family. Can't get them over until we're in the Lodge, unfortunately. Glad to have met you, Mr Napier.'

'Give Mr Ismay my best wishes. And when he *is* in the Lodge, if he wanted any help with all those fish—'

'Hah! I'm sure he'd be delighted.' Lloyd put his hat on. 'I'll mention it, sir. And hope to see you over there one day. I go through there, do I?'

The flap in the counter: Napier went ahead to raise it and

let him out. Remarking as he did so, 'I don't know how long you want to be over here, of course, but you know there's a dock strike coming, do you? Of course, if you wanted a nice long stay with your family—'

'I wouldn't take such advantage, sir. I'm really very lucky to have this post with Mr Ismay. No, I might cut my stay short, in fact . . . But one other thing I'm sure he'd like me to mention – a *very* good turn you did him – our Mrs Maguire, whom you sent to him?'

'I *what*?'

'Mrs Maguire – you gave her a letter of introduction—'

'She's *there*?'

'Very much so, and he's – tickled pink, as the saying goes. All we're waiting for is a typewriter to arrive. But she's an *extremely* nice young lady . . . Anyway – goodbye. A pleasure to have met you . . .'

Napier returned slowly to his desk. Sat down slowly too, and sat for a moment or two immobile, looking at the telephone. Then he pulled open a desk-drawer, found and brought out a card – business card, of sorts.

'Getting through your quota, are you, Napier?'

Fawcett. Napier put the card down beside the telephone. 'By and large, I am.' He shook his head. 'Some of 'em are pretty awkward, though.' The next on the list had an address in Hammersmith. He took the receiver off its hook, and dialled.

Sergeant Donovan was a man of soldierly bearing with a greying beard trimmed short around his jawline. Dark green uniform, highly polished black boots and belt. Mrs Nagle had let him in and brought him up to the big room where Ismay was going through papers, Eileen making notes on the backs of sheets that had been pruned out for discarding.

'Thank you, Mrs Nagle. Good morning, Sergeant. What

brings you back so soon? Oh – this is Mrs Maguire – my secretary.'

'How d'ye do, ma'am. Lodging at the O'Neills, I believe.'

'I am indeed.' She smiled at him. 'And they're looking after me very well.'

Not 'letting it show' at all, George Henry might have been pleased to note. In fact she'd felt only the smallest twinge of anxiety – guessing the sergeant would have come about his gun-running problems again, not about anything to do with her. In her imagination when they came for her it would be that English sergeant: the one with the luxuriant, russet-coloured moustache and sideboards and the rather striking table manners.

Ismay was waiting for Donovan to state his business. Donovan aware of it, and looking awkward. Clearing his throat and glancing at her, then back at Ismay.

'Might we have a word on our own, sir?'

'I'm sure there's nothing you'd want to tell me that couldn't just as well be said in front of this lady, Sergeant.'

'All the same, sir – and may I say, no offence intended, Mrs . . .'

'I was wanting a word with Mrs Nagle anyway.'

She told her in the kitchen, 'They're talking secrets up there. At least, the sergeant is. Matters unsuitable for our delicate ears, Mrs Nagle.'

'It would be about the guns they're after bringing ashore over the quay below, no doubt.'

'Do you believe they really are?'

'Ah, bless you, no, 'tis just silly gossip.' Shrugging contemptuously: a well-rounded woman, grey-haired, a widow in her fifties. She added, 'But if the *poliss* is needing to waste their time – why, good luck to 'em, but they shouldn't come wasting it for himself above there. But you see, why Donovan wouldn't spout his nonsense in front of you, Mrs, is you're close with the O'Neills now, and he has it in for Michael. For no good reason *I* know of . . . That's a turbot you're looking at and it's your lunch today, though just hours ago wasn't it still cavorting in the sea, poor devil. Billy Haines was by here with it earlier.'

'On the quayside there?'

'Where else?'

'Which of those cottages is yours, Mrs Nagle?'

'Sure you wouldn't spot it, except from higher up. See the three that are in line along the edge there? My house is the other side of them and to the right a bit – I look out on the bay, not down into the inlet where I may say them others still dump their slops. Listen though, they're coming down, already.'

Steel studs scraping on the stone treads of the stairway: and Donovan's voice – 'Thank you for your cooperation, Mr Ismay, and I'll see you later.' And from Ismay what sounded like, 'I don't know that you will. You'll have your own food and drink with you, I suppose?'

'Oh God, yes . . .'

Mrs Nagle murmured, as the front door slammed, 'Else he'd die of hunger and thirst, far as *I'm* concerned . . .'

Ismay came through to the kitchen. 'Mrs Nagle, is that a turbot?'

'It is so, and it's for your lunch what's more.'

'I'm hungry already! I'm *famished*!'

'That's a beautiful fish, all right . . .'

Upstairs again, Ismay told her, 'Better not discuss this elsewhere, but there's no reason you shouldn't know what that was about. Same subject as before, more or less. A ship – cargo ship – which is in Galway docks now unloading, was sighted early yesterday from Hag's Head – over there, in Clare, near the Cliffs of Moher – and according to the coastguard took longer than it should have in rounding the Arans – on the seaward side of them, where it was out of sight – and they suspect that during that time it may have transferred a consignment of rifles to a trawler. There were a few in that vicinity, apparently. So, further theory or speculation is that although the ship re-appeared and steamed in up Galway Bay, they expect the trawler would carry on fishing for another day or night or two, rather than nip in quickly and obviously, so a landing may therefore be expected tonight or tomorrow night or the night after even – and *here* he still believes. I queried it, and he said rather huffily "We do have our sources of information, Mr Ismay" – as a result of which he and two of his minions are planning to camp out in our tower tonight.'

'Just three of them?'

A nod. 'But with more of them at Carraroe, whom they'd whistle up. Chap on a bicycle'd go for them – it's less than a mile. Anyway it's better than having dozens of 'em swarming all over the place.'

'You *shouldn't* be telling me, should you?'

'Nonsense. Only thing is, better not say anything to the O'Neills. I've no reason to distrust them myself, but friend Donovan – who I would say is not the brightest in the land—'

'You mentioned it before. He doesn't like them.'

'Let's keep this to ourselves anyway. You won't have seen anything, they won't be here till after dark. And I really don't want to be caught up in local feuds. On the other hand, if Donovan asks for help in upholding the law, what can I say?'

Charles Napier finished his treacle tart. He was at the end of the table where he'd sat twice when he'd had *her* with him: and the first course today, believe it or not, had been Irish stew.

But Sergeant Collindale had *not* put in an appearance. Just as well, perhaps. If questions were asked afterwards, possibly at Bruce Ismay's behest, it might be better that one had not imparted the information surreptitiously across a table in a luncheon room. In fact, in the interests of remaining on good terms with Ismay, it would be better if the police had got on to it through some other line of inquiry altogether. If Ismay was so pleased to have her there, and grateful to one for having sent her to him – even though of course one *hadn't*, that letter having been drafted at her request and addressed to the White Star manager in Cork.

He paid, leaving twopence as a tip.

Not tell them? Stay out of it?

Crossing the top end of Trafalgar Square, he paused to buy a newspaper – the *Standard*, its front page devoted entirely to the already much heralded transport workers' strike. It was all very much still 'on', apparently. A mass rally was being organized for Sunday – 26th May – here in this square. There was to be a march from the London docks, led by a band playing the 'Marseillaise', speeches by union leaders and by the MPs Horatio Bottomley and George Lansbury. The unions' demands included acceptance of a closed shop, uniformity in rates of pay and recognition of the National Federation. That fellow Lloyd probably *would* find himself stuck over here for a while.

Why the 'Marseillaise', he wondered. What had any strike here to do with Frogs?

Cockspur Street, and the distinguished portals of White Star. He went through to the back, hung up his bowler and paused for a word with a colleague before returning to his desk. The card was there where he'd put it beside the 'phone; Sergeant Collindale had left it, but the extension number in Scotland Yard was Inspector Tait's – Collindale's superior in the murder squad. Though what Eileen Maguire could possibly have to do with murder . . . He glanced around: no one in earshot, no Fawcett hovering.

He lifted the receiver, murmured the number to himself as he dialled.

Eileen told Lorna that evening, having no reason to be close-mouthed with her as Michael had been, having in fact promised she'd pass on anything of interest that she heard – 'Donovan and two others are quartering themselves in the Glashnacally tower tonight, and there'll be more of them on call in the barrack at Carraroe. You didn't hear of it from me, though.'

'So who told me?' She was at the table, picking bones out of a piece of salmon that Mrs McKaig had left with her; Eileen was at the sink peeling potatoes. Shrugging: 'God knows. Gossip you picked up in the shop, maybe.'

'And what do you think I should be doing with it? What would Michael do if he was here?'

'I thought you'd be interested, that's all. But since you're not – well, you wouldn't want to know the why or where-fore either, I suppose.'

'Ah, well. The workings of the brains of such as Donovan are always of some interest. Amusement, at least. Could be he's heard Michael's over on Inishmore?'

'Might that have anything to do with it?'

'Only that Donovan has his eyes on stalks for whatever the poor lad gets up to.'

'I'm still surprised he never mentioned he was going over there. He must have decided on it yesterday at least – or even Saturday, when I was with him in the launch. I mean, when he'd arranged for Mick McGurk to see to the pots – *and* doing whatever he was doing to the boat's engine yesterday – wouldn't that have been in preparation for it?'

'He'd have been doing the overhaul in any case. Most Sundays, he's doing that. Don't ask me *what*, mind you, he still does it. He's a man that keeps his own counsel when he can, he was never one to go about announcing his intentions. Besides, seeing it's not fish alone as takes him there, he wouldn't think to mention it to *you*, I dare say.'

'Why not?'

'A young lass in Kilronan he likes to think might favour him. 'Twas only by chance and tittle-tattle I heard of it. But as if *you*'d care, eh?'

'I assure you I would not. I'd wish him luck. I'm not interested in any man now, Lorna – and even if I was, Michael would be too young for me. He's great, altogether, but in the past month I've lived – oh, a lifetime, is how it feels.'

'Tell me why Donovan's spending the night on that roof?'

'It's to do with a ship that's in Galway docks now but spent longer than they thought it should behind the Arans, time enough to have off-loaded into a trawler, of which there were some about – and the trawler'd wait an interval before it came in, they think.'

'In here? That's to say Glashnacally?'

'Or Rossaveel, I suppose.'

'It's a simpleton, he is.' Chuckling, shaking her head. The salmon was about as boneless as she could get it, ready to be poached, she was looking round to see how Eileen was doing with the spuds. Eileen telling her, 'Donovan called in to ask permission for the night's vigil – which Mr Ismay said yes to, of course. I wasn't supposed to hear it; Mr Ismay told me about it when your man had left us.'

'And did he tell ye when those dastards don't come tonight he'll be up there again tomorrow? And Wednesday? Thursday, then?' Another cackle of amusement. 'Holy Mother of God, ye'd not *believe* it, would ye?'

On Tuesday morning she was at Glashnacally shortly before nine. Everything was as normal; obviously there'd been no excitements during the dark hours. It was another beautiful day, with only a moderate wind from the southwest, and high cloud. Ismay told her he'd heard Donovan and his men leaving soon after first light – on bicycles, the way they'd come last night after dark.

'He left a note downstairs to inform me that they'll be back tonight. I suppose *he* thinks he knows what he's doing.'

Sometime during the day or possibly tomorrow a lad would be coming to start putting shelves and cupboards into the ground-floor room that was to be Eileen's office. He was the son of a friend of Mrs Nagle's, who'd recommended him. Ismay had spoken to Donal Cleary on the telephone last night, to make sure he'd have no objection – which he hadn't, since as Ismay had remarked almost anything you did to the place would improve it. Mrs Nagle herself had meanwhile coaxed a certain amount of hot water out of the cranky old boiler and had an idea of what might be done to get better results still; there was a man over at Rossaveel she'd thought of, who might see his way to tackling it, and she'd be sending him a message through Mick McGurk when Mick next stopped by. Mick's brother would have been the perfect man for it, but hadn't he taken himself off to Cork now.

Eileen, at Ismay's suggestion, spent some of the morning taking measurements and roughing out a plan for the shelving and cupboards. The boy hadn't come by lunchtime though. Lunch was haddock – Eileen reflecting that if it was true that fish built brains she'd very soon be bulging with them – and after it she got down to exercising her Pitman's shorthand. There'd been a postal delivery yesterday and some more arrived at midday – by bicycle, sent down by Lorna, the cyclist being Liam Hegarty, who wore a cap backwards on his head and was part-time postman and part-time fisherman. Anyway, Ismay was dictating a few replies – trying her out as much as anything, she guessed – Eileen having to make do with the backs of unwanted correspondence and a pencil she'd found in her shoulder-bag. In the light of all of which Ismay had agreed that a shopping trip to Galway was essential. He had no idea whether any stationery or other office gear might be coming with the typewriter, but suspected that it might not; certainly hadn't thought of it himself, until now.

'Later in the week, Eileen. You might make a list, meanwhile. Shorthand notebooks, pencils, pens, typing and copy-paper, envelopes, carbon, blotting-paper—'

'Typewriter ribbons too – but not knowing what sort of machine—'

'Get a selection, and we'll return the ones we don't want later. Shouldn't be long before the thing turns up, in any case.' He reached to touch wood. 'I'll ask O'Bryen's advice, which shop or shops—'

The telephone rang. Eileen got up and went to it. It was *much* too low on the wall. Donal Cleary must be a midget, she thought.

'Mr Bruce Ismay's residence.'

'Ah. *Ah* . . . Might – er – might Mr Ismay be available, if you please?'

Irish voice, male; and a lot of crackling on the line.

'If you'd just hold on a minute, I'll see. Who is it calling?'

'Ah – well . . . My name's O'Keeffe. I have not had the pleasure of making Mr Ismay's acquaintance, but it's a – a rather private matter.'

In other words he wasn't going to tell *her* anything. She said again, 'Hold on, please.' Ismay was coming. She put her hand over the mouthpiece – conscious of a hollow in her stomach, an expanding sense of fear – and told him evenly, 'Somebody called O'Keeffe, I'd guess long-distance. Says you don't know him and it's a private matter.'

He took the receiver from her, stooped to the mouthpiece as she'd had to. 'Ismay here.'

Behind her then as she went back to the other end of the room, she heard, 'Yes. Bruce Ismay. Your name is O'Keeffe, I'm told . . . Yes – that was my secretary—'

She turned: guessing: *knowing* . . .

He was staring at her, looking startled. 'That is correct – yes. But how on earth—'

'All right – County Inspector . . . Yes. Yes, of course she is. But exactly why it should be of concern to you . . .'

More rapid speech from the other end now. Ismay in that awkwardly crouched position and with the receiver at his ear, and still with his eyes on her. An expression of astonishment: eyebrows hooping up into his forehead . . .

'No – you listen to *me* now! One, I am in excellent health and in no *danger* whatsoever. Despite your local man here – Donovan, by name, a sergeant – thundering around in his hobnailed boots and spending his nights on my roof here. Eh? Oh, watching for gun-runners. Some bee he has in his bonnet that they'll be landing rifles on the quay here. Indeed yes, and he's coming back tonight . . . But this ridiculous allegation—'

'No. She is not living here, she's lodging in Costelloe with a Mrs O'Neill, who is as respectable and and almost as charming as Mrs Maguire herself. I can tell you beyond a shadow of doubt, Inspector – *County* Inspector – this is a colossal blunder on your part!'

'On Scotland Yard's part then. I can positively assure you—'

Eileen had sat down, was toying with the pencil. Ismay listening, grunting now and then but saying nothing. Eileen's bag was on the table, where she'd left it after rummaging for the pencil: she moved it first to her lap, then to hang by its cord from the chair-back.

'Very well, When he does get there, you'd *better* bring

him over. But take my word for it – what? A *warrant*
for—'

'It's incredible. Simply incredible . . .'

'Yes, of course she'll be here!'

'Tomorrow afternoon or evening, then. Tomorrow,
Wednesday . . . No, not the slightest need, you stay there
and bring him – if you *have* to, that is – couldn't you possibly
telegraph them, tell them what I've said – that it's rubbish.
I'm perfectly all right and Mrs Maguire is—'

More gabble. And he'd shrugged. 'Very well. If you
have to, you have to. It's sheer nonsense, and I may say
an infernal nuisance – quite apart from—'

'All right. Good *night*.'

He'd hung up. Straightening, staring at her down the
room's length.

'Know what that was about, do you?'

'I'm sure I have the gist of it.'

'Did you come here to kill me?'

She looked down at the bag, and nodded. 'Yes. And – in
London—'

'You're supposed to have killed some man there.' He was
coming back towards her. 'A warrant has been issued for
your arrest, and an inspector from Scotland Yard's on his
way over – or will be shortly. O'Keeffe was offering to
come here ahead of him – to ensure my safety by what he
called "detaining" you immediately, pending the arrival of
the other chap. I said – you heard me – no, not necessary.
Was I right, or—'

'Of course you were right. *Are* right.'

An inspector, though. *Not* the gluttonous sergeant.

Ismay sat down where he'd been before: pulled a pipe out
of his pocket, fiddled with it without looking at it – without
taking his eyes off her – and put it down on the table. Touching the little curly ends of his moustache – as if to make sure
it was still there. 'You *don't* want to kill me now?'

'I said – you were right, I do not.'

'When did you change your mind?'

'I think the day I arrived in Costelloe. Wednesday. To be honest with you, I felt terrified of it suddenly. Then I began to feel as if I'd been – I don't know, unconscious, drugged or – well, out of my mind somehow. Like having been concussed, maybe. Then when I came here – Thursday – when I met your man Lloyd down there, I wasn't sure what I was about at all, whether I could or couldn't, or—'

'Wait a minute. When you asked them in Cockspur Street to give you a letter of introduction—'

'It was an excuse to be around there. I could go back and ask for it – and for the vouchers for my train and ferry – oh, and I had a story why I needed to stay in London for a while – I was after you then, all right – that staff entrance in the passage—'

'Good Lord . . .'

She gestured apologetically. 'I think I *was* – unbalanced. But I didn't feel I was. I simply hadn't questioned it. I'd sworn to Frank I'd do it. It was – *seemed* – natural, *proper* even – I mean there was no question in my mind at all, no – well, no *option*!'

'Yes.' Reaching for the pipe. 'If it makes this any easier for you, I may as well tell you that in some ways it's less of a shock to me than you might expect. I've had death threats, as well as abuse. In your case – well, when we first met, here in this room – it did actually enter my mind, naturally I've been alert to the possibility that sooner or later one of the letter writers might turn up. But long before the conclusion of that interview I'd dismissed the notion. Your personality and manner, and the letter – and of course having heard of you from young Napier . . .' Tobacco pouch now – a soft-leather roll, from a trouser pocket. 'Frankly, it hasn't occurred to me since. To that extent, it *is* a shock.' Looking down – with the pipe's bowl inside the pouch, filling it. 'How were you going to do it?'

'With this.' She tipped her bag out, on the table. The pistol slid out first, then other small items which she scooped back. Ismay leaned forward peering at it.

'Neat little weapon, I must say. Is it loaded?'

'Yes. Do you know about firearms?'

'A little. Magazine in there – holding about – six?'

'Seven. But six in it now.' She pointed with a fingertip: 'That's the safety-catch: it's on "safe" but if you turn it to the red dot it's ready to go off. It's a Browning.'

'American. Did you get it over there?'

'In London. I asked in a pawnbroker's shop and a really nasty, slimy person said he could get me one – a pistol, *any* pistol – and he'd said ten pounds, no more, meet him the next evening he'd have it. So I met him – a Saturday this was – and he took me to a really squalid basement flat, to show it to me. Then he began arguing about the price, but changing completely suddenly and offering it for nothing – he put his arms round me, in that filthy place sort of all over me, up close and – well, this was jammed here between us, in my hand but his hand over mine – all I was doing was trying to push him away, struggling to get free—'

'It went off.'

She nodded. Deep breath . . . 'I think into his heart. And – blood all over. And – this was rather terrifying, actually – when we'd got there there'd been a street-girl coming out of it with a man – I began to realize *then*, I think, it was what the place was used for – and after I'd got away I was in the Strand getting a hansom cab and there was the same girl getting out of it – and she recognized me, you see, spoke to me. I'm sure it must have been through her they somehow—'

'Very likely. But with a good lawyer to defend you—'

'I'm not so sure. I've no witness, it'd be only my word,

how it happened. And I couldn't deny I was buying this thing in order to – well, you know.'

'Before these policemen come I'll have a word with O'Bryen. At the very least, get his advice on it.' Putting down the pipe, unlit, beside the pouch. 'I'll call him now. And whatever I can do – or he says I could do—'

'Despite the fact I'd intended to kill you?'

'One, you changed your mind. Two, the fact several other people had the same idea – threatened it, at least – suggests it might not have been entirely unjustified. You I'd guess probably more than any of them. I still can't *imagine* how you'd have felt – perhaps for the child especially.'

'In the lifeboat – I didn't tell you this – the blade of the steward's oar quite near where I was hit a floating body. Floating or just submerged. It was a child's – may have been Tommy's—'

'You didn't actually see it?'

'No, but—'

'Surely, at least a thousand to one against!'

'No. Even mathematically much less than that. But it was the way the others tried to assure me it was quite different – older, and – I don't know, only that I shut my mind against it, I *had* to believe it wasn't – and now I wish I'd looked, wish to *God* I had!'

'The fact is you didn't. I think you should leave it at that. Stop trying to see it in your imagination, Eileen. Isn't that what you're doing?'

'It comes into dreams – often. Me just sitting there, and—'

'Eileen – face this – he couldn't have been alive, could he?'

'No – it's not *that*, it's—'

'I'd say it's torturing yourself unnecessarily. May I selfishly change the subject now?'

'Of course.'

'Tell me this – if you can . . . At what stage did you decide you'd kill me?'

'I think when I saw you on the deck.'

'The boat-deck?'

'The *Carpathia*'s. You were with that Dr McGhee. Who treated me too, incidentally, had me on laudanum. Before that though, Frank and I did see you on the *Titanic*'s boat deck. You were shouting "Lower away, lower away!" while male passengers were being kept off or ordered off – as Frank was. I was in the boat then—'

'*Your* lifeboat? Where I was shouting at them to start lowering?'

'No, but somehow I had it that way in my mind. I've realized since I must have been – dreaming it, sort of. But we'd seen you doing that, sort of dancing about and howling at them, then Tommy was running away – Frank not being allowed into the boat with me so he was after passing him over to me – then they were both *gone* – and the boat going down with me in it. I told you this, didn't I, I was trying to get out, and the women sitting on me!'

'And you later saw me on the *Carpathia* alive and well. Your husband and child, as you say, gone.'

'I promised Frank then. I suppose that night.'

'I don't blame you in the least, Eileen. I can tell you that quite honestly. If you'd found a carving-knife and gone for me there and then . . . In fact I'd invite you to shoot me now – well, you could, I suppose, that thing's a lot nearer you than me – except I admit I'd much sooner stay alive. And second time round, they *would* hang you for it. But I'd deserve it – from your view of it I would, I see that clearly.' He was preparing to get up: paused, nodding towards the pistol. 'Why have you kept it – and six bullets in it still – if it's several days since you decided not to use it?'

'Decided not to use it on *you*.'

'On who, then?'

'Better than hanging. Or even the trial and everything surrounding it.'

'I'll call O'Bryen. I think he'll be at Costelloe Lodge, I'll try there first.'

George Henry had listened to Ismay's guarded appeal for help – that he needed legal advice and please would he – O'Bryen – come over while Eileen was still here.

'Don't want to discuss it over this thing. So if you could . . .'

'I'll be with you shortly.'

Ismay hung up too. 'He's coming.'

She'd thought he might. He'd said not to involve him, but she wasn't – Ismay was. Involving him only as a lawyer, too – which he'd allowed that she could do anyway. His Morris car rolled into the yard after less than half an hour's wait: it had felt like longer to her: she'd seen the car approaching and called out, 'Here he is!', Ismay's comment as he joined her at the window being, 'Sort of chap you can put your shirt on. Bear up now, I'm sure he'll help us.'

'You say help *us*.'

'Yes. Us. We'll get you out of it somehow. Just damn well *have* to.'

George Henry strode in, then, had simply walked in and up the stairway, no waiting to be admitted . . .

'So what's the trouble?'

Ismay began to tell him, and she took over – recounting what he already knew, in fact. George Henry meanwhile refusing a cigarette but accepting a cigar, watching her closely through the haze of it and occasionally putting in a question. Then a hard look at Ismay: 'She comes with that intent, and you're after letting her off scot-free?'

'There's no such intent now, and God knows she had reason.' A shrug: 'At any rate in her own mind she had. I'm just lucky she didn't get a crack at me earlier. But the point is – this call from O'Keeffe – as I said, they're on their way, with a warrant. Here tomorrow afternoon – if the Scotland Yard man's taking the Kingstown ferry in the morning.' He added, 'Unless of course the strike holds that up.'

'We can't be looking for miracles of that sort. In the long run it wouldn't help us much in any case.' George Henry told Eileen through a drift of smoke, 'Twenty-four hours we have – please God. We shouldn't count totally on that, even – miracles can apply both ways, remember. What it comes down to is we need whatever time we have. Tell me this now: if it was for you to decide, would you say it was an accident or self-defence?'

'Accident. All I was doing to defend myself was trying to push him off me. I'd never touched a firearm in my life and I wouldn't have then if I could've helped it. He'd been showing me how it worked, the safety-catch and that – then handed it to me to see for myself. How he'd left the safety – on or off – I had no idea. Next minute wasn't he half smothering me, the weapon up between us because of the way he was forcing himself on me – his other arm round behind me here, d'you see—'

'Accident. *I'd* have it proved, all right. At least – you ran from the scene because you were scared of course—'

'Out of my wits!'

'We'd get us a man in London, and the way I'd direct him – given a judge that didn't have a blood-lust or a particular hatred of us Irish . . .' To Ismay almost privately: 'For the best man we could get in London would there be funds available?'

'Yes. Within reason. I'm no millionaire.' He'd neither hesitated nor even glanced at Eileen. George Henry said, 'An immediate problem however is that if there's a warrant already issued—'

'O'Keeffe did say this fellow was bringing one.'

'Then they'd take her the minute they got here, and if

the warrant's made out as it should be there'd be nothing I could do to stop them. You'd have a bad time to go through before anything got better, Eileen. They'd get statements out of you and there might be words in 'em you'd never uttered. So we need time now – you and me together – to prepare *exactly* what our defence will be. So, I want you to come and see me in my Galway office, for that purpose. Mr Ismay has informed you of these allegations and that the fellow'll be here in a day or two – those are the very words you used, Bruce, I'd ask you to remember them – a day or two, that's how you understood it from O'Keeffe – so she'll be visiting me in a normal and legitimate manner – you telephoned me to make an appointment for her.'

'Telephoned you where?'

'Didn't you just catch me at Costelloe Lodge? And did I not say let her come to my office in the morning at nine thirty? I'm on my way to the city now – wasn't I on the point of leaving when you called. Eileen, now listen. I'll arrange a ride in there for you. Not with me, that wouldn't do: too personal, it might look like you and I were out to deceive, connive like. It has to be my profession I'm exercising, not favours I'm doing to friends and especially not to attractive young women. I'll be in Galway, so, expecting you in the morning. Just between us, this fellow who'll be giving you the ride in will take you to a place where they'll give you a bed for the night, and a meal I dare say. But that's nothing I'd know about, you'd have found it for yourself.'

'Extremely kind – really very, *very* kind – but could I not somehow get myself to Galway in the morning?'

'No. Because O'Keeffe might have changed his mind and be on his way this minute, or he might put Donovan on to it – and that'd sink us. He could've hung up the telephone after that talk you had and thought to himself now what if she ups and shoots him dead and makes herself scarce before we get to 'em – which she might, knowing it's all up with her now – wouldn't *I* be for the high-jump then, he'd ask himself? So – no, you come up to Galway tonight, Eileen. The luck of it is that I believe I know who might be more than ready to collect you in an hour or so. Could you get yourself now to the O'Neills'?'

'I could – I have Lorna's bike here.'

'That's that, then. And I'll be off. I'll be off now. Mr Ismay—'

'Bruce.'

'Bruce, then. Sorry, I was being the pompous lawyer with his client. What I was about to say, more or less – I'll make no secret of it that you'll be paying whatever legal costs may be involved. I'll do my best to see you get off lightly, but you see it's not only the money, it's the fact it'll do no end of good for our side of it. Her intended victim dipping in his own pocket to get her off – conceive the effect of that on judge and jury!'

'By Jove, that *is* a point!'

'On my way out now if you don't mind I'll take the chance of a word with Suzie Nagle . . .'

He had a further word or two with Eileen too: having seen Mrs Nagle: Eileen waiting out there with her bicycle, badly *wanting* a private word with him. They met beside his Morris, George Henry pausing with a hand on its open door.

'I know, Eileen, I know, you're feeling desperate . . .'

'No. Well – yes. But listen – if I'm in Galway and the ship's there—'

'You will not be in Galway. Only we have to allow your man inside there to be convinced absolutely it's where you've gone. Listen to me now, so. I'd have stopped along the road there but I'll say it quickly now. Ride to the O'Neills', and pack a bag. Not for Galway – you know where for – but allow Lorna to think it's Galway you're

away to. Take what you need but nothing you can do
without. What you leave behind will leave her no doubt
you're coming back. It'll be Dr Murphy coming for you –
Brian Murphy you met on Sunday? I'll be seeing him myself
in ten minutes: and what he'll do, Eileen, is he'll bring you
back *this* way – having a call or two to make before he sets
out for the city – that's the way Lorna'll understand it—'

'Why can't Lorna be told the truth?'

'She could. But she's a decent, God-fearing woman, and
such folk lie better when they believe it's the truth they're
telling. See, though – Murphy'll bring you to Suzie Nagle's
cottage behind the inlet there: when he gives you the word
jump out, run inside, don't show yourself again. Suzie
knows you'll be there.'

'Two days – Thursday still?'

'Yes, yes . . . But listen while I *think* now. When a few
hours is gone tomorrow and you've not kept the appointment with me, I'll call your man here and tell him seems
you've done the disappearing trick. That way his visitors
won't hang around – they'll have no reason – and he won't
know what he's telling 'em's not the truth. This is just off
the top of my head, you understand, but – ah, well, here's
himself coming out to us. Eileen, good luck to ye – keep
your nerve, bear in mind you're our golden goose, we're
not lettin' the damn *pol*iss have ye.'

'I think you're—'

'Hold on – one more small thing – the big hat you had
with you Sunday – give it to Brian Murphy, would you?'

'But why on earth—'

'To keep the sun off the young lady he *will* be taking to
Galway with him?'

18

'Mrs Maguire!'

'What?' Rolling over on the mattress of folded blankets: Mrs Nagle had offered her her own bed but in the first place she'd have had to sleep doubled-up and in the second, why should the poor woman have sacrificed her own comfort? Eileen felt as if she'd been flat out for hours. Probably had . . . 'What is it – what's the time?'

'Come see – come *see* now!'

'See what, though?'

'Here. Look. Uh?'

Mrs Nagle, bulkily blanket-wrapped, at the end window nodding southward. South end of her living-room cum kitchen, this was. From the window in the longer wall you looked out across the bay to Rossaveel; from this end the view was along the coastline to Curraglass Point or southeastward past Rossaveel Hill to the Ordnance Tower.

Eileen getting her brain working and her eyes into focus, more or less. Some sort of ship or boat out there: moonlight brightening the white dappling around its stem.

Trawler – coming in, and not showing any lights.

'What's the time?'

'Gone two. Don't those fellers know there's *poliss* on the tower here, Christ almighty's sake? George Henry O'Bryen knew there'd be! Well, *didn't* he!'

'How would he have let *them* know it? Have you been up long, watching?'

'No, but I wasn't sleeping all that much either, I'd have been taking a look from time to time like. Won't you put a blanket round you, Mrs, before you catch your death?'

She took one from her bedding. She was in her slip, wasn't in fact cold at all. Bemused, rather. Remembering that by now she'd disappeared in Galway City: might be on her way east to Dublin or south to Cork, Brian Murphy having taken the niece of George Henry's cook into Galway with him, wearing that floppy hat that was supposed to be an effective disguise, for God's sake, and that when she hadn't called on George Henry in his office by mid-morning he'd be telephoning Ismay to tell him she must have decided to disappear. So one place she certainly was *not* was here at Glashnacally, Mrs Nagle telling her as she rejoined her at that window, 'It's stopped, I think. Though with the moon one minute shining and the next – holy God, did you see *that*!'

'What—'

Beside her now: and it was Michael's launch she'd seen. Its shape was quite distinctive, with that shelter he'd built on the front of it. But the moon gone again, behind cloud. Mrs Nagle gasping, 'Might he have taken leave of his senses? Surely to *God* . . .'

'It was his boat, all right.'

The trawler with Michael's launch in close company had come through the narrows: their distance from here would be – she guessed – about half a mile. Not much more. The trawler lying stopped there – if it was, as Mrs Nagle had thought from as much as she'd seen in that last splash of moonlight: and the launch up close to it on this side.

Having entered close together: the trawler maybe aiming
to screen the boat from the coastguard station? If they'd
left so much as a single lookout there, which they might not
have. But Donovan on the tower there, feasting his eyes on
every move, for Christ's sake!

'They'll get him, won't they.'

'I'd say they will. If he's carrying what he should not be.
Pray God he's not. Although there's plenty of room for it in
that boat of his . . .'

'If they do get him now—'

'There goes *your* voyage. Just a minute though, hold
on . . .'

Forcing up the window – trying to. Small window with its
timber swollen or warped like those in the big house were.
And she'd not be wanting to make a noise by hammering
at it, draw attention. Eileen moved closer to help: it seemed
to be at the top that it was stuck. Getting the heels of both
hands on it there: 'Ready, so? Push – *now* . . .' Thinking
they *would* find a way: George Henry would, she being his
golden goose, please *God* he would. So many good people
being with him – *all* of them for instance who'd been around
that lunch table. Except Ismay: except for him, every one of
them. The window shifted: opened. A small bit of a creak,
was all the noise it made. The moon showing through
again meanwhile – a dim radiance brightening rapidly as
the cloud-cover first thinned then cleared. The trawler had
by no means stopped when Mrs Nagle had thought it had,
had come on higher up the bay, half a mile up and with
Michael's launch this side of it – less easy to make out,
being lower to the water and its shape distorted by its own
pitch and roll, the south wind driving the waves in with it
and moonlight dancing on those fast-moving ridges.

But now – she put a hand out to Suzie Nagle's arm.
'Getting his sail up!'

'Why would he do that?'

'If his engine's failed, he'd need to. But from where he is, and the wind where *it* is . . .'

The trawler was turning away to starboard. To get itself into the Rossaveel quay, she guessed, by way of the channel between the rocky area around Illaunawehichy and the jetty there. It was in a position to, all right. Unless it was going to turn about completely, go back out?

'Does he have his sail up then?'

'If he's steering *this* way—'

'Well – I'd say he might be . . .'

'Then he's sailing across the wind and the sail'd be kind of end-on to us here. It's a brown sail too, doesn't show up so much. He couldn't hold much closer to the wind than that – that boat and the sail he has on it – he was teaching me, or I should say trying to.'

'I did hear you was out with him.'

'I'll bet you did. The villages all around would have, wouldn't they? He *will* make it I'd say, from there. Although why couldn't he have gone with the trawler into Rossaveel . . . Then she thought – he'd have been in the lee of the hill there. But – in *this* wind, surely – and if he'd known about this attendant congregation of constabulary and coastguard . . . As he *would* have, didn't I warn him and Lorna myself? But – unless his engine *had* just failed? If they'd had him in tow and he'd cast off to come in on his own – and Glashnacally easier for him, for some reason?

A roaring sound – from seaward. Rattling, roaring, loud on the gusting wind.

Michael knew it for what it was: a ship letting go its anchor. And the only thing it could be was a coastguard cruiser. Which must have been well-handled enough, to have got in so close behind them without them spotting it outside there somewhere. Could have been lying hid in Greaterman's, maybe – which would constitute what you might call a near-miss and the coastguards' *exceptionally* bad luck – although they wouldn't know it yet. He remembered the names of the cruisers that had been seen on this coast in recent years: *Argus*, *Colleen*, *Squirrel* – and the bigger one, *Thrush*, a former gunboat, eight hundred tons or there-abouts. The others only about half of that. There was just one place this fellow could have anchored – southeast of Curraglass, mid-channel where there was never less than thirty feet of water – as well as room for a vessel of that size to swing at anchor.

Wouldn't matter, as long as there was no rush now, as long as the SS *Baltimore Princess* wasn't finishing before Thursday. The coastguard wouldn't be leaving their cruiser there anything like two days, for God's sake: especially when it had come on a wild-goose chase like this one. He had the black solidity of the Glashnacally quay in sight over his launch's port bow – the sail swelling darkly out to starboard hiding the mouth of the inlet and the pier from him. No visible presence or movement on the quay. Wouldn't be, of course. Donovan would go berserk if one of them moved too soon or even sneezed, at this stage. Although he did now have the gift of that cruiser like a cork in the bottle too: she'd have her boats in the water by now, bluejackets ready to intercept any craft attempting to escape seaward. *What* a lot of trouble they'd been put to, the damned eejits. All arising from Donovan and his pals listening at keyholes – in fact listening at one too many. Donovan you'd bet barely controlling his excitement up there now, the bounder.

Judging the distance wasn't all that easy in the dark – the moon being covered again – but he'd have known with his eyes shut where the steps were. Just to make it easy for all concerned. Averse to the thought of scraping her against the wall though, even in as good a cause as this preferring to play it safe by a yard or so. He'd have help enough, soon enough. And the time might just as well be – *now* . . .

He let fly the sheet. Helm over, swinging the launch's bow – the tabernacle shelter doing its bit as a brake against the wind, dead into the fierceness of it. Sail fighting him like a wild animal, sheets thrashing: she was at a standstill and at this moment bow-up with the broken white and inky black heaving and battering at her, lashing over too and spouting between her and the quay's sheer wall: Donovan's whistle making its shrill noise heard above it all – then his scream: 'Take this line, O'Neill!'

A crash, as one of them jumped from the steps and tumbled over the gunwale, sprawling. To forestall a panic dash for freedom? Lights up there on the quay now – bull's-eye lanterns and storm-lamps – they'd have been sleeved until this moment – and behind and amongst them them, uniforms. He'd caught the line, and the creature that had sprung aboard had another across up for'ard to haul the bow in. All right, so let them do the work; Michael left the helm, to get the sail down and inboard.

'Where's it stowed, so?'

Donovan: on the lowest step, getting his trousers wet while his lantern probed around the inside of the boat. Michael had the sail down and temporarily lashed, and was putting rope fenders out before she could do herself damage. Shouting at Donovan – there was a whole battery of lamps above them along the quayside now – 'Where is what stowed, and by what right is that bugger trampling around in my launch?'

'How come you're fetching up here this time of night?'

Stupid question, indicative of his having sensed by now that he'd been had: at least had begun to *suspect* the donkey's prick he'd made of himself. He'd know it a lot better in a few hours' time. Michael asked him, 'A law against berthing here at night, is there?'

'I'll have your answer, O'Neill. I've a dozen men here, and twenty at Rossaveel!'

'To keep you safe from *what* would they be?'

'I'm warning you, O'Neill!'

'Warn away, man, warn away! I'm in from sea, is all. By the mercy of God and the kindness of Charlie Gilmore – who was shifting through Gregory's Sound towards Black Head and saw me where I'd broke down just out from Kilronan, and gave me a tow in, bless him. I doubt he would have put in at all except only to bring *me* in. Oh, he'll have fish to land, but—'

'Broke down, you say.'

Bull's-eye beam on the engine cover. Wishing to God, no doubt, that it was a crate of rifles. But there'd be a dozen or more cases on the strand or up to the road even by this time. Michael said, 'I'll see to it when there's daylight. Could be water in the fuel, I was shipping a bit out there, so I was.'

'And doing what else out there?' Donovan had jerked a thumb to his man, ordering him up out of it. 'Fishing, you clearly were *not* – so—'

'My business in Kilronan, *Mister* Donovan, is personal and private, not your concern at all. Ask away, I'm not discussing it with ye, even . . .'

Eileen moved between one window and another. It was a bright day but a wild one, with the gulls whirling like scraps of paper on the vortex of the wind and gusts of salt-spray reaching even this far up; the sun, well in evidence much of the time, was competing with two separate layers of cloud that were moving in different directions, although the one you'd be feeling if you were out there was from the southwest again: higher, slower-moving cirrus from the west. She was alone in the little house, and there was nothing to be seen out there except windswept water and cloud and the sea running white along the coastline,

bursting over the rocks at the top end of the bay; she
had no view of Gashnacally quay from this small window
through which she and Mrs Nagle had watched Michael's
approach – until the boat with the dark sail on it had gone
out of sight – where you couldn't see on account of the
other cottages – but she was thinking it might still be
there, at the quay. Nothing out of the ordinary seemed
to be happening at Rossaveel either, that she could see.
A rowing boat had come across an hour, hour and a half
ago, to Glashnacally, and she'd guessed it would be Mick
McGurk at the oars, with the boat – a punt, Frank would
have called it – bouncing and rolling across the seaway;
McGurk might have been coming, she guessed, either with
fish for Glashnacally and the cottages or to see Michael –
if he was still there, or attend to the launch if it was there
and he wasn't. If for instance he'd been arrested, or gone
on foot to Costelloe, or – God knew. In any event, McGurk
– if that had been him – she'd never set eyes on him except
at a distance in a boat, but Michael had spoken of him,
especially the way he'd go out in any kind of sea and
weather – whoever it was, anyway, had rowed back over
to Rossaveel after about half an hour. As much *in* the waves
as on them, for as long as he'd been in sight at all. All *she*
had to do, she reminded herself about every other minute,
was sit tight and curb her anxieties, the most obvious of
which was that if Michael was out of it – which please God
he was not, or would not be for long – how long she'd be
stuck here, with the police coming from Dublin to arrest
her, and the ship loading cargo another two days yet. Biting
her lips, pacing the room, most of the time at one window
or another but taking care not to get too close, be sighted
from other cottages or by anyone wandering down this way
from the road. Michael *might* have been arrested, or might
have got himself into Costelloe, might even have pushed
off in the launch and got over to Rossaveel while she'd

been asleep – likewise Mrs Nagle, after all that excitement they'd both slept soundly. If he was free, she thought, he'd know where *she* was, because he'd surely have got in touch with George Henry: but knowing it, of course, he'd stay well clear, so while she might hear of him she'd not hear *from* him. Any word there was, would come with Mrs Nagle. Though where *she*'d get it . . . Well, she'd know whether or not the launch was there, for one thing; and she'd have spoken with Mick McGurk most likely. But – eleven o'clock almost, she'd been gone two hours.

Keep your nerve, hadn't George Henry advised. And – *bear in mind you're our golden goose . . .*

Didn't they *kill* the golden goose?

By this time, Eileen Maguire would have failed to show up for her appointment at the lawyer's office. He'd go through the motions probably of telephoning Lorna O'Neill to enquire had she left for Galway yesterday as she'd intended. All Lorna knew was that Eileen had had to get herself to Galway to see George Henry, and that she'd been setting out to walk to Rossaveel – from where Lorna had suggested she might get a lift in a fish-lorry into the city – when Dr Murphy had very luckily happened to come by, and him on *his* way into Galway.

Someone coming by *here* now: footsteps scrunching on the cinder path. Mrs Nagle, she guessed, but wasn't showing herself at any window without being sure. She put herself behind the half-open door of the washroom instead: washroom containing a tin tub for ablutions as well as laundering, and no window, only ventilation slots high up. There was only the ground floor to this cottage, no stairs and, as with the O'Neills', of course the lavatory was outside. Which meant that Eileen wouldn't be using it more that she absolutely had to: short of utter desperation, safer to hold on for the hours of darkness, if necessary with gritted teeth.

'You there, missus?'

The front door had been opened and was now pushed shut. Eileen came out assuring her, 'I haven't run away.' Mrs Nagle had fish wrapped in newspaper in her basket, and looked excited.

'Would y'ever *believe* it?'

'I'll tell you when I hear it.'

Pulling off her headscarf . . . 'There was a landing of – well, they're saying rifles – two cartloads, when they had 'em on shore – this past night, over by Derryrush. Do you know where Derryrush is?'

'No—'

'Kilkieran Bay? So. At the top, the north end of it. The road passes close to the water there, and they'd have had it all away and hid – oh, in two shakes like. So while Donovan's crowd was all here and at Rossaveel – d'ye see?'   -

'What Michael was doing, then.'

Smiling, nodding approvingly at Eileen's quick grasp of it . . . 'Him and the trawler that came in with him – her skipper's Charlie Gilmore, as fine a man as ye'd ever meet. See, Michael had his story ready, how his engine broke down—'

'And it had not?'

'Not at *all*. And now he has it mended, who'd say different? While Donovan and that rabble's gone tearing off Kilkieran way, they'll be searching every house and barn for fifty mile around, you bet – while that ship we heard drop her anchor – a coastguard cruiser, Michael said—'

'One thing – would Donovan not have seen right at the start there was no transport brought here? Like lorries as you were saying at the other place?'

'There *was*, see. There was Pat Sweeney's big old peat-cart he'd left just up the road there – and no peat-cutting while the ground's rock-hard as it is – and Don Hegarty's van on the corner – his own corner and every right to be!'

'They'd thought it all out, then. But where's Michael now?'

'Didn't he beg a ride home in a van the coastguards come in? The *po*liss was on bicycles, all of 'em, but – sure, he was back I don't know how not long past daylight and he's below there now. Mick McGurk brought him a piece of tube he asked for – for the look of it, see, the repairs, so-called. What was I after saying then . . . Ah, yes – the cruiser's pulling up its anchor. Mr Ismay himself was telling me – wasn't he studying it from the tower. Sure I had a look myself, it'll be gone by now for sure.'

'Has Mr Ismay spoken with George Henry at all, d'you know?'

'Of that I have no knowledge whatsoever. But Micky McGurk was after telephoning him from the other side there somewhere. What about I couldn't tell ye, but he'll be back directly, Michael said. Despite it's gusting the bejasus, on and off. Now – this here – herrings – is for our tea, but I must go back to prepare lunch for himself. For you there's the left-over from last evening – if that'd do ye?'

Ismay's lunch, to his surprise, wasn't fish but mutton chops, with baked potatoes. Mrs Nagle told him she'd got the chops from a neighbour; she'd thought he'd like a change from fish once in a while. He'd replied that he appreciated her thoughtfulness, but when the fish was as delicious as she'd been serving up these last few days he personally wouldn't mind if he never saw meat again.

Especially – he didn't mention this – when the meat was as tough as his chops had been.

'Strange goings-on in the night, Mrs Nagle?'

'They was that, sir.'

'And that ship – which has gone now—'

'Coastguard cruiser. Michael was saying it was the *Squirrel*. Gone nosing up Kilkieran way now, Jack Sheehy from

Lettermore was just saying – where there *was* stuff landed, by all accounts.'

'Guns, you mean?'

'What they're saying. It might explain the goings-on, too – though I'm sure I don't know how.'

'I've heard nothing at all, of course. Not even from Sergeant Donovan.' A smile: 'His day off, perhaps. But no post, no telephone.'

'This big old place is twice as empty without herself, sir, don't you find?'

'Well.' Looking at her in slight surprise. 'Yes. Yes, it is . . .'

He went up to what Eileen had called 'the big room', was filling a pipe when the telephone jangled. Putting pipe and pouch on the table, he went to take it, guessing first that it might be O'Bryen and then at the last moment as he stooped to it, O'Keeffe perhaps – either to say they were on their way or that the Scotland Yard man had been delayed.

'Ismay here.'

The Galway operator's voice: 'You're through, caller.'

'Thank you. Bruce – George Henry here. Listen – bad news. She didn't come. And no word from her either. I've spoken to Brian Murphy – 'twas he who gave her the ride in, I had reason to believe he'd be setting off about that time – and he dropped her outside a place that has rooms to let, and she waved him goodbye but then evidently did not go in. That's been checked, I sent a lad round, they'd never heard of her. What's more she'd asked Murphy before this where was the railway station. So, I'm sorry to say, Bruce, there's only one conclusion open to me. You've not heard from her yourself, I suppose?'

'No. No. Damn it, I can't quite take this in. I wouldn't have thought it was in character at all. Without a word, just—'

'I did observe certain small signs of panic. When I was

speaking with her in your yard there – before you came out – wasn't I just saying "Keep your nerve now, girl." It's the worst she could have done, d'you see – sure as eggs they'll get her – if not this week, next week – Dublin, Cork, wherever – or back over, maybe – and it won't help her case at all that she'd have done this. If you *should* hear from her now—'

'I'll implore her to get in touch with you. But – oh, *damn* it—'

'Any news *I* get, I'd call again. I'd intended returning to Costelloe tonight, but—'

'Keep in touch anyway, let me know where you are?'

'I will. I will. You've not heard from O'Keeffe?'

'When I do I'll tell him what's happened and put him on to you. All right?'

'What I was going to suggest – exactly. So long, now . . .'

Ismay hung up. Straightening, with a hand to the small of his back, massaging it. Muttering to himself, 'Damn it to *hell*!'

Eileen must have lost her head completely. Despite having been offered a great deal of support. Just panicked. On top of all the other misery, of course: from which she'd have been struggling for the past five or six weeks to 'keep her nerve' – and not making a bad job of it either. O'Bryen was of course dead right – you didn't have to be a lawyer to see that she wasn't helping herself by running away. They'd see it as virtually an admission of guilt. And running away from help – from *friends*, the silly girl . . .

But she was *not* a silly girl. In fact, rather a special girl. With a head on her shoulders and – real guts, he'd have thought, as little as ten minutes ago would have *insisted*. It hurt him, rather. Putting a match to his pipe, drawing the flame into an overall surface glow. Balkan Sobranje, his favourite, the flavour of Latakia a real delight. Thank heavens he'd brought a good stock of it and asked Lloyd to bring a few more tins back with him. Exhaling: muttering to himself, 'Oh, Eileen, Eileen . . .' Looking down at the papers she'd been working on with him, recalling the deftness of those slender fingers and shocking himself with the brutal fact that she would *not* be rejoining him here – ever: that this wasn't just a temporary interruption to their relationship, but the finish of it.

Practicalities now, though. Ring O'Keeffe and tell him, save him the journey?

Couldn't: had no number. The Dublin exchange might track him down, but come to think of it he'd probably still want to come – or the Scotland Yard man would, would want to discover all he could about her, maybe pick up her trail from here. Might well be on their way, in any case.

So – nothing to do but bloody well *wait* . . .

He was looking across the room at a table against the wall between the two right-hand windows, on which he'd been keeping a few bottles and glasses and a jug of water: focusing particularly on a bottle of Irish malt whiskey which O'Bryen had brought along with him the other day. He'd remembered that Ismay invariably drank Scotch, and told him, 'Now you're here for good, please God, you'd be better off doing as the Romans do. I'm sure you'll be surprised. In my own opinion this one's magnificent.'

He hadn't tried it yet. But in all the circumstances: and not being inclined to even so much as glance at any of that correspondence . . .

He decided against it. Tonight, perhaps. In fact tonight for sure. But, alone here – entirely, you might almost say *dramatically* alone now – if one started drinking in the afternoons –

The telephone startled him. Moving swiftly to it, thinking *Eileen*? If she'd had second thoughts, returned to her senses?

'Ismay here.'

'You're through, caller.'

'Mr Ismay, this is Mrs O'Neill . . .'

Eileen back there?

'Good afternoon, Mrs O'Neill.'

'I thought I should tell you, sir – I had the *po*liss here, demanding where is Mrs Maguire, and from here they was going on to you at Glashnacally. There's two constables and two other gentlemen, one from Dublin and the other an Englishman. They'll be with you directly, I'd say.'

'Thank you very much, Mrs O'Neill.'

'Is Mrs Maguire all right, sir? Wasn't she after seeing George Henry O'Bryen in Galway City?'

'She was, yes. What did you tell them?'

'Why, the truth, sir, that she'd taken herself off to Galway. I hope she *is* all right, sir – such a *nice* young lady—'

'Yes indeed. I hope so too. Thanks for letting me know.'

Leaving the telephone, drawing hard on his pipe: it was all right, still going. Checking the time, and thinking of warning Mrs Nagle that the place would soon be crawling with police. Or *po*liss. Then thinking of the tower, the view from there up the straight road past Clynagh – to see them coming. No particular reason – except that moving was better than just just standing about . . .

Mrs Nagle had mentioned that Mick McGurk was coming back over from Rossaveel and sure enough he was in sight soon after, the punt soaring and plunging across the whitened water of the bay, for seconds at a time actually disappearing in the troughs. That day in the launch Michael had said that fond as he was of young Mick, the lad was bone-headed in his defiance of rough seas, was always ready to visit the pots no matter how hard it was blowing. Michael himself was no stay-at-home, but he'd warned Mick time and time again that one of these rough days he'd drown himself. He was as strong as an ox, of course.

He'd made it all right this time, anyway. He and his punt had gone out of sight around the end of the pier, he'd have been there at the quay with Michael these last fifteen minutes now.

Except he wasn't. He was at the front of Mrs Nagle's house and Eileen had been off-guard, careless, hadn't heard anyone coming until there he was staring at her through the front window, she standing like a dummy gazing back at him. He'd gestured towards the door then: she went to it, let him in.

'You're Mick McGurk.'

A smile. No word – he spoke Irish more than English, Michael had said. But it was a strikingly pleasant smile. He wasn't by any standard handsome. Crude, blunt features, and a mulish expression under a thatch of light-coloured hair that hung over his low forehead in a thick fringe. Really, a mule was about the closest comparison. Broad, deep-chested, but more mule than ox. While that smile – and both of them being Michael's friends . . . She'd induced him to shake hands, and realized in so doing that he was wet through – clothes and all.

'Michael says to tell you – the mackerel is running.'

It took a couple of breaths in and out to sink in. Wide-eyed by then: '*Now*? In *daylight*?'

A mulish nod, and movements signifying urgency as well as certainty. She'd drawn back: 'But the ship – in Galway, loading – he said *Thursday*!'

'*Orleâin Arainn.*'

Aran islands – in the Irish. Michael's stamping-ground. Accept it, go with it. Anyway, what option did she have? She nodded: 'I'll get my gear.' The sailcloth bag, kitbag-style, that Lorna had provided for her Galway trip. There were only a few items to stuff into it: first and foremost her shoulder-bag with its vital contents. Then struck by a premonition about open boats and high winds, she took

those things and some others out again in order to get at
the grey coat, which still had faint markings where she'd
scrubbed at bloodstains. She put the other things in and tied
the lashing at the top, put on the coat while allowing Mick
to lead her to that small end window, where he pointed
down into the inlet – at least, the slope down to the inlet
– beyond the privy and Mrs Nagle's potato and cabbage
garden and to seaward of the nearer of those three cottages.
She'd seen that down-slope to the rocks – seen it from the
road, also from the tower up there – remembered it as being
extremely steep: precipitous, lower down dropping sheer to
the rocks, which in present conditions would be awash and
foam-swept: and down there you'd have the inlet itself –
twenty or thirty feet in width and deep enough for boats
to get in there to the steps.

'Sure you'll find it aisy, Mrs!' Mule nodding encouragingly . . . To the back door then – his hand on her arm:
if she hadn't gone willingly – alarmed, but willing – he'd
probably have dragged or carried her. From the open door
– the force of the wind had tried to hold it shut against
him but it would have taken a hurricane to do that – she
pointed at the privy, told him in Irish, 'For me, there first, I
must stop there.' She ran for it, flung herself inside, forced
the door shut and pushed the bolt across before he could
wrench it open and pull her out. Knowing a last chance
when she saw one: and with some idea of the distance to
the Arans, not to mention the exertions she was likely to
be put to now – here immediately and then in Michael's
launch, no doubt. Arans as so to speak first-base, she
guessed – until the ship finished loading and put out to
sea, and she'd be taken off from there. It was all this *could*
be aimed at, surely . . . Then she was out, Mick grabbing
her with an urgency that made it plain he was going to
make up for lost time now. All very well for *him* . . . They
were past the other cottages and on the grass slope then –

grass, nettle, thistle and low scrub – and where it steepened he pulled her down to slither beside him feet-first – glad of the thickness of the coat purchased a month ago in New Rochelle, New York, although it tended to ride up with her skirt. Spindrift flying even this high, barely halfway down; and soon enough spray like bursts of rain. Not much to be concerned about, when her guess was that within minutes she'd be expected somehow to get across the inlet to the pier. Again, what *else*? Wind hammering in full-blast meanwhile, booming like thunder – she could have screamed her loudest, nobody but Mick here would have heard her: might *well* have screamed, in the course of that last sheer drop into the welter of sea swirling over rock. At least down here they weren't in sight of any habitation – unless you'd call the tower on the big house 'habitation' – but out of sight *and* sound and thank God on her feet: Mick pointing at a figure – Michael's, of course – crouching on the pier's steps – where he'd be out of sight of anyone beyond him there – the quay for instance, where as usual he'd have his launch. He was crouching with a line in his hands – a rope – Mick's skiff on the end of it, the rope to the boat's bow staying it from being washed on to these rocks here. Eileen seeing the sense of it all right, but only if she could get – if Mick could get her – into that skiff: which surely would mean swimming or at the very least wading – which explained why *he* was soaked, she realized, if this was the way he'd come. Which it had to be. She looked round at him – he'd shouted something: stooping then, gathering her up – unresisting, the last thing she wanted was to make it harder for him – to sling her across his shoulders. He had her sail-bag over the left shoulder, that hand up holding it in place out of the wet and her face pressed against it: he was at first stepping, then leaping, from one rock-surface to another, into the boil of sea.

*   *   *

Ismay saw the RIC motor coming, now passing the nearer of the two mottes this side of Clynagh Lodge. It looked like a big old thing, could even have been a Rolls, though older by several years than the Silver Ghost he had in London (and was leaving there for the time being for Julia to use). Up there on the road coming south its bonnet and headlamps were reflecting the sun in brilliant flashes.

The wind was truly savage, up here on the tower. With his back to the blast of it, before going down to meet them he was tapping out the smouldering dottle from his pipe on the crenellated wall. But then a shift of focus – same direction but longer range, down into the inlet beyond the pier, focusing – at first by chance and with his thoughts elsewhere – on a boat – row boat, dinghy really – that was being held on a rope against wind and sea like a huge fish hooked and fighting, while a man who must have waded out to it from the far side of the inlet was tipping another human figure – girl, woman – in over its transom. The girl clambering forward then: he'd tossed a bundle to her and was now heaving himself in head-first over the transom too. Another figure had magically risen into sight close to the end of the pier – must have come up the steps on that other side but was now transferring the strain of the line to a bollard, taking a quick turn around it – and hauling in now, the man in the boat having got a pair of oars out and begun to row – powerfully, making headway at once: he had the help of that line's pull of course but it was still an astonishing performance.

It was Michael O'Neill, on the pier's end. In profile instead of back view suddenly, and thus recognizable. And the girl –

Ismay jerked upright – as if he'd been shot. She was in the boat's bow and looking up at Michael but effectively *this* way too: calling and waving to him – to Michael – and *laughing* . . .

Eileen.

He thought, *I'm dreaming* . . .

Thinking about her – as he had been, rather intensively, since O'Bryen's telephone call – then "seeing" her in some altogether different female? Hardly credible in itself though that one could hallucinate or fantasize to that extent: but that simply could *not* be Eileen!

It was, though. Beyond doubt, it was. He'd begun to raise his hand, to wave and yell down to her – being more or less invisible to her up here, he supposed – and against the sun at that.

He'd lowered the hand, was standing back a little.

Eileen escaping. She'd transfer into young O'Neill's launch at the quay – O'Neill was coiling in his line there now, Eileen herself must have cast it off from the boat's bow, now they were clear of those rocks and about to round the end of the little pier . . . Escaping to *where*, though? And by what physical means or agency could she have got to where she was now – having disappeared in Galway City?

Well. Michael and his aunt were to some degree protégés of O'Bryen's. One was aware of that. Also that O'Bryen was as artful as a sack of monkeys but essentially good-hearted. So plainly she was *safe*, in whatever extraordinary exercise this was, and certainly not taking part in it against her will.

Even if he'd leaned over and yelled down at her, he doubted she'd have heard him over the racket of the wind . . . There was a yell behind him then though, which *he* heard all right: 'Hah, Mr Ismay! Wasn't I searching for you all over!' Mrs Nagle – from the head of the spiral stairway. Ismay turning to her and in so doing shifting his position, putting himself in front of her, effectively barring her from coming forward any closer to the surrounding wall – from where if *she*'d looked down . . . She was shouting,

'You have visitors below – *po*liss. Two dressed normal like, and two constables – from Dublin they say they are. The big feller, his name's O'Keeffe, county inspector he said he was, was asking where was Mrs Maguire and I told him she was away to Galway. Now 'tis yourself he's asking for.'

'I'll come down.' He gestured, politely. 'After you, Mrs Nagle. Go ahead.'

He'd been trying to get O'Bryen on the telephone for the Scotland Yard man – Tait – who wanted to talk to him, but George Henry's secretary had said he had clients with him and would call back shortly. He'd given her the number, told her it was urgent police business, and hung up.

O'Keeffe turned from the window. A large, genial character, ginger-haired though balding. It was his own motorcar, that old Rolls: had been his uncle's, who'd sold it to him for a song, and it was now his pride and joy he'd told Ismay when Ismay'd joined them below in the yard and asked about it. There'd been chat about last night's gun-running, at that stage, a matter in which O'Keeffe had shown intense interest. County Inspector was one up from District Inspector, apparently: the next rank up was Assistant-Inspector General. Beside him Inspector Tait, his junior in rank, looked much older, with his stoop and profile rather like a camel's. They'd left the two uniformed men down there, poking around and peering into the wrecked stables, inspecting the Siddeley in its barn – perhaps, Ismay guessed, alerted by their superiors to the possibility of the woman they'd come for making a bolt for it.

O'Keeffe said, 'Must be a fine view from your tower.'

'Well, it is. Only thing is, this wind'd blow your head off.'

Would be just about blowing *their* heads off, for sure. They'd have pushed off in the launch by now. If Michael had put her in that little shelter in the bow she'd be out

of sight from all directions except from right astern –
as it would be now from here, of course. And from the
coastguard station down there – even to a lookout with a
telescope, if she stayed under cover there they'd get by all
right. In Michael's shoes, he thought, he'd have given her
the sail to cover herself with.

But he certainly wasn't inviting anyone to go up and
admire the view.

'Mr Ismay?'

'Yes.' Getting himself together. 'Sorry. I heard what you
said, though. But you see, Inspector, I'd have had no right
– authority – to make her wait here for you. Much as I've
enjoyed her company, in the short time she's been with me.
No charge has been laid against her – any that had been
would be bunkum anyway—'

'No, sir. Very far from bunkum. I have every reason to
believe she came here to kill you!'

'In a single word, man – bollocks. Or if you prefer it,
balderdash. As I was saying – no charge laid, but after your
call she knew something of the sort was imminent—'

'You warned her?'

'Of course, I told her as much as O'Keeffe here had told
me. She'd answered the telephone anyway, she was here in
the room during that conversation. I say again – no charge
laid, a threat of arrest – isn't any subject of His Majesty when
threatened by the Law entitled to seek legal advice?'

'Pity she changed her mind and didn't take some.'
O'Keeffe was filling his pipe, a cherry-wood. 'Doesn't
exactly proclaim innocence, taking to her heels – if you'll
forgive my saying so.'

'She must suddenly have panicked. You do know she
was on the *Titanic* – lost her husband and little boy?
Then this threat – which I can only see as trumped-up
nonsense—'

'Oh, come, sir.' Tait – pushing his lower lip in and out.

'"Trumped-up" implies something discreditable – which I'm sure it was not your intention—'

'Cautioning *me* now?'

'Not in *any* sense, sir. But if I might explain: it was my assumption – oh, two weeks ago – that she had *a* victim in mind. She'd gone to some lengths to acquire a pistol – with which by the way she shot the person who was selling it to her—'

'I don't believe it. That girl couldn't shoot anyone. If you knew her – spent half an hour with her, even . . .'

Spend half an hour with her now, he thought – his mind away again, with *her* – you'd be bringing up whatever you had for lunch. Imagining how it might be in that open launch, practically home-made – he knew about O'Neill's reconstruction of it – plugging into a head sea and a wind gusting at maybe fifty miles an hour . . .

'Fact remains – ' Tait still on track – 'I have with me a warrant for her arrest on that charge. Two weeks ago, you see, all we knew was that the unidentified killer – a female – was at large and armed, sufficiently determined already to have killed once, and logically must have had some other victim in view. Then, aware of her identity—'

'Aware how?'

'If I might continue – but we prefer not to reveal our sources of information, sir – knowing her identity, we were able to elicit from officials at White Star—'

'Which officials, and what pointed you that way in the first place?'

' – discovered – as you say, the *Titanic* background. What had pointed us towards White Star was the fact that she was here with you, that Line's former managing director, who we were aware had been the target of some – criticism – held responsible by *some* for the considerable loss of life. Lives, we learned, including those of Mrs Maguire's husband and small son. Well – you can see the logic?'

O'Keeffe removed the pipe from his mouth for long enough to comment, 'Logical to me, for sure. As an outsider to the case, of course.'

'Seemingly so, I dare say.' Ismay shrugged. 'But there's no substance to it.' He was at the nearer window, his back to his visitors. Wishing George Henry would get a move on. He thought they'd still be in sight from the tower, although they might be getting close to rounding Curraglass. After which – well, anyway, the mere sight of a boat even with two people visible in it wouldn't tell them anything, but it might spark a thought, a possibility . . . Although it hadn't, immediately, in his own mind – even when he'd seen her, recognized her, he'd hardly taken it in. But then, he'd *known* she'd gone to Galway: these two didn't, had only his word for it. He turned back to them: 'My White Star people in London had given Mrs Maguire a letter of introduction to our manager in Cork. She's a stenographer with good secretarial qualifications, and needed a job. She had a glowing reference from her previous employer – in Cork – which she showed them, I believe, in asking for that letter – and the young man who provided her with it happened then to come down to me at Southampton – bringing documents I needed – and in the course of conversation he told me about her – her personal *Titanic* tragedy and her need of a job. I remarked that I'd be wanting secretarial help up here, and when he next saw her in London he told her this – and where I'd be, Costelloe – and *that* is what brought her here. Not – homicidal intentions, of which I must point out you've no *evidence* at all!'

'I still – ' Tait shook his head – 'with all respect, sir – still find the logic – which fits in reasonably well with everything you've just told us—'

'Another thing I'll tell you—'

Telephone. He went to it.

'Ismay.'

'Ye're through, caller!'

A female voice: 'Hold the line for Mr O'Bryen, would ye, please?'

He looked back at Tait. 'Holding for O'Bryen.' The camel was out of its chair, lurching towards him. 'Thank you very much.' He took the receiver: and George Henry must have been on the line by then, the inspector was introducing himself even before Ismay had moved away – to where O'Keeffe was asprawl in the only comfortable chair there was in the whole building. Removing the pipe from his mouth: 'You were saying – another thing you'd tell us?'

'Yes. If I can remember . . .' At that window again though, re-conjuring his picture of her in that boat, her upturned, laughing face as she waved to O'Neill: not only laughing, in that wildly cavorting dinghy, not only tremendously *alive*, but actually *beautiful* . . . He turned back to O'Keeffe: while Tait at the phone was managing to inject a monosyllable now and then into George Henry's flowing monologue. He told the Irishman, 'The fact is – although you might find it difficult to comprehend – that the *Titanic* experience turned out to be more of a bond between us, than anything disruptive. I'll admit to you that when she arrived here my first concern was that it might prove otherwise – that she might find it difficult if not impossible to work with me. We went over all the salient points – well, really quite analytically. Including my own degree of responsibility for this or that, the several contributary factors. And the outcome was – well, it's another thing that I'd say stands enormously to her credit – a complete *lack* of animosity of any kind.'

'Right.' Pipe in again, for a few puffs. Then out, and a suggestion of a smile. 'If I may say this, you sound almost as if you hope our friend there does *not* lay hands on her!'

'Do I. Do I, indeed . . .'

Tait said, returning from the telephone, 'He hasn't heard from her. He guesses she'd have taken a train to Dublin, Limerick or Cork.' Lower lip out, back again. 'Or Glasgow or Timbuktu, he then suggested. Oh, and he's convinced of her innocence.' A glance at Ismay. 'Very much your own position, sir.'

'O'Bryen's a much respected lawyer, in these parts.'

O'Keeffe nodded. 'As far away as Dublin, even, we've heard of him.' He looked at Tait. 'So what now? Home, is it?'

'Home. Pausing in Dublin to set such wheels as one can in motion – if you please, and thank you for all you've done already. We might stop at the O'Neill place again, have a quick look through the things she left behind. Would you mind? Just in case there's *something* . . .'

From the tower ten minutes later Ismay saw in one glance that the quay was empty – both boats gone – and in another that there was nothing afloat between here and Curraglass Point and nothing in sight beyond it – except a morass of tumbling sea under racing cloud.

He hoped the launch was sound and that Eileen was a good sailor. She'd need to be a brilliant one. In any case they'd be well out by now. Eight or ten miles, he supposed, to Inishmore. But heading directly into wind and sea – that wind, that sea – how long? Four hours? It might take that long, he imagined. Three, anyway. With Michael keeping a sharp look-out, one might hope, for the coastguard cruiser. He would, obviously: and he'd see it before it saw him, surely. They might not have any great interest in him or his boat anyway: that was one of the wheels which the inspector would *not* have thought to 'set in motion' – touch wood. Not the least reason he should have either – thanks largely to George Henry's cunning Irish heart.

Seeing it from George Henry's angle for a moment –

for the sake of understanding what he'd been up to. Irish girl – personable, attractive. In an English catastrophe in which many Irish including her own husband and child had drowned, then in England in some trap set by an English crook, and now English police eager to take it out on her – even maybe hang her. So – George Henry to the rescue; in some style, at that. No wonder people around here loved him. Mrs Nagle's comment a day or two ago for instance: 'Ah, he's great *al*together!' But Eileen's face again then: the strength in it, sensitivity as well: and a memory accompanying that close-up – the trip they'd made to Kilkieran and Ardmore Point, when he'd seen her leaning into the wind that was battering at them from across three thousand miles of ocean – she with her eyes shut, lips moving – he'd been moved to say to her after they'd started back – in fact had left Kilkieran village behind again – 'I was thinking there of the band still playing, right to the end. I tell you, I revere the memory of those men. And for my own behaviour, I *cringe*.'

She'd touched his hand where it rested on the steering wheel. He'd looked her way quickly enough, but by then her face had been averted – with (he'd *thought*, but it might have been imagination, *his* emotion) a tear or tears on that smooth curve of cheek. It was real enough in his visual memory now anyway, as he left the tower and carefully descended the worn steps into the echoey, empty building. A glass or two of George Henry's special Irish malt, he thought, might help.

Factual Note

━━━◆◆◆━━━

Bruce Ismay moved into Costelloe Lodge in 1913 and lived there until 1936, although the house he bought originally was burned down in the post-1918 Troubles, along with the coastguard station; it had become the Fenians' (by 1919, the IRA's) standard practice to destroy 'the big house' and 'the coastguard' in any particular locality. The Lodge's handsome replacement was built in 1922 to a design by Sir Edwin Lutyens.

Ismay died in 1937 and his American-born widow subsequently put up a memorial to him, which stands in the garden between house and river and is scrupulously maintained by the present owners. The inscription on it is fond and laudatory; while the only man I've met who actually knew him told me (in 1998), 'Oh, he was a *very* decent sort of fellow.' I mention this because derogatory statements have been made about him by other writers seizing on the fact that at the time he was made a public scapegoat for the tragedy. As a recent example, Dr Robert Ballard wrote in 'The Discovery of the *Titanic*' that Ismay 'became a recluse and eventually died a broken man' – a statement for which my own researches suggest there is no justification whatsoever.